# My
# Mother's
# Photograph

# BOOKS BY LAURA SWEENEY

DOVECOTE COTTAGES SERIES

*My Grandmother's Secret*

*My Great-Aunt's Diary*

# My Mother's Photograph

## Laura Sweeney

*bookouture*

Published by Bookouture in 2025

An imprint of Storyfire Ltd.
Carmelite House
50 Victoria Embankment
London EC4Y 0DZ

www.bookouture.com

The authorised representative in the EEA is Hachette Ireland
8 Castlecourt Centre
Dublin 15 D15 XTP3
Ireland
(email: info@hbgi.ie)

ISBN: 978-1-83618-948-0
eBook ISBN: 978-1-83618-947-3

*For my Golden Girls*

# PROLOGUE
## ROSE

June 1945

I stood at the back door of Pebble Cottage. The salt-laden breeze from the sea carried the shrieks and squeals of the children enjoying the Dovecote victory party on Beachfront Road. The garden looked like an allotment, but the vegetables I'd grown had kept me going throughout the war. I hadn't had time to get the Anderson shelter taken down or the lawn re-laid. For almost five years, I'd loved this view over Dovecote, the bay, and the lighthouse. It would be hard to leave, but it wasn't mine any more.

I let out a long sigh before going back into the house, shutting out the joyful racket. Inside, Pebble Cottage was cool and calm. Over the past few weeks, I'd busied myself with clearing out the cottage. Most of my personal things had either been thrown away or placed in my suitcase, which was now sitting at the foot of the stairs. Looking around, it was almost as if I'd never lived here.

I paused at the mirror, holding my fair hair away from my face as I slipped a loose pin back in place. I caught my own eye, and my lips curved upwards. There was more than a little excitement flickering in the wide blue eyes looking back at me. Having fixed my hair, I crossed the small sitting room and picked up the plain postcard on the mantelpiece. It had arrived in response to the letter I'd sent just after VE Day.

> *Rose, meet me at King's Cross station, London, at 1 p.m. on the 1st of June. I have a plan. Love D x*

I draped my coat over my arm, picked up my suitcase, and gave the sitting room of Pebble Cottage one last fond look. I locked the front door and posted my key through the letterbox, glancing at the small stained-glass window to the left of the front door. There was no going back now. I was going to miss the old place, but I was taking the happy memories with me.


Halfway along The Promenade, I stopped outside The Seaside Café. The café had once been my pride and joy. But now, looking up at the pink and yellow sign above the front window, I was ready to let it go. Then I remembered the photographs.

My heart thudded against my ribs as I looked back towards Pebble Cottage. How could I have forgotten the envelope of photographs hidden beneath the loose floorboard under my bed? Well, there was nothing I could do about it now. They'd have to stay there. A little piece of me left behind to prove that I'd been there at all. And if anyone did find them, then they'd be a clue as to why I decided to leave.

The toot of a train whistle jolted me out of my reverie. I adjusted my hat and set off towards Dovecote train station. It was time to leave the first place that had ever felt like home. My future was waiting for me.

# ONE

## SARAH

April 2017

The afternoon sun glinted off the split front windscreen of Sarah Portman's orange and cream 1960s Volkswagen Campervan as she coaxed it over the stone humpback railway bridge and into Dovecote. The long drive from Manchester had done nothing to improve her mood, or the running of the van's ancient engine. Even the classic rock blaring out of the radio was starting to irritate her, so she thumped the volume dial to silence the screaming guitars.

With a sigh, she pulled into the car park next to Dovecote's grey stone, green-gabled train station and climbed out of the van, stretching her aching back.

'You stay there, Dad,' she said to the wooden box in the passenger-side footwell. She shook her head at the absurdity of talking to a box of ashes as if it were still a living, breathing human being. The van door creaked as she slammed it shut.

It was only a few steps from the car park to the low stone wall that bordered the pebbly beach. Sarah stood at the wall, her hands thrust into the pockets of her black jeans, the breeze ruffling her short black hair. With everything that had happened, she'd not had time to re-dye it, so the purple streaks were growing out. She glared at the sea, grinding her teeth. Ten years ago, she'd turned her back on this place and vowed never to set eyes on the treacherous, cold, grey sea ever again. And yet, here she was, aged thirty-three, back in the town where her heart had been ripped to shreds.

'I'm only doing this for you, Dad,' she whispered.

Following the curve of the beach, her eyes fell on the pink awning and white wrought-iron tables and chairs of The Seaside Café, halfway along The Promenade. She chewed the inside of her cheek. It was bad enough that her father, on his death bed, had requested his ashes be scattered into the sea from the rocks at the base of Dovecote's lighthouse. But he'd also made her promise that she'd go and see her mother and tell her he was sorry. Sarah's stomach tied itself into a knot. That was a reunion that could wait until the morning. She turned her back on the sea and returned to the van. Back in the driver's seat, she frowned at the wooden box.

'Why did you do this to me, Dad?' she asked. 'You know I'd do anything for you, but this is a step too far.' She turned the key in the ignition. The van's engine spluttered and coughed but eventually caught, and she drove out of the car park.

Not much had changed in Dovecote in the ten years she'd been gone. The Royal Oak was still on the corner of Blythe Avenue and the High Street, with Harrington's Bookshop on the opposite corner. Las Gaviotas, a tapas restaurant, was new. Her chest tightened when she glanced at Crawford's Opticians on the High Street; that was one place she wanted to avoid. Turning into Blythe Avenue, she passed the tall, wrought-iron gates of Victoria Park where she'd spent a good portion of her formative years doing the things teenagers do in the dark. She supressed a grin at the memories of those happy days before she'd learnt how hard life could be. The old patch of scrubland between the park and Dovecote Museum was now a building site, so she couldn't see the back of The Seaside Café. She drummed her fingers on the steering wheel. Maybe after a good night's sleep she'd feel ready to face her mother.

The van struggled up the steep road to the camping and caravan park at the top of the cliff.

'Come on, old girl,' Sarah muttered, giving the steering wheel a gentle rub.

The caravan park was almost deserted. The Easter holidays had been and gone, and summer was a few months away, so Sarah was given the 'prime' corner plot. Anyone else would have described the view of the sparkling blue sea and the pretty town as breathtaking, but for Sarah, everything she could see felt like a knife in her chest. As evening fell, the warmth of the spring sun faded and the lights along The Promenade cast their glow onto the stony beach. Sarah sat in the doorway of her van, wrapped in a blanket, cradling a cup of coffee. In the gloom, she could pick out the landmarks of her life, including the now-illuminated windows at the back of Pebble Cottage. Her mother was probably at home, making herself some supper, before settling down for a night in front of the TV. Sarah could see the inside of the cottage so clearly in her mind – but she shut it out. If she started reminiscing, it would take her to the dark place she'd been avoiding for the last ten years.

'I'm sorry, Mum,' Sarah whispered into the salty night air. 'I'm sure you don't want me here any more than I want to be here, but I'm doing this for Dad.' She put down her coffee cup, her stomach churning. Her mother wouldn't be the only person unhappy to see her again after so many years.

Sarah woke with a start, her heart thumping and her pillow drenched in sweat. She'd not had *that* nightmare in years. The interior of her van was cast in silvery moonlight and she could hear the waves slapping the foot of the cliff. Reaching for her headphones, she drowned out the sound of the sea with a blast of Meat Loaf's 'Bat Out of Hell'.

In her dream, she'd been falling, the sea rushing up to meet her. Hands reached out for her, but she couldn't reach them, no matter how hard she tried. Her own scream had woken her.

Returning to Dovecote was bringing everything she'd worked so hard to bury deep down inside back to the surface.

With a huff, Sarah got out of bed and set the camping kettle on the single-ring stove. Opening the van door, she put on her heavy boots and threw a fleece jacket over her pyjamas. Soon, mug of tea in hand, she sat at the door and watched the sky turn from inky black to mauve, pink, and finally pale blue. The early morning sun set the windows of the houses on the seafront ablaze, and glinted off the gently undulating waves as Dovecote slowly came to life. A milk float pootled along Beachfront Road and up the High Street, and the first train of the day pulled into the station to pick up a few early risers commuting the hour and a half to London.

A wave of nausea turned her stomach, and she glanced at the wooden box containing her father's ashes.

'I'm so sorry, Dad. But I just can't do this.' Angry tears dripped from her eyes, and she wiped her cheeks with the sleeve of her fleece. 'I'm sorry to let you down – I hope you'll forgive me.'

It only took Sarah fifteen minutes to dress and pack everything away in the van. That was the benefit of travelling light – you could pick up and leave quickly. Back in the driver's seat, the wooden box safely stowed in the passenger footwell, Sarah heaved a deep sigh.

'Come on, Dad, let's get you back home to Manchester. That's where we both belong.'

She turned the key in the ignition. The van's engine coughed once and died.

'Come on, you heap of junk,' Sarah pleaded, giving the steering wheel a thump for good measure. 'Okay, I'm sorry,' she said, a little more gently, when the engine spluttered but didn't catch. 'You're not a heap of junk. Now will you please start? One more try. Come on, please...' Nothing. She couldn't help the rueful laugh that escaped her mouth. 'Well, so much for beating a hasty retreat. I'm not going anywhere.' She glanced at the wooden box. 'Is this your doing, Dad? Fine, you win. I'll go and see Mum. But I'm not going to see Daphne or Jake, or Heather or Rob... Definitely not.'

She was locking the van doors when Paddy, the site manager, came jogging up, wheezing and red-faced.

'She won't start, huh?' he puffed, leaning against the front of the van. 'Want me to call the garage and get them to send someone up to take a look?'

Sarah's mouth instantly dried up. 'No!' She coughed. 'I mean, no it's okay. Thanks. I'm sure it will be fine. Um, I'll sort it out.'

Paddy waved away her words. 'Nonsense, the garage is only at the bottom of the hill. They'll be here in minutes.' He laughed. 'They're probably just sitting around doing nothing anyway.'

They? Sarah began to breathe again. If there was more than one mechanic at Dovecote's only garage, then maybe it wouldn't be...

Paddy had already whipped out his phone and was chattering away. Sarah chewed the skin around her thumbnail.

'See, no bother,' Paddy said triumphantly. 'One of the lads will be up around ten or eleven.'

'Oh, right. Thanks. Look, um, I have an appointment.' Sarah gestured in the rough direction of the town.

Paddy nodded. 'No problem, I'll wait with the van.'

Sarah flashed him a quick smile as she passed over her keys. It wasn't as if there was anything worth nicking from the van anyway. All her valuables, including the locked wooden box containing her dad's ashes, were coming with her, in her favourite David Bowie tote bag. The tote bag was like armour; as long as she had Bowie with her, she could cope with almost anything. But going back to where she grew up and seeing her mother for the first time in ten years was going to be pushing it.

The winding path took Sarah from the caravan park down the steep slope of the cliff and onto Fisherman's Walk. The old telephone box at the end of the road had been given a fresh lick of red paint, but the phone inside – which hadn't worked since Sarah was a teenager – had been replaced with a defibrillator, of all things. At least it had been repurposed for something useful. The row of semi-detached whitewashed cottages lining the cobbled street hadn't changed a bit, though. Sarah supposed that when you were a couple of centuries old, the odd decade here and there didn't make much of a difference. She ticked the names of the cottages off as she passed, running her hand along the white wall bordering the neat little gardens: Mermaid Cottage, Barnacle Cottage, Shell Cottage, Driftwood Cottage, Coral Cottage. She came to a stop outside the last cottage on the street, where the cobbles gave way to the smooth concrete of The Promenade.

Pebble Cottage had looked the same for as long as Sarah could remember. The lilac wooden frames of the peeping windows and the slate-tiled porch were slightly wonky, and the moss-dotted roof sagged in the middle, as though slumped wearily with age. The flowerbed underneath the sitting-room window was full of bright yellow daffodils nodding their heads in the ever-present sea wind that funnelled through the narrow street. The two-hundred-year-old stained glass in the small window to the left of the front door glistened in the sunlight. On the opposite side of the road was a terrace of narrow, grey stone houses each adorned with a vibrant hanging basket. It was a picture-postcard perfect street. She patted the lilac-painted wooden gate and turned away. Her mother wouldn't be home; she'd be at the café.

Sarah stepped onto The Promenade. As a young girl, she used to run along the concrete path, trailing her hand along the turquoise railings. She'd learnt to ride a bike here, only accidentally cycling down the steps to the beach once. She still had the scar on her knee.

Dovecote Museum was closed, and Sarah paused to read the notice pinned to the front door.

*Grand re-opening June 2017! Come and see our brand-new extension and visit the recreation of Dovecote's World War Two air raid shelter.*

She'd be long gone by June. With any luck, the van would be fixed, and she'd be on her way back to Manchester tomorrow. She slowed as she approached The Seaside Café, halfway along The Promenade, near a set of steps that led down to the beach. It was a blustery day, so there was no one sitting at the tables outside. But the morning sun glinted off the small panes of glass that made up the large front window.

'Come on, you can do this,' she muttered, patting her lucky tote bag and psyching herself up to fulfil the promise she'd made to her father.

She ducked into the narrow alleyway between the café and the museum when the café's door opened and three laughing women stepped out onto The Promenade. Sarah vaguely recognised the one with long, wavy brown hair. Molly? Was that her name? Sarah had a hazy recollection that she ran the bookshop on the High Street. The other two – one with shoulder-length auburn hair and the other a tall redhead – she didn't know. They walked away towards Victoria Park and Sarah rested her head against the wall for a moment. She couldn't avoid every-one; Dovecote was far too small for that. But limiting contact with the people she knew would make it so much easier to slip away unnoticed, one last time.

Steeling herself, she entered the café, making the bell above the door tinkle. The slight woman with a grey bob and reading glasses that hung around her neck, didn't look up from the table she was clearing.

'Hello, Mum,' Sarah said.

Janice Portman turned quickly. The pink flowery teacup in her hand slid to the floor and smashed into fragments.

# TWO

## ROSE

September 1940

There was quite a commotion outside the red-bricked Brighton Parochial Offices on Prince's Street. A group of people stood near the sandbags that were piled up outside the building. Their raised voices suggested one couple's wedding day wasn't going to plan. It was hard not to stare. I arched an eyebrow at Martin, and his deep-brown eyes widened in response. His hand was clammy in mine as he led me through the front door and up the stairs to the ceremony room.

There were more couples gathered in the hallway at the top of the stairs. Some had families around them, laughing joyously. Others had a weary anxiety in their eyes that their smiles couldn't hide. The brides whose husbands-to-be were in uniform looked the most worried. I was relieved to not be one of them. Telegraph operators were classed as a reserved occupation, so Martin was currently exempt from conscription. How long that would last was anyone's guess; the rules seemed to change daily. I took a single pink carnation from my bouquet and pinned it strategically over the Post Office logo on the breast pocket of his work suit. There had been no sense in wasting clothing coupons on a wedding suit that he probably wouldn't ever wear again. He looked down at the flower and then back at me. When our eyes met, a small smile pulled at his thin lips. He was nervous. I wanted to kiss him, but he didn't like showing affection in public, so I resisted the urge. Once we were married, it would be different: then it would be quite acceptable for us to kiss in front of others.

Like most young girls, I'd dreamt of gliding down a church aisle in a frothy dress and long veil like a princess. Instead, I was standing in a corridor in a registry office wearing a navy-blue two-piece that was a little too big for my narrow shoulders, and a pearl comb in my fair hair. I'd spent the morning teasing my straight hair into neat rolls, but I hadn't used quite enough hair fixative and the wind coming off the sea had left me with wisps of blonde around my face. I glanced in the mirrored panels on the wall of the corridor. The wisps were unfashionable, but they softened my face and drew attention away from my slightly too-long nose.

The bride in front of us turned sideways, revealing the swell of her stomach behind the large bouquet of greenery clutched in her hand. At least Martin and I didn't have to worry about that. Martin, being the traditional sort, had decided that such activity was best kept until our wedding night. *Tonight.* The swirling in my stomach was either nerves, or excitement. I was distracted by Martin's friend, Brian, stomping up the stairs.

'There he is,' Brian called out, grasping Martin's shoulder. He was a big man, tall and broad with large hands, and bushy eyebrows on a heavy forehead. He reminded me of a bear. 'Never thought I'd see you throw your life away, Martin.' Brian's loud laugh echoed around the corridor, and I shrank back against the wall. From his tone, it was clear he wasn't joking.

I'd only met Brian once before. One evening, I'd been

standing outside Martin's Post Office, waiting for him to finish for the day, when Brian had come storming out of the building, nearly knocking me over. When I'd mentioned this to Martin, he'd said that Brian was cross because he was spending the evening with me, rather than at the pub. If Brian didn't like me much, the feeling was mutual. When Martin said he wanted Brian to be a witness at our wedding, my heart sank. But Martin didn't seem to have any other friends, so I swallowed my feelings and smiled instead. That's what women did, wasn't it?

Brian's hand was still resting on Martin's shoulder. It didn't look like Martin was going to introduce us, so I bent my head and examined my rapidly wilting bunch of pink carnations.

The door to the ceremony room opened and a newly married couple emerged, the bride's mother wiping her wet cheeks. The pregnant bride in front of us glanced at the man dressed in a Royal Air Force uniform next to her and they went into the room. I hoped she was marrying for love and not just because he'd got her in the family way. The poor chap would probably be back in the sky tomorrow, taking out German fighter planes and trying to avoid being shot down.

'Sorry. Am I late?'

It was such a relief when my friend Maggie bounded up the stairs, wiping her hands on her dark green skirt. She had a streak of flour in her red hair, and a warm smile on her round, freckled face.

'Tried to get away early but old Frobisher is in charge today. You know what he's like.' Maggie gave me a kiss on my cheek. 'Well, not that *you* have to worry about that any more. I say, it's not going to be the same without you.'

Up until yesterday, Maggie and I had worked together at Frobisher's bakery on the outskirts of Brighton. For three years, we'd got up before dawn to spend hours baking, sorting, and packing loaves of bread. At the end of my final shift, I'd handed in my apron and my hair net to begin my new life as a married woman. Every day since Martin had proposed, I'd thanked my lucky stars I'd met such a kind, considerate, hard-working, and handsome man. So many women seemed to be saddled with lazy brutes who they despised.

Maggie smiled at Martin and raised an eyebrow at Brian, who was still holding on to Martin's shoulder. 'Well, aren't we a jolly little group?'

I caught the hint of a frown cross Brian's face before he smiled. It wasn't a pleasant sight; he smiled as though it pained him to. Martin didn't say anything. But that wasn't unusual. He was the quiet sort. So many men were awfully loud and crude and boisterous. But even at the young age of twenty-one, Martin was calm and peaceful and quiet.

Maggie tugged at my arm and put her lips close to my ear. 'You are happy, aren't you Rose? If you're not, it's not too late to change your mind.'

I shot her a look but then softened my face into a gentle smile. 'I am happy, Mags, I promise.'

'It's just that you're only nineteen...'

I sighed. 'Age means nothing these days, Mags. We could all be dead tomorrow.'

She squeezed my hand. 'Isn't that the truth? All the best, Rose.'

At that moment, the door to the ceremony room opened, and the expectant newly-weds appeared, relief on the bride's face. Her baby wouldn't be born on the wrong side of the blanket now.

It was our turn. I was getting married.


In a matter of minutes, I went from being Miss Rose Partridge to Mrs Martin Wilton. It's funny how you can change your entire identity with just a few words and a signature. It was quite unnerving to leave the Parochial Office an entirely different person to the one I'd been when I entered. Outside, I kissed Maggie goodbye, with promises to keep in touch and visit soon. Brian shook my hand without looking at me and slapped Martin on the shoulder again. He whispered something in Martin's ear and took off down the road. Good riddance. I hoped I'd never see him again.

And then it was just the two of us. That was that. We had no celebration meal arranged, no cake, no photographer to capture our happy day. As neither of us had parents, we'd decided not to have any fuss. I'd been orphaned at the age of six when both my parents were taken by tuberculosis, and Martin's parents had been killed in a road accident at the start of the war. Unaccustomed to driving in a blackout, they'd been involved in a head-on collision with a truck and died instantly. If we'd tried to have any sort of celebration, their absence would have been too much to bear. Being so young when I lost my parents, I wasn't sure what they would think of me getting married. I hoped they would have been happy that I was being looked after.

We walked slowly, hand in hand, up the hill towards the train station. We passed the Post Office where Martin and I had first met. I'd only gone in to send a telegram for Mr Frobisher. Yet that day changed my life forever. I had been quite surprised, but secretly thrilled, when the handsome man behind the counter asked if I'd like to go the pictures with him. It was his deep-brown eyes that did it for me. The colour of dark chocolate: I could have happily drowned in them. Martin had been the perfect gentleman that evening, kissing me softly on the cheek as he dropped me off at my rented room just off Brighton seafront. We went out twice more before he kissed me properly, and then asked me to marry him. Even though his proposal had come out of the blue, I said yes without thinking about it. He'd even gone down on one knee and presented me with his mother's small, but lovely, diamond ring.

Was I in love with him? Yes, I suppose I was. But more importantly, I was safe with him. The war, the bombs, the noise of the overhead dogfights, the predatory men that hollered from darkened doorways as I made my way to the bakery in the early hours before dawn, or home from a late shift in the blackout, couldn't touch me when I had Martin next to me. And that was why I'd said yes.

I glanced down at the thin gold band on my ring finger, also Martin's mother's. Rings were so expensive these days, I didn't mind not having my own. Martin's father had, apparently, never worn a wedding ring, so Martin's hand was bare. I'd get him one as soon as we had the money.

The light was fading by the time we collected our two small suitcases from the storage room at Brighton station. We boarded the train bound for the seaside town of Dovecote, a few miles down the coast. I'd never been to Dovecote, but Martin had been born and raised there. On his parents' deaths, he'd inherited their cottage and the café they had run. He described it as a pretty town and assured me that I'd like it because it was a quiet, peaceful sort of place. A tingle of excitement ran up my spine. I wasn't sad to be leaving Brighton and the memories of a lifetime of foster homes.

Just as the train trundled out of Brighton station, the air raid siren sounded. I gripped Martin's hand as shockwaves from bombs hitting concrete and brick rocked the carriage. That was another reason I was happy to say goodbye to Brighton; Dovecote probably wasn't high up on the Germans' target list. I squeezed my husband's hand and settled back into my seat. I was safe, I was loved, and I was happy.

# THREE

## SARAH

April 2017

'Well, this is unexpected,' Janice said, bustling around the café, turning the sign on the door to closed, sweeping up the remnants of the smashed teacup, and wiping down the counter. Sarah stood frozen to the spot. Her stomach was tight, and her scalp prickled. 'Lovely, of course,' she added, glancing up at Sarah. 'Just unexpected.'

'Mum...' Sarah began.

'Tea? Sticky bun?' Janice said breezily. 'Sit down, would you?'

Sarah sank into the nearest chair, hanging her tote bag and its precious contents on the back. She hadn't said yes to the tea and bun, but nevertheless they appeared in front of her. Her body tensed as her mother placed a warm hand on her shoulder.

'It is wonderful to see you, love.' Janice's smile didn't quite meet her eyes, and Sarah could see doubt and a little worry in the lines across Janice's forehead before she turned and disappeared back behind the counter and began wiping it down again.

'Mum, will you come and sit down?'

Janice twisted the cleaning cloth in her hands.

'Please,' Sarah added.

A silence extended as Janice pulled out the chair opposite Sarah. The words Sarah needed to say to her mother bounded around in her head, but refused to form into any sort of coherent order. In the end, it was Janice who broke the silence.

'Ten years is a long time, Sarah.' The undertone to Janice's words pierced Sarah's mental armour and a wave of guilt washed through her chest. She looked down at the bun on the plate and picked a currant off the top.

'I know,' she said eventually, to the bun. But when she looked up, there was a soft smile on her mother's face.

'I've missed you.'

'You have?' She had missed her mother too. But she'd buried those feelings; they hurt too much. They'd been subsumed by the stronger sting of grief and pain, and she'd lumped all the feelings together. But now, sitting in The Seaside Café where she'd grown up, they were pushing at her ribcage again. The sugary sweet smell of the sticky bun wasn't helping. It was sensory overload, and she forced her mental shutters back down and resisted the urge to run.

'Mum, there's something I need to tell you about where I've been and why I'm back. I don't know how you're going to feel about it.' Sarah looked up at her mother, who suddenly looked tired, and old. The family cottage hadn't aged, but the ten years Sarah had been gone were marked on her mother's skin. 'When I left.' She held up her hand when Janice opened her mouth to speak. 'No, I don't want to talk about *that*.' Janice closed her mouth and Sarah continued. 'I travelled around for a year or so. I tried London, but it was too loud. I tried a small village in the Scottish Highlands, but it was too quiet. I eventually ended up in Manchester. Long story short, I found Dad.'

Janice's eyes flashed and her usually rosy cheeks paled. 'You found Neil?' Her quiet voice shook, and Sarah almost reached across the table to take her hand.

'Yes, I did. And for the last nine years I've lived near him and...' Sarah hesitated. 'And Pete. We became close. He understood me.'

'Oh.'

'Are you angry?'

'No!' Janice paused for a moment and then smiled. 'No, of course not. I'm glad you found somewhere safe.'

Sarah looked down at the table again. 'Dad died in February. He fought off lung cancer three years ago, but it came back. This time, there was nothing anyone could do.' She swallowed down the ball of grief in her throat. No one, not even her mother, would ever see her cry. She raised her head at the scraping of the chair against the wooden floor. 'Mum?' Her mother turned and Sarah almost gasped at the sight of tears rolling down her cheeks.

'It's so silly,' Janice said, leaning against the café's mahogany counter, wiping her eyes with a tea towel. 'We've been divorced for thirty years, and we've not spoken to each other in all that time.' She sniffed and flung her hands in the air. 'And yet hearing he's gone still does this to me.' She picked up the cleaning cloth again and set to the countertop with renewed vigour.

Sarah kept quiet; she had no idea what to say.

Janice was wiping down the coffee machine when she spoke again. 'How is it forty-five years since we met?' she whispered. She looked over at Sarah. 'In 1972 I was working at a café in London, having left Dovecote ten years earlier to go to cookery school. I hadn't even wanted to go to my friend's house party.' She was gazing into the middle distance now and Sarah said nothing. Her mother had never told her this story before. 'The minute Neil walked into the room, I was smitten. It was his piercing blue eyes and his David Cassidy haircut. And that lovely, soft Yorkshire accent.' Janice jolted back to the present and set to the coffee machine again. 'When your sister came along, he insisted we get married. We came back to Dovecote, bought Pebble Cottage – which was cheap because it was almost derelict – and this café, which had been closed since the end of the war. Ten years later, you arrived, and we bumbled along for a few more years. But then he left. And now here we are.'

Sarah couldn't help but smile at her mother's breezy summary of nearly fifty years. But then her father's words came back to her. *Tell your mother I'm sorry.* The memory of that day, when he'd lain in the sterile hospital, grey and emaciated, gave her shivers. She got up and went behind the counter to join her mother.

'Dad's final wish was for me to come back to Dovecote and scatter his ashes in the sea from the rocks around the lighthouse.'

Janice hiccupped. 'The lighthouse rocks? Gosh. That's... um...'

'I know, it threw me too.' Sarah looked down at her hands. He'd been very specific about the location, which was making all of this even harder. 'He also asked me to—' She was cut off by a knock on the café door. A woman with long, straight brown hair, wearing an oversized beige cardigan with fluffy cuffs was peering in through the glass. A huge Afghan hound sniffed around at her feet. Janice glanced at Sarah, who was already backing into the kitchen, before making her way around the counter and over to the door.

'What are you doing closed, Mum?' the woman gabbled as she barrelled through the door, leaving the dog outside. 'Is everything okay?'

Sarah stepped out from her hiding place in the kitchen. 'Hi, Daphne.'

Her sister froze, her eyes wide. She looked between Sarah

and their mother before finally finding her voice. 'What is *she* doing here?' Daphne cried, placing a hand on Janice's arm.

'Dad's dead,' Sarah snapped. 'Not that you'd care.' It was probably a little cruel to break the news so abruptly to her sister, but Daphne had been scathing about Neil since the day he'd left Dovecote.

Daphne paled slightly and drew a sharp breath. But she gathered herself and huffed. 'Is that the only reason you've come back? To tell us?' She glanced at Janice, who was wiping fresh tears from her cheeks. 'Well, congratulations, you've upset Mum all over again. Clearly, you've not changed in the last ten years. So now you've told us, you can go. We don't need you here, making our lives difficult.'

Sarah stomped across the café and picked up her tote bag. 'Fine by me,' she said sharply. As she passed, she placed a hand on Janice's shoulder. 'Dad wanted me to tell you he was sorry.'

'Don't leave, love,' Janice whispered, and Daphne rolled her eyes.

'Let her go, Mum. She'll only cause trouble.' Daphne turned to Sarah and arched an eyebrow. 'Seen Rob yet?'

Sarah inhaled sharply and narrowed her eyes. 'Screw you, Daphne.'

The door of The Seaside Café slammed behind her.

# FOUR

## ROSE

September 1940

I took Martin's hand in mine as we exited Dovecote's delightful grey stone station, and I got a first look at his hometown, my new home, in the gloom of a hazy twilight. There was an oddly grim set to his pursed lips, and I gave him a peck on the cheek. That raised a small smile.

'You don't mind moving to Dovecote, do you?' he asked as we crossed the road. I was glad he knew the way. In the near-dark, the small town felt quiet and calm. Beyond the barbed-wire-topped railings that bordered the path on which we walked, I could hear the swish of sea on pebbles. What I couldn't hear were any anti-aircraft guns, or air raid sirens. It was as though a heavy weight had been lifted from my shoulders. I leant close to my husband.

'It makes sense, Martin. What's the use of paying for lodgings in Brighton when Pebble Cottage is sitting empty here?' I instantly regretted my choice of words. Had I just insensitively reminded him of his loss? 'Do *you* mind?'

The muscles in his arm tensed and he blew out a puff of air between his teeth. 'Well no, I suppose not. But I do still want to carry on working in Brighton. I shall have to, otherwise I might find myself as cannon fodder in some godforsaken field. It's not that I am opposed to fighting for my country or doing my bit. You know that.'

'Of course, darling.' Martin would go and fight if he was forced, but *only* if he was forced. He wasn't a coward, by any means, but he was as relieved as I was that he was in a reserved occupation.

'I am doing my bit. Telegrams need to be transmitted and received, after all. Now more than ever, in fact. And I have friends in Brighton I wish to continue to see.'

I immediately thought of Brian. The way he had clasped Martin's shoulder at our wedding bothered me. But then the memory of the air raid sirens screaming out over the sound of the train as we left Brighton rolled my stomach. Martin had rescued me from that horrific reality; the least I could do was allow him to continue to see his friends. For my part, I was determined to leave everything that had happened in my life until now firmly behind me. There would be new people to meet and new friends to make here in Dovecote. And perhaps a family of my own. The prospect of *that* made me a little wobbly on the inside. A curious mixture of anxiety and something else I couldn't quite put my finger on. Was that something I really wanted?

I was soon distracted from my thoughts as Martin drew me to a halt outside a single-storey stone building standing alone halfway down The Promenade. It was opposite a set of steps that would have led down to the beach, had there not been a large boulder in the way. In the shielded light from Martin's small torch, I could just about make out the shape of a dark door and small panes of glass making up a large front window.

Martin angled his torch upwards, and I saw the painted sign above the window. It read *Ursula's* in plain block lettering.

'My parents' café,' Martin said by way of explanation. 'My father named it for my mother.'

'Oh,' I said, relieved that I'd not said out loud that I thought Ursula's didn't seem like a fitting name for a café on the beach. The location deserved something a little jollier.

'I shall probably sell it.' There was a hint of sadness in Martin's voice.

'Oh, no. You mustn't,' I said softly. There was something about the café, even in the dark, that called to me.

'But I won't have time to run a café as well as working at the Post Office, Rose.'

I looked up at the building again and my mind was flooded with images of flowers in baskets, pretty crockery, and a counter laden with sweet treats. 'I'll run it.'

'You? But Rose—'

'I'll do it. I can bake, after all. And I can pick up the ins and outs of ordering stock and the suchlike. You'll help with the books. It would be such a shame to let it go, Martin.'

He lowered his torch. 'I'll think about it. Come on, we should get inside.'


Arriving at my new home on the cobbled Fisherman's Walk in the blackout meant I didn't really get a good look at the semi-detached cottage from the outside. There were two small windows on the upper floor, and one to the right of the front door downstairs. The tiny window to the left of the front door looked like it might be stained-glass, but it was impossible to tell in the dark. The roof of the porch was slightly wonky, and the front door creaked as Martin opened it. He made no attempt to carry me across the threshold. Perhaps it didn't occur to him, seeing as Pebble Cottage wasn't a new home to him.

The moment he turned the light on inside, having drawn the blackout blinds, I was in love. It was like no home I'd ever known, and even without a fire in the huge stone hearth, there was a feeling of cosiness and warmth. We were standing in a neat sitting room. The stairs to the upper floor rose from the left, and a red upholstered sofa with turned legs and a matching armchair were arranged around the fire. A beautiful walnut-veneered wireless radio sat atop a mahogany sideboard against the far wall. Wooden beams crossed the low ceiling, and the walls were painted a buttery yellow. The exposed floorboards creaked underfoot.

'So, here we are,' Martin said. There was a curious look on his face, almost nervousness. I stopped looking around the room and stepped into his arms. He held me more loosely than I'd expected him to, and a morsel of doubt nibbled at the edges of my mind.

'Would you like to show me upstairs?' I had never tried to sound alluring before and, as the words left my mouth, I wasn't sure I'd succeeded. I angled my face up to his, waiting for his kiss, but it never came. Instead, he cleared his throat and stepped away.

'Perhaps we should get things arranged down here first,' he mumbled. 'I'm not sure what level of provision we have in the kitchen.'

I placed my hand on his arm. 'I'm a little nervous too,' I said, my voice wavering slightly. Relief flooded his brown eyes. 'I know what we both need.' From my handbag, I retrieved the bottle of Gordon's gin Mr Frobisher had gifted me as a wedding present. 'Just to help with the first-time nerves.'

Martin blushed, but then disappeared through the archway into the kitchen and returned with a couple of glasses. I poured us each a generous measure. It might take us a while, and a little liquid courage, to adjust to married life, but we'd get there. It was reassuring to see that Martin was just as anxious about our new life together as I was. After all, we'd only known each other a few months. It would get easier. We'd work it all out in time. It would all be fine.

Why did I sound as if I was trying to convince myself?

# FIVE

## SARAH

April 2017

Sarah's tote bag banged against her hip as she stomped back down The Promenade. She gave the bollard at the end of the path a kick. The old stress reliever from her teenage years didn't quite work the same now. Why did Daphne have to turn up just when things had been going okay with her mum? She'd not expected her mum's tears, though.

Sarah made her way down Fisherman's Walk. She had only been three when her parents separated, so she didn't remember what the atmosphere had been like between them. Her dad had never wanted to talk about it. She had no memory of them ever arguing or anything like that. Pausing at the lilac-painted front gate of Pebble Cottage, she frowned. Her parents must have loved each other at some point, surely, or they wouldn't have lasted fifteen years. She tapped the top of the wooden gate. Not that it mattered now. It was all in the past.

Pulling the strap of her tote bag higher up on her shoulder, she glanced up at the small windows on the upper floor of the cottage. The one on the left had been her bedroom until she was about eight. She'd moved into the bigger room at the back once Daphne moved out. The cottage was so peaceful and still. Yet, even just standing at the gate, the memories held within the thick whitewashed walls seeped into her bones. Daphne was right: she wasn't needed here, and she didn't need to be here. As soon as the van was fixed, she'd get out of Dovecote, and this time it would be for good.

The wooden gate that led to the caravan park creaked as Sarah pushed it open. She faltered at the sight of a man with his head in her van's engine. He must have heard her footsteps on the gravel, as he spoke without moving from under the bonnet.

'The problem is your starter motor.' There was a soft Welsh inflection to his words.

Sarah moved her mouth, but no sound made it past the constriction in her throat.

'I've taken the starter out and given it a good clean, but no joy. I think you might need a new one, which could take time to...' His voice petered out as he pulled his head from under the bonnet and turned to look at her.

'Hi, Rob,' she rasped. The instant she'd come through the gate, she'd known it was him. How could she not, when she knew every contour of his body? He still favoured T-shirts that were slightly too tight and showed off his toned arms. The familiarity of his voice had knocked her sideways. He swallowed and blinked his sapphire-blue eyes a few times. The ten years looked good on her estranged husband. Thirty-five suited him – but then, he had the sort of bone structure that meant he was always going to age well.

'Sarah?' He stared for a moment, seemingly fixated on Sarah's turquoise nose stud. Then he puffed out his cheeks and turned back towards the van. 'Your spark plugs are badly corroded, your fan belt is on the way out, and your battery's not holding charge.' He didn't look at her as he gathered his tools, which had been strewn across the patch of grass behind the van. 'I'll get one of the boys to come up with the truck and bring it down to the garage. I want to take the engine out and make sure there's nothing else going on.'

'Okay.'

Rob gave her a long look as he got into his car, and she shrank back slightly. Then he ran his hand through his dark brown, wavy hair, and muttered something rude. He drove off, leaving Sarah standing by her stricken van with a pounding heart and sweaty palms.

She barely had time to throw her clothes and toiletries into her holdall before a tow truck pulled up and a large, bald man with an array of tattoos on his meaty arms climbed out.

'Morning,' he said, nodding at Sarah. 'I'm Kev. Don't worry, we'll get her sorted out. She's a right beauty.' He set to work getting Sarah's van hitched up to the truck. At his request, she provided her phone number and signed the paperwork. 'Can't say how long it will take to get the parts. But we'll be in touch.'

'Oh, right. Thanks,' Sarah managed to mumble as Kev climbed back into the truck. He gave her a toot of the horn and a wave as he disappeared down the road towards the garage.

With a grimace, Sarah lifted her holdall onto her shoulder and picked up her tote bag in the other hand. Checking the contents of the bag, she groaned.

'Seriously, Dad? I bet you're having a right laugh about all of this. Well, it's not funny.' She stepped onto the path down the cliff into town, hoping the rooms at The Royal Oak weren't fully booked.

She gave Pebble Cottage a sideways glance as she passed, her steps slowing. The street was in shadow at this time of day, yet Pebble Cottage always seemed to glow. Sarah tilted her head slightly to the left. The lilac paint around the upstairs windows was flaking, and the flowerbed under the sitting room window contained as many weeds as daffodils.

'I know what you're thinking.' Sarah's head snapped around at the sound of her mother's voice. 'The old place is looking shabby around the edges. Daphne and Adam do what they can to help, but work and Jake keep them busy.' Sarah swallowed back a snort. Her perfect sister, and her perfect GP husband, weren't so perfect after all. Janice nodded towards the house. 'Cuppa? Or are you heading somewhere?' She eyed Sarah's bags. 'Don't tell me that's the same David Bowie tote bag you used to carry around when you were fifteen?'

Sarah looked down at her bag. 'No, it's not. That one finally fell apart not long after Bowie died last year. Dad bought me this one last Christmas.' She coughed to hide the wobble in her voice. 'Actually, I was walking up to The Royal Oak to see if they have any rooms. My campervan has given up the ghost. It's been taken into the garage. Dodgy starter motor, apparently.' Sarah sighed at Janice's raised eyebrow. 'Yes, I saw Rob, and no, I don't want to talk about it.'

Janice patted Sarah's arm. 'Well, you're not staying at the pub when your bedroom's sitting empty.'

Sarah shook her head. 'Oh, no. I...'

'Don't be daft. Come on in, love. I've been waiting to see you for so long. It will be nice to have you home.'

A hard lump formed in Sarah's throat at that word. *Home.* What did it even mean any more? Where *was* home these days? Wherever it was, it certainly wasn't Dovecote.

'Daphne will be thrilled,' Sarah said, pursing her lips as Janice pushed the gate open

'Leave her to me. She's just touchy at the moment. There are changes happening at the Dovecote Medical Centre and they're not sure what it all means for Adam's job. It's a stressful time for them both. I'm sure she didn't mean what she said.'

Sarah followed her mother up the short path to the door of Pebble Cottage, her legs leaden. This had not been part of her plan.

Janice was still chatting away as they stepped inside. 'You'll hardly recognise Jake now. He's a big lad, tall. Loves football. Do you remember Adam's sister, Natasha? Her daughter, Alice, is growing up into a lovely girl. Was Natasha dating Tim Jackson, the postman, when you left? Well, they got married about eight years ago. Natasha helps me out at the café most days. I'm getting too old to be on my feet all day.' Janice's voice grew muffled as she moved under the archway and into the kitchen at the back of the cottage, leaving Sarah standing in the sitting room, her bags at her feet.

It was all just as she remembered. The stone fireplace, the beams across the low ceiling, the squishy floral sofa and matching armchairs, the coat hooks by the stairs, the mahogany sideboard, the creaking floorboards. There was even the familiar scent of jasmine and apple blossom in the air. The edges of Sarah's mind tingled. It was hard to keep all her memories locked away. She closed her eyes for a moment and drew a few deep breaths. The memories kept pushing, demanding to be acknowledged.

'You'll remember the Prentice family, up at Dovecote Manor, of course. Both of their boys are back home in Dovecote now.' Janice's words were punctuated with the sound of the kettle being filled and mugs being taken out of the cupboard. Sarah couldn't bring herself to respond. 'Violet Cooper died last year, sadly. She was ninety-one.' Sarah's gaze flicked to the painting on the wall above the sofa. A closely packed group of white-sailed Cornish working boats bobbed on a blue-green choppy sea, but it was the boat in the middle of the group with its dark-red sail that Sarah loved. In the bottom corner were the initials 'VC'.

'And Lily Morrison, remember her? She died the year

before, and her husband not long after. Their grandson, Harry, is good friends with Jake. Nice boy. Speaking of which, his parents, Grace and Ben, split up. That was sad, but they're still friends. They come into the café quite a lot.'

'Uh-huh,' Sarah mumbled as she moved across the rug to the fireplace. From the mantelpiece, she picked up a photograph in a silver frame and a cold shiver ran down her spine. The photo was of a little girl with mousy-brown hair. She was only three years old, but her wide blue eyes gave her the look of a wise old owl. She was sitting on the front wall of Pebble Cottage, her little legs dangling, holding a bucket and spade. Sarah's heart thumped and her hands shook slightly as she gazed at her daughter's innocent face. She turned slowly, still holding the photograph as her mother came into the room.

'I don't know if you've seen that the museum is being expan — Ah.' Janice came to a stop. The tray, filled with mugs of tea and a plate of shortbread, trembled in her hands.

'It's a nice photo of Faith,' Sarah said, squeezing the words past the lump in her throat. She blinked away a sudden wetness in her eyes. As she returned the photo to the mantelpiece, she found herself launched back ten years to the last time she'd stood in the sitting room of Pebble Cottage – the day of her daughter's funeral. The day before she'd run away.

# SIX

## ROSE

September 1940

I woke early the next morning, my body still in tune with the routine of pre-dawn starts at the bakery. The night before tumbled through my aching head. That the deed was done was probably the best I could say for it. We'd eventually find our way. I'd heard enough married women chattering on the bread packing line to know that it took a few goes to find out what worked.

Not wanting Martin to see me without my face on and with my hair looking like a bird's nest, I quietly went about my morning routine. He snored on, oblivious to my pottering about the house. I explored every nook and cranny of Pebble Cottage. We had everything we could need here. The cottage had a lived-in feel, and I found myself thinking back to the original owners – probably a fisherman working out of Dovecote, and his family. No doubt there were a few stories held within the thick, stone walls.

As I rearranged the contents of the kitchen cupboards, I could feel Ursula's café calling to me, urging me to have a go at running it. What did I have to lose? I wasn't going to sit around all day while Martin was at work.

After putting my own belongings where I wanted them – a photograph of my parents on the mantelpiece and a couple of books on the small table in the alcove by the sofa – I stepped out into the back garden. It was an oddly shaped patch of land with too many angles. The garden was dominated by the curved, corrugated roof of an Anderson shelter dug into the lawn, and the sloping rise of the grass-topped cliff to the left. Directly ahead, beyond a brilliant white lighthouse standing proud on a rocky outcrop, was nothing but sea. The salty breeze tickled my cheeks. If I looked round the corner of the cottage, I could see the whole of Dovecote, including The Promenade we'd walked along the previous evening. I was itching to explore, and to go down to the café again.

'Morning!'

I was startled from my daydream by a cheerful voice from over the chest-height stone wall dividing the gardens. It belonged to a round-faced woman with blonde curls tucked up under a headscarf.

'Oh, hello,' I replied. She was a few years older than me, maybe mid-twenties.

'I'm Maureen,' she said, giving me a wave. Her arms were sturdy. She looked as though she was no stranger to hard, manual work. 'I'm guessing you must be the new Mrs Wilton.'

'Rose,' I said. 'And yes, we were just married yesterday.' A sudden panic widened my eyes. Had we been awfully loud? I didn't think so, and the walls seemed pretty thick. But still, the cottages *were* semi-detached. Maureen burst out laughing, a loud, raucous laugh that wobbled her ample chest.

'You needn't look so worried, love. I didn't hear a peep. I'd be more worried that you'd be kept awake by Stan's snoring. That's my brother. He could wake the dead, the noise he makes. Even worse when he's been down the pub.'

I let out a breath. 'Oh. No, not a peep.'

'Good old stone houses, these,' Maureen said, looking up at her own cottage. While the wooden window frames of Pebble Cottage were painted in lilac, hers were a light green. 'Coral Cottage was my ma and pa's. Pa didn't come home from the last war, and Ma got taken by the flu a couple of years ago. Her lungs had never been strong. It's just me and Stan now. He does the scrap collecting around Dovecote. Been mightily busy since this war started. I help him out most days.' She stopped suddenly. 'Oh, you mustn't mind me, love. I could talk the hind legs off a donkey. Now, have you everything you need?'

'Actually, I don't like to ask, but I don't suppose you've any tea and milk going? I'll replace them once I get my ration book sorted and get registered with the shop.' My stomach growled, reminding me that all I'd put in it since the previous lunchtime was several tots of gin. 'It's the first thing on my to-do list, I promise.'

Maureen held up her hand. 'You wait there.'

She returned a moment later and handed over a wooden crate. Inside was a tin of tea, a new tin of powdered milk, a loaf of bread, a half-pound of lard wrapped in paper, a tin of spam, two rashers of bacon, two eggs, and a bag of apples.

'There you go, love. That should see you through until you can get yourself up to the shops. You newly-weds have better things to be doing than standing in line at the grocers,' she said with a wink. I blushed.

'Are you sure? Thank you so much. I can give you the money for it.' I could hear my voice beginning to wobble. Maureen's gift was beyond any kindness I'd ever experienced. Dovecote was already finding a home in my heart.

Maureen shook her head, and a blonde curl escaped from her headscarf. 'Think of it as a wedding present. The apples were free anyway. Reverend Douglas lets locals take what they want from the vicarage orchard, as long as no one takes advantage, you know. And a fella over the other side of the park keeps hens, and he'll happily give you a few of his eggs in exchange for a pack of cigarettes. You'll come to know our little ways of getting by, Rose. Now, get inside and cook that husband of yours some breakfast, or it'll be the shortest marriage in history.'

I couldn't help but chuckle as I closed the back door behind me and put the kettle on the stove to boil. I was gasping for a cuppa. The upstairs floorboards creaked, so I found a frying pan and dropped a lump of lard in it. If I'd learnt anything from years in foster homes and boarding houses – other than that the only person I could rely on was myself – it was that the smell of frying bacon could entice any man out of his bed.

I cradled my cup of tea as Martin mopped up the last specks of egg yolk and bacon grease with a piece of bread. It was the first meal I'd cooked for us. It might have been basic, but it was a good start. I smiled to myself. We were on our way to becoming a proper couple, in our own little home.

'That was lovely, Rose. And how kind of Maureen. I remember her and Stan, growing up. Mother didn't let me play with them. She said they were too rough.' He rubbed his left eyebrow. 'But my mother was a snob.'

'How long is it since you lived in Dovecote?'

'Seven years. I left at fourteen to start at the Post Office, as a telegram boy. I chose to lodge with an eccentric old aunt, rather than spend what little money I was earning on getting the train back and forth to Dovecote every day. I wanted to save up as much as I could to be free and independent. When she died, my aunt left her house to the Seaman's Mission charity, so I had to move out. As it happens, she'd always had a thing for sailors. But at least by then I'd been promoted to desk clerk at the Post Office and had a steady wage and savings. I didn't need to come home, cap in hand.' His smile lit up his eyes and I swooned, just a little. In the early morning sunlight, he had a touch of Jimmy Stewart about him. 'And then I met you.' He kissed me lightly on the nose. 'I'm going to go and get a newspaper,' he said, rising from his chair.

'Oh, I'll come with you. If you don't mind. I want to see the café in the daylight.'

I stood at the gate of Pebble Cottage as Martin locked the lilac-painted front door. The roof of the cottage sagged slightly in the middle, like an old sofa, and some of the tiles were adorned with patches of moss. Maureen had a lovely row of roses lining her front path. I'd have to bring our front garden up to scratch. The flowerbed under the sitting room window was empty, apart from a few sad-looking woody stumps of what might have been lavender bushes. I gave Martin a smile as he joined me at the gate and looked back at the house.

'I know it's only small and rather old, but will it be alright for you? Even just for now?' he asked.

'Martin, it's perfect.' He offered me his arm, and I wrapped my hand around his elbow. 'I love the cottage, and I love you.'

He blushed, but didn't reply.

I unwrapped my hand from around the crook of Martin's elbow as we drew to a stop outside the café. The sun reflecting off the windowpanes distracted from the dark grey paint of the door and the sign above the window. Seeing *Ursula's* in such dark, forbidding paint made my heart sink.

'It's in such a lovely location,' I said, trying to hide my disappointment at how shabby and dreary the building looked in daylight. Martin rooted around in his pocket and pulled out a key. He inclined his head towards the dismal grey door.

'Do you want to see inside?'

I held my breath in anticipation as he turned the key in the lock and pushed open the door. He stood, hands on hips, as I stared, agog. It was so dull. The floor was covered in a scuffed beige linoleum, the square wooden tables were bare, and the chairs were flimsy and mismatched. There was no colour: everything was beige or brown.

'Just as I remember,' Martin said from behind me. 'Well, why don't you have a look around and I'll fetch the paper. I'll pick you up on the way back.'

I could only nod as I wound around the tables. Not a single one of them was level, they all rocked, and the tops were sticky. A spider had built an intricate home across the front of an old Welsh dresser against the back wall. There were no pretty plates or curiosities on display. The one saving grace was the beautiful mahogany counter that curved away from the door and ran along the left-hand wall. With a dollop of polish and some elbow grease, it would come up lovely.

On the wall behind the counter, on a series of long shelves, were rows of brown mugs and teapots. They were like something you'd find in a school canteen. Through a doorway on the back wall, I found a narrow but well-stocked kitchen. In the cupboards, there was every size and shape of mixing bowl and baking tin you could need, and a large gas oven which flickered into life when I turned the dial. A narrow door led to a storeroom lined with shelves and a working refrigerator. In a box shoved under the worktop in the kitchen, I found porcelain teacups and teapots in mismatched floral designs and pastel colours. This was what I'd imagined the café to be like. Pinks and yellows and mint green. Flowers and polka dots. White lace tablecloths and carnations in bud vases.

'Found something?' I was momentarily startled by Martin's voice and nearly hit my head on the countertop as I stood up. I held up one of the teacups. 'Oh, those old things. Mother stopped using those in the 1930s. She thought they were frightfully old-fashioned.'

'I think they're divine. What have you got there?'

Martin held aloft a bottle of sherry. 'Wedding present from Mr Ingram, who owns the newsagents. It's a small town, and word does get around. He asked after you and I said you'd be in to make your acquaintances soon. He also asked if we were intending to reopen the café. Everyone has been missing it for the past year, since it's been closed.' A slight shadow crossed his eyes. It was the first time I'd seen any reaction from him about what had happened to his parents. I hoped being back in Dovecote wasn't painful for him. Maybe I'd find an occasion when I could encourage him to open up about it.

I put the cup down, before I dropped it. 'And what did you say?'

To my surprise, Martin put down his paper, cigarettes, and the bottle of sherry and wrapped his arms around my waist. I looked up at him, desperate for his next words. 'I said,' he kissed my forehead, 'that my wife was very much looking forward to doing so.'

Speechless, I kissed him.

'Just one thing, darling,' I said, batting my eyelashes a fraction as we locked up the café and headed towards Pebble Cottage. 'I was thinking of maybe, if you don't mind, changing the name.'

'What's wrong with Ursula's?' Martin bristled. 'You want to erase my mother's name from her café?'

I rubbed his palm with my thumb. We'd not had a disagreement thus far. We'd scarcely been together long enough to row. And I didn't much fancy starting one.

'I was just thinking that, with the beach closed off, it might be enticing for people to come to the café and feel as though they're by the sea.'

Martin's frown deepened. 'Hmm. And what were you planning on changing the name of my café to, might I ask?'

'The Seaside Café,' I said. The name had come to me while I looked out beyond the turquoise railings of The Promenade to the blue-grey waves that lapped the stony beach. He grunted a little but didn't let go of my hand.

'I'll think about it,' he said.

For now, that was good enough for me. I was going to have quite the challenge on my hands transforming the café into the one in my imagination. But I had a plan, and *I* would make it work. No matter what.

# SEVEN

## SARAH

April 2017

Despite the flood of memories triggered by being back in her old bedroom, Sarah slept deeply and was woken by the early morning sunlight streaming in through the light curtains. The bedroom looked out over the back garden of Pebble Cottage, with its irregular-shaped lawn that gave way to the rise of the cliff. Having drawn back the curtains, Sarah was faced with an uninterrupted view of the sea, and of the tall, bright-white lighthouse standing proud atop steep jagged rocks buffeted by the waves. She turned her back on the view and drew a steadying breath. She couldn't avoid the lighthouse; it would be visible everywhere she went in Dovecote, shimmering in the sun. A waft of freshly brewed coffee lured her downstairs.

Janice was already up and busying herself. A batch of her infamous sticky buns was waiting to go into the oven down at the café.

'Good morning, pet. Sleep well?'

'Yes thanks,' Sarah said, pouring herself a cup of coffee and buttering a slice of toast. 'It was weird being back in my old room.'

Janice sat down at the round pine kitchen table next to her. 'So, what are your plans? Are you going to scatter your dad's ashes today?'

Sarah struggled to swallow her mouthful of toast. 'I don't know. I was thinking maybe I'd just bring him back to Pete, once my van is fixed.'

'Did Pete not want to scatter Neil's ashes with you?'

Sarah watched her mother sweep a few crumbs off the table into her hand. 'He...' she hesitated. 'I think he felt it was best if he didn't come down to Dovecote.'

Janice got up and tipped the crumbs into the sink.

'Well, if you've nothing else to do, why don't you come and give me a hand at the café? You could hide out in the kitchen if you need to.'

Sarah stared at her mother, but her face was inscrutable, and her dark brown eyes widened innocently. 'Alright. I'll come down.' She didn't fancy being cooped up in the cottage, crammed as it was with memories she was in no hurry to relive. At least she could keep her hands busy at the café.


At The Seaside Café, before opening time, Sarah dusted the shelves of antique teapots and other knick-knacks that had found their way into the café over the years, while Janice finished off the buns and made a few other cakes. As she worked, Sarah allowed herself a few moments of nostalgia. The café had been her home growing up, just as much as Pebble Cottage. She'd worked Saturday and Sunday mornings to earn money for cinema trips and CDs. After leaving school, she'd found a lovely job in the office at Bayview Care Home, but still helped at the café on the weekends. As much as it didn't feel like it now, the café had been in her blood once.

The duster fell from her hand as another memory flared. She and Rob had brought their newborn daughter into the café for her first outing. Every customer had crowded around Faith's pram to coo and fuss over her. And they were right, she was a little dote, all pudgy cheeks and rolls. It had been a crisp autumn day and the leaves on the trees in Victoria Park, next to the café, were burnt orange and russet. The photograph on the mantelpiece of Pebble Cottage swam back into her mind.

Sarah shook the memory away, exchanged her duster for a damp cloth, and set to scrubbing the coffee machine. For the past ten years, she'd kept herself busy to keep the pain and the anger buried. Being back in Dovecote was no reason for that to change.

A clatter of metal, a loud thud, and a cry of pain sent Sarah running into the kitchen. On the floor, surrounded by mixing bowls and utensils, was Janice, pale-faced and grimacing.

'Are you alright, Mum? What happened?' Sarah asked, kneeling down next to her mother. Janice's right leg was stretched out in front of her, her foot bent at a nauseating angle.

'I don't know.' Janice's voice was quivering. 'One moment I was carrying the bowl over to the sink, the next I'm down here.'

'Do you want to see if you can get up?' Sarah slipped her hands underneath Janice's armpits, but as soon as Janice put any weight on her right foot, she fell back down again.

'It's my ankle,' she said, tears brimming in her eyes.

Sarah swept a strand of hair from her mother's face. A thin line of bright-red blood trickled down Janice's temple.

'It looks like you banged your head, too. You're bleeding!'

Janice raised her fingers to her head. 'Am I? Oh!' She slumped against Sarah's body. 'I'm a bit dizzy.'

'I'm calling an ambulance.' Sarah whipped out her phone and dialled. As she spoke to the call handler, she wrapped Janice's coat around her shoulders. She'd started to shake. 'They'll be here in a few minutes,' she said, slipping one of the chair cushions from the café underneath Janice. 'You don't want to catch a chill from the cold floor.' Janice didn't reply. Her skin was a sickly grey-green colour, and she was still trembling. Sarah cradled her and pressed a folded paper napkin against the cut on Janice's head. 'You know, I was thinking earlier about all the good times we had, here in the café, you and me.' That drew a small smile from Janice. 'I'm sorry for bolting the way I did.'

'Don't worry, love,' Janice whispered. 'I'm just glad you're back.'

Outside the café, the flashing blue lights on The Promenade gave Sarah the excuse not to say anything more.


Daphne raced towards the café just as the paramedics were moving Janice into the ambulance. As she drew to a halt, she glared venomously at Sarah, who was already sat beside Janice in the back.

'What did you do, Sarah?'

Sarah rolled her eyes. 'Mum slipped and fell in the kitchen, Daffs. I know you'd love it if I'd pushed her, but it was an accident.'

'Don't call me Daffs,' Daphne snapped. 'You know I hate it.'

Sarah shrugged. 'All the more reason for me to do it.'

'I don't have time for your childish games,' Daphne hissed before turning to the paramedic. 'I presume you'll take my mother to Brighton General Hospital?'

'Yes, we will,' the blonde-ponytailed woman said calmly.

'My husband, who is my mother's GP, and I will follow in the car. That way we can bring Mum home.' She shot a look at Sarah 'I'd like it noted that I have power of attorney, my sister does not.'

Janice feebly pulled the respirator mask from her face. 'Oh, for goodness' sake Daphne, I've hurt my ankle. I'm not about to die.'

The paramedic replaced the mask. 'Now, Mrs Portman,' she said. 'Don't be getting yourself all worked up. We need you to keep calm.'

As the ambulance trundled along The Promenade, Sarah squeezed her mother's wrinkled hand. 'I think Daphne and I bring out the worst in each other. I'm sorry.'

Janice just shook her head.


Sarah made herself scarce the minute Daphne and Adam arrived at the hospital. If they wanted to get on everyone's nerves by being in the way and making demands about Janice's care, then she was happy to leave them to it. She sat in the A&E waiting room, cradling a black coffee from the shop in the main foyer. Hours ticked slowly by, and eventually Daphne and Adam appeared at the double doors and went in search of sustenance, without even glancing at Sarah. Everyone was so used to her not being around that they'd clearly forgotten she was there. She hurried through the doors and found her mother sitting up in bed with a cup of tea.

'Hello, love,' Janice beamed as Sarah approached. Clearly, she'd been given some pretty hefty pain relief. A red-haired nurse with *Mandy* on her name badge gave Sarah a smile and bustled away.

'Sorry, I just couldn't, you know,' Sarah said, inclining her head in the direction Daphne and Adam had gone. 'How are you feeling?'

Janice giggled. 'On top of the world. I have no idea what's in this' – she lifted the hand with the canula in it – 'but I like it.'

'What are you like, Mum? Any news on your ankle?'

'It's fractured, but not too badly. They're hoping I'll get by with a boot rather than a cast. But I'm just waiting on confirmation.' She beckoned Sarah closer. 'I'd quite like to go home. I don't like hospitals. I haven't ever since, well...'

The memory came in such a rush that blue dots swam in front of Sarah's eyes. All the time she'd been sitting in the waiting room, she'd tried really hard not to remember that day, or the look on the doctor's face when he'd gently told her and Rob that the doctors had done everything they could, but... The noise that erupted from her had not been human. It had been an animalistic howl from deep down in her core. The sort of sound only a mother could make.

Back in the room with her own mother, she bit her lip. No tears. Push it down. Lock it away.

There was an uncomfortable silence in Adam's car as he drove everyone back to Pebble Cottage. Daphne barely looked at Sarah, and Sarah stared out of the window, with her arms folded tightly across her chest for the entire journey.

By the time they'd got Janice inside and settled in one of the armchairs by the fireplace, with her ankle raised on a footstool, everyone's stomachs were starting to rumble. Sarah ventured up to the chip shop on the High Street, which everyone agreed did the best chips. She returned laden with packages of battered fish and bundles of chips that gave off a mouthwatering aroma of salt and vinegar.

'Here we go,' she said, handing around warmed plates piled with golden fish and mountains of thickly cut chips. Daphne poured out four cups of tea from the pot and they all tucked in. They were all clearly starving hungry, as no one said a word for a while. It was Adam who broke the silence.

'So, Janice.'

Was he using his 'doctor voice'? Sarah shuddered slightly as Adam and Daphne exchanged a look. She might have been imagining it, but there seemed to be an odd vibe between the couple. Maybe all was not well in their marriage. They'd hardly said a word to each other since leaving the hospital.

Adam cleared his throat and ran his slender fingers through what was left of his sandy hair. He'd lost quite a lot of it in the ten years since Sarah had seen him. There was genuine concern in his grey eyes behind the thick glasses. His forehead was permanently creased, so it was hard to tell if he was frowning. 'Daphne and I think it would be a good idea for you to move into Bayview Care Home for a few weeks. Just until you're able to put weight on your ankle. I spoke to them earlier, and they do have space – and you'd be made very welcome.'

Janice threw her fork down on her plate. 'Absolutely not.'

Daphne placed a hand on Janice's arm, stroking it gently. 'Now, Mum, don't be difficult. I have a very busy few weeks coming up, what with Jake's football and cricket clubs, and several Parent-Teacher Association meetings and events. I have to take Treacle to the groomers and to the vet for her annual injections. Jake has a dentist appointment. I just don't think I'm going to be able to look after you. And you can't be left on your own. How would you manage? You can't even get up the stairs.'

'I am *not* going into an old folk's home.'

'But Mum—'

'Sarah's here,' Janice said, and three pairs of eyes turned sharply in Sarah's direction. 'She'll look after me. Won't you, love?'

'Sarah?' Daphne spluttered. 'Sarah can't look after you. And she'll be disappearing off as soon as her van, or whatever it is, is fixed.' She sniffed. 'I don't think—'

Before she could stop herself, the words tumbled out of Sarah's mouth. 'I'm happy to stay as long as Mum needs me.' She got up and gathered the empty plates, stacking them in her hands with the skill of someone who'd been waitressing for ten years. She hurried into the kitchen before anyone spotted that she was breathing a little too heavily. What was she saying? Her mother could be incapacitated for weeks – months, even. She did *not* want to stay in Dovecote for that long. The raised voices from the sitting room blurred in her ears as she set about filling the sink with hot, soapy water.

'No! And that's final.'

Sarah couldn't help but grin at Janice's firm tone. She had forgotten that her mother was a woman with an iron will, when the mood took her. She turned away from the sink as Daphne cleared her throat behind her.

'Well, Mum's made up her mind.'

Sarah dried her hands on a tea towel. 'As she has the right to. She's not a decrepit, feeble old woman, Daphne. And you can't treat her like a child.' From the look in Daphne's eyes, Sarah knew she'd said too much. Daphne took a step towards her and lowered her voice.

'How on earth would you know how Mum should be treated? You've not been here.'

Sarah squared her shoulders. 'Well, I am now. And I *will* look after her.' She reached for a mug and wiped it with the towel.

'Do you even know how to look after anyone but yourself?'

Sarah's hands tightened around the mug. Her mouth moved, but no sound came out. Her eyes watered and she turned away.

Daphne placed a hand on her shoulder, making Sarah flinch and drop the mug into the sink. 'I'm sorry. That was an awful thing to say. I didn't mean it. I'm just worried about Mum and...'

Sarah shrugged off her sister's hand. 'I think you should leave,' she said addressing the soapy water.

'Look, I'm sure you and Mum will be fine. But you can't do it all on your own, so I'll be around, and we'll see if we can get one of the carers from Bayview to call in.'

'Fine.'

'I'll come back tomorrow.'

'Yeah.'

'And I'll see if Natasha can cover the café.'

'Okay.'

'Thanks, Sarah.'

'Whatever.'

Sarah watched her sister's reflection in the kitchen window as she walked under the archway into the sitting room. She barely heard Adam and Daphne's goodbyes or the front door of Pebble Cottage closing behind them. It wasn't only Daphne's insinuation that Sarah only cared about herself that was making Sarah's heart beat so loudly she could hear it in her ears, it was what she'd said about finding a carer from Bayview. The universe had already conspired to reunite her with her estranged husband. Was she also about to come face-to-face with her former best friend?

# EIGHT

## SARAH

April 2017

Daphne had been right about one thing – Janice couldn't get up the stairs. She'd tried, later that evening, with Sarah's help, but she couldn't do it. Her good leg wasn't strong enough for her to hop up the steep stairs, and shuffling on her backside wasn't working either. The sky outside was morphing from blue to purple and Sarah was standing in her mother's bedroom with a screwdriver in her hand. A knock at the front door sent her scurrying down the stairs.

'I'm sure that bed comes apart, Mum. I just have to work out...' Her voice faded as she opened the door. Rob had a bouquet of flowers in his hand and a nervous expression on his face. He ran his fingers through his hair as the light hanging from the porch roof glinted in his eyes.

'Hi.' He rubbed his stubbled chin.

Sarah's heart stopped for a moment. He was wearing his wedding ring. She hadn't noticed if he'd been wearing it when she'd seen him at the campsite the previous day. She glanced down at her bare hand. She'd asked her dad to hide her rings away, years ago. She had no idea where he'd put them.

'Hi,' she said.

'Um, I heard about Janice's accident.'

Sarah stepped aside to allow Rob to cross the threshold. 'Right.'

'Rob!' Janice cried, her face lighting up. 'How lovely of you to come round.'

He handed Janice the flowers before giving her a light kiss on the cheek. 'What have you done to yourself, Janice? Honestly, what did I tell you the last time I came round? You need to slow down.'

Janice flapped her hand at him and handed the flowers to Sarah, whose stomach performed somersaults as she went into the kitchen in search of a vase. Rob and her mother had always got along really well. It was hard to imagine anyone not getting on with Janice, and Rob was pretty easy-going. Clearly her vanishing act hadn't changed that. It sounded as if he was a regular visitor to Pebble Cottage. She snipped the cellophane wrapper from around the flowers and filled a sea-green vase with water. Outside the kitchen window, the beam from the lighthouse swept in a wide arc, illuminating the cottage's garden at regular intervals. She shoved the bouquet of roses, daisies, and tulips into the vase. She wasn't envious that Rob and her mum were still friends. Well, maybe she was, just a little bit. But she'd be gone again once her mum's ankle was better. It wasn't any of her business who remained friends in her absence.

'Your mum was saying she can't get up the stairs and you're trying to bring her bed down here,' Rob said, with a hint of amusement as Sarah carried the vase of flowers back into the sitting room and put it down on the coffee table. 'Do you want a hand?'

Sarah bristled. 'No, thanks. I can manage.'

'Sarah,' Janice said gently. 'Let Rob help.' The pleading look in her mother's eyes made Sarah sigh.

'Okay, fine.'


Between them they managed to dismantle Janice's bed and bring it downstairs. Sarah made sure to avoid eye contact with Rob as they moved the sofa to underneath the window. That sofa held memories of the early days of their relationship within its flowered upholstery. As Rob was putting the bed back together, Sarah went back upstairs under the guise of vacuuming the now exposed patch of floorboards – but really, it was to get away. Being near her practically-if-not-legally-ex-husband made her light-headed and confused. It would have been easier if the years had aged him terribly or if he'd become obnoxious and nasty. But he was still so damned good-looking. And nice. And kind. And all the things she'd loved about him. But the dark memories pushed the light ones away. It had been *his* fault. She had to keep that at the front of her mind, otherwise he was too dangerous.

As she pushed the vacuum cleaner across the area of the floor previously hidden under the bed, a floorboard lifted and then caved in on itself.

'Oh, for crying out loud,' Sarah tutted as she turned off the vacuum cleaner and knelt down on the floor, reaching into the hole to retrieve the board. 'There better not be spiders down here,' she muttered as she groped in the darkness. Her fingers closed around something papery; she grasped it and pulled it out into the light. It was a very dusty, yellowed envelope. She wiped it with her sleeve and dust flew up her nose, making her sneeze. She lifted the flap, trying not to sneeze again. Inside was a bundle of black and white photographs, around four inches square. In the first photograph, two women were sat in a garden, the curved roof of a shed or something behind them. Their hands were very close together. Sarah turned the photo over. On the back, in neat, small writing was an inscription:

*September 1943 – Me and Rose in the back garden at Pebble Cottage.*

Sarah's eyes widened. Pebble Cottage? She peered more closely at the picture. It was hard to see in monochrome, but yes, that could be the cliff rising up at the end of the garden. How exciting. Photographs belonging to a previous resident, perhaps? But what were they doing hidden in an envelope beneath a loose floorboard? She reached for the next photo, but Rob's voice calling up the stairs brought her back to the present.

'The bed's done. Can you bring down the pillows and stuff? And your mum's nightdress.'

Sarah got to her feet and rubbed the dust from the knees of her jeans. Stuffing the envelope of photos into her back pocket, she gathered up the bed linen and went back downstairs. The sitting room looked even pokier with a double bed taking up most of it. The two armchairs, one of which still cradled her mum, were backed up against the stairs.

'It's only for a short while,' Janice said, surveying her sitting room. 'I'll be able to manage the stairs in no time.'

Sarah dumped the linen down on the bed. 'There's no rush, Mum. Better to take your time and let your ankle heal properly. You can't see the telly from there.'

'Ah, no problem,' Rob said clambering over the sofa. In a matter of minutes, he'd moved the television, and the table it lived on, to the opposite end of the sofa, near the front door. 'There. Is that alright, Janice?'

'It's perfect, love. Thank you, both.'

Rob rubbed his hands together and turned to Sarah. 'I don't know about you, but I could do with a pint.' The invitation was clear in his eyes and Sarah shrank back from his gaze.

'I can't leave Mum on her own,' she mumbled.

'Nonsense,' Janice cried. 'Just pass me my book and the remote and I'll be right as rain here. I've got my crutches; I can get as far as the downstairs toilet if I need to. Go on, you've earnt a drink or two.'

Sarah narrowed her eyes at her mother. What was she up to? Janice blinked back innocently, and Sarah huffed. 'Just one. I'll be back in an hour, Mum.' As she grabbed the spare key to Pebble Cottage, she remembered the envelope of photographs. She placed them down on the sill of the stained-glass window at the bottom of the stairs. 'Remind me to show you what I found upstairs,' she said. She bent down to kiss Janice's cheek, and her mother whispered in her ear.

'He's missed you.'

The blood drained from Sarah's face. That was exactly what she had been afraid of. Surely, he couldn't still have feelings for her, not after all this time?

If he did, her life was about to become a lot more complicated.

# NINE

## ROSE

June 1941

It had taken six months of hard work, but The Seaside Café had opened for business a few short months ago. I already knew it was the best thing I had ever done. Every morning when Martin had left for a day on the telegram machine at the Post Office in Brighton, I'd donned a pair of old overalls I'd found in the garden shed at Pebble Cottage and got to work. I'd pulled up the grim, beige linoleum and sanded and polished the beautiful parquet floor underneath until I could see my face in it. I'd stripped all the tables back to bare wood and varnished them. Maureen's brother, Stan, from next door, had kindly got me a couple of rolls of cream wallpaper covered in little pink flowers. I'd painted the back wall cream. Several spiders had been evicted from the old Welsh dresser, which I'd cleaned until it looked brand new.

The awful brown teapots were taken down and replaced with the antique ones I'd found in the box under the kitchen counter. They were different sizes, colours, and shapes, and I thought they were beautiful. Just before Christmas, I'd bumped into Sister Margaret, one of the nuns who ran Bayview Convalescent Home, and bartered an exchange of the brown teapots for twelve white bud vases the convalescent home had no use for. The injured soldiers in their care didn't mind a boring brown teapot.

I'd washed and scrubbed and polished and painted and varnished until my hands were red raw.

Then in the evenings, I went home to Pebble Cottage and waited for Martin. His workday finished at five o'clock, but most evenings I didn't see him until almost eight. He'd developed a habit of stopping for a drink in one of the pubs between the Post Office and the station. I didn't mind, particularly if it meant that his friend Brian never saw fit to sully Dovecote with his presence. I was starting to feel as if Martin and I didn't fit together, although I couldn't put my finger on why.

I turned this question over and over in my head as I walked along The Promenade on the morning of what was promising to be a delightful summer day. Already the sun was bathing the stony beach and glistening off the sea. The seagulls were up and squawking as they swooped and dived in the breeze. I sighed contentedly as I approached the café. The pastel pink on the window frame and the door were so welcoming. The day I'd climbed up a tall ladder, lent to me by Stan, and sloshed pastel pink over the hideous grey, had been the day the café truly became mine.

Martin had never expressly given me permission to rename it, but I did it anyway. He didn't argue or complain. By then, his habit of a few drinks after work had become entrenched, so I suppose he'd thought better of kicking up a fuss. Mr Crawford, who owned the opticians on the High Street, had put me in touch with the signwriter he'd used. Thankfully the chap hadn't been called up, and he did a marvellous job, for a very reasonable price.

Every day, when I read the words *The Seaside Café* in delicate, looping yellow script above the window, my heart swelled. I slipped my key into the lock, excitement bubbling in my chest at the prospect of another day of raising smiles with tea and cakes.

I was just putting the first batch of teacakes out on the counter when the bell above the door tinkled and Reverend Douglas entered.

'Morning, Rose,' he said with a smile and a tip of his hat.

'Morning. The usual?'

'Oh, yes please. Looking like a glorious day out there today,' he commented, folding his tall body and long legs into a chair.

I busied myself with making a pot of tea and toasting a teacake. 'Yes, it is. They were talking on the wireless this morning about the German invasion of the Soviet Union.' I sighed. 'It's never going to end, is it?'

Reverend Douglas gave me one of his reassuring smiles. It lit up his otherwise sharp face. 'Have faith, Rose. There will be an end.'

'Hmm,' I said, putting down his tea and cake. 'But at what cost? And will any of us be left to see it?'

He had picked up his paper, but put it down and motioned for me to join him. The café didn't officially open for another half an hour, but Reverend Douglas and I had developed this little routine whereby he'd call in for breakfast while out on his morning constitutional. I allowed it, seeing as he was my uncle.

It had been quite the shock, the first day he'd come into the café with his wife Gladys and, after staring at me for several minutes, enquired whether I was acquainted with, or indeed related to, an Anne Partridge. He only asked, he explained, as I looked so like her. I had her eyes. Well, when I confirmed that Anne Partridge was my mother, who had died some thirteen years previously, he'd burst into tears. He later explained, having been fortified with strong tea, that he was my mother's brother. They had fallen out not long after my birth, over the contents of my grandfather's will, and hadn't spoken since. He hadn't even known she'd died. That evening, I'd examined the only photograph I had of my parents closely. My mother and Reverend Douglas had the same long, thin nose.

We'd become good friends since then. Making up for lost time, as he'd put it.

'Now, Rose. This is most unlike you. Whatever is the matter?'

I rested my elbow on the table and cradled my chin in my hand. 'I don't really know. Just silly things, I suppose.'

'Everything alright with Martin, is it?' Douglas had an uncanny knack of knowing what was bothering people. A handy skill in his profession, no doubt. He didn't wait for a response before continuing. 'Don't start fretting, my dear. Pebble Cottage will be filled with the patter of tiny feet when God decides the time is right.'

I blushed as my stomach contracted. That was not the issue at all. In fact, it wasn't entirely surprising, but nonetheless a relief, that I hadn't fallen pregnant. I wasn't ready. Of course, I understood that it was expected that we would have children, but just not yet. That would have required partaking in more intimacy than Martin and I did. Occasionally, if he came home from the pub in a good mood, he initiated it, but most of the time he just fell into bed and started snoring. What concerned me slightly was that this suited me perfectly well. I should have been upset about his lack of interest, but I really wasn't. Again, there was that feeling that we didn't fit. Or perhaps the two of us were somehow broken.

I was also not completely naïve. It had crossed my mind that Martin's real reason for staying in Brighton late into the evenings, and his lack of interest in me, could be due to him seeing another woman. I'd quickly dismissed the thought. He wasn't the sort. And there were never any traces of lipstick or scent, or any of the other telltale signs I'd heard other women say had given their wandering husbands away. I was certainly not going to reveal any of this to my uncle, man of the cloth or not. So instead, I just gave him a smile.

'You're right. Perhaps God is just giving me time to get the café up and running,' I said with a light laugh.

'You've become quite an integral part of the community. I don't know what we'd do without you. Especially since the bakery closed down.' The sudden closure of the bakery up on the High Street had been a boon for The Seaside Café. Being the only establishment where people could buy bread meant I could get enhanced supplies of ingredients, and reduced rates on the gas and electric bills. But, even with very reliable suppliers, it was getting harder to source the essentials. The cost of sugar had gone through the roof.

'Well, it's nice to be needed.'

'You're more than that, Rose. You're a vital service, both for our stomachs and our souls.'

'I don't wish to tread on your toes in that regard,' I laughed again.

Uncle Douglas gave me a wink as he drained his teacup. 'The soul is nourished in various ways, Rose. Sometimes a warm teacake and a pot of tea can give more succour than a sermon. Right, time for me to be on my way. Don't forget where I am if you need anything. Anything at all.'

I turned the sign on the door to *Open* and stood in the doorway inhaling the sea air. With a small, but contented sigh, I went back behind the counter. There were souls that needed nourishing. If only the success of the café was mirrored in my marriage. There was a wall forming between me and my husband, and I didn't know what I could do about it.

# TEN

## SARAH

April 2017

Pools of light dappled The Promenade, and the lights strung up between the lampposts cast their glow on the grey pebbles of the beach beyond the turquoise railings. Over the other side of the bay, Sarah could see lit windows in the cottages along Beachfront Road, and the row of lights marking the steps that snaked up the cliff towards Dovecote Manor. She paused just outside The Seaside Café and placed a shaking hand on the railings. A cold shiver ran up her spine, chilling her blood. Fighting a rising tide of anger, pain, and grief, she stared out at the black sea to where the lighthouse, and the rocks on which it stood, loomed in the darkness. Those rocks were where it had happened. Where Faith had died.

'It took me months before I could even look at that view,' Rob said, making Sarah jump. She had completely forgotten he was there. 'But I've made my peace with it. I've even been out there a few times.' The beam from the top of the lighthouse arced over the beach, illuminating his face. For a split second, she wanted to physically wipe the concerned look off his face. She didn't need his pity.

'Well, good for you,' she spat.

'Sarah. I didn't mean—'

'I don't want to talk about it. Not with you.'

'Okay. Well, how about that drink?'

They walked in silence along The Promenade, and up the High Street. As they approached The Royal Oak, Sarah's skin began to crawl. The pub would be full of people who knew her. She drew to a halt outside Harrington's Bookshop, on the opposite corner.

'What's wrong?' Rob asked, his eyes wide.

'I don't think I can deal with seeing everyone,' Sarah replied, shaking her head.

Rob glanced across the road and then back to Sarah. 'Okay, not the pub. As we're already halfway there, why don't you come back to mine for one drink? Just one. Please?'

Would going back to her former marital home be better or worse than the pub? The obvious, and sensible, response to his invitation, was no. But there was something about the look in Rob's eyes that stole that word from her mouth.

'Just one.' For a split second, she thought Rob was going to take her hand as they turned into Blythe Avenue, and then down the narrow lane between the terraces of Victorian houses, and out onto Courcey Road. She had no idea what she would have done if he had.

Standing outside the red-brick, mid-terrace, two-up-two-down house on Courcey Road, Sarah's palms were clammy. She stuffed her hands into the pockets of her jeans. Maybe The Royal Oak would have been the lesser of two evils. What she should have done was stay at Pebble Cottage and spent the evening with her mother, looking at the old photographs she'd found.

What she *really* should have done was stay in Manchester.

Rob nudged her with his elbow. 'Just one drink, Sarah. Please?'

She chewed the inside of her cheek and looked up at the window of what had once been their bedroom. Every fibre of her body was screaming at her to run away from this obvious portal to her past. She wouldn't get far. Rob had the keys to her van, which was probably in bits in his workshop anyway. But he had that look in his eyes again; the look that said, 'I need you.' She had never been able to resist that look. Rob had opened the front door and was standing just inside, waiting. Sarah pulled her shoulders back and walked right smack into her old life.

The hallway smelt of the fresh paint coating the off-white walls. There was still masking tape on the skirting board, and a scrunched-up plastic sheet at the bottom of the stairs.

'Sorry, it's a mess. I wasn't expecting to have visitors.' Rob grimaced as he indicated the decorating supplies, before leading Sarah down the narrow hallway to the kitchen-dining room at the back of the house. Not that she needed to be led; she could find her way around the house with her eyes closed. She'd walked the floor in the deep darkness of the middle of the night with a restless Faith in her arms enough times. 'I've slowly been redecorating over the last few months.'

'Oh, right.'

'Red or white?'

Sarah could tell from the tone of Rob's question that he remembered, and didn't really need to ask. 'Red. Always.'

Rob's lips parted in a slow smile as their eyes met, and a moment steeped in memories passed between them. Sarah looked away as Rob poured two large glasses from the bottle. Had it really been fourteen years since they'd first shared a bottle of wine – and a decade since their last? The night-time beach party where they'd met and ran into the sea screaming with laughter nibbled at the edge of Sarah's consciousness, but she pushed it away. She'd fallen for him quickly, and hard. She wouldn't let that happen again, no matter how much the deep blue of his eyes called her to lose herself in them. Taking the glass of wine from him, she swallowed back the apology that pushed at her lips. It was too late for that now. He had one to make too, but it didn't seem to be forthcoming.

She stifled a sharp intake of breath as she followed him into the small sitting room. It didn't look anything like the room she'd last seen ten years before. The green carpet was gone, and the original floorboards had been buffed and varnished. The battered old yellow sofa that had taken up the whole room had been replaced by a much neater grey one. Of course, the biggest difference was that the room wasn't crammed with toys. Sarah forced a tiny sip of wine down her constricted throat. She pushed away the question she wanted to ask. If he *had* redecorated Faith's room, it was better that she didn't know. A sharp pain stung her chest. Not that she could imagine going into that room either way.

'So?' she said, leaning against the arm of the sofa, trying to maximise the distance between them in the small room.

'So,' Rob replied. 'You've been in Manchester for the last ten years.'

Sarah studied the contents of her wine glass. 'The last nine years. With Dad and his husband, Pete.'

'Yeah, Janice told me that earlier, while you were up in her bedroom. That's good.'

'Is it?'

Rob shrugged. 'I mean it's good that you reconnected with him. I guess it must have helped. I was sorry to hear that he died.'

They both drank their wine in silence. When Rob reached for the bottle and topped up her glass, Sarah didn't complain.

'So, um, I'm guessing it's not the first time you've redecorated in ten years?' She really didn't want to open the door to the past, but what else did they have to talk about? As long as he didn't mention Faith, she could cope.

'No, it is.'

'Really?'

Rob put his wine glass down and turned towards her. 'When you first left, I vowed not to change a thing, so that when you came back you wouldn't think I'd tried to erase you. Or Faith.'

And he'd done it. He'd lifted the stake and driven it straight into Sarah's heart. Hearing him speak their daughter's name chilled her bones.

'As the years went by, I found I couldn't change anything. If I didn't change the wallpaper, or the sofa, or our bed, then it felt like you were still here. A few months ago, the hall radiator developed a leak and had to be replaced. The new one is smaller than the original, so I had to paint the wall. Once I started, I couldn't stop. It felt like I was letting myself let go. And then you turned up. If I'd known splashing a tub of off-white emulsion on the walls would bring you back, I'd have done it years ago.' His half-smile was almost apologetic.

'Have you been—'

'Waiting? Yes. I've been waiting for you to come home for ten years.' His voice was soft, and he spoke into his glass.

Sarah drained hers as a wave of emotions swept over her. 'Well, then you're a fool.' The moment the words left her mouth, there was a change in the atmosphere. Rob slammed his glass down on the table. He got to his feet and looked out of the window at the dark street. Sarah put her glass down quietly and stood. She had her hand on the door when he turned back, fury in his eyes. She met his glare with equal ferocity. The familiarity of the tension between them made her muscles ache. They stared each other down for a long minute.

'A fool?' he growled. 'I believed you would come back.' He rubbed his forehead. 'I loved you. You were... you *are* my wife,

Sarah. Of course I waited for you.' He paced the tiny space like a caged lion; his hands balled into fists. The air was heavy.

'I was never coming back,' she said through gritted teeth. 'And I never gave you, or anyone else, any indication that I would. So, if you're stupid enough not to realise we were over ten years ago, that's not my fault.'

'You didn't exactly make it clear you weren't coming back. As I recall, you told me, and everybody else, nothing. One text to your mum so we knew you were alive. That was all we got. Everyone who loved you was just left wondering and waiting. You have no idea how hard it was for all of us.'

His words hit her right in the chest, but the impact wasn't enough to quell the rage bubbling inside her. 'At least you had each other. Who did I have?'

'And whose fault is that?'

'My daughter *died*.' The shout rattled her rib cage.

Rob stopped pacing and stared at her, stony-faced but with wildfire in his eyes. '*Our* daughter. You don't have a monopoly on grief, Sarah. And we could have had each other.'

Sarah almost laughed. 'Yeah, right. Come on, Rob. Admit it. We were falling apart long before Faith...' Her voice cracked and failed. There was a pressure in her sinuses and behind her eyes. No tears. She'd shed enough tears in this house. She gulped down the rising tide and her words came out coated in sadness. 'We'd stopped loving each other way before.'

Somehow, although she'd not realised it, she had crossed the room and was standing right in front of her husband. His body heat radiated against her bare arms. The hurt and pain of all that had happened between them thickened the air, shortening their breaths. They locked eyes and the ground slipped out from under Sarah's feet. And then – so fast that she didn't even know who had made the first move – they were kissing. It was hurried and forceful. Rob's hand was in her hair at the back of her neck, his other arm around her waist. His touch was electric.

'I never stopped loving you,' he murmured when their lips parted for a moment.

'Oh, God,' Sarah mumbled. Her pulse thundered in her ears and a red-hot desire rose up in her stomach. She fumbled with the buttons of his shirt as he tugged her T-shirt out of the waistband of her jeans... A loud message alert from her phone brought them back to earth. Sarah disentangled herself from Rob's embrace and pulled her phone from her bag.

> *Hi, love. I hope you and Rob are having a nice time. Just to say, I don't mind you staying out late, but don't forget I'm sleeping downstairs when you come home.*

She looked up from her mother's message at Rob, a wave of guilt coursing through her chest. God, he looked so good with his shirt half undone and his wavy hair tousled. Her heart fluttered. He didn't need to say anything for her to know what he was thinking. What was *she* thinking?

'I have to go,' she said suddenly, throwing her phone back in her bag and reaching for the door handle.

'Sarah?'

She turned and raised her hand. 'No. Just. No. Oh, God,' she groaned.

He didn't follow her into the hall, or out onto the street. When she looked over her shoulder as she crossed Courcey Road, he wasn't watching her from the window. What had she done?

# ELEVEN

## SARAH

April 2017

The brightness of the sun the following morning meant Sarah could hide the redness of her eyes behind her sunglasses as she walked along The Promenade to The Seaside Café. The events of the previous evening had kept her awake most of the night, and when she'd finally fallen asleep, she'd had that nightmare again – the one where she was falling and no one could catch her. She tried to push it all out of her mind. There were bigger things to focus on, like keeping the café running while Janice was out of action. Although, she had been quite impressed at her mother's determination to get herself up, washed, and dressed without any help. It was a good job her parents had fitted a downstairs bathroom when Sarah was little. Otherwise, Janice would have had to go into Bayview. The thought churned Sarah's stomach. Reuniting with Rob was one thing, but the thought of seeing...

'Sarah?' The call from the woman with bushy ginger hair outside the café pulled Sarah back to the present. 'Oh wow! It *is* you. Gosh, you've not changed.'

'Hi, Natasha.' Sarah couldn't help but smile. Natasha Jackson, Adam's younger sister, hadn't changed either. She was still bright-eyed, bubbly, and dressed head-to-toe in vibrant colours.

'Are you sure you don't mind holding the fort for the morning?' Sarah asked as she unlocked the door and flicked on the light.

'Oh no, not at all. How is Janice doing?'

'She's doing fine. Obviously, her ankle is still very sore, but she's determined not to let it get her down.'

Natasha chuckled as she pushed her magenta-framed glasses back up her small nose. She pulled a pink and white striped apron off the peg in the kitchen and slipped it on over her canary-yellow cardigan. 'Well, that's our Janice. Nothing much ever fazes her. I hope I'm that sprightly when I'm in my seventies.'

'Yeah, me too. That's why I need to stay at home with her. Not because she needs help, but because I know she'll try and do something daft if she's not supervised.'

Natasha fired up the coffee machine and began setting up the till, so Sarah dragged the white tables and chairs outside. 'We might need to pull the awning out,' she said, when she went back in. 'I think it's going to be a warm one.'

'Oh, that will be nice,' Natasha said, going into the kitchen. She removed a stack of envelopes from her bag and handed them to Sarah, who had followed her into the narrow space. 'Tim brought the post while I was waiting.'

'Brill, thanks. I'll take these home to Mum. That should keep her out of mischief for a while. Right, do you have everything you need?' she asked, dropping the post into her tote bag. Neil's ashes were sitting safely on Sarah's old desk in her bedroom back at Pebble Cottage. Who knows what he might have thought about that.

Natasha looked around. 'Milk? Yes. Cakes? Yes. I'll get another couple of tea loaves out of the freezer. Bread? Yep.

Eggs?' She opened the large fridge. 'Yep. No sticky buns though.'

'Mum hasn't given you the secret recipe, then?'

'Nope.'

'As soon as she's able to stand for long enough, I'll see if I can convince her to make a batch and I'll try to keep a close eye on what she's doing. You know, I watched her make those buns throughout my entire childhood, and I never saw what she put in them to make them so good.' Sarah scuffed the floor with the toe of her black boot. 'When I was away, I tried to recreate them. But I could never get them exactly right.'

'It's a mystery,' Natasha said with a giggle as they went back out of the kitchen and into the main café area. 'Oh, the kids are here!' There was a trio of teenagers peering in through the door, and Natasha waved. 'You probably don't remember my Alice,' she said, crossing the café and unlocking the door. But Sarah barely noticed the girl whose smile matched her mother's, or the boy with thick-rimmed glasses who was holding Alice's hand. She couldn't take her eyes off the taller boy with mousy-brown hair and lanky limbs. His school tie was already loosened, and he had a football tucked under his arm. The kids were chatting away, but Sarah could only stare at her nephew, Jake. He must have felt the weight of her gaze on him, but when he looked over at her, there was no hint of recognition on his face. He'd not seen her since he was three years old. It was hardly surprising that he didn't know who she was. And whose fault was that?

Sarah ducked back into the kitchen, where she rested her head against the cool stainless-steel fridge. She rubbed her eyes and tried to steady her rapid breathing. Faith had only been a few months younger than Jake. She tried to imagine her daughter grown up and running around Dovecote with her cousin, but the image failed to materialise. She would have been so beautiful, of that Sarah was sure. She'd had her father's eyes.

That familiar pressure built up again in her sinuses. No, there could be no tears. If she started to cry, she wouldn't be able to stop.

She tentatively emerged from her hiding place and let out a long, relieved breath. The kids were gone, and Natasha was replacing the wilted daffodils in the bud vases with fresh carnations.

'Alice brought these,' she said, indicating the vibrant pink flowers. 'I told her she could come down after school and help out for a while. If Janice doesn't mind? She'll probably just sit in the corner on her phone the whole time. I think the boys have football after school. Or maybe it's cricket. Daphne will know. I can't keep up with all of Jake's hobbies. Harry is a nice boy. Alice would kill me for saying it, but I think there's a little romance going on there. His mum, Grace, was in my year at school. Of course, you'd know her seeing as she's best friends with your Rob's sister, Rachel.' Natasha suddenly stopped and put her hand to her mouth, realising what she'd just said. 'Oh sorry, Sarah. That was so insensitive of me.'

Sarah mustered a tight smile. 'It's fine.' Natasha busied herself with fluffing the net curtains on the window and rearranging the cups on top of the coffee machine. She had everything under control and Sarah was only getting in the way. 'Well, I'd better get back to Mum. Just call if you need anything.'

'Will do. Tell your mum not to worry. Everything will be absolutely fine.'

Sarah managed a grateful smile. 'Thanks.'


When Sarah walked through the front door of Pebble Cottage, she nearly knocked her mother over.

'Sorry, Mum. I didn't expect you to be standing behind the

door.' She plonked her tote bag down on the sofa. 'What have you got there?'

'An envelope I found on the windowsill. I don't remember putting it there.'

'You weren't trying to get up the stairs, were you?'

Janice looked down at her feet, one of which was encased in a heavy blue support boot.

'Mum! Oh, it's the photos.' That was what Janice was holding – the envelope of photos Sarah had found the day before. What with everything that had happened with Rob, she'd completely forgotten about them. 'I found them under a loose floorboard yesterday after we moved your bed. I didn't get a chance to look at them properly.'

They sat down in the armchairs that had been pushed back against the stairs to make room for Janice's bed. Sarah pulled the first photo out of the envelope.

'This first one was taken in the back garden, here at Pebble Cottage, in 1943,' she said, passing the photo to Janice. 'There's a note on the back. One of the women is called Rose. Any idea who they are?'

Janice peered at the photo. 'Not a clue. Must be the people who lived here back then.'

'Yeah,' Sarah said, taking out the next photo. It was of one of the women from the first photo, but she was standing on The Promenade, leaning against the railings with the beach behind her. Her head was tilted back, and she looked like she was laughing. Sarah turned it over. '*October 1943 – Rose on The Promenade.*' She passed it to Janice, who put it down on the coffee table squeezed in between the two armchairs. 'Here's Rose again,' Sarah said, handing Janice a third photo. This time Rose was sitting on a patch of grass, her legs stretched out and her feet bare. 'Is that the Victoria Park bandstand in the background?'

'Oh yes, I think it is,' Janice said. 'I'm surprised that wasn't torn down for scrap during the war.'

'Those vintage dresses are really popular again,' Sarah laughed. 'Look at the pin curls in her hair. Here's another one of her. Must have been taken at Christmas.' She paused before passing it to Janice. Rose was standing next to a rather sorry-looking Christmas tree. There was something about her that was familiar. Maybe she was a relative of someone who lived in Dovecote now, or maybe she just had one of *those* faces? She was very pretty. 'She seems quite young,' she observed, giving up on working out what it was that was making her look twice at Rose's face. 'Whoever she is.'

'Indeed.'

'Oh, crikey,' Sarah cried at the next photo before turning it so Janice could see.

'Oh,' Janice echoed. It was another photo of Rose and the unnamed woman, but it wasn't easy to see which was which, as they were mid-kiss. And it was no platonic peck on the cheek, either. 'I... um... well, I wasn't expecting that.'

Sarah giggled. 'No, me neither. They're having a proper snog there. Well, well. I kind of want to find out who they are now. Oh, last one. Strange to think these may not have seen the light of day for seventy-odd years.' The photo was of Rose again. She was sitting up in what could have been a hospital bed, and in her arms was a newborn baby, securely wrapped in a bundle of blankets. Sarah turned the photo over and her heart nearly stopped. Her voice trembled as she read out the inscription. '*10th March 1942 – Rose and Janice at Bayview.*'

Sarah stared at her mother, and her mother stared back.

# TWELVE

## ROSE

June 1941

A few weeks after my heart-to-heart with Uncle Douglas, at half past ten on the dot, Dora Stephens came into the café, carrying a string shopping bag with a manila envelope inside. Today, her long chestnut-brown hair was set in waves and pinned back from her pretty oval face. There was the slightest trace of rouge on her cheeks. Her peach lipstick matched the nail varnish on the tips of her delicate fingers.

'Good morning, Rose,' she said, a little shyly, approaching the counter. I never saw her talk to anyone else in Dovecote, and no one ever joined her for her morning cuppa. I wondered if she was a little lonely. Well, one thing was certain, no one was ever going to feel unwelcome at The Seaside Café. I knew from years of being an outsider what that felt like, and how much it hurt.

'Hi, Dora. Right on time as usual.'

She laughed along with me. 'Ah, well, I like a routine. It reminds me of being at school. I would like someone to ring a bell for me when it is time to stop working and have lunch.'

'Just a tea today, or can I tempt you with a sweet treat?'

Dora examined the teacakes, and the golden syrup sponge I'd baked that morning. 'They do look lovely, but just a tea. Thank you.'

I brought the tea over to the table she always sat at; the one near the back by the Welsh dresser. She turned her cornflower-blue eyes to me and smiled. She had such a captivating smile.

'So,' I said, desperately searching for a reason to talk to her. 'Seen any good films lately? I've not been to the pictures in ages.'

Dora shook her head. 'Me neither. I just don't have time. Work keeps me so busy.'

'That's a shame. What is it that you do?'

She glanced at the manila envelope in her shopping bag hanging from the chair beside her. 'I'm sorry, Rose. I can't...'

'Oh, goodness. I'm so sorry. I should know better than to be asking such questions at a time like this. Please, forget I asked.' My face was burning as I ran back behind the counter and into the kitchen. How idiotic. But all the same, the fact she couldn't tell me what she did was intriguing. It must be something to do with the war or the government. Maybe she was a spy? I nearly laughed out loud. What on earth would a spy be doing in Dovecote? The very idea was ridiculous. She was just a sweet, beautiful young woman who came into my café every morning for a cup of tea.

The rest of the day passed as the days do. The sun shone in the windows of the café all day, and people came, had tea, and went off about their business again. It was one of those days where the war seemed very far away.

I closed the café at three o'clock as usual and meandered down The Promenade. I'd prepared a cottage pie that morning before work, so all I needed to do was put it in the oven for dinner. It was mostly potato on top of a thin layer of ground beef and carrots in gravy, but it would do. There were two slices of golden syrup cake left, so those were coming home with me for afters. I had a couple of hours to myself before Martin got home. Perhaps I might start digging up more of the lawn, so I could put another row of carrots in. Or I could just sit in the garden with my book and quietly enjoy the sun. It wasn't that he was noisy, but he was always *there*, rustling his paper or tapping his foot against something. But that was what marriage was about; putting up with the little things to benefit from the bigger things, like having someone to hold hands with during an air raid siren.

I turned my key in the lock of Pebble Cottage, pushed open the front door, and came to an abrupt halt.

'Martin! Gracious, you startled me. What are you doing home so early?' He didn't get up from the sofa. He barely looked up at me. Then I saw the piece of paper in his hand and the redness of his eyes. 'Oh.'

He hauled himself to his feet. It seemed to take him a lot of effort just to move. 'It's not as bad as it could be,' he said with a slight shrug. His voice was hoarse, as though he'd been crying for a long time. 'I'm not being called up to the Front, at least.'

I raised my hand to my chest. 'Oh, that's a relief.'

'The letter says I'm to get the ten o'clock train from Euston to Dundee on Tuesday, where I will be given further instructions. It's from the General Post Office Headquarters.'

'And you go next Tuesday?'

'I shall struggle to get to Euston by ten in the morning. Perhaps I should go up the day before.'

'And stay in London?' My head was filled with the news headlines about the bombing raids. Every morning for eight months, the newspapers had been full of reports of the damage, and of the dead. The papers were calling it the Blitz. My knees gave way, and I landed heavily on the sofa. 'Do you have to go?'

Martin took my hand and pulled me to my feet. He held me close, and we swayed slowly to music only we could hear.

Later that night, after we made love, he whispered into the dark, 'I'm going to miss you.'

He said the words so softly and quietly, I wondered whether they were for me at all.

# THIRTEEN

## SARAH

April 2017

'Mum?' Sarah gathered the photos into a bundle and put them back in the envelope as her mother reached for her crutches and hobbled into the kitchen. Sarah followed. 'Do you—'

'Do I what? It's a coincidence, Sarah. I'm sure Janice was a popular name back then.' Janice flicked on the kettle. 'Is Natasha alright at the café?'

'She's fine. But, Mum—'

'And how did it go with Rob last night?'

The kettle gurgled as Sarah's stomach knotted itself. 'Fine. We had a chat. But never mind that. Mum, that picture of the baby. That's *your* birth date.'

'So?'

Sarah took two mugs from the cupboard above the kettle and threw a teabag in each. 'You don't think it might be you?' The kettle clicked off and Sarah poured water and a generous splash of milk into the mugs.

Janice laughed. 'Don't be silly. Of course that's not me. As you know very well, my mother's name was Gladys.'

'But you were also born at Bayview on the tenth of March, 1942.'

'Well, yes.'

Sarah placed the two mugs down on the round pine table that had been in the cosy kitchen of Pebble Cottage much longer than Sarah had been alive. If the table could talk, it would have quite the tales to tell. Arguments, break-ups, homework, meals, laughter, tears, secretive sips of alcohol; a whole history of a family had unfolded around that table. It had a few marks on it to prove it. Sarah ran her finger over a long gouge she'd made in the wood, by accident, with a screwdriver when she was twelve. 'And you're not even a little intrigued about there being two babies born the same day, both called Janice?'

Janice took a sip of tea. 'Nope.'

'Really? I am.'

'Look, Sarah. I admit, it's strange. But stranger things have happened than two babies born on the same day with the same name. There are probably hundreds of Sarahs that share your birthday.'

'Yeah, but from the same small town?'

Janice put down her mug. 'Sarah, love. I was born in Dovecote to Gladys and Douglas Legg. You know all of this. My dad was the vicar at St. John's. I grew up at the vicarage until Mum died when I was twenty, and I went to cookery school in London, where I met your father. Your grandad retired and moved down to Cornwall not long after. He passed away just before Daphne was born. A few years later Neil, Daphne, and I came back to Dovecote and moved into Pebble Cottage.'

'And the name Rose doesn't ring any bells? Or you never knew of another Janice the same age as you, in your class at school?'

Janice patted Sarah's arm. 'No, love. There were no other Janices that I knew of.' She glanced out of the window. 'Now, look, it's a beautiful spring day. I'm going to sit out in the garden for a while. I don't get much time to enjoy it, so I'm going to make the most of not being able to do much else.'

There was a photograph in a frame on the mantelpiece, next to the picture of Faith sitting on the front garden wall, and Sarah picked it up. In all her years, she'd never really taken a good look at it and had just accepted it for what it was – a photograph of her grandparents holding their baby daughter on the day of her christening. Now she examined every detail. The baptismal font was absolutely the one at St. John's Church, on the other side of the railway line. It was the same font Sarah herself had been baptised in, and where Reverend Clive had baptised Faith. Sarah glanced at the other photograph and a tight pain squeezed her chest. She carefully took the photo of Rose and the other Janice out of the envelope and held it close to the framed photo. It was impossible to tell if it was the same baby. Not only were the babies obscured by blankets and christening robes, but all babies looked the same when they were that small. Sarah huffed as she put the framed photo down. Maybe her mother was right, and it was just a weird coincidence.

As she returned the photo to the envelope, Sarah flicked through the collection again, stopping at the one of Rose and the other woman kissing. It was brave of these young women to take photographic evidence of something that was a taboo at the time. They must have known that if anyone had seen the photo, it would have landed them both in very hot water. Maybe that was why it was hidden under the floorboards. A shiver ran up Sarah's spine. How much would it have meant to her teenage self to see this photo – to see proof that the thing she both craved and feared was real? She might have felt a little less alone, and found it easier to accept that she was attracted to both girls and boys. Or at least, it might not have taken her as long to realise what was going on. And to think this photo was hiding under her mother's bed all that time. She smiled to herself. Pebble Cottage clearly had a colourful history.

'I'm just going to nip out to stretch my legs,' Sarah said as she slipped on her denim jacket and leant out the back door. 'Will you be alright for an hour?'

Janice looked up from her book and pushed her reading glasses up onto her head. 'Of course. Meeting Rob again?'

'No, I am *not*. I'll be back soon.' Her mother's lips pressed into a tight line. 'If I had my way, I'd never see him again,' Sarah grumbled to herself.

But the kiss? Oh, the kiss had been good. It was nostalgia, that was all. As good as the past might look through rose-tinted glasses, it was the past for a reason. Anything she and Rob might have had, might have been, needed to stay firmly there.


The spring sun sparkled off the sea and laughter spilled onto The Promenade from Victoria Park, along with the heady scent of spring flowers. Sarah poked her head into The Seaside Café, which was nicely busy but not packed. Natasha smiled and gave her a thumbs-up, before waving her away. Everything was under control.

It would have been lovely to be able to stand at the railings of The Promenade and look out over the water, but she still hadn't forgiven the sea for taking her daughter. She thumped the railing with her fist. Each morning when she opened her bedroom curtains and caught sight of the white lighthouse, she was reminded of her father's dying wish. But she couldn't do it. She couldn't go out there, to those rocks. No, her dad was going back up to Manchester, and back to his husband, as soon as her van was fixed. That way she could avoid the past forever.

Sarah turned away from the beach, and the squawking seagulls, and made her way up the High Street. Her feet took her past the newsagent, the tapas restaurant, the bookshop, and the pub. It was only when she was safely beyond Crawford's Opticians, on the other side of the road, that she crossed the High Street. As she passed the chain coffee shop at the end of the road, a woman with long blonde hair stepped out, nearly knocking Sarah over with her pram.

'Oh, sorry,' the woman said. Sarah mumbled an apology back before hurrying away, her chin pressed tightly into her chest. With any luck, her sister-in-law's best friend wouldn't have recognised her. As she reached the bend in the road, just before the stone bridge over the railway line, she glanced back. Grace Curtis was staring at her. Brilliant. In about thirty seconds, Rachel Davies would know that her brother's estranged wife was back in Dovecote. If Rob hadn't already told her, of course. Nothing stayed secret for very long around here.

Sarah glanced up at the twin red-brick buildings of Bayview Care Home, perched on the hill that rose steeply beyond the top of the High Street. Well, there were some things that had managed to stay secret. And would forever.


Something compelled Sarah to cross the stone bridge over the railway onto Brighton Road. With a deep frown, she let her muscle memory guide her under the lychgate of St. John's Church and along the path to the graveyard behind. The woman kneeling over Faith's gravestone didn't look up as Sarah approached, but the large brown Afghan hound sitting on the grass got up and trotted over, her shaggy ears flopping as she walked. She had a good sniff of Sarah and nuzzled her long, narrow snout in her hand, clearly deciding she was friendly.

'Treacle? Where did you...?' Daphne stood up and turned around. 'Oh.'

'Hi. What—?'

'*Someone* has to keep Faith's resting place neat and tidy.

You certainly weren't going to do it. Treacle, come here.'
Daphne brushed past Sarah.

'Hey, wait. You look after Faith's grave?'

Daphne glanced back at the headstone. 'Mum and I take turns. Rob comes up here sometimes too, but he finds it hard. Even after all this time.'

'Thank you.' Sarah blinked back sudden tears. 'I really mean it, thank you.'

Daphne huffed and crossed her arms. 'Look, I'm sorry for what I said the other day. And for being such a cow to you since you came back. I just... I've spent the last ten years looking after Mum, bringing up Jake, dealing with Adam working all the hours under the sun, and just trying to keep everything going. And I know my grief was nothing compared to yours, but I lost my sister as well as my niece. I missed you.'

'You *missed* me?' Sarah raised an eyebrow. 'I thought you'd have been glad to see the back of me. We never really had that whole sister vibe going on.'

'I think that was partly due to our age difference. But it was also because I was jealous. I'd been Mum and Dad's only focus for eleven years before you came along. I should have grown out of it, I know.'

'I think we hit rock bottom when we were both pregnant at the same time.'

Daphne rolled her eyes. 'Yeah. God, I was awful. Adam and I had spent years trying, so when we finally had a baby on the way, I wanted everyone to focus on me. I wanted it to be my time.'

'And then I got pregnant by accident, and stole your limelight. Sorry about the timing, I didn't do it on purpose. We were planning on waiting a few years.'

'It should have brought us closer together, but instead I pushed you away. I'm the one who should be sorry.'

They stood in silence for a moment watching Treacle chase a squirrel up the ancient oak tree in the middle of the graveyard.

'How long do you think you'll stay?'

Sarah shrugged. 'At least until Mum is back on her feet. I said I would, and I'll not go back on my word. Beyond that, I don't know. Dovecote isn't my home any more, Daffs.' Her sister flinched and Sarah gave her a small smile. 'Sorry, it's an old habit.'

'Well, maybe I don't hate it as much as I make out. But I'll only take it from you; I wouldn't let anyone else call me that. Truce?'

'For Mum's sake.'

Daphne moved as if to hug Sarah, but stopped at the last minute. 'Come on, Treacle, home time.' Treacle bounded over obediently, and Daphne glanced back at Faith's headstone. 'I'll leave you to... You probably have a lot to say to her.'

'I talked to her every day from the moment I knew I was pregnant with her, and I've never stopped, even after she died.'

When Daphne was out of sight, Sarah lowered herself down onto the grass next to her daughter's grave and rested her head against the cold marble. A hot pressure built up behind her eyes and this time, she didn't try to stop the tears from running down her cheeks.


Sarah could hear voices in the back garden as she approached Pebble Cottage. She threw her jacket on Janice's bed in the living room and went through to the kitchen. As she stepped out of the back door, the petite, wiry woman who was sitting with Janice turned around, and the wind was knocked out of Sarah's chest. A broken van had brought Sarah into contact with her estranged husband and led her back to her childhood home. Now a fractured ankle had brought her former best friend to the garden of Pebble Cottage.

# FOURTEEN

## ROSE

August 1941

I probably should have been concerned at how easy it was to adjust to life without Martin. It was as though a weight had been lifted from my shoulders. Not that I let on that that was the case. When customers asked how I was bearing up, I would sigh dramatically and widen my eyes and say that I was missing him, but managing, and that it was a price worth paying to win the war, or some such platitude. Invariably, they told me I was very brave. But I had my café and my friends. I was completely fine without my husband. I was rather tired, though. June and July had been scorchingly hot and dry and, even without any summer tourists visiting Dovecote, The Seaside Café had been very busy. August had started out wet, and the forecast was for more of the same. The rainy days would give me a chance to get my breath back.

As the café was quiet, I closed up half an hour early. I usually closed at three. The Ministry of Transport had issued me a poster to put up, urging housewives to finish travelling by 4 p.m. so as to leave the buses, trams, and trains free for war workers. It was a hideous bright yellow with large red writing, and it looked quite out of place in the café. Rather than display it, I'd decided to close at three so at least I couldn't be held responsible for any housewives still being out and about late into the afternoon. I was just turning the key in the door when Dora came running up, panting slightly, but with an excited smile on her pink lips.

'Oh, Rose, you're closed.' Her smile faded. 'I wanted to show you my new camera.' In her hand, she held a square cardboard box, about the size of a gas mask case. A gust of wind blew in from the sea, bringing with it a few light spots of drizzle. I unfurled my umbrella and held it above our heads.

'Why don't you come back to Pebble Cottage with me? You can show me there.'

Dora blushed. 'That would be lovely.'

We huddled together under my umbrella as we walked, our shoulders brushing against each other. I'd never noticed her perfume before. It was light and almost sweet, with hints of vanilla and honeysuckle. We crossed the threshold of Pebble Cottage a moment before the heavens opened, unleashing a downpour that pelted the windows of the cottage like a drum beat. Dora placed the box down on the round pine table that dominated my kitchen and withdrew a chrome and black leather camera from inside. It meant nothing to me, but the glint in Dora's eye gave away that it was something special.

'It's a Leitz Leica from 1939.' She held it up to the light with the same reverence with which Uncle Douglas held up the chalice during Communion on Sundays at St. John's. But then her cheeks flushed, and she placed the camera back down on the table. 'My grandmother sent it to me from Switzerland.' She looked at me with wide blue eyes. 'I wouldn't have bought something German-made. You won't tell anyone, will you?'

I shook my head. 'I couldn't care less where it's from, Dora, as long as it makes you happy. But don't worry, I shan't breathe a word.'

Her shy smile was back. 'Thank you.' She glanced out of the kitchen window. 'Blast this weather; I'd love to take some photographs outside.' She looked down at the table again. 'Apologies, I get quite excited about cameras.'

'I like seeing you get excited. I do worry about you sometimes, Dora. You come into the café every day and sit so quietly. You look a little lonely. I know what it's like to feel as if you don't belong somewhere.'

'You do?' Dora's eyes lifted to mine.

'I grew up in a string of foster homes from when I was six, Dora. I know very well what it feels to be alone. Do you have friends that you see?' I placed a hand on her arm.

'I have you,' she whispered, the blush on her cheeks darkening as our eyes met. There was something in hers that I couldn't read. The clock on the mantelpiece in the sitting room chimed the half hour, and she moved her arm from under my hand. 'I am sorry to disturb you, Rose.' Dora placed the camera back in its box and gathered her belongings.

'You don't have to rush off, Dora. Won't you stop for a cup of tea, or a sherry?' Suddenly, I couldn't bear for her to leave.

'That is very kind of you. Perhaps next time.' She was struggling to look me in the eye.

'You are welcome to call in any time, Dora, here or at the café. I mean that. We are friends, are we not?'

'I hope so,' she said, a small smile returning to her lips. It widened. 'I would like that.'

I laughed lightly. 'Me too.' Perhaps we were both in need of a friend.

'But today, I must go. I have some work to catch up on.'

'I understand,' I said, leading her to the door. It was still pouring down, and I handed her my umbrella. 'Here, take this. Otherwise, your lovely hairstyle will be ruined.'

'Thank you, Rose.' Our fingers brushed as she took the umbrella from my hands. Our eyes met again for a moment and then she looked away, almost coyly. 'See you on Monday.'

'I'll have your tea ready for half past ten.'

'Perhaps I might be naughty and have a teacake too.' There was a giggle in her voice. I watched her run across the cobbles of Fisherman's Walk before she disappeared into the tight maze of streets that led to Blythe Avenue. I watched the space she had vacated for a moment. My skin tingled slightly where our fingers had touched.

The rain was replaced by persistent drizzle the following morning, and I was wondering why I'd bothered to drag myself out of bed and open up at all. The café was empty. I was sampling a small slice of an eggless ginger cake I'd made from a recipe in *Woman's Weekly*, as an experiment, when the bell above the café door tinkled.

'Hello, Rose.' Betty's sing-song voice filled the café as she swept up to the counter, her uniform cape nearly knocking over the bud vase on a nearby table. I'd become very fond of Betty Jones, who lived on Beachfront Road with her mother, Sheila. Betty instantly brightened any room with her bouncy brown curls, sparkling eyes, and loud giggle. She was my age and, having recently completed her nursing qualifications, was training to become a midwife while working at Bayview Convalescent Home. She eyed up the ginger cake and bit her lip. 'No, I mustn't. These uniforms are ghastly at the best of times – they're completely unforgiving if you're carrying an extra pound or two.' She spotted my half-finished slice, making me blush.

'Just quality checking,' I said, giving her a conspiratorial wink. 'And I missed breakfast so I was feeling a little queasy. The cake has perked me right up.'

'I'm not surprised. Ginger is rather good for settling the stomach. Anyhow, I can't stop. I'll be done for if Sister Margaret sees me in here in uniform. I've already had one ear-bashing for being late this week. Any further misdemeanours and she'll have me out on my rear end. I was just stopping by to say Roger is taking me to a dance at The Old Ship Hotel in Brighton tomorrow afternoon, if you fancied joining us?'

'Who's Roger? What happened to Graham?' Betty's romantic entanglements were a constant source of entertainment. I struggled to keep up with who she was stepping out with, it changed so frequently.

Betty flapped her hand. 'He got shipped out to somewhere. I told him I wasn't going to wait around. Do come to the dance. It will be jolly good fun, and you don't ever come out.'

I stifled a yawn. It did sound like fun. 'Sorry, Betty. I'm so tired, I doubt I'd be much company. Oh.' A wave of dizziness overtook me, and I reached for the counter to steady myself. In a flash, Betty was at my side, guiding me to a chair.

'Are you alright?' She felt my forehead and placed a finger to my wrist. 'If you don't mind me saying, you do look a little peaky.'

'I'm just tired. Been overdoing it, I think.'

Betty pursed her lips. 'Did you say you'd been feeling queasy?'

'Well, yes. But I didn't have breakfast. Although now I think of it, I wasn't all that bright yesterday either, or the day before for that matter.' I frowned. How long had I been feeling unwell?

Betty sat down on the chair next to me and gave me an exasperated look. 'Do you think you'd best see the doctor?'

'Whatever for? I just need a few days of rest.'

'Rose.' Her tone was almost scolding, and I stared back at her in confusion for a few minutes before it hit me.

'Oh, goodness,' I said, my hand automatically going to my stomach. 'You don't think... Oh, heavens.'

Betty grinned. 'I'd bet my entire clothing coupon book on you being pregnant, Rose. Get up to the doctors as soon as you can. And start taking it easy. Get someone to help you with the café. You can't be on your feet all day if you're pregnant. You'll need to rest.' With that, she swished out of the café, her giggle trailing in the air as she went.

It was all well and good her being happy about this. Having a baby in the middle of a war, while being on my own, had not been a part of my plan.

# FIFTEEN

## SARAH

April 2017

Heather's hug nearly knocked Sarah clean off her feet. For a small woman, she was surprisingly strong. When Sarah eventually disentangled herself from Heather's embrace, she could see tears gathering in Heather's dark-brown eyes. Her soft, cloud-like afro framed her face, which the intervening years had shaped from round into a heart.

'I can't believe you're actually back,' Heather said, drawing her sleeve across her cheeks, leaving wet tracks across her flawless, smooth skin. 'It's so good to see you.' She frowned, and Sarah shrank back a little from the glare. 'You could have called me, or messaged me, or done something in the past ten years.' She shook her head, making her gold hoop earrings jangle. 'Ah, I can't stay mad at you. Come here.' She hugged Sarah again.

'It's good to see you, too,' Sarah gasped, her breathing constricted by Heather's embrace. 'When Daphne said she'd arranged for someone from Bayview to come down and check in on Mum, I had wondered whether it would be you.'

Heather grabbed Sarah's hand and squeezed. Her touch

immediately transported Sarah back to teenage summer days spent together on the beach, or wandering through The Lanes in Brighton, gazing in wonder at the gold and diamonds in the jewellery shop windows. 'Of course it was going to be me. Especially when I heard you were home.'

Sarah's chest tightened. There was that word again: *home*. It jarred in her mind. She couldn't connect it to Dovecote or Pebble Cottage, or anywhere, really. The sound of the word made her feel strangely empty.

'Look, this is my last job of the day, so *we* are going for a drink. That is not even a question, Sarah. I need to hear about everything you've been up to.'

Sarah scrunched up her nose. Why was everyone so keen to get her to go to the pub? The doorbell of Pebble Cottage interrupted her answer.

'Oh, that will be Sue,' Janice said.

Sarah only just got to the front door before her mother, who had become surprisingly speedy on her crutches. Sue Prentice stood on the doorstep holding a casserole dish. 'Oh, hello, Sarah,' she said pleasantly. 'Your mum said you were back.' Sarah raised an eyebrow at Janice, who smiled sweetly at her. 'Janice, dear. How are you?'

'Oh, you know, bearing up.' Janice raised one of her crutches and wiggled it in the air. 'Got the hang of these things at least. Come on through and we'll have a cuppa.'

'I brought a chicken casserole. Didn't know how much cooking you'd be able to do,' Sue said, following Janice into the kitchen with a rustle of her wax jacket. Sarah cringed inwardly. She should be doing a better job of looking after her mother. Heather appeared in the sitting room, where Sarah was still standing by the open front door.

'Pub?' Heather asked.

Sarah glanced towards the kitchen. The sound of the kettle boiling accompanied by bright laughter made her smile. 'Pub.'

. . .

The Royal Oak had looked the same from the outside for as long as Sarah could remember, and the inside hadn't changed much either. Everything, from the maroon carpet to the huge stone fireplace, flicked a switch in Sarah's brain, reigniting memories that warmed her insides like hot chocolate.

As they made their way to the bar, Heather put her hand on Sarah's arm and nodded towards a table of people.

'Hang on, Sarah. I'll be back in a moment.' Sarah followed Heather for a few steps, but hung back as she approached the table. 'Hey, guys.'

Everyone around the table greeted Heather with a smile. The three women were the same ones Sarah had seen coming out of The Seaside Café, laughing, on her second day back in Dovecote. Now that she got a good look at the brunette's face, Sarah could see she *was* Molly from Harrington's Bookshop. The blond man with an earring might have been the younger of the Prentice brothers, Harrison. Heather was pointing back towards Sarah, who looked away. Her eye was caught by a poster stuck to the wall behind the bar. It was the same one she'd seen pinned to the door of the museum, advertising the recreated air raid shelter. She had a vague memory of a history lesson at school when they'd been taught that the cellar of The Royal Oak was used as an air raid shelter during the Second World War.

'Sorry.' Heather was back beside her. 'I usually meet up with Harrison, Molly, Aoife, and Emily for a drink every Friday, so just wanted to let them know why I'd not be joining them. I'd introduce you, but I want to keep you for myself. For now, anyway.' That was fine with Sarah. Socialising with people from school, or meeting new people, was not high on her list of priorities.

Just as Heather and Sarah reached the bar, the pub seemed

to go quiet, and Sarah caught a not-very-subtle whisper in a distinctive Irish accent.

'*That's* Rob Davies's ex-wife? Fit mechanic Rob?'

Sarah resisted the urge to turn around, the hairs on the back of her neck bristling.

Beside her, Heather groaned. 'Sorry, that's Aoife. She has no filter.'

Aoife wasn't wrong; Rob was undeniably easy on the eye. A momentary flashback to him standing in what was once their sitting room, with his shirt unbuttoned and his hair tousled, jolted Sarah's nerves. He was also, technically, still her husband, so Aoife could keep her thoughts about him to herself. A tendril of guilt squeezed her chest as she recalled what Rob had said about waiting for her. She pushed the thought away. It wasn't her fault that he'd chosen to wait for her rather than find someone else. She had expected him to move on. Regret nudged her conscience. Maybe she should have told *him* that.

Sarah and Heather settled at a table by the stone fireplace, each cradling a glass of red wine. Suddenly, Sarah found herself tongue-tied. There was so much she didn't want to talk about. Not in the pub. Not yet.

Searching for a conversation topic, and remembering the discovery she'd made, Sarah was just going to tell Heather about the photographs and the mysterious Rose and Janice, when Heather spoke first. 'Did you and Rob get divorced? Your mum said you were going by your maiden name now.'

'No, we never did.' Sarah swallowed a large mouthful of wine. 'I am still Sarah Davies. But, when I left, I wanted to put everything about my life in Dovecote behind me, so I started going by Portman. It hurt too much to use Faith's surname.' She bit her bottom lip. No tears. Heather had seen enough of those.

'Have you seen him? Since you've been back, I mean.'

'Yeah. My camper van broke down, and guess who came to fix it?' She let out a short, sharp laugh. 'It was very awkward and weird.' And that was before he'd helped move her mum's bed, and Sarah had very nearly ended up in his. Heather did not need to know about that.

'I'll bet.'

'It's all been pretty much as I expected,' Sarah said, picking up her glass and examining its contents. 'Mum was cautiously happy to see me. Rob was... I don't really know.' The memory of him with his shirt half-undone blazed in her head. Thank God for her mother's text that night. She shuddered. 'And Daphne was furious. You're the only one who seems genuinely happy to see me. And I don't deserve that. I know I hurt you too when I ran away, leaving a trail of devastation behind me. I'm sorry.'

'I knew how much pain you were in, don't forget.' Heather paused and gave Sarah a look brimming with compassion and understanding. Sarah's shoulder muscles slackened a fraction. Heather scrunched up her nose. 'But, yeah, it hurt, and I've missed you like crazy. With everything that had happened, I wasn't really surprised you felt like you needed to get away. And, hey, it wasn't as if it was the first time you'd broken—'

'So, it's true.' Sarah's head whipped up to find a red-painted talon pointing at her. 'You're back.'

'Hi, Rachel,' Sarah said, trying to keep her voice steady. She wasn't afraid of Rachel Davies, but she also wasn't in the mood for a confrontation.

'Don't give me "hi".' Rachel's eyes flashed. Ben Curtis was standing slightly behind her with Grace, concern in his blue-grey eyes. Sarah had a brief flashback to the trio in their school uniforms. Grace glanced at Ben, who placed a hand on Rachel's shoulder. Rachel shook it off and swished her long, silky brown hair out of her perfectly made-up face. 'How dare you show your face in Dovecote after what you did to my brother?'

'What I did? Your brother is no saint, you know.' Sarah got to her feet. Heather tried to pull her back down, but she yanked her shirt out of Heather's grasp.

'It was an accident,' Rachel snarled. They were almost toe-to-toe now. Or rather, court shoe to Doc Marten. 'Stay away from Rob, or so help me I'll—'

'You'll what?'

'Rach, leave it,' Ben pleaded, taking Rachel's hand.

'Come on, Rach, let's just get a drink,' Grace added. Sarah shot her a look.

Rachel's lip curled and her eyes narrowed. 'Leave Rob alone. You've done more damage than you know. Stay away from him.'

Sarah bristled. Rachel had always been able to wind her up far too easily. She flicked an eyebrow. 'Too late.'

Rachel lunged at her, grabbing a fistful of Sarah's hair. Sarah swung an arm, and her open hand collided with Rachel's face. The slap rang out through the now-silent pub.

'That's enough,' Declan, the barman, hollered over the curses Rachel and Sarah were flinging at each other. A firm hand gripped Sarah's shoulder, and when Rachel let go of her hair, and she looked up, it was to see Declan holding them apart. 'I'm not having this in my pub.' He looked from Rachel to Sarah and back again. Ben had grabbed onto Rachel, but she was struggling against him, hissing like an angry cat. Sarah growled at her. 'You,' Declan said, pointing at Rachel, 'go and sit over there.' He pointed to the farthest table. 'Heather, sort her out,' Declan added, and Heather's hand closed around Sarah's.

'Sit down, Sarah,' Heather said softly, and the red mist that had descended on Sarah lifted just enough for her to see the pleading look on Heather's face.

'It's alright,' Sarah spat, throwing a loaded look in Rachel's direction. There was a bright red mark on Rachel's cheek. 'I'm leaving.'

. . .

Outside, there was a slight chill to the sea breeze coming up the High Street. Sarah stood on the pavement, her heart racing and her blood boiling. Who did Rachel think she was?

'Hey.' Heather's soft voice made Sarah turn. 'Are you okay?'

'Fine,' Sarah snarled. Heather reached for Sarah's hand, but she pulled away. 'Not now, Heather.'

Heather stared down at the pavement. 'Okay, sure. No, it's fine. I mean, you know, we're not what we used to be to each other. But I'm here if you need a friend.'

'I don't.'

Sarah muttered a curse as Heather walked away up the hill, her head bowed. She shouldn't have snapped at Heather. It wasn't Heather's fault Rachel had touched a raw nerve. Sarah followed up the hill, but took the turning before Heather's, into Courcey Road. The minute anyone told Sarah not to do something, it made her more determined to do that thing than ever before. And Rachel had told her to stay away from Rob.

# SIXTEEN

## ROSE

March 1942

Betty was right. I was pregnant. I finally gave in and handed over the running of The Seaside Café to Maureen when my ankles swelled up and I couldn't bend to pick up a dropped teaspoon. I couldn't have managed to keep working at the café for so long while pregnant without her help, or that of Aunt Gladys – and of course, Dora. Dora stopped by the café every day after work, to give it a thorough clean and prepare it for the following day, always with a smile on her face. Maureen would arrive at opening time and stay all day, making sure I took regular breaks and didn't overdo it. She was a fast learner too, and in no time had picked up everything she needed to know.

I also wouldn't have been ready for this baby if it hadn't been for the generosity and kindness of the whole of Dovecote. Not a day went by without someone dropping off a hand-knitted blanket or a parcel of baby clothes. Maureen's brother, Stan, presented me with a refurbished pram he'd collected from one of the big houses along Brighton Road. Uncle Douglas sanded down and repainted an old cot he found in the attic of the vicarage. I had worried about being on my own, but I needn't have. The Dovecote community looked after me like I was family. On more than one occasion, my pregnancy hormones got the better of me and I burst out crying as someone who I only knew in passing handed over another bundle of clothes, or a pair of handmade mittens.

Betty kept a close eye on me too, constantly checking my progress against her textbooks. She was almost a qualified midwife, and she was shaping up to be a very good one. Although the diagrams she showed me, and the detail with which she gleefully explained the birthing process, sent me into a tailspin. But I did laugh when she said it was too late to back out and that the baby was going to come out whether I liked it or not.

The only dark cloud that hung over me was that Martin hadn't come to visit. Not even for Christmas. He had written, of course, and his letters were lovely. He'd expressed his excitement and fear at our impending arrival and had apologised that he wouldn't be there when the time came. Well, he wasn't the only absent father-to-be. Hundreds of men would be away from home for the birth of their children. That was just one of the many sacrifices we had to make for the greater good. There was nothing to be done about it, so there was no point moping. I just had to get on with things. No matter how frightened I was.

As the Americans had now entered the war, after what happened at Pearl Harbor, transatlantic communications were even more vital. That was what Martin was doing now, tucked away in Scotland: monitoring communications. I was proud of him for doing his bit, but also relieved he was relatively safe. Dora had taken a photograph of me and my bump, which I sent to him.

.   .   .

Around ten o'clock in the morning on the tenth of March, I developed an intense desire to wash the windows of Pebble Cottage. Maureen came rushing out of Coral Cottage next door when she saw me waddling about with a pail of water.

'What in God's name do you think you're doing?' she cried. 'You're due to give birth any day now. For crying out loud, Rose. Put down that bucket and get back inside and put your feet up. Look at the size of those ankles! Good gracious.'

I only made it as far as the front door of Pebble Cottage before a sharp pain tore through the underside of my stomach. 'Oh,' I gasped, reaching for the door frame. 'Oh.' Before I knew it Maureen's strong arms were around me, guiding me back into the house. Another pain caused me to groan. There was a funny feeling between my legs, and I looked down to see a puddle on the sitting room floorboards. 'Oh.' It was all I seemed to be able to say.

Maureen didn't have the same problem with words. 'Heaven's above. This baby is not hanging around. Stan!' she roared out the front door. 'Bring the van around right this instant, we've got a baby in a hurry to meet its mother.' She glanced back at me. I was sweating and panting as the pain began again, seeming to rip my insides apart. 'Steady on, Rose. No need to panic. STAN!' Stan honked the horn of his van in reply.

How Stan made it the length of Dovecote in what seemed like a matter of seconds, I shall never fathom, but I was delivered in one piece into the waiting arms of Sister Margaret at Bayview Convalescent Home. Maureen had rung ahead from the phone box at the end of Fisherman's Walk to let her know I was on the way. I hadn't wanted to give birth at home. I needed people around me. It was Betty who'd suggested I ask Sister Margaret if I'd be allowed to have the baby at Bayview. Sister Margaret had been delighted to oblige. They loved a birth at Bayview, apparently.

. . .

My daughter arrived at two o'clock in the afternoon on the tenth of March. She screamed Bayview down from the minute she entered the world, but stopped the instant Betty placed her in my arms.

'Well done, Rose,' Betty whispered. 'She's beautiful.' I could see there were tears on her cheeks. Sister Margaret appeared behind Betty and placed a hand on her shoulder.

'And well done you. We never forget our first delivery,' she said to Betty. 'You'll probably go on to deliver hundreds more babies, but this one will always be special.'

Betty wrung her hands. 'I'll tell you one thing, my nerves are all over the place. The moment I'm out of uniform I shall be having a very stiff drink.'

I tuned out their conversation and concentrated on the tiny, helpless bundle in my arms. I'd never known love like it. The moment I set eyes on my daughter's little scrunched-up face, I'd felt a rush of emotion so visceral, I could almost taste it. There was something else amongst the love. Fear? Yes, I was nervous and frightened. What kind of world would there be left for her after the war? And what kind of mother would I be? Could I even do it? What if I let something happen to her? What if something happened to me and she was left without a mother, just like I had been?

Sister Margaret reached for my baby. 'Let's get her cleaned up and make you a cup of tea. And don't worry, Rose,' she added, with the wisdom and intuition of someone who'd cared for many new mothers. 'All you can do is your best. And all she really needs is your love. The rest will work itself out.'

Fortified by tea, toast, and a nap, I was sitting up in bed, gazing at my daughter asleep in her little cot beside me, when Sister Margaret poked her head around the door.

'Are you feeling up to a visitor?' When I nodded my reply,

Sister Margaret held the door open, and Dora came in. Over the previous nine months, she'd lost some of that shyness she'd once had. Her eyes were bright, and she held her head high.

'Dora.' I smiled as she came to the side of the bed and gave me a gentle hug. 'How lovely to see you.'

'Maureen told me the news,' Dora whispered, glancing into the cot. 'And I thought maybe I should come and take some pictures. You will want one to send to Martin as soon as possible.' It was only then I noticed the camera in her hands. Her long fingers were tipped with pale pink nail enamel, which matched her shell-pink lipstick perfectly.

I glanced down at my bare nails, and remembered I didn't even have a dusting of powder on my face. 'Oh, gracious. I don't think I'm in any fit state to be photographed. I haven't done my hair or anything.'

'You look radiant,' Dora said.

'Well, if you don't mind. Thank you, that's a lovely thought.' I ran my fingers through my hair to smooth it out a fraction, and scooped my daughter out of her cot and held her so that her face could be seen. It was only then that I noticed the small fold in the skin at the top of her right ear. Martin had one, too.

Dora must have taken half a dozen pictures, and I felt a little guilty about using up so much expensive film. But she waved away my concern.

'Not at all. It is not every day that you get to take such special photographs.' She put the camera back in its case.

'Would you like to hold her?'

Dora visibly stiffened and took a step backwards. 'Oh, no. Really, I am not experienced in holding small babies. Have you decided on her name yet? I suppose you are waiting for Martin to help you choose.'

The baby let out a whimper. I cuddled her a little closer and she settled back down. 'We discussed it in our letters. He said it was up to me. I'm sure he would have liked to name her after his mother, but I don't think she looks like an Ursula.'

Dora frowned. 'I agree. And it's quite old-fashioned. What do you want to call her?'

I stroked my baby's cheek. Her skin was as soft as a ripe peach. Her little red lips were scrunched up in a pout. 'Janice. I don't know why. It came to me early one morning when I was baking some teacakes at the café. What do you think?'

'It's perfect.' Dora's smile lit up her eyes. 'I'd better leave you to get some rest. Don't worry about anything. Maureen and I have everything under control at the café. All your customers are going to be delighted to hear your good news.'

'Thank you for coming to see me, Dora. And for taking the photographs. I will send one to Martin as soon as I can. You really are a wonderful friend.' Dora blushed, and when she hugged me goodbye, she placed the lightest of kisses on my cheek. It was a little like being kissed by a spring breeze.

Janice wriggled in my arms, and I settled down to feed her. I stroked her head while she suckled. Sister Margaret appeared at the door again.

'I've sent one of the office girls down to the Post Office to dispatch a telegram to Scotland. Martin will know the joyous news very soon.'

'Thank you, Sister Margaret. I do hope he'll be granted leave.'

And if Martin did come home, what would he make of his daughter? And what would this tiny, beautiful bundle mean for him and me? Would she bring us closer together, or would she drive us further apart?

# SEVENTEEN

## SARAH

April 2017

Sarah breathed heavily as she stomped up Courcey Road. How *dare* Rachel? As she knocked on Rob's door, her anger defused into nervousness. But it was too late. She could hear his steps coming to the door; she couldn't run away.

'I just had a run-in with your sister at The Royal Oak,' Sarah said when Rob opened his front door, bemused.

'Oh.'

'When I say a run-in, it was more of a fight.'

'A fight?' Rob raised his eyebrows.

'She pulled my hair. I slapped her.'

Rob ran his fingers through his hair. 'You'd better come in.'

'What I don't understand is where she gets off telling me to stay away from you,' Sarah grumbled, following Rob into the kitchen. 'I know she's your older sister but you're a grown man. Surely you have a right to see whoever you want.' Rob poured two glasses of red wine. 'Presuming that you want to see me, that is? Say the word and I'll go.'

'No, don't go,' he said, handing her a glass. He sat down at the kitchen table and rubbed his eyes. 'Rachel is very protective of me.'

'No kidding.'

'Listen, Sarah. For once would you just *listen*? Please?'

'Wow,' Sarah huffed. 'I'm listening.' Rob's eyes glowed an even more brilliant blue in the muted light of the kitchen, and Sarah mentally dampened the spark that ignited somewhere in the pit of her stomach.

'The morning after Faith's funeral...' He paused. 'No, it wasn't the morning. It took me until mid-afternoon to realise you hadn't just gone to the shops, or down to your mum's. Around two o'clock, I started to panic. I called Janice. She very gently told me that you'd sent her a text.' He laughed. It was a mirthless, hollow sound and Sarah's chest tightened. 'I still remember her exact words. She said, "She's gone away for a while, love. She's safe but she just needs some space."'

'She told you what I asked her to tell you.'

'Those words broke the last thread of whatever was holding me together. I'd buried my three-year-old daughter and now my wife had left me. The person I needed most had just upped and left, without a word. Sarah, I was a mess. You don't want to know how much I was drinking, and what else I was taking to try to numb the pain.' Sarah looked up from her glass. Rob's eyes were dry, but she could see pain and hurt scored in the fine lines around his eyes and the deep furrow of his brow. 'I don't think it's an exaggeration to say that I probably wouldn't have survived if it hadn't been for Rachel. I was only twenty-five, and I didn't know how to express what I was feeling, never mind cope with it. Rachel helped me put the broken pieces of myself in the right order so I could begin to live again. I wouldn't be here if it weren't for her. If she's not happy to see you, it's only because she doesn't want to see me hurt again.'

Sarah briefly closed her eyes, trying to fight off the wave of guilt that threatened to swamp her. Of course, she'd known that her disappearing would have hurt Rob, but she'd not expected him to take it *that* badly. Maybe everyone hadn't been as happy to see the back of her as she'd thought they would be. Maybe she had been loved more than she'd realised. She drew a shaking breath to banish the immensity of those thoughts. They were for interrogating another day – or preferably never.

'It doesn't give her the right to start a fight with me in the pub.'

'No, you're right, it doesn't. And I'll have a word with her about that. Are you okay?'

'I'm fine, thanks. I left a red mark on her face, though.'

'She'll live. What's that?' Rob reached across and plucked something from Sarah's hair. He showed it to her. It was about half an inch long and bright red.

'Ha! Looks like she's also missing a false nail.'

They drank their wine in a silence punctuated by the hum of the fridge-freezer. Sarah had reached the bottom of her glass when she spoke again.

'And what does Rachel think about what happened out at the lighthouse that day?' It was spiteful of her to ask, of course it was.

Rob got up from the table and picked up the two empty glasses. Sarah followed him over to the sink, where he set the glasses down before turning back to her. The colour had drained from his face. In contrast, Sarah's cheeks were burning. The anger had reignited, and it rampaged around inside her, looking for a way out.

'Of course your sister would accept your explanation and be on your side. But I'm not.' She slammed her hand down on the countertop, making Rob jump. 'It was *your* fault, Rob.'

'It was an accident, Sarah. No one was to blame.' His voice wavered, and Sarah couldn't stop herself going in for the kill.

'You were!' she cried. 'It was your fault. You weren't watching her. You let her fall from those rocks. It's your fault. Yours!' Her fists pummelled his chest, and he grabbed her wrists and held on firmly, but not tightly.

'Sarah, stop this.'

'You killed her!'

'No, I didn't, Sarah. It was an accident. It happened so quickly, there was nothing I could do.' When she stopped fighting against his grip, he released her wrists. He looked away for a moment and Sarah backed off. Breathing heavily, she slumped against the larder. She'd kept those words locked away for ten long years. Now they were out, they'd left a gaping hole.

Eventually, she dared to look up at Rob. His brow was heavy, and his mouth was set in a firm line. He folded his arms across his chest and narrowed his eyes. 'But while we're talking about blame,' he said, his voice dangerously low. 'Don't forget, *you* were meant to be there. I wasn't supposed to be looking after two three-year-olds on my own.'

'*You* decided to take Faith and Jake out to the lighthouse.'

'You promised them we'd go, and then left me to choose between breaking that promise or taking them on my own. You knew how obsessed Faith was with the lighthouse back then. She was desperate to go out there with Jake. I couldn't tell her no.' He unfolded his arms, crossed the kitchen, and looked deep into her eyes. 'You're as much to blame as I am.'

His words punctured her chest and buried themselves in her heart. 'How dare you!' she hissed.

His glare softened and he hung his head for a second. 'I shouldn't have said that,' he said softly.

Whatever Sarah was about to say next, it went straight out of her mind when she looked into his eyes again. The world went into freefall around her as the space between them shrank.

Their lips were almost touching, when she suddenly turned her head. It took her a moment to find her voice.

'I have to go.'

'Why?'

She pushed him away, but her hand lingered on his chest. 'Because this' – she let her hand fall – 'is wrong.' Sarah shook her head, a little sadly. 'And you know it.'

Rob leant back against the kitchen counter, his head in his hands. When he pulled his hands away from his face, there were tears in his eyes. 'I love you,' he whispered. Sarah opened her mouth to reply, but shut it again without a word. She walked up the hall without looking back, and closed the front door quietly behind her.

As she made her way back towards Pebble Cottage, tears dripped down her cheeks. What Rob had said about Faith's death being as much her fault as his only hurt so much because, deep down beneath the burning rage and stinging grief, she knew it was true.

# EIGHTEEN
## ROSE

March 1942

Having been released from Sister Margaret's care only the day before Martin was due home, I paced the sitting room of Pebble Cottage. Should I go out to meet him, or wait indoors until he turned his key in the lock? I settled on waiting at the open door for him. I was relieved that he was able to come at all, even if it was only for a short visit. Two days was better than nothing.

In the distance, I heard the toot of the steam engine as it pulled into Dovecote station. It was a bright spring day, and a warm breeze funnelled down Fisherman's Walk. I stood in the doorway, cradling Janice, who was wrapped snugly in the yellow blanket Maureen had knitted. I didn't know where she could have got such soft wool, but I was incredibly grateful and touched that she'd used something so precious for Janice. How was she nearly two weeks old? Already, the time was passing by too quickly. The sound of footsteps on the cobbles made me look up from Janice's sleeping face.

'Hello, Rose.' I hadn't expected Martin to run up the path and sweep me up into his arms, but I also hadn't expected him to hesitate nervously at the gate. It had been a little over nine months since he'd left, but it felt a lot longer. It was nice to hear his voice.

'Hello, Martin.'

He gave me a kiss on the cheek and followed me inside, dropping his bag at the foot of the stairs. He glanced around the room before looking down into my arms.

'Well, here she is.' I pulled back the edge of the blanket so he could get a good look at his daughter's face. 'Would you like to hold her?'

His chocolate-brown eyes widened. 'I don't trust myself to. She's so tiny.' There was something in the way he was looking at Janice, as if analysing her features. Was he wondering if she was his? The timings were very tight. We must have conceived her the night he got the news of his deployment.

'She has your eyes, Martin,' I hinted, moving into the stream of sunlight coming through the sitting room window. 'And a little fold on the top of her ear, just like you.' Hopefully that would be enough to reassure him. I also hoped he trusted me and knew I wouldn't dream of betraying him.

'I think she looks more like you.' He rubbed his chin and sank down into the sofa. I sat down beside him.

'Here, hold out your arms.' He did so and I lowered Janice into them. 'Just mind her head.' As if on cue, Janice opened her eyes and looked up at her father. 'See, she knows who you are,' I whispered, not daring to shatter the stillness that had fallen on the room. In that moment, we were the only three people in the world.

'Hello, Janice,' Martin said softly. I wiped a tear from my eye.


'Oh, that's perfect,' Dora said from behind her camera that same afternoon. 'Martin, just move in a fraction. That's it. Rose, the blanket is covering Janice's face a little.' I tucked the edge of the blanket down. 'Lovely. And smile, everyone.'

Martin and I stepped away from the baptismal font to where Uncle Douglas was standing by the front pews. He'd gone all out and put on his best vestments for Janice's christening. The inside of St. John's Church was filled with spring sunshine. Bunches of daffodils graced the windowsills along the south aisle. The windows on that side had a lovely view over Dovecote and the sea.

Uncle Douglas reached his arms out. 'Would Dora kindly take a photograph of me and Gladys with Janice? It's not every day that one gets to baptise their great-niece.' The joy on his face made my insides glow. When he smiled, I could see my mother in him. I allowed myself a moment of pride that it was the presence of *my* daughter that was making him so happy.

'Or to baptise their own goddaughter. I know it's not the done thing, so thank you,' I said, handing Janice over to him for the second time that day. When he'd held her earlier, and poured the blessed water over her head, she'd scrunched up her face as if preparing to wail, but hadn't made a sound. Uncle Douglas placed a warm hand on my arm.

'In times of emergency, it is absolutely acceptable. If being in the middle of a war isn't an emergency, then I don't know what is.'

'If anything were to happen to Martin and me, you would be her only family,' I added. That was why I'd asked him to be Janice's godfather. I hadn't even thought twice about asking Dora to be her godmother. She'd been to see us in Bayview every day, and I think she was almost as in love with Janice as I was. To Janice, she would always be Auntie Dora.

'Don't be thinking like that,' Uncle Douglas said. His face became serious as he stood by the font with Gladys. 'But know that I will always be here for you, and for Janice. In whatever capacity you need me to be.'

Once the photographs were taken, we filed out of the church, and I lowered Janice into her pram.

'Are you sure you won't come over to the vicarage for a cup of tea?' Auntie Gladys asked, for the umpteenth time. I hated to refuse her kindness. Luckily, Douglas intervened.

'Now, Gladys, leave them be. Martin is only home for two days. They need to spend time together, just the three of them. We'll have plenty of time to spend with Rose and Janice. Poor Martin has to be back in Scotland tomorrow night.'

Gladys took Martin's hand and gave it a squeeze. 'Come home for longer next time, would you?'

He gave her a shy smile. 'I'll try.'

Dora had slipped away quietly, so Martin and I walked along Brighton Road and over the railway bridge. At the top of the High Street, we paused to look down the hill towards the beach and the sea. Beyond the cliff, the white lighthouse rose up from the steep, jagged rocks at its base, shimmering in the heat haze.

'I can't imagine a more perfect place for Janice to grow up,' I said as we started down the hill. 'I'm so glad we came to Dovecote, Martin. Aren't you?'

'Well, yes, I suppose so.'

I nudged him with my elbow. 'I know Brighton is special to you. It's where you got your first taste of freedom. But this is your home. And now it's your daughter's home, too.'

He wrapped an arm around my waist. 'Of course it is. And as long as you're happy, I'm happy.' He kissed me lightly on the forehead as we stepped onto The Promenade and his hand tightened around my waist. My stomach swooped a little and my cheeks flushed.

'I'm sorry, Martin. I don't think I'm able for any sort of' – I dropped my voice – '*intimacy* tonight. I'm not fully healed from... you know.'

He didn't remove his arm. 'I understand.'

'I must have been very good in a past life to end up with a husband as caring as you.'

'I don't know about that.' He let go of my waist. I was instantly colder. 'Actually, I've been somewhat nervous about tonight. I don't want to disturb Janice, and' – he paused and fidgeted with his jacket buttons – 'I've become quite used to sleeping on my own. Perhaps it would be better if I took the spare room tonight?' A weight lifted from my shoulders. Truth be told, I'd been dreading him tossing and turning next to me all night. If I had missed him, I'd not missed his snoring.

'It's probably the only way you'll get a good night's sleep,' I said. 'I'll be up every few hours to feed Janice anyway. And you have a long journey tomorrow. I wouldn't like to send you back to your post exhausted.'

The time and distance apart hadn't helped us fit together. If anything, it had made our shapes even more incompatible. It would be different, of course, when the war was over, and he came home for good. Then we'd be a proper family, wouldn't we?

# NINETEEN
## SARAH

May 2017

The Seaside Café provided Sarah with a welcome distraction from Rob and the past. She and Natasha soon developed a routine, with Natasha out front and Sarah hiding in the kitchen. Making cheese toasties and putting endless trays of scones in the oven gave her something to do with her hands.

Her ear was always pricked, waiting for a familiar voice to drift into the kitchen. Rachel she could cope with; she could just blank her. Heather? She probably owed her an apology. Rob? Her stomach churned at the thought of him casually coming in for a coffee or a sticky bun. What was wrong with her? Why couldn't she spend five minutes with Rob without throwing herself at him?

With a groan, she set another batch of fruit scones out on a wire tray to cool. Kev from the garage had messaged to say they were still waiting for a part to arrive from Germany, so she couldn't leave. Even if she could get in her van and go, she'd promised her mother she'd stay. The squeak of the hinge of the back door made her turn around.

'Hi,' said Daphne, pulling off her raincoat. The forecast was for showers but, as was so often the case, Dovecote wasn't sticking to the script, and the morning had been bright and sunny. 'I thought I'd come in and give you a hand.'

'No PTA meetings or events today?'

'No, thank goodness. I've had it up to here with it all.' She raised her hand and tapped her forehead. 'Between you and me, I'd rather not be doing it. But there's a certain expectation of the wife of the local GP. You've got to be part of the community and seen to be doing good things. Maybe Adam is right, and we should move somewhere bigger.' She put a hand to her mouth. 'Oh... I wasn't...'

'You're thinking of moving away?' Sarah handed a freshly made ham and cheese toastie out to Natasha. Her stomach growled; she'd have to make herself some lunch in a minute.

'It's just something that might be on the horizon. With the planned restructure of the Dovecote Medical Centre, Adam's been looking elsewhere and has been offered a job in Birmingham. I've not said anything to Mum yet. You know how she gets.' Daphne rummaged in the fridge and emerged with a tub of tuna mayonnaise.

'Mum mentioned you were kind of stressed about some changes. Do you want to go?'

Daphne put down the tub and reached for the bread. 'It would be a good career move for Adam.'

'That's not what I asked. If you're making a tuna sandwich, I'll have one too.'

'I know, but it's the only answer I have right now.' The frown lines on her forehead deepened. Sarah said nothing as Daphne made their sandwiches and wrapped them in foil. 'Shall we take these down to the beach?'

Sarah's insides constricted. 'I... um...'

'Come on.' Daphne took hold of Sarah's hand. She'd not done that since Sarah was a little girl. 'It's a lovely day, and you can't avoid it forever.' Daphne leant through the archway. 'Sarah'll back in ten minutes, Natasha.' Sarah rolled her eyes as Daphne bundled her through the back door.

'I'm not avoiding it. It's just that looking at the sea makes me angry. As for scattering Dad's ashes by the lighthouse, that's not going to happen.'

Daphne's eyebrows shot up. 'You're not going to grant his final wish? I mean, you knew him better than me...' Daphne's words petered out as they crossed The Promenade.

'I'm going to bring him back to Pete. It's the right thing to do.' Sarah hesitated at the top of the steps to the beach, watching Daphne descend.

'You mean the easy thing?' Daphne called back from the bottom of the steps. 'Come on, or I'll give your sandwich to the seagulls.' A fat seagull sunning itself on the stones eyed up the sandwiches in Daphne's hand. Sarah blew out a breath and clambered down the steps.

'See, that wasn't so hard,' Daphne said as they sat down on the stone bench against the wall, halfway along the beach. Daphne handed Sarah one of the foil packages. 'From what I hear, it's not only the sea that's testing your temper. Mum told me about Friday night at The Royal Oak.'

Sarah grimaced. 'I had hoped she hadn't heard about that. How did she find out?'

'Come on Sarah, you know nothing stays quiet in this town. I think Harrison Prentice told his mum, who then told Mum.'

'For God's sake. Rachel started it.'

Daphne chewed a bite of tuna sandwich. 'Sarah you're thirty-three, not three. Stop sulking.'

'I'm *not* sulking.'

Daphne laughed. 'You are *so* sulking. Listen, Sarah, I'm not going to say I know how you're feeling, but I can imagine it's not been easy for you being back here, where it happened. But you have to understand, while you've been away, life has gone on.'

'It just feels like the last ten years haven't happened, like I'm back to square one.'

Daphne squeezed Sarah's knee. 'You're not. But even if you feel like you are, it's not the worst place to start from.'

'I don't resent you or Jake, Daffs. I just wanted you to know that.' Sarah got up from the bench and walked down towards the water's edge. She picked up a flat, grey stone, with a line of white running across it. She flung it into the foaming waves, somehow holding in the scream that bubbled in her chest. She sank to her knees, her breaths coming in short, shallow bursts. A warm hand touched her shoulder.

'Better?' Daphne's voice was soft and kind. 'Come on, we should get back and let Natasha take her break.'

The lunchtime rush was over, and Natasha came into the kitchen where Sarah and Daphne were just about on top of the tidying up.

'So many people are asking for Janice's sticky buns. The look on their faces when I say we don't have any.' She shook her head. 'It would break your heart.'

Sarah exchanged a look with Daphne. 'What do you reckon, Daffs? We've both seen Mum make those buns a hundred times. Surely we can come up with something similar. I'm guessing she's not given you the recipe, either?'

'No, and I've asked her for it, but she just says she'll pass it on when she retires.'

'Right,' Sarah said, clapping her hands together. 'Natasha, please could you make us a couple of strong coffees? This could be a long afternoon.'

The first batch they made were too doughy, the second too sweet. Sarah was putting a third attempt in the oven while

Daphne bagged up the rejects to take home for Jake. Natasha had long since closed the café and gone home.

'If this lot isn't right, I'm giving up. I never want to see another raisin as long as I live,' Sarah said with a grunt as she closed the oven door.

'Sarah?' Daphne asked, putting down the bag of buns. 'What you said on the beach earlier, about not resenting Jake?'

'Uh-huh?'

'Thanks. It means a lot to me.' She took a few deep breaths. 'Have you seen Jake since you've been back?'

'Yeah, he stopped by the café the other morning on the way to school. He was with Alice and some kid with glasses.'

'That will be Harry.'

'Oh yes, that's what Natasha said. I don't think Jake knew who I was.'

Daphne's gaze dropped to her hands. 'We didn't know if we'd ever see you again, so we haven't really mentioned you around Jake. I'm sorry.'

Sarah bit back her first response. When Daphne put it like that, it was hard to be mad at her. How could she expect Jake to know her, when she'd run out on all of them?

She folded her arms across her chest. 'It was tough, seeing Jake and Alice all grown up. I just kept thinking about Faith, how she would be the same age, and how they would have had a blast hanging out together.'

'They really would have. And I can't imagine how hard that is for you.' Daphne paused, visibly shuddering. 'No actually, I can imagine. You're the strongest person I know, Sarah. I'd have crumbled into a heap and never recovered if it had been Jake that day.' Daphne knelt down to look in the oven door at the buns. Sarah watched her sister closely. She'd always thought Daphne saw her as nothing more than an annoyance. Daphne looked up and caught Sarah staring at her. 'That's not to say that running away was the right thing to do. Mum and I would have looked after you, if you'd stayed.'

Sarah swallowed a lump in her throat. They wouldn't have looked after her if they'd known the truth about where she was that day, and why she wasn't out at the lighthouse with Rob and the children.

Daphne put a hand on Sarah's arm. 'I'll bring Jake down to Pebble Cottage one evening, so you can meet him properly. I know it's a few years too late, but I'll tell him about his Auntie Sarah.'

'Don't tell him too much.' Sarah's voice cracked. She needed to change the subject before she spilled her secret to Daphne. 'Did Mum tell you we found some old photographs hidden under the floorboards in her bedroom?'

'No! How exciting. Anyone we know?'

Sarah shook her head. 'They're mostly of a woman called Rose, who must have lived in Dovecote during the war. There's one of her and another woman, taken in the back garden of Pebble Cottage.'

'Oh, that's amazing. I wonder if we could find out who she was. There might be relatives who would like to have the photos.'

'Wait until you hear the weirdest bit, Daffs. In one of the photos, Rose is sat up in what looks like a hospital bed holding a newborn baby. It's pretty obvious she's just given birth. We both know that look.'

'Yeah,' Daphne laughed. 'I looked like I'd been dragged through a hedge backwards in the photo Adam took of me and Jake. But there's a certain radiance in a new mother's face, isn't there?'

Sarah cast her eyes down for a moment, willing the ache in her chest away. Daphne nudged her gently. 'You were telling me about Rose.'

Sarah pulled herself back to the present. 'This is where it's gets weird. According to the inscription on the back of the photo, the baby is called Janice – and the date is Mum's birthday.'

'Gosh, that is a coincidence.' Daphne looked in the oven at the buns. 'Hmm, they're not golden enough on top. Did you brush them with egg wash?'

'No, I forgot. Never mind the buns, Daffs. Aren't you intrigued?'

'By what?'

'By the photo. What if the baby *is* Mum?'

'Oh Sarah, don't be ridiculous. It's just a coincidence. I'm taking the buns out.'

'Go for it. Mum is not even remotely interested in the photos either. But there's something about Rose that—'

'That what?' Daphne put the tray of buns down on the counter. A few of the raisins were burnt. 'No, these aren't right either. I give up.'

'She looks kind of familiar.' Sarah reached to get a knife out of the drawer to cut into the latest batch of buns, but the drawer handle came off in her hand. 'Oh, great. Hang on, I think I saw a screwdriver in the storeroom dresser the other day.'

The Welsh dresser crammed against a wall in the storeroom had once stood in the café, but Janice had moved it so she could fit in a few extra tables. It had become a dumping ground for all sorts of bits and bobs over the years, and Sarah rifled through the cupboards and drawers, looking for the screwdriver. The middle drawer was looser than the ones either side, and when she pulled on it, it came all the way out, revealing the screwdriver right at the back. 'For goodness' sake,' she muttered. 'What is it with me and drawers today?' As she wriggled the drawer back into place, a piece of paper fluttered down onto the floor. With the screwdriver in one hand, she picked up the paper and wandered back into the kitchen.

In the light, she could see it was actually a photograph stuck to a very thin piece of paper, folded in half to look like a greetings card. The photo was of a grand, but rather overly ornate mansion, with a large tree in front of it. Sarah opened the paper.

*Dearest Rose,*

*Even if the well runs dry, we'll always have tea. Merry Christmas.*

*Love, Dora*

She blinked a few times. 'A Christmas card to Rose. But what a strange message – it makes no sense. And who's Dora?' A switch flicked in her brain. 'Oh, I wonder if she's the other woman in the photo?' Daphne wasn't listening. Sarah slipped the card into her tote bag. If the writing in the card was the same as on the back of the photos, she'd have the answer to at least one of her questions.

'I should be getting home,' Daphne said, reaching for her raincoat. The forecast showers had never arrived.

'Yeah, me too. Sue has been keeping Mum company all day, and I suspect Heather will have been and gone by now.'

'Has it at least been nice, seeing Heather again after all this time? You two were inseparable for so many years.'

Sarah's pulse pounded in her ears as she locked the back door behind them. 'Yeah, I guess.'

'You know, we've talked more today than I think we ever have. It's been good.' Daphne did up the buttons of her coat and then looked at Sarah, who avoided her sister's gaze. 'I don't want to keep bringing it up...'

'But you're going to.'

'Yeah, because there's something that still bothers me. Where were you the day of Faith's accident? And don't tell me you were at work, because that was the first place someone went to try and find you.'

Black dots swam in Sarah's peripheral vision and her hands were clammy. She pushed past Daphne and sprinted down the narrow alleyway to The Promenade, leaving her sister staring after her. She almost ran all the way to Pebble Cottage.

She'd been so sure she'd covered her tracks ten years ago. She had been so sure everyone had believed her lie.

# TWENTY

## ROSE

May 1943

The sun was streaming in through the windows of The Seaside Café from an unbroken blue sky. With the door open, I could hear playful squeals and laughter from Victoria Park. Only the drone of the occasional aircraft overhead shattered the illusion that it was a perfectly ordinary late-spring day. Violet, the young woman who worked at Harrington's Bookshop on the High Street, was having tea and toasted teacakes at the table by the window with a pretty blonde woman with astonishingly green eyes. I vaguely knew her face, but not her name. The way they bent their heads towards each other and let their knees touch under the table made me wonder if they were more than friends. If they were, then it was brave of them to show it in public, even if they did think they were being discreet. They looked so happy together. Had I ever looked at Martin the way Violet was looking at her companion? I shook my head and let out a deep sigh as I ran a cloth over the counter. He'd never given me a starry-eyed glance either.

Janice laughed from her pram, beside the Welsh dresser. She astonished me every single day. Now fourteen months old, she was trying to walk, and her gurgles were becoming proper little sounds. Mama was her favourite word, closely followed by 'ake', which I took to mean cake. She hadn't mastered 'Dora', so she just squealed and laughed when Dora came near. I wasn't sure how to introduce the concept of Dada, but I'd have to teach her before Martin's next visit, or he'd be upset. At least he asked after her in his bland and sporadic letters. But Janice and I were getting by just fine. She was still beautifully pudgy and squishy. When I pressed my lips against her bare tummy and blew raspberries, she dissolved into fits of giggles. Every customer who came into the café was greeted with gummy smiles and offered a bite of soggy teacake from her doughy hands. The only time she cried was when I wheeled her pram out of the café and locked up to go home.

Violet and her friend got up and left, and I yawned as I cleared and wiped down their vacated table. I was a little tired these days. Janice was the most precious little bean in the world, but I did wish she would sleep a little more. She was rather too fond of the night-time for my liking.

'Shall we call it a day, young lady?' I asked, giving her a cluck under her chin.

'Ake.'

I laughed. 'No more cake. Well, maybe we'll bring some home for after tea.'

Having cleaned the kitchen and the café, turned off the lights, and pulled down the blinds, I locked the front door behind us and set off down The Promenade towards home. The pram bounced over the cobbles and by the time I reached the gate of Pebble Cottage, Janice had fallen asleep.

Maureen was out in the front garden of Coral Cottage, pruning her rose bushes. She stood and stretched as the gate of

Pebble Cottage creaked. 'I'll have Stan put some oil on that hinge for you, Rose.' She threw her pruning shears into her basket. 'You're home early. Everything alright?'

'Fine, Maureen, thanks. It was dreadfully quiet in the café, so I thought I could spend the afternoon harvesting some of my carrots. If I leave them much longer, they'll go over.' I'd developed a knack for vegetable growing. Good job, too, as fresh veg were getting rather hard to come by, if you didn't grow your own.

'And how's the little lady?' Maureen leant over the low wall between our gardens and peered into the pram. 'She really is the image of you.'

'Yes, I'm beginning to think so. Although that might be because I'm struggling to remember the finer details of Martin's features. Is that awful? Please don't tell anyone I said that. Gosh, people would think I was a most dreadful wife.'

'No sign of him coming home for a visit, then?'

'I keep hinting that he ought to. Otherwise, Janice won't know him. But he doesn't seem keen. I know it's a frightfully long journey but, truth be told, it hurts a touch.' I bit my thumbnail for a moment. 'It's not as if he's in the forces or overseas. He gets leave, plenty of it, but he always seems to find something better to do with it than come home.' I sighed deeply. I tried not to think about Martin much. It only caused me to become bitter and resentful. And it didn't do much for my self-esteem either. Once again, there was the feeling that we just weren't right for each other. Maureen's response was drowned out by the mournful, haunting wail of the air raid siren. Janice immediately started crying. Tiny black dots appeared on the horizon.

'Blimey!' Maureen shouted over the siren. 'This could be a real one.'

'Come on, then,' I replied pushing the pram through the front door. 'Best get into the shelter.' Maureen and Stan didn't have their own Anderson shelter and, as mine was big enough for a family, they often waited out raids with Janice and me. Stan usually had a pack of cards in his pocket and Maureen never tired of rocking Janice for me.

'I'm right behind you, love. Stan's up at Bayview, trimming some overgrown hedges for Sister Margaret.'

Once safely inside the shelter, we sat on opposite bunks, and I held Janice close to my chest. It sounded as though the aircraft were right overhead. It was a good job it was so dim in the shelter that Maureen couldn't see me shaking. At least Janice had stopped crying, although she was looking at me with wide eyes. The rat-a-tat of the anti-aircraft guns along the coast punctured the air, and the engines faded away to the west.

'Brighton again,' Maureen said. 'Poor things.' A brief silence. And then we heard it. A single aircraft engine getting louder and louder. Then the dreaded whistle of a bomb falling through the sky.

'Get down!' Maureen shouted, throwing herself over me and Janice. I didn't so much hear the explosion as feel it vibrating through my chest. I stifled a scream and held my breath waiting for another one, one that might rip right through the corrugated roof of the Anderson shelter and blow us all to smithereens. My heart was in my mouth, but all that came was the long, single note of the all-clear.

'I'm not sure I want to look,' I said as Maureen got up and went towards the door.

'I don't think they got us. But it was close. Come on, if it's bad news it's best to get it over and done with.'

I let Janice suckle my little finger as Maureen and I stepped out into the garden, exhaling loudly at finding both Pebble Cottage and Coral Cottage still standing. But there was a crackling sound in the distance, and a large plume of smoke coming from the direction of Victoria Park. There must have been terror in my eyes, as Maureen reached for Janice. 'The café?' she said, bouncing Janice on her hip.

'Stay here with Janice,' I called, already racing towards Pebble Cottage.

'Rose, wait. It's too dangerous!'

I barely heard her; I was already out the front door.

The Seaside Café was still standing. There were a few tiles missing from the roof and the glass was gone from the window in the back door. But the square of tall, double-fronted town-houses behind, that stretched up to Blythe Avenue, was a blazing pile of rubble. Over the roof of the café, through the thick smoke, I could see remnants of wall poking into the sky like a jagged finger. A pink curtain flapped from a windowpane only half-encased in brickwork. A single bed dangled from the sloping upper floor of a house that had been split in two, exposing the interior like a doll's house. Fire engines and ambulances clanged, and muffled shouts filtered through the crackling flames. I coughed as the wind changed direction, blowing black smoke towards the beach. I wiped my gritty eyes and was about to turn for home when a soft voice called my name. On the low wall that separated Victoria Park from The Promenade sat Dora. She had her string bag full of manila envelopes and her camera case at her feet. Her hair and face were streaked with dust.

'Dora,' I called, rushing over and kneeling down next to her. 'Are you alright? Are you hurt? Were you...?'

'Mrs Marshall and I just made it into the basement in time. Not everyone did.' She looked up at me, and for the first time I saw fear in her eyes. 'It's all gone.'

I wrapped her in my arms and held her close. Her small body trembled as her tears seeped into the fabric of my dress.

'Oh, Dora, you've had quite the shock. Come home with me

and we'll put the kettle on.' I couldn't tell whether it was me or Dora that was shaking more as we made our way down The Promenade. In a single moment, my little cocoon had been shattered. I'd felt so safe in Dovecote, yet I'd come so close to losing everything.

# TWENTY-ONE

## SARAH

May 2017

In the few days since leaving Daphne open-mouthed outside The Seaside Café, Sarah had kept her head down, avoiding her sister at all costs. She'd given Pebble Cottage a thorough spring clean, once Adam had moved Janice's bed back upstairs now Janice was so adept at using her crutches that she'd been able to master the stairs. And she'd spent hours just looking at the photos of Rose and, presumably, Dora. The handwriting on the Christmas card matched the writing on the back of the photos, which only made Sarah more intrigued about who these women were.

Janice refused to allow Sarah to drive her to her hair appointment and her crutches clicked on the concrete as they made slow, but steady, progress along The Promenade. The flowerbed between The Promenade and Queen's Parade was full of bright yellow daffodils and vibrant red tulips. The bell above the door of Aoife's hair salon tinkled, and Janice sank gratefully into the leather chair inside the door.

'Janice!' Aoife cried. 'How lovely to see you. How's the ankle?'

'Getting there, Aoife.'

'Well, you're looking grand.'

'Apart from the mop that is my hair.' Janice fingered her grey bob.

'Sure, we'll get that sorted out in no time. Come on over.'

Janice hauled herself out of the chair and hobbled after Aoife. She glanced back at Sarah. 'Won't be long, love. Are you going to wait?'

Sarah glanced out of the window. 'I think I might have a browse in the bookshop.'

'Oh, lovely. While you're there, can you pick up something for me? Molly will know what sort of thing.'

She hadn't meant anything by that, Sarah knew. But the implication that Sarah didn't know her mother's reading preferences stung.


Making her way up the High Street, she avoided Crawford's Opticians. She'd apologise to Rachel when Rachel apologised to her. Rachel had never liked her. Sarah had the feeling that Rachel thought she'd trapped Rob by falling pregnant. Well, Rachel could think what she liked. She gave Molly a slight nod of recognition as she entered Harrington's Bookshop. Molly smiled back. Everyone in Dovecote knew who she was, and what she'd done. Well, they knew some of it. Sarah could feel Molly's curious gaze on her as she perused the shelves of paperback fiction. She couldn't pick something for Janice, much to her annoyance, so she shifted her focus to the thriller section, looking for something dark. The bell above the door tinkled.

'Hmm, dark and creepy. Sounds about right.' Sarah whipped around at Heather's voice. There was a curious half-smile on

Heather's lips, and her left eyebrow was raised in a gesture so familiar to Sarah that it made her chest constrict. She was looking at the book in Sarah's hands. Sarah shoved it back on the shelf.

'I, um, hi.'

'Calmed down yet?'

It was Sarah's turn to raise an eyebrow. She bit back a sarcastic retort and sighed instead. 'Yeah.'

'Good, in that case do you want to go for a coffee?'

'Sure. Mum's getting her hair done. I've got time.'

'Once she and Aoife get chatting, you've probably got time for a full three-course dinner.'

'I just need to get her a book. But I'm not sure what.'

'Why don't you ask Molly?'

Sarah glanced over at the counter, where Molly was obviously pretending not to listen. 'I guess.'

Heather laughed. 'Honestly, Sarah. It is totally okay to ask people for help, you know. You really need to get on board with that. Hey, Molly,' Heather added, placing a bag of books on the counter. 'A few donations from Bayview for the second-hand bookstall at next week's church fete for you.'

Sarah's heart skipped a beat. She'd hoped to avoid all the annual Dovecote events that would trigger memories of the happiness she'd lost, and where she'd have to engage in small talk with people who might ask where she went, and why. She'd forgotten about the church fete.

'Oh, brill. Thanks, Heather. Hi, Sarah.' Molly swept a lock of brown hair back behind her ear. 'If you're after something for Janice, the latest Jill Mansell is out in paperback. She's not read it yet.'

Daphne was right: everyone knew everything about everyone in Dovecote. The idea was terrifying and comforting at the same time. Could she ever live in such a small place again?

Not while she had secrets that needed to be kept.

. . .

It felt borderline treacherous to be having coffee in the chain coffee shop at the top of the High Street. Sarah could feel the weight of everyone's attention in there on her.

'I'm sorry about the other night. God knows what your friends must think of me.' Sarah stirred her latte.

'It must have been a surprise for Rachel to see you again.'

'So, you're on her side too?'

Heather threw up her hands. 'Whoa, I'm not on anyone's side. Look, Sarah, you left a deep wound when you left. For the past ten years, the people you hurt have been trying to stitch it up. You've come along with a scalpel and opened it right up again.' She reached across the table and grasped Sarah's hand. Her skin was warm and soft, and the touch sent a tidal wave of warm memories washing over Sarah.

'Daphne asked me where I was that day.' Sarah spoke into her coffee.

'Did you tell her?'

'No.'

Heather sucked in her cheeks and raised her eyebrows. 'Okay.'

'I don't want to talk about it.'

'You brought it up.' There was the hint of a laugh in Heather's voice. She was very used to Sarah's habits.

Minutes of silence ticked by. There had been a time when Sarah could have told Heather anything; and had. Now, when there was so much she needed to talk about, she couldn't find the words. The photograph of the two women kissing floated into her head.

'I don't suppose you know of anyone called Rose or Dora who lived in Dovecote during the war?'

'What?' Heather jolted, as though Sarah had interrupted a deep thought.

'Sorry, that came out weird. I found an envelope of old photographs hidden under a loose floorboard in Mum's bedroom. They were mostly of a woman called Rose. I'm pretty sure they were taken by someone called Dora. The handwriting on the back matches a Christmas card sent to Rose, which I found in the café.'

Heather frowned and blinked a few times. 'Wow, that's very random.'

'I think Rose had a baby at Bayview, but I wondered if either woman could have lived at Bayview in their later years. I don't remember any residents called Rose or Dora when I was working in the office after we left school. What about in the last ten years?'

'Doesn't ring any bells.'

Sarah hesitated – but then, if there was anyone who she could tell about *that* photo, it was Heather. 'There's a photo of them kissing. And I don't mean a little peck on the cheek, either.'

Heather let out a low whistle and grinned. 'Ooh, how interesting.'

'Maybe they were there before our time.'

The tightness in Sarah's jaw eased as Heather caught and held her gaze. The memories of their time swirled in Heather's brown eyes. A heavy silence fell – broken by the ping from Sarah's mobile.

'Mum is finished and waiting at the salon. I'd better go and meet her. Otherwise, she'll try to walk home on her own.'

'She needs to be resting that ankle.'

'You try telling her that.'

They slurped down the dregs of their coffees. Sarah wouldn't say so out loud, but the latte hadn't been anywhere near as good as Janice's. Outside the coffee shop, Heather placed a hand on Sarah's arm. The lightness of her touch made Sarah's breath hitch in her chest.

'I just had a thought. There's a lovely lady at Bayview called Maureen. She's probably old enough to remember Dovecote in the forties. She might be able to shed some light on your mystery women? Her memory's as clear as day, and she'll be thrilled to have someone new to chat to.'

'That would be great. I'll drop in at some point.'

'If you come to the church fete next week, she'll be there.'

Sarah groaned. 'Yeah, I'll probably be there. I presume it's not changed much in the ten years I've missed?'

'Oh, I think you might be pleasantly surprised. There was a gin stall last year. That went down a treat!'

Heather placed the softest kiss on Sarah's cheek, setting off a chain reaction in Sarah's nervous system that made the tips of her fingers tingle. Heather looked as though she was going to say something, but changed her mind. Sarah watched as she walked away across the road and up the sloping driveway towards Bayview Care Home. Twin tendrils of guilt and regret twisted around Sarah's heart. How deep was the wound she'd inflicted on Heather, and how much had it hurt to have it ripped open?

Back at Pebble Cottage, Sarah sat cross-legged on her bed. Outside, the sun sank down behind the cliffs to the west of Dovecote, turning the sky lavender. A seagull's call echoed down the chimney and out of the black cast-iron fireplace. Her mother had wanted to block up the fireplace when she'd redecorated the room for Sarah to move into when Daphne moved out, but Sarah wouldn't let her. It was such a romantic feature of the cottage, and the gothic decoration was perfect for Sarah's taste.

The six photographs were spread out in front of her. Whoever this Dora was, she had meticulously noted the dates on the back of each, and Sarah turned them over and rearranged them into date order:

*10th March 1942 – Rose and Janice at Bayview.*

*August 1943 – Rose in Victoria Park.*

*September 1943 – Me and Rose in the back garden at Pebble Cottage.*

*October 1943 – Rose on The Promenade.*

*December 1943 – Rose in the sitting room at Pebble Cottage.*

*December 1943 – Me and Rose under the mistletoe.*

Sarah turned the photographs over carefully, one at a time, a sense of uneasiness sitting heavily in her stomach. The first time she'd flicked through them, she'd presumed the one of Janice was the last in the collection, but it was the earliest one. After March 1942, Janice just vanished. What if the name *was* just a coincidence, and something had happened to the Janice in the photograph? That would explain why her mother had never come across the other Janice.

Sarah picked up the second to last photo. Rose was standing next to a very spindly looking Christmas tree. Garlands of paper rings were draped over the tree and the occasional bauble dangled from the branches. Sarah could make out the edge of a familiar mantelpiece. Rose's fair hair was pinned back from her face in curls. Her nose turned up at the end and she had big, round eyes. She was smiling: her lips were full, and her two front teeth overlapped slightly. She was dressed casually in a jumper and wool skirt. There was something in her smile, the way it touched her eyes, that was so familiar.

Sarah glanced up at the photograph on her dressing table. Sarah couldn't fathom why her mother insisted on displaying it. It was over thirteen years old, having been taken of herself and her mother on the morning of Sarah's wedding. Sarah tried not to dwell on her own image, her knee-length 1950s-style ivory dress, or the wildflowers in her hair. Instead, her eye was drawn to Janice's smile, the way it touched her eyes. Hauling herself off the bed, she held the photo of Rose up to the photo of Janice. Even though Janice was significantly older than Rose, the similarity was unmistakable. But it didn't make any sense.

A message alert from her phone interrupted her pondering, and she rolled her eyes. Speaking of things that didn't make sense.

*Hi. Just to say we've been told there's an issue with the part we need for your van, so we're sourcing an alternative supplier. We'll get it as soon as we can.*

Sarah groaned. The three dots were wiggling. Rob was still typing.

*Also, I think we should probably talk. How about dinner at Las Gaviotas one evening?*

On the one hand, dinner with Rob did not appeal. On the other hand, tapas did. She drummed her fingers against her phone for a few minutes before slipping it back into the pocket of her jeans, leaving Rob's question unanswered. As for the photographs, they left Sarah with unanswered questions of her own.

# TWENTY-TWO

## ROSE

May 1943

I had just put Janice down for her afternoon nap when Dora slipped in through the front door of Pebble Cottage. It had been a couple of days since the bombing that had destroyed 24 Blythe Avenue, where she had been lodging, and we were all still quite shaken up. The café was closed while the broken windows and damaged roof tiles were replaced. Dora gave me a sad sort of smile as she put her camera down on the sideboard next to Martin's parents' wireless.

'I was able to get close enough to get some pictures this time. The street is still crawling with firemen, and a demolition team have been called in to knock down the rest of what is still standing.'

In the immediate aftermath of the bomb, some of the other houses and odd walls had come crashing down, and the few that remained had been deemed dangerous. What had once been a whole block of beautiful townhouses was now a pile of rubble in a large crater.

Dora took off her shoes and massaged her stockinged feet.

'There's no chance of salvaging anything now. Poor Mrs Marshall has lost everything. Including all her photographs and mementoes of her late husband.'

I wanted to point out that Dora had lost everything too, but she only ever thought of others. She was a deep well of kindness and compassion.

'Have you heard from Violet?' Violet Saunders had been last seen running from Blythe Avenue on the evening of the bombing, after discovering that her mother had been pulled from the rubble, badly injured. I could hazard a guess as to where she had been when her home was hit, but it wasn't my place to say. All I could hope was that the blonde girl she'd been having teacakes with that morning was looking after her now. Dora's eyes filled with tears.

'No. Oh, the poor thing, orphaned now, of course. It could have been even worse. Thank goodness her mother saw fit to evacuate her two young boys when she did. It makes me feel quite ill to think what could have happened to them.'

My stomach lurched, and I found myself climbing the stairs and pushing open the door to the box room. With Janice's cot in the tiny room, there wasn't much space for anything else, except an old dressing table and a chest of drawers which Stan had sanded down and varnished for me. I stood over the cot, watching Janice's chest rising and falling as she slept.

Dora had followed me up the stairs, and was hesitating at the door.

'Do you think there will be more bombings?' I asked, not daring to tear my eyes away from my baby.

'I don't know. Probably.'

My trembling hands gripped the side of the cot so tightly, my knuckles started to turn white. Dora's warm hand on my shoulder made me look up.

'I have to get her out of here, Dora. It's not safe. I want to keep her safe.' My voice wobbled.

'Where would you go?'

'Me?'

'You'd have to go with her, Rose. She's much too young to be sent away on her own. And she needs you to be safe, too.'

I pushed my fingers through my hair. I hadn't thought of that. But I couldn't leave the café. I was needed in Dovecote; Dora had said it herself, and so had Uncle Douglas. But the thought of another bomb made my insides quiver.

'I don't know what to do,' I wept. Dora put her arms around me and the wool of her cardigan muffled my sobs.

'Why don't you ask your uncle?' Dora said, gently. 'He'll know what to do.'


Uncle Douglas had been understanding of my predicament but had, after some thought and some prayer, advised that the best thing for Janice was to arrange for her to be evacuated. My heart swung like a pendulum – one moment determined that I couldn't let my baby out of my sight, the next adamant that a German bomb was going to come through the ceiling of Pebble Cottage and take her away from me permanently. At least if she was evacuated, it would only be a temporary separation.

Martin had been worse than useless. His only contribution to the debate, exchanged via a chain of letters, was to say that I should do what I thought was best. That was all well and good, but I didn't know what *was* for the best. If I kept her at home and the worst happened, it would have been my selfishness that had put her in harm's way. But how could I live without her smiles, and sloppy kisses, and half-formed words? She was walking now, unsteady but determined. My little Janice was going to be the sort of girl who didn't let anything stand in her way.

But the decision had been made and the wheels set in

motion. Uncle Douglas had called in favours and made impassioned pleas to the powers that be. And now here we were, two weeks later, on a bright June morning with seagulls circling in an unbroken blue sky, on the platform of Dovecote station. I'd dressed Janice in her best clothes, tied a pink ribbon in her hair, and packed her favourite belongings into a small suitcase. Dora had given me a copy of a photograph she'd taken of Martin, Janice, and me on the day of Janice's christening. I'd slipped it into the case along with one of my headscarves, which I'd sprayed with my favourite perfume. All I could hope was that Janice wouldn't forget me. I held her tight now, as she sat on my hip. I bent my head and kissed her cheek. I drew her smell deep into my lungs, imprinting it onto my memory. Above the noise on the platform, I heard the familiar click of Dora's camera. It would be a dreadful photograph of me; I had tears streaming down my face.

'Mrs Wilton?' I lifted my head to a kind-faced evacuation officer and nodded. 'And you must be Janice?' She tickled Janice under her chin, making her giggle. 'You're doing a very brave thing, Mrs Wilton. We cannot afford to get complacent about children's safety. With the damage our boys are inflicting on the Germans, we can expect reprisals and, as you well know, we on the south coast are right in the firing line.' She looked at her clipboard and frowned. 'We prefer to evacuate the mother as well, when the child is so young.' I didn't need her to tell me that; I would have preferred it too. But I couldn't expect Maureen to take over the café, on which Dovecote relied so heavily, not when Stan needed her too. 'But never mind, things are what they are.' She tucked her clipboard into her large bag and reached out. This was the moment that had kept me awake every night for a fortnight. The instant Janice left my arms, a cold shiver ran through me, as though a piece of my body had been sliced off. 'Now, don't worry about a thing. Janice's host family are lovely, and they have experience of looking after very young evacuees. I will deliver her to them personally; you have my word.'

And then my baby was gone. Off on a journey that may save her life. Dora and I stood on the platform as the train left the station. As the last carriage disappeared, Dora wrapped her arm through mine and guided me away. If it hadn't been for Dora, I might have stood on that platform until the end of the war.

# TWENTY-THREE

## SARAH

May 2017

Janice's ankle was healing well, so she'd been able to do a huge amount of baking for the church fete. Sarah loaded box after box of cakes, sticky buns, and scones into the boot of Janice's red Vauxhall Corsa, and then helped her mother into the front seat.

'How come the church fete is being held at Bayview this year?' Sarah asked as she turned the car around on Fisherman's Walk and headed up towards Blythe Avenue. A new car park had appeared at the back of the museum. The extension looked almost done. The three weeks Sarah had been back had flown by. If only the part for her van could be in as much of a hurry. She still hadn't replied to Rob's text, and he'd not asked again.

Janice was down to one crutch, which she'd propped against her leg. 'The work being done on the church hall roof and on the vicarage means that there isn't space up there, so Bayview offered their gardens in exchange for a portion of the funds raised. I think they're donating it to dementia research.'

'I did wonder what was going on at the church hall with all

the scaffolding when I went up to...' She couldn't finish her sentence. Janice reached over and squeezed Sarah's knee.

'You can just drop me off if you don't want to stay.' Janice shot Sarah an understanding look. Sarah swallowed hard.

The last time she'd been at the annual Dovecote church fete was a week before Faith's death. Faith had loved running around and having a go at the games. Even though it was being held in a different location, and in May rather than August, it was still going to be a fertile ground for a flood of memories. No matter how much Heather insisted it had changed. She was also in danger of running into Rachel, or Rob, or Daphne, who Sarah had been avoiding since she'd run off that day at the café. And, as it was at Bayview, Heather would definitely be there. The prospect of seeing her should have been a comfort, but the ghost of Heather's kiss on her cheek lingered. She cleared her throat, which was strangely dry.

'No, of course I'll stay,' she said, turning into the steep winding driveway up to the red-brick Edwardian Bayview buildings. 'For a while, anyway.' Until the urge to run away got too strong.

The back gardens of Bayview Care Home were a hive of activity. People bustled across the manicured lawn and between the flowerbeds full of roses, peonies, dahlias, and delphiniums, carrying trestle tables and boxes. In the middle of it all, clipboard in hand, directing operations, was Helen Bretherton, Reverend Clive's wife. Even though Sarah hadn't seen her in over ten years, with her grey perm and colourful hand-knitted cardigan, Helen was instantly recognisable. She peered over her half-moon glasses at Sarah.

'Hello, Helen, which table is the cake stall?' Sarah asked. Her arms were starting to ache under the weight of the boxes full of baked goods. Helen consulted her clipboard and pointed over to a table near the back entrance to Bayview. 'Over there, please. Oh, are those Janice's sticky buns?'

'Yes. Mum was able to stand long enough to make some. She still hasn't divulged the recipe to me or Daphne.'

Helen peered at Sarah again, as if only now seeing her properly. 'Gosh, it *is* you. I wasn't sure, but then who else in Dovecote has purple streaks in their hair and a turquoise nose stud?' The laugh in her voice and her gentle smile told Sarah that she wasn't being judgemental, just stating the obvious. It was true, Sarah had always stuck out. 'Welcome home – it's nice to see you again, Sarah. Keep one of those buns aside for me, would you? I've assigned a couple of ladies from church to help on the stall, if that's alright with your mum?'

Why did everyone seem to be so sure Dovecote was her home? Sarah filed the question for later, much later. 'I'm sure it will be fine, Helen, thanks. She'd rather do it all herself – you know what she's like – but she still needs to be taking it easy. Right, I'd better go and put these down and unload the rest.'

Reverend Clive arrived, looking flustered and mopping his bald head, just as the last string of bunting was being tied around the stalls. He called for quiet, and a solemn hush fell across the garden. It was only interrupted by the chirping of a blackbird in one of the hazel trees.

He rested his hands across his rounded middle. 'Once again, you have done yourselves proud. Thank you for all your hard work. Let us pray.'

As everyone bowed their heads, Sarah took a surreptitious look around. The edge of her mouth twitched as she spotted Heather in the care home doorway. Their eyes met and Sarah looked down at her feet. It was like being back in a school assembly all over again.

· · ·

With Janice happily in charge of the cake stall, bossing about the two ladies from church, Sarah went for a wander around the fete to test Heather's claim that she'd be pleasantly surprised. Also, getting away from the cake stall meant she could slip away quietly if she spotted anyone she'd rather not talk to – namely Rob. There were all the usual stalls – a tombola, a few raffles, various crafts – including sinister-looking hand-knitted duck-shaped tea cosies, Molly's second-hand books, and tables of homemade jams and chutneys. There was no sign of any gin, though. Perhaps lessons had been learnt from the year before. Her stomach rumbled as she debated buying a jar of homemade pickled onions and a jar of pickled eggs. They were only two pounds a jar, and she'd not had a proper pickled onion or egg for years. Having paid for the jars and slotted them into her tote bag, she turned away from the table and bumped straight into Rachel.

'Oh, sorry,' Rachel said. Then she realised who had walked into her. 'Oh, it's you.'

'Hi.' They stared each other down for a moment.

'Look,' they said at the same time.

'I'll go first,' said Sarah. 'I never intended to meet up with Rob. The only reason I came back was to fulfil my dad's dying request for his ashes to be scattered in Dovecote.' Sarah bit her lip. Neil's ashes were still on the desk in her bedroom. She couldn't just leave him sitting there; she needed to get him back to Pete sooner rather than later. 'My plan was to scatter his ashes and then disappear again without seeing anyone. But things worked out differently.' She paused and drew a breath. She had to try to make amends, for Rob's sake. 'Rob told me what happened after I left, and how much you did for him. Thank you for looking after him.'

Rachel shrugged slightly. 'He's my brother.'

'Yeah, I know. But still. Anyway, we are where we are, I guess.'

'He gave me a telling-off, you know.'

Sarah had to smile. 'It probably wasn't our finest hour, for either of us. Did you manage to get your nail fixed? I found it in my hair.'

'Oh, is that what happened? I'm sorry.'

'Me too.'

Rachel turned to walk away, but paused. 'He's glad you're back. I hadn't realised he would be. He's too soft for his own good sometimes. I think he's forgiven you.'

'I don't deserve that.' Sarah looked down at the grass. Had she forgiven him? The flicker of anger that sparked in her chest answered her question. But if that was true, why had she kissed him?

Rachel spoke again, breaking through her jumbled thoughts. 'No, you don't. But that's between you and him. Just, please don't hurt him again.'

As Rachel walked away, Sarah rubbed her chin. That hadn't been too bad. They would never be friends, she and Rachel. But as long as weren't tearing strips off each other, that was progress.


Next to a particularly colourful flowerbed, Sarah spotted Heather chatting to Harrison Prentice at a stall decked out in rainbow bunting. Dovecote had come a long way if there was now a Pride stall at the church fete. Perhaps that was Heather's promised pleasant surprise. An elderly couple walked past her, each sporting a rainbow sticker. Had her father known he'd have been welcomed in Dovecote, maybe he would have come back.

Heather's hair was tied up in a bright yellow scarf, revealing the soft, dark brown skin of the back of her neck. Sarah's knees went unexpectedly weak. It was just the memories, she told herself, nothing more.

'Sarah!' The call of her name stopped her in her tracks.

Reverend Clive was waving at her. He clasped her hand between his. 'How lovely to see you. How are you?' It struck Sarah that he was the first person to ask her that since she'd been back. It was a nice change from 'What are you doing here?' She swallowed down the lump in her throat.

'Fine, thanks Clive.'

'I was sorry to hear about your father. I didn't know him well, but I remember him being a good man.'

Sarah welled up, but bit her lip to stop the tears spilling over. 'Thank you. I was glad I got the chance to get to know him, once I'd tracked him down.'

Clive nodded sagely. 'And—'

'Yes, I've been to see Faith's grave. Daphne and Mum have done a wonderful job taking care of it. Of her.' If she kept talking to Clive, the dam was going to break. What was it about him that made her want to release all the emotions she'd been keeping so carefully contained for so long? He patted her hand.

'It is marvellous to see you back. It will do your mum the world of good to have you home. And Daphne, Adam, and Jake too.' There was *that* word again. Home. Every time someone said it, another splinter embedded itself in Sarah's heart. Clive looked her in the eyes, and she couldn't turn away. 'I'm always here if you need a chat, Sarah. About anything.' Before Sarah could respond, Clive let out an exclamation. 'Oh! I almost forgot.' He reached into the hessian bag hanging from his wrist. 'I found this in the attic at the vicarage. It was buried under a pile of old moth-eaten vestments. Must have been left there by one of my predecessors, and forgotten about.' He handed Sarah a dusty shoebox tied with string. A brown label tied to the string simply said 'Janice.'

'Oh. Right, I'll give it to Mum.'

'I haven't looked inside – I assume it's nothing particularly important.'

The photograph of Rose and the mystery of the other Janice sprang into Sarah's mind. 'Clive?'

'Yes, dear.'

'When did you first come to Dovecote?'

He stroked his double chin. 'February 1982. I remember because it was just before the outbreak of the Falklands War and, having previously been a chaplain in the RAF, I was quite relieved to be moving away from the front line, as it were. Why do you ask?'

'Oh, no reason. I just wondered whether you had ever met Reverend Douglas Legg, my grandfather. But I think he retired in the late sixties.'

'I know the name, of course. But no, I took over from Reverend Quinn. He left rather suddenly, and I was parachuted in.' He laughed. 'Not literally. Thankfully my involvement with the RAF didn't extend to being pushed out of planes. Was there something in particular you wanted to know about your grandfather?'

Sarah shook her head. 'Just curious.'

'Well, you're more than welcome to stop by the vicarage and have a rummage in the archives. Although you might want to wait until after the roof is done; everything's very dusty at the moment.'

'Thank you.'

'I'd best go. I'm not allowed to stand still for long. Have to get round and see everyone. Take care of yourself, Sarah. Remember, you know where I am.' And he was gone, swallowed up by a huddle of adoring grey-haired ladies.

Heather looked up and watched as Sarah crossed the lawn towards her.

'Hey, you. What were you chatting to the good Reverend about?'

'Oh, nothing. He was just asking how I was.'

'Do you still fancy having a chat with Maureen? She's looking forward to meeting you.'

Sarah glanced over her shoulder. Janice was deep in conversation with someone. 'Yes, I'd love to.'

Heather led her to a paved area under the shade of a tall oak tree. An elderly woman with suntanned skin and sturdy arms sat in a wheelchair next to a wooden picnic table. A few grey curls peeked out from under her floral headscarf.

'Maureen,' Heather said brightly, sitting down at the table. 'This is Sarah, who I told you about.'

Maureen regarded Sarah closely, with the intensity of a hawk, then sat back in her wheelchair. 'So, you're Sarah. Yes, I can see your mother in you.' Her eyes narrowed. 'I also see a kindred spirit. Like all runaways, we always end up coming home.'

Heather shot Sarah an apologetic look, but Sarah laughed. She liked Maureen immediately.

'Hello, Maureen. I don't know if Heather has mentioned it, but I need your help. You might be the only person who can clear up a mystery for me.'

'Huh,' Maureen grunted. 'More like the only one ancient enough and with enough marbles left to remember the old days. Go on then. What have you got?'

Sarah pulled the envelope of photographs from her tote bag and drew out the one of Rose leaning against the railings on The Promenade. 'I don't suppose you know who this is?'

Maureen picked up the photograph and held it close to her eyes. She looked at it for a long moment before putting it back down on the table. 'Oh, indeed I do. That is Rose Wilton, who lived at Pebble Cottage and ran The Seaside Café during the war.'

# TWENTY-FOUR

## ROSE

August 1943

The summer eventually came in a blaze of sunshine. The Seaside Café was so busy that I didn't have much time to dwell on missing Janice. Sleep was hard to come by, and not just because of the hot, sticky weather. On clear nights, I spent hours at my bedroom window looking up at the stars, willing them to watch over her and keep her safe. By the light of the moon, I re-read the monthly letters that came from her host family in Carlisle, giving me updates on how she was doing. She was growing so fast, and I was missing so much. But it was a small price to pay for her safety.

I couldn't have borne an empty house, so I was grateful Dora had accepted my invitation to lodge with me. She was such a quiet, serene presence and I found myself looking forward to closing the café for the day, knowing she was waiting for me at Pebble Cottage.

The temperature had peaked over the bank holiday week-end, and we'd had a terrific thunderstorm. I locked the café door behind the last customer of the day, and was sweeping the floor when a light tapping on the window made me look up.

'Dora!' I gasped, opening the door and letting her in. She had her camera with her, as usual. 'Why aren't you working?'

She gave me a shy smile. 'I have the day off. It's such a beautiful day, I thought I'd take some photographs. I was just heading to Victoria Park and wondered if you wanted to join me?'

'I was going to go home and potter about in the garden. I think my latest batch of peas are ready for picking. But your idea sounds much better.'

We walked, arm in arm, along The Promenade and up the steps into Victoria Park. There was a lot of activity over at the allotments and a gaggle of young boys were kicking a football around on the bandstand. We found a small patch of grass and sat down. I kicked off my shoes and let the grass tickle my aching feet before stretching my legs out. *Click.* I turned my head to find myself facing Dora's camera. *Click.* It was strangely enjoyable, being the focus of her attention.

'I hope you don't mind,' she said, her blue eyes sparkling in the sunlight. 'But you're such a natural in front of the camera, and you looked so relaxed and, dare I say it, happy.'

I plucked a daisy from the grass and twirled it between my fingers. 'It feels wrong that I should admit to it, what with Janice being so far away, and Martin of course. But I do feel rather content, I suppose. Does that make me a terrible mother and wife?'

Dora rested her head against my shoulder and a strand of her brown hair fell across my chest. 'Rose, I've heard you weeping late at night. I know you miss Janice terribly.'

'I miss Martin, too.' That was a little bit of a lie. I couldn't even remember the last time I'd received a letter from him. Which was worse: that he hadn't written, or that I hadn't noticed he'd not written?

'I'm sure you do. But they are both relatively safe. I think it's quite alright that you take the little moments of contentment. We all should. Otherwise, we will all go quite mad.'

'You've never spoken of any sweethearts, Dora. I don't know how some lucky chap hasn't claimed you.'

Dora smoothed her tartan skirt with her delicate fingers, but didn't reply.

'I'm sorry, have I said something hideously insensitive?'

'No,' she eventually said, as she lifted her head from my shoulder. 'I'm afraid there's just nothing to tell.'

'Really? I find that hard to believe.'

Dora looked down at her hands for a moment, and then a smile spread slowly across her lips. 'Well, there was someone while I was at university in Oxford. But then I got recruited and left. That was the end of it.'

I knew better than to ask about what she had been recruited into. We'd been sharing a home for three months and I was still none the wiser as to what she did all day. 'Have you kept in touch?'

'No. It was... complicated.'

'Oh. I see.' I didn't see at all, but it seemed like the right thing to say. Dora lay down on the grass and closed her eyes, so I didn't push for details.

Lily Morrison, who lived on Beachfront Road next to Betty, walked past, her little girl skipping along next to her. As I watched the little girl smile up at Lily, I felt a crushing sadness, and also a dose of shame.

'Dora?'

Dora tilted her head towards me. 'Yes?'

'You don't think I'm a bad mother, do you?'

Dora sat bolt upright, and a frown creased her forehead. 'Of course not. Whatever made you ask that, Rose?'

I poked at the grass with my forefinger. 'I just see mothers with their children and wonder whether I'm bad and selfish for having sent Janice away.'

'Oh, Rose. You chose to have Janice evacuated for her protection. Lily has chosen to keep her child at home. You both had your reasons for those decisions and neither choice is that of a better mother than the other. Please, Rose, don't torture yourself over this. Everything will be fine in the end.' She lay back down on the grass and I gazed out to sea. Dora was right, as always. What would I do without her steady dependability, and permanent optimism?

'Do you know what I would like right now?' she half-whispered a moment later.

'What?' I leant closer so I could hear her. Her skin smelt of glycerine soap.

'A daiquiri.'

'A what?'

Dora sat up again and dusted a few bits of grass from her blouse. 'It's a cocktail made of rum, lime juice, and sugar. Mummy told me about them in her last letter. They had them at a party.'

'Sounds very fancy. I'd say if you tried to order one at The Royal Oak, Derek would look at you like you'd grown a second head. But he might be able to rustle up a gin and lime.'

Her smile widened and a glint of mischief flared in her eyes. 'Shall we?'

'Go to the pub? I don't know, Dora. It's not really a place for women.'

'Come on, Rose. You're a respectable married woman who runs her own business. I'm... well... I shall be with you. Come on, let's be rebels. The whole world's gone mad, who cares if a couple of women go into a pub?' She stood up and pulled me to my feet. I didn't want to let go of her hands.

.   .   .

Derek, the bald, tattooed, chain-smoking owner of The Royal Oak placed two gin and limes down on the counter and Dora handed over a few coins. I hurried her over to a table tucked up against the side of the stone fireplace.

'There's more people in here than I thought there would be,' I said, trying to look around without appearing like I was looking around.

'It's marvellous,' Dora giggled. Over by the bar, a group of men laughed loudly. One of them caught my eye and smirked. I'd seen him and his lot skulking around town in their sharp suits, colourful shoes, and trilby hats. I knew they were black-marketeers, and I didn't trust them as far as I could throw them. I shuddered, but turned my attention back to Dora, only to find she was gazing at me. My cheeks flushed.

'You know,' I said, running my finger along the rim of my glass. 'I barely know anything about you. We've been friends for a while, and you've hardly told me anything. I know you can't tell me about your work, but what about before the war?'

She flashed me one of her shy smiles. 'There's not a lot to tell, really. I was born in London. Mummy and Daddy met at some soirée or other. Daddy came over from Zürich to England at the end of the last war. He's a psychiatrist and was here to study. At school, the only thing I was really good at was languages.'

'Being brought up by parents who spoke two different languages must have helped.'

'I suppose. I knew some Italian and French from a young age.' She lowered her voice to a whisper. 'And of course, German. After school, I went up to Oxford. I was only there a couple of years before the Foreign Office found me.'

I had been right; it was government work Dora was doing. She probably shouldn't have even told me that much.

A shadow loomed over the table, and Dora and I looked up to find a red-faced, heavy-set man staring down at us. Or rather, at Dora. I was familiar with most of the Dovecote residents, but I'd never seen him before. His piggy eyes narrowed, and he raised a meaty finger, almost jabbing her in the cheek.

'I've seen you around,' he growled. 'With your camera. Foreign, aren't you?'

'N... n... no,' Dora stuttered, before composing herself. 'I'm from London.'

The man brought his fist down hard on the table, knocking over my glass. Gin and lime sloshed all over the table. 'You're one of *them!*' He was shouting now, and beads of sweat formed on his podgy forehead. 'I reckon you're one of them fifth-columnists, giving away our secrets to the enemy.' I reached for Dora's hand across the table, and we tried to stand, but he gripped Dora's shoulder and forced her back into her seat.

'Get your hand off me,' she managed to say. I was rendered speechless and quivering. I could see his grip tightening. 'Please.' It was a whisper this time.

'Oi, mate. She said get off.' The red-faced man turned at the voice behind him and was met with the clenched fist of one of the spivs. The punch sent him sprawling to the floor. Dora and I leapt to our feet.

'It's traitors like *her* that got my son killed,' he whimpered, wiping a trickle of blood from his split lip with his sleeve. He muttered something else that I didn't quite catch as he staggered to his feet. By the look on our rescuer's face, it wasn't something that was fit for ladies' ears. As he stumbled away, the crowd, who had fallen silent, turned back to their drinks. The man who had thrown the punch straightened his pinstriped suit jacket and held out his hand to Dora.

'Reg Harris,' he said. 'Are you alright?' There was an unmistakable Cockney twang to his voice, and he dropped the 'H' from his surname. Dora shook his hand and nodded. 'Don't you be worrying about what the likes of him says.' I could see tears in Dora's eyes. Then Reg turned to me. There was a glint in his eye. 'It's Rose, isn't it? You run that little café down on the seafront. Nice little money-maker, I reckon.'

'I'm Mrs Wilton, and yes, my husband owns The Seaside Café,' I replied. Something about the way Reg was looking at me made my skin crawl. It was like he was sizing me up, like a piece of meat in a butcher's window. I supressed a shudder, reminding myself that, despite his good deed, he was a black-market operative, a thief, and a rogue. Everyone knew him. He could get you pretty much anything you wanted, for a price. I tried not to think about where it all came from.

'I'm very pleased to meet you,' he continued. The feeling was not mutual. 'That oaf has spilled your drinks. Would you permit me to buy you lovely ladies a replacement?' He didn't take his eyes off me, and my gut tightened.

'Thank you for your assistance,' I said, threading my arm through Dora's. 'But I think we should be leaving.'

'Next time then, Rose.' Reg grinned. His words dripped honey, but his eyes flashed. I didn't like the look on his face one bit.

Dora held my arm tight as we made our way down The Promenade and home to Pebble Cottage. She watched nervously out of the front window while I went into the kitchen and put the kettle on.

Perched on the edge of the sofa, Dora wrapped her hands around the warm cup and rested her elbows on her knees. There were wet tracks on her cheeks.

'I suppose I shouldn't be surprised that's what people think of me. I've not really made an effort to get to know people. And I suppose I do look rather odd, walking around with my envelopes and taking pictures.' She looked down at her tea. 'It's so frustrating. I'm proud of who I am, and of my heritage. But people don't always appreciate the distinction between Swiss

German and German. As you can imagine, it's best if I keep my father's nationality under wraps.'

'I don't think anyone truly believes you're a spy, Dora. That man's son was killed in the war. He's clearly angry and looking for someone to blame.'

Dora put down her cup and turned to face me, pulling one foot up under her. 'You're very good to say so, Rose. Goodness knows, it would be worse if I went by my actual name, and not my mother's maiden name.'

'Now that I know your father is Swiss, I do wonder how your name is Stephens.'

Her mouth twisted into a lop-sided smile. 'It's Müller, and it's why my parents moved to America just before the war.'

'I shan't tell a soul.'

'I know.' Her long fingers toyed with the hem of her skirt. Her nails were painted an oyster-shell pink. 'I want to tell you what I do all day, up in your spare room, Rose. But I can't. It's not about trust, it's about safety. Mine, and yours.'

'You don't have to prove yourself to me, Dora. I trust you.'

'And I, you.'

The moment our eyes met, something fundamentally shifted, not just in me, but in the universe. I'd never known a feeling like it. It was as though I were an iron filing and she, a magnet. I was suddenly very aware of my own heartbeat and my insides were flooded with warmth.

The instant our lips met, I knew my life would never be the same again.

# TWENTY-FIVE

## SARAH

May 2017

'Oh yes, I remember Rose. She was a lovely, friendly girl. Terrifically frightened of bombs though.' Maureen sat back in her chair and laced her thick fingers together over her ample chest. 'I knew her husband, Martin Wilton, as a child. I was only a few years older than him, but his mother, Ursula, was frightfully snobbish. Martin wasn't allowed to play out on the street with the rest of us. He moved away as soon as he could. Got a job in Brighton at the Post Office, I believe. His parents were killed in a car accident at the beginning of the war. We thought Martin would come home after that, but it wasn't until about a year later that he turned up, new wife in tow.'

'Rose?'

'Aye, Rose. She was a delightful neighbour. We lived next door then, in Coral Cottage. Rose and I often chatted over the back wall. She loved to potter about in the garden, planting vegetables and whatnot, when she wasn't working her fingers to the bone in that café. Then Martin got transferred, up to Scotland or somewhere. A couple of months later, Rose finds she's having a baby. Bit of a shock to her, I think. Stan and I did what we could to help. She was determined to keep The Seaside Café running.'

'Rose owned The Seaside Café?' Sarah asked. That explained why she'd found the Christmas card from Dora there.

'Martin inherited it when his parents died. It was in their family for years.'

A shiver ran down Sarah's spine. Pebble Cottage and the café! *If* that baby was her mother... She refocused on Maureen. 'Was Stan your...?'

'My brother. He was a great bear of a man. And he'd do anything for anyone. He worked for the council, going around collecting scrap for salvage during the war, and then found work building new houses after. That's why we left Dovecote at the end of the war, you see. So he could work on the big building sites just outside London. He got mesothelioma in 1970. He died ten months after being diagnosed. They said it was the asbestos in the scrap metal he collected and sorted. Of course, it was used in those damned post-war houses he was building, too.'

Sarah and Heather exchanged a glance, and Heather placed a hand on Maureen's knee. 'I'm sorry, Maureen.'

Maureen patted Heather's hand. 'Thanks, love. He's been gone a long time, but I still miss him.' Sarah knew that feeling.

'So, Rose had a baby she named Janice,' Sarah prompted. She needed Maureen to confirm that the baby in the photo was Rose's.

'No, love, Rose's baby was called Janet. Similar, but no, definitely Janet. She was a sweet baby, so happy and always smiling.'

Sarah rummaged in the envelope for the photograph of Rose holding the baby, her heart racing. 'Are you sure, Maureen? See here, on the back of this photo it says, "Rose and Janice".'

Maureen took the photo from Sarah's hand and examined both the front and the back closely. 'Well, I never! Would you look at that? I've not thought about those days for quite some time and at some point, I must have got her name muddled up. But now you say it...' She grunted. 'Huh, I guess the old memory isn't as sharp as I thought. Happens to the best of us.' She handed the photo back to Sarah, who took out the photo of Rose and Dora in the back garden of Pebble Cottage.

'And do you know who this woman is?' Sarah showed Maureen the photo. 'I think her name might be Dora, but I'm not sure.'

Once again, Maureen held the photo close to her eyes. Sarah's stomach dropped. Maureen was her only chance of finding out who the women were, but could she trust the old woman's memory?

'She was a friend of Rose's. Moved into Pebble Cottage with Rose after the bombing in May 1943. A rogue German bomber, aiming for Brighton, got lost and dropped one on Dovecote. Flattened a load of townhouses on Blythe Avenue. Nearly took out Victoria Park and The Promenade, too. The cottages survived, the café had some minor damage. I was in the shelter in Rose's back garden with her and little Janet. Sorry, Janice. I can still hear the sound of the confounded thing screaming towards us. I was sure our number was up. Unsettled us for a time, that did.'

'And this woman moved in with Rose after that?' Sarah prompted, before Maureen could go off on another tangent.

'Yes, Dora something or other. I couldn't tell you her surname if my life depended on it. Bit of an odd one. She'd go out every morning with an envelope in a string bag and then come back again, still with the envelope. You rarely saw her in between times, and you could set your watch by her. Never said a word to anyone.' She paused and then tapped her temple. 'That's it, she used to take photographs. The gossip was that she was a spy, but I didn't think so. Stan didn't either. Rose seemed to like her, anyhow.'

'What happened to Rose and Janice? And Dora?' Sarah leant forward, determined not to miss a single clue or detail from Maureen's words.

Maureen gazed into the middle-distance for a moment. 'To tell the truth I'm not sure.' She shook her head. 'We bumbled along through the war. Stan and I said goodbye to Rose a few days after VE Day, and Martin wasn't home by then. At the time, I thought we might come back to Dovecote, but it didn't work out that way. I only came back home a couple of years ago – to die, I suppose. Still here, though. I got my telegram from The Queen last year. I expect I'll probably snuff it soon. About time, really.' She glanced over at the cake stall. 'Funny how I misremembered Rose's baby's name. If I'd remembered correctly, I might have thought it interesting that there was a Janice running the café. I might have questioned whether she was Rose's Janice. Would have made a right fool of myself, seeing as your mum is old Reverend Douglas's daughter.' She laughed, but then tilted her head to one side. 'I wonder what happened to Rose and the rest of them?' Maureen seemed to shake the thought away as she slapped her knees. 'Right. Heather, love, wheel me over to the teas, I'm gasping. Nice to meet you, Sarah.'

'You too, Maureen. And thank you.' Sarah sat back in her chair, the noise from the fete becoming a muted hum as she let Maureen's words sink in. Those photographs had opened up a whole history she knew nothing about. She glanced over at the cake stall. Was Rose really a relative of hers? Were the two Janices actually the same person – her mother? And if Rose had been married to Martin Wilton, where did Dora fit in? Maureen's final question lingered and made Sarah's fingers twitch with excitement – what *had* happened to Rose, and the rest of them?

# TWENTY-SIX

## SARAH

May 2017

Sarah had barely shut the front door of Pebble Cottage when Janice rounded on her.

'What were you talking to Maureen about for so long?'

'Just stuff.' Sarah put down the bags and empty cake boxes. 'I got some pickled eggs and pickled onions.'

'Don't give me "just stuff". I know Maureen used to live next door years ago. You were asking her about that Rose woman, weren't you?'

'So?'

Janice sighed and lowered herself down into the sofa, resting her crutch against the arm. 'Why are you so concerned about some woman who is probably long dead, and who is nothing to do with our family? Is it because of the photo of her kissing that other woman?'

Sarah rolled her eyes and put her hands on her hips. 'It's more to do with a certain baby.' She eyed her mother. 'Who could be you.'

'Sarah Davies!' Janice barked. 'That woman is not my

mother. My mother was Gladys Legg, and that's the end of it. I don't want to hear another word about it.' If she could have got up and stormed out of the room, she would.

'Sarah Portman,' Sarah muttered, as she went into the kitchen to sort out the cake boxes. She filled the sink and started washing out the containers. How could her mum not care that her entire past might be in question? How was she not intrigued? Maureen had said that if she'd remembered Rose's baby was called Janice, she might have made a connection between Rose's baby and Sarah's mother. Surely there must be other people in Dovecote who remembered Rose, who *had* made that connection? Was she missing something? Or was everyone else? She plunged another cake box into the hot water. If she was going to get answers, she needed to find more people who'd known Rose.

Sarah's stomach growled as she put away the last of the cake boxes, and she reached into her tote bag for the jar of pickled eggs. Her hand closed around cardboard. She'd completely forgotten about the shoe box Reverend Clive had given her.

She handed a peace offering of a mug of tea and a slice of fruit cake to her mother, and sat down beside her. She placed the box on the coffee table.

'What's that?' Janice asked, peering at the box.

'Clive gave it to me. Said he found it in the loft at the vicarage, under some old vestments. Reckons it must have been put up there and forgotten about. It's got your name on it.'

'Hmm. Hand it over and I'll have a look. If it's my old school reports, they can go straight in the bin.' A plume of dust rose off the lid as Janice undid the string and lifted it. She looked down into the box for a moment, a frown creasing her forehead.

'What is it, Mum?'

'I don't know. Papers of some description. But I'm getting a funny feeling. Here.' She handed Sarah the box. 'You have a look.'

Sitting on top of a folded, yellowed piece of paper was a length of pink ribbon. Sarah pulled it out of the box and raised a quizzical eyebrow at her mother. Janice shrugged. For a split-second, Sarah considered putting the lid back on the box, but they'd gone too far to stop now. She placed the ribbon down on the coffee table and reached into the box again, her fingers almost itching. The first piece of paper was folded in four, and Sarah opened it up, her mouth dry.

'Mum, it's your birth certificate.'

'My what?'

It was hard to make out the writing on the yellowed page, but Sarah squinted.

'*Tenth of March 1942, Bayview Convalescent Home, Dovecote. Name: Janice Ursula.*' Sarah glanced at her mother. Janice's eyes had widened, and her mouth was firmly set in a thin line. Sarah turned back to the page.

'*Sex: female. Name and surname of father: Martin Wilton.*' Her voice cracked. '*Name and maiden surname of mother: Rose Wilton, formerly Partridge. Rank or profession of father: Telegraph Operator of Pebble Cottage, Fisherman's Walk, Dovecote, Sussex.*'

All the air had been sucked out of the room. Sarah looked up at her mother. 'Mum?'

'I don't understand,' Janice whispered. 'I... I... It can't be. No, it just can't be.'

'There are two more pieces of paper, Mum. Do you want me to see what they say?'

'I don't know. I can't think.' Sarah took her mother's hand in hers and squeezed it gently. Janice nodded, slowly. 'Yes. Go on.'

Sarah unfolded the second piece of paper. 'This one looks like a baptism record. *St. John's Church, Dovecote. Janice Ursula, daughter of Martin and Rose Wilton. Twenty-fourth of March 1942.* Signed by Rev. Douglas Legg.'

Janice opened her mouth, but all that came out was a stran-

gled cry. Sarah unfolded the last piece of paper. At first glance,
it looked much like the birth certificate, but it wasn't. The paper
quivered as Sarah held it and read it out. *'Date and country of
birth of child: Tenth of March 1942, England. Name and
surname of child: Janice Ursula Wilton. Name and surname,
address and occupation of adopter or adopters: Reverend
Douglas Legg, St. John's Vicarage, Dovecote, Minister of Reli-
gion. And his wife Gladys Legg, of the same address. Date of
entry: fifth of September 1945.'* A photograph had fallen out
from between the folds of one of the certificates and fluttered to
the floor. Sarah bent to pick it up. It was the same baby as in the
photograph on the mantelpiece, but she was being held in
Rose's arms. The man standing next to Rose looked decidedly
nervous. Sarah passed it to her mother, who barely gave it a
glance.

'I don't understand,' Janice whispered, before dissolving
into loud sobs that wracked her slight body. Sarah wrapped her
arms around her and held her tight. She couldn't speak.


The kettle had not long boiled when Daphne arrived,
summoned by Sarah. There was no way she was going through
this with Janice alone. Sarah pressed a mug of heavily-sugared
tea into Janice's hand.

'What's going on?' Daphne asked, looking from Janice to
Sarah and back again. It was obviously on the tip of her tongue
to ask what Sarah had done this time. Clearly Sarah bolting
from the café had brought Daphne's distrust of her back to the
surface. 'Are you alright, Mum? Is it your ankle? Do you want
me to call Adam?'

'Sit down, Daphne.' Her sister looked up in surprise at
Sarah's use of her proper name. The colour drained from her
face as she sank into an armchair. 'Do you want to tell her,
Mum?'

Janice's cheeks paled. 'I don't think I can.'

Sarah sat down on the couch next to her mother and took a deep breath. 'At the fete earlier, Reverend Clive gave me an old shoe box that he found in the attic at the vicarage. It had Mum's name on it. We opened it and what we found inside, well, it's kind of turned everything upside down.'

'Spit it out, Sarah.' Daphne shot her an impatient glare.

'Long story short, Mum isn't who she thought she was. It looks like Douglas and Gladys Legg weren't Mum's biological parents, but her adoptive ones. Mum's parents were Rose and Martin Wilton, and they lived here, in this cottage. We also know that Rose Wilton ran The Seaside Café during the war.'

'That's ridiculous,' Daphne snorted. 'Nonsense.'

Sarah held up the box, to which the certificates and the ribbon had been returned. The photograph was still lying on the coffee table. 'Birth certificate, baptism record, and adoption certificate.'

Daphne's hand flew to her chest. 'I... Oh...'

'Yeah, you know those photos I found?'

Daphne sucked air in through her teeth. 'Rose?'

'Our grandmother.'

'I'm... I don't know what to say.' Daphne got up and paced the small sitting room a few times before reaching for the photograph on the mantelpiece. 'But surely your parents would have told you if you were adopted, Mum?'

Janice shook her head and looked down into her mug of tea.

Sarah's eyebrows flicked upwards. 'You'd think so, but apparently not. According to the baptism records, Reverend Douglas Legg baptised Mum. Here.' Sarah held out the other photograph and Daphne blinked at it a few times. 'Same day, same church, same baby. Except that photo,' – Sarah indicated the loose photo in Daphne's hand – 'is Mum with her parents. Hang on!'

'What?' Daphne asked.

'Give me that a second. There's something written on the back.' Daphne handed back the photo and Sarah turned it over. '*Dora Stephens*. That's crossed out. It says *Dora Müller* underneath.'

'Isn't Dora the woman who sent that Christmas card you found at the café?'

'Yes! And if Maureen's memory is accurate, she's also the woman in the photograph with Rose. Why is her name on the back of this one, it's not on any of the others?'

'How on earth did Mum end up being adopted by the vicar who baptised her? What happened to Rose, and Martin? And who on earth is Dora?' Daphne was pacing again.

'Find out.' Both women turned at the force of the command from Janice. 'Find her, Sarah. Find my mother.'

# TWENTY-SEVEN

## ROSE

August 1943

I ducked down behind the counter as Reg Harris, in his trilby as always, walked past The Seaside Café, and glanced in. The way he'd looked at me in the pub the day before sent a shiver down my spine. I let out a long breath as he carried on walking. At least the feelings he drew up in me were clear and easy to understand.

But I got shivers of a different kind when I thought about what had happened with Dora. Where to even start? I was a married woman. What was I doing kissing someone else? And a woman, too. I threw the cloth in my hand down as that same warmth seeped through my body, turning my knees to jelly. I knew there were women who loved other women. But how could I be one? I was married to Martin. We'd conceived a child, eventually. Was there a reason I was relieved that Martin hadn't seemed keen on regular intimacy? Or that I didn't miss sleeping next to him? My head was going to explode. And Dora? Why had she not told me? Had she always known she was that way inclined?

'Oh, God,' I said out loud to the empty café. My hand flew to my mouth. What would Uncle Douglas think? Well, he'd never know, would he? It was just a one-off. It only happened because of how upset Dora was after that awful encounter with that man in the pub. It wouldn't happen again. Why did that make me feel strangely empty? It had been the most beautiful kiss I'd ever had. I pulled myself together as the bell above the door tinkled and Betty swept in, having left her bicycle propped against the window.

'Hullo, Rose. Just thought I'd stop by as I've time before my next patient. A nasty case of varicose veins. It's all glamour in district nursing, I tell you. Oh, can I have one of your teacakes? I'll take it back up to Bayview and have it on my break later.' Her fingers played with something in her pocket. 'I say, Rose, be a love and keep watch while I have a cigarette around the back. We're not allowed to be seen eating or smoking in uniform, but I'm gasping.'

'Only if I can have one too.' I locked the front door of the café, flicked the sign to *Closed*, and ushered Betty through the kitchen and out the back door. From the little alleyway along the back of the café, I used to look up at the windows of the big houses on Blythe Avenue. But they were gone now, as were the people who had died in the bombing.

'Since when did *you* smoke?' Betty asked, passing me a cigarette.

'Since right about now.' I sat down on the back step and hugged my knees to my chest. Betty leant against the back wall. 'Betty?'

'Hmm.' Betty exhaled a long puff of smoke.

'Do you think it's wrong for girls to like each other?'

She frowned in confusion. 'You what?'

'You know what I mean. In a more-than-friends kind of way?'

Betty took another long drag. 'Budge up.' She sat down on

the step next to me. 'I've never really thought about it. Each to their own, I suppose. Can't say it's something that appeals to me.'

'Well, no, I didn't think it would be.'

She looked off into the middle distance for a moment. I took a tentative drag. How anyone could enjoy this was baffling. It was revolting.

'I know that there's more of it going on now,' Betty added, glancing at me out of the corner of her eye. My cheeks flared. 'With so many boys away, girls are trying out alternatives. If you get my drift. I think for most of them, it doesn't mean anything. It might do for some, I suppose. What's brought all this on, then?'

I stubbed out my cigarette. 'Please don't breathe a word to anyone. Please, Betty, I mean it.' She nodded earnestly, but there was a hint of hunger in her eyes. She loved any sort of drama or gossip. 'Promise?'

She sighed. 'I promise.'

'I kissed someone, last night.'

'A girl?'

'It was only a kiss, nothing more.'

'And?'

'And, well, I can't stop thinking about it. I... I quite liked it.' I couldn't look at her.

Betty finished her cigarette. 'How long since you last saw Martin?'

My chest tightened. 'Almost a year and a half.' Had it really been that long? And Janice had been gone almost two months. I knew whose absence left a bigger hole in my life.

'Blimey. In that case, I'm not surprised you needed a little attention. I don't think I could go eighteen days without a kiss, never mind eighteen months.'

'Do you think that's all it is?'

'Ever hear the saying "any port in a storm"?'

'Well, yes.'

'If I were you, I'd be sending a telegram to that husband of yours telling him to get back home on leave quick-smart.' She patted my arm. 'You're just a little lonely, Rose. I shouldn't think on it too much. You'll be right as rain after a week of marital bliss. Oh blast, I'm late for my patient. Must dash.' And with that, she was gone, off down the alleyway towards The Promenade. I got up and dusted myself down. I needed a cup of tea.

I thought about what Betty had said as I stirred my tea. She was wrong; I wasn't missing Martin. We'd not written to one another in over a month. So no, I would not be sending a come-to-bed telegram to my husband. But what *was* I going to do?

# TWENTY-EIGHT

## SARAH

May 2017

Chaos had broken out at Pebble Cottage in the moments after Janice's plea to Sarah to find the mysterious Rose. Voices were raised, and Daphne had slammed the door on her way out. When Sue Prentice unexpectedly called by, Sarah had taken the chance to slip out. She avoided the beach; the sound of the waves in the fading light was too much for her overloaded brain. She needed a distraction from mothers, daughters, and lost years. So, she headed to Victoria Park instead. Something drew her past the bandstand and across the lawn towards the cricket pavilion in the far corner. Back in her youth, the pavilion had been a dilapidated magnet for graffiti and hormone-fuelled teenagers. It was all clean and tidy now. There was glass in the previously boarded-up windows and the missing tiles had been replaced on the roof. She checked over her shoulder as she ducked around the side of the building.

She found what she was looking for on the back wall of the pavilion. *SP+HR*. Carved into the soft wood with the sharp end of a compass. The heart surrounding the pair of initials was wonky. This was a secret declaration of love, one for no one's eyes but her own. She hadn't even known what it meant to be in love with another girl back then, or even if it counted as love. But her heart had wanted what it wanted. Years after she'd scored their initials onto the wall of the Victoria Park pavilion, she'd brought Heather to show her. Hidden from the world, they'd kissed for the first time behind this building. And their love had remained hidden in the dark, secretive and furtive, but deep and real. More real than anything Sarah had experienced before, or since.

Sarah had her phone in her hand and her finger poised to write a text when an incoming message startled her back to reality.

> *I can't be dealing with all this, Sarah. I know you'll do whatever you want, but in my opinion, the best thing to do is just forget it all.*

Sarah rolled her eyes as she replied to her sister's text.

> *I'll do whatever Mum wants. It's not up to you or me. I doubt we'll find Rose or Martin anyway.*

She shoved her phone into her pocket and wandered out into the park, dragging her feet along the gravel path. She couldn't begin to understand how her mum was feeling. Maybe she'd change her mind about finding Rose in the morning. But that photo of Rose and Dora kissing gnawed at Sarah, leaving her with an aching need to find out the story behind the picture.

Deep in thought, Sarah turned out of the gate from Victoria Park onto Blythe Avenue, and walked onwards. After a couple of minutes, she came to with a jolt. She'd crossed Blythe Avenue and was on Courcey Road, outside Rob's house. There was a light on in the sitting room, the yellow warmth seeping through the gap in the curtains. Behind the curtain would be a glass of wine, a supportive arm, and maybe more. There was something about the way he'd kissed her. Even after so many years, the thought of it made her skin tingle. But she couldn't allow herself to give in, not while there was so much Rob didn't know. With leaden legs, she trudged back towards the High Street.

The heady smell of warm garlic wafted from the door of Las Gaviotas. The intimate tapas bar was a new addition to Dovecote since Sarah had left. Beyond the burgundy-velvet-draped windows, marble-topped tables were surrounded by brown-leather chairs. The red shades on the table lamps produced a cosy, sultry, ruby glow. How long had it been since she'd been out for dinner with someone? Too long. She pushed open the door and took her phone out of her pocket.

Rob arrived ten minutes later, looking better than he had a right to in a tight T-shirt that showed off his firm muscles. Sarah swallowed a gulp of Rioja. This was either a brilliant idea, or a spectacularly stupid one.

'Hi,' he said, pulling out the chair opposite Sarah and sitting down.

'Hi.' She poured him a glass of wine. Her cheeks flushed at the memory of their last meeting, when she'd had a complete breakdown and thumped him repeatedly. 'Look, I'm sorry about the other day. I just lost it.' She glanced down at the tabletop. 'I guess it's been harder coming back than I thought it would be.'

'No harm done. But I've been worried about you. You're still angry, aren't you?'

'I think I always will be. But let's not talk about that tonight. Let's just chat.'

'I'd like that.'

They both gave the menu their full attention for a moment,

and it wasn't long before the table was groaning under the weight of small plates of *calamares fritos, patatas bravas, chorizo frito, champiñones al Oloroso*, and *morcilla*. While Sarah told Rob about the photographs, the shoebox, and the complete unravelling of everything she, her sister, and their mother had ever known about their family, a second bottle of Rioja arrived.

Rob skewered a piece of crispy calamari. 'That's intense, Sarah. Is Janice alright?'

Sarah pushed a sherry-sautéed mushroom around her plate. 'She wants to find Rose. I can understand why. I'm sure she must have a million questions.'

'Yeah, like how she ended up being adopted by the Leggs and why they never told her?' He topped up Sarah's glass. Her head was fuzzy. Her insides were warm. 'But also, how has Janice got through life so far without a birth certificate? I had to send mine off to get my passport.'

'I wondered the same thing. Mum said that Douglas and Gladys arranged her passport when she was little and she just kept renewing it. When she and Dad got married, she used her marriage certificate to change her name, and of course never changed it back.' Sarah shrugged. 'I suppose once you've got a passport that covers everything else off.'

'Fair enough. Surely, she would have asked to at least see her certificate, though? Out of curiosity if nothing else.'

'I guess not. And to think it was buried up in the attic all this time. I wonder if my grandad ever realised he'd left it behind when he moved away from Dovecote?'

Rob couldn't answer that question.

'I don't suppose the name Dora Müller or Dora Stephens means anything to you?' Sarah asked a few moments later.

Rob speared the last chunk of chorizo. 'Nope. Why?'

'Her name was on the photograph in the shoebox. Maureen identified the woman with Rose in a photo taken in the garden of Pebble Cottage as Dora. It had "Rose and me" on the back.

So I'm guessing she took the photos I found as well as the christening ones. There's just something about the name Dora Müller. Like I've heard it somewhere before.'

The sun had fully set, and darkness pressed against the restaurant windows. Sarah had no idea how long she and Rob had sat looking into each other's eyes when he cleared his throat.

'So, um...' He had the look of someone desperately trying to find something neutral and bland to talk about. 'Didn't you used to be big into photography at one point? Am I remembering that correctly?'

'Yeah, I was. It fell by the wayside when Dad got ill. Pete needed my help looking after him. Between that and working shifts at the pub, I never had time. I didn't even bring my camera with me to Dovecote. I think I left it at Dad and Pete's house...' Sarah suddenly thumped the table and reached for her phone. That was it! That was where she'd seen the name Dora Müller before. She scrolled through her emails and facepalmed herself when she found the one from a photography society she'd long since forgotten why she'd joined. 'I can't believe I didn't realise,' she said. 'Here it is. *An exhibition, talk, and book signing with renowned photographer Dora Müller (95) to celebrate the release of her latest book. Monday 22nd May 2017.*' She passed her phone to Rob and he scrolled through the email.

'Is that Dora?'

Sarah grabbed her phone back. On the screen was a photograph, just one of the many due to be displayed as part of the exhibition. It was of Rose, and she was standing outside The Seaside Café. 'No. *That* is Rose Wilton. The woman who, if those documents are what we think they are, is my maternal grandmother.'

Rob let out a low whistle. 'I think you need to go to that exhibition.'

'Absolutely.' Sarah read on further into the email. 'Oh,

there's one small problem.' Her shoulders dropped. 'The exhibition is being held in Alpensee, the town in the Swiss Alps where Dora lives.' She drained her wine glass. 'I guess that's the end of that.' Her bottom lip started to wobble, and she bit it. Rob reached across the table and placed his hand on hers, sending a shockwave up her arm and across her chest.

'Come on, let's get you home.'

The fresh air hit Sarah the moment they left the restaurant. Suddenly her tongue was too big for her mouth, and her feet didn't feel connected to the pavement. There was one thing she was sure of, though, and it consumed her. At the bottom of the High Street, on the corner of Queen's Parade, Sarah stopped abruptly, and when Rob paused next to her, she kissed him. The force of her kiss pushed him back against the window of Aoife's hair salon.

'I want to go home, Rob,' she said, slurring slightly when she finally released him. 'Not to Pebble Cottage. Take me back to *our* home.'

He ran his hand gently through her hair, and onto the nape of her neck. The touch of his fingers on her bare skin sent fireworks through her body. She needed him. He removed his hand and looked into her eyes.

'Believe me, Sarah, I'd really like to do that. You have no idea how much I want you. And I'm fighting every single impulse when I say this, but no. Not tonight. You are far too drunk. I'd wake up in the morning with a knife in my chest and you'd hate me more than you already do.'

'I don't hate you.'

'Come on. Your mother is going to kill me for bringing you home in this state.'

'Mum loves you. She always has.'

He took her hand in his and guided her across the road and onto The Promenade.

At the gate of Pebble Cottage, Rob gave her a light kiss on

her forehead. 'Drink some water before you go to bed, or you're going to have a monster of a hangover tomorrow.'

She just about managed to slip her key in the front door lock, but paused when Rob called out to her again.

'Sarah?'

'Yeah.' Standing on the front step was like standing on the deck of a ship in the middle of a storm.

'If it's money stopping you from going to Dora's exhibition, I'll take you.'

'You would?'

'Yeah. If it would make you happy.'

'Okay.'


Sarah's eyes hurt when she opened them very late the next morning. But she was in her own bed, alone. She let out a groan and buried her head in her pillow as the night before came back to her in hazy chunks. She'd kissed Rob. Again. Thank God he'd been sober enough to stop it from going any further. She rolled over onto her back and tried to focus on the ceiling, but closed her eyes again when the ceiling refused to remain still. They flew open a moment later.

She'd agreed to let him take her to Switzerland. Absolutely not.

There was no way on earth *that* was going to happen.

# TWENTY-NINE

## SARAH

May 2017

In the absence of anywhere else to turn, Sarah found herself in her sister's sitting room the following evening, asking Daphne for advice. Adam had taken Jake to the cinema. Sarah still hadn't been introduced to her nephew. Clearly, Daphne didn't trust her yet. Not surprising, seeing as each time they made headway in repairing their dysfunctional relationship, Sarah did something weird. Like running off when Daphne asked a very reasonable question. Or unearthing documents that turned their mother's world upside down.

'What did Mum say?' Daphne handed Sarah a mug of coffee. The first sip went some way to calming her churning stomach.

'She's all in favour. I'm not sure whether it's of me potentially meeting Dora, or of me spending time with Rob.'

'Hmm.'

'Urgh. I must be in a mess if I'm asking *you* what to do.'

'Ha! Yeah, well. It's probably about time I played the older sister rather than the spoilt first child. How do you feel about it? Really.'

'I want to go. I don't know if Dora will be able to tell me anything about Rose. But she seems like a good place to start.'

'And Rob?'

'Daffs, I kissed him.'

'You can blame the wine.'

'What would you do?'

'Me? I have no idea. I've never been in that kind of mess, Sarah.'

Sarah laughed. 'No, I guess not. You've pretty much got your life sorted.'

Daphne examined her hand for a moment, focusing on her wedding ring. 'Yeah, well.' There was something unsaid in her eyes, and Sarah raised an eyebrow. She was reminded of the weird vibe between Daphne and Adam on the day of Janice's fall.

'Is everything okay, Daffs?'

Her sister flashed a weak smile. 'Of course. Back to you and Rob. Honestly, I think it might do you some good to spend time together. But away from Dovecote, and all the memories and reminders of what happened that day. Remember, you did love him once.'

'And what if I find I still do, despite everything?'

'Do you think you do?'

Sarah put her head in her hands. 'I don't know. Maybe. No.'

'Hmm.'

'Would you stop making that noise?' Sarah said with a laugh. 'You sound like Mum. I'm going to have to go, aren't I? For her sake.'

Daphne nodded. 'She needs to know the truth. Obviously, she can't go, not with her ankle. I'd go, but Jake's got exams and Adam needs me here.' There was that look again. But Sarah didn't repeat her earlier question. It was one thing to go to her sister for advice; the reverse would never happen. And Sarah couldn't blame Daphne for that. Nobody in their right mind would, or should, ever ask her for advice about anything.

'I'm not going to let him pay for it all, though. I can't bring myself to be that beholden to him.'

'Mum will help out.'

'She said she would.'

'Well, then. I guess you're going. And Rob's going with you.'

Sarah lifted her mug to her lips. 'Heaven help me.'

The following day, Sarah left Natasha at the café and walked the few yards to Victoria Park. Heather had responded to her rambling text the night before with a demand to meet for lunch. The moment she saw Heather sitting on the bench by the bandstand, the midday sun glinting off her gold hoop earrings, she was catapulted back into the past. Back to a time before her faith in the world had been shattered, when she had still believed a happy ever after was possible.

'That text was unhinged,' Heather exclaimed, as Sarah sat down beside her. 'Run it past me again.'

So, Sarah did. She told her about the shoebox, and about Rob's offer, but left out how she'd tried to get into Rob's pants. And she relayed Daphne's advice.

'You do know that Daphne is absolutely right, don't you?' Heather said when Sarah stopped to draw breath.

'Part of me does.'

'You and Rob need time away from Dovecote to talk things through. Otherwise, neither of you will ever fully heal.'

'Losing a child is not the sort of thing anyone ever fully heals from.' Sarah crossed her arms.

'I meant fully heal from the breakdown of your marriage. Sarah, your grief is yours. Only you can carry that. But you need to sort out what happened between you and Rob, even before Faith's death. Just promise me one thing, would you?'

'What's that?'

'Go easy on the vino. And don't do anything you're going to regret. But also, I think you're going to have to tell him the truth.'

The blood drained from Sarah's face. That was the one thing she was hoping to avoid. 'I can't.'

'You *have* to. I know you feel guilty; I can see it in the way your shoulders hunch up around your ears. I can hear it in your voice any time that day is mentioned. You have to tell him, otherwise it's going to keep eating you up inside. You've said you're not sure whether you have feelings for him. It's obvious he still has feelings for you. So, before something happens, he deserves to know.'

Sarah rested her elbows on her knees and cradled her chin in her hands for a long moment. She tried not to look out at the sea, but the position of the bench meant there wasn't much else to look at. The lighthouse shimmered in the heat haze. If that was where Neil wanted his ashes scattered, then who was she to deny him that? It still seemed beyond possible that she could go out there to those rocks. And even if she could bring herself to do it, would that mean she'd have no further reason to stay in Dovecote? Was she delaying the inevitable for some reason other than wanting to avoid the place where her daughter had died?

Eventually, she rested her head on Heather's shoulder. The world looked different from sideways on.

'Why did you never tell Rob where I was the day Faith died?' she asked softly. Heather shifted her shoulder and Sarah lifted her head.

'Because it wasn't my place to tell him, Sarah. But I think it's time you did.'

When Heather reached for Sarah's hand and held it, Sarah didn't pull away.

# THIRTY

## ROSE

August 1943

By early afternoon, the day after *that* kiss, I couldn't bear the silence of the empty café any more. I'd been on my own most of the day, which was becoming normal. Not even Uncle Douglas had come in. I wasn't surprised that Dora had given The Seaside Café a wide berth. Thankfully, Reg hadn't reappeared.

Since the Blythe Avenue bombing, the streets of Dovecote had been noticeably quieter. People were afraid. For almost four years, we'd carried on, bullish and determined not to let the war break our spirits. But the lone bomber had done exactly that. I wondered how the people in London and the other cities that had suffered so much were able to carry on at all. If I'd lived in London, I would have probably crawled into a hole and just let myself die, rather than live with the constant fear. At least Carlisle was being spared, which meant Janice was safe, and happy, if the letters I got were anything to go by. I supressed a shudder and offered a plea to the heavens for the madness to end as I locked the café door.

I paused and leant on the railings of The Promenade, my thoughts returning to Dora. I'd been thinking about her all day. Why now? Why me? Was she as confused as I was? Breathing heavily, I turned towards Pebble Cottage. The only way to find the answers to my questions was to ask her. But how did one start a conversation of that nature?

Dora was in the kitchen of Pebble Cottage, buttering a slice of toasted National Loaf. That bread was the bane of my life. A few customers had kindly remarked that mine was better than their attempts. Probably because I still had some white flour that I substituted for a portion of the wholemeal. But my stocks wouldn't last much longer and my wholesaler had said there wouldn't be any more. The sooner this war ended, the better. And preferably before I had to stop selling food at the café altogether. I fought off my bleak thoughts.

Dora was wearing a cream blouse with a delicate lace fringe on the neck and cuffs, and a knee-length navy wool skirt. Her small feet were encased in a pair of fashionable Burlington dark grey suede shoes from Freeman, Hardy and Willis. I recognised them from an advert I'd seen in the paper. Looking at her in the sunlight streaming through the kitchen window, everything I'd worried about no longer mattered. The same warmth that had flooded me the instant before our kiss returned, and I yearned to touch her again. But I faltered.

'Tea?' I asked, moving towards the stove. As if tea was going to fix this.

'Yes, please. Would you like some toast?'

'No, thank you.' We were being so damned polite to each other. I put the kettle down on the stove and went over to the table, placing my hand on her shoulder. She didn't turn around. 'Dora?'

'I...'

'Can we talk? Please.'

'Alright.'

We sat side by side on the sofa. The gap between our knees simultaneously too big and too small. I had to say something before I either lost my nerve or kissed her again.

'Last night—'

'I'm so sorry, Rose. I never should have kissed you.'

'Are you... a... lesbian?' There was a word I never thought I'd hear myself say.

Dora looked at me with big wide eyes the colour of a spring sky. 'Yes, I am. It is who I am. Who I have always been. Rose, will you hear me out if I tell you everything?'

'Of course.' I wanted to take her hand in mine, but I resisted.

'When you asked whether I had a sweetheart, I didn't tell you the whole truth. There was someone, someone very special. A girl called Mariella. She was a fellow student at St. Hilda's College. We would have both been sent down if anyone had discovered we were more than friends. We were very much in love, Rose. We were so young and so in love that we didn't even worry about the future, about what would happen to us when our studies finished. I broke her heart when I had to leave. I was recruited by the Foreign Office. They needed translators and I, as you know, am fluent in not only German, but Italian, French, and Russian too. I had no choice. We cried together the night before I left. We kept in touch for a while, but then she wrote to tell me she'd met someone else. And what could I do? I had to let her go.'

'Could you not have at least stayed friends?'

Dora shook her head sadly. 'Her mother sent me a telegram just before I was sent to Dovecote to tell me Mariella had been killed in an air raid.'

'Oh, Dora. I'm so sorry.'

'I never thought I would fall in love again. Until one day, I walked into The Seaside Café and saw you.' She looked down at her fingernails, today a vibrant cerise. Her cheeks burned.

'You... Oh.'

'Why do you think I came in for a cup of tea every day that I could have made at home? I wanted to see you. To talk to you.' She looked up at me. 'I am sorry for embarrassing you.'

'You haven't embarrassed me.'

The hesitant smile she gave me almost wrought tears from my eyes.

'Rose, I like you very much. But I understand that you are not like me, and I don't expect you to requite my feelings. I promise I will never behave like that again. If you wish me to move out, please just say so. I will not be offended. Rather, I would not stay for a moment longer if I knew it would offend you.' She got up from the sofa, having not touched her tea or toast. I reached out and took hold of her hand. Her skin was as soft as silk.

'I don't want you to move out.'

'That is very kind of you.' She pulled her hand out of mine. 'I will keep to my room.'

'Dora...'

But she was already gone up the stairs. The soft click of her bedroom door could have been the clang of a prison cell.


For three days, the only hint I had of Dora's presence was the soft click of doors and the occasional waft of glycerine soap or vanilla. She altered her routine to avoid me and stopped coming to the café. I missed her. For three nights, I tossed and turned, unable to sleep. On the fourth night, it dawned on me. I loved her, body and soul. And I wanted her. It was an alien concept, to want someone. In the dark, I realised I had never wanted Martin. I admitted to myself that I didn't love him, either. I was so grateful that he'd given me my daughter, but when I thought of him, of his body, there was nothing. Worse than nothing, there was a feeling of emptiness, of frustration. I didn't despise him. He was too good a person for that. But he left me cold. Dora, with her blue eyes and soft skin, warmed me. Holding her image in my head lit a spark deep down inside of me, and it could not be extinguished. More surprisingly, I had no desire to extinguish it. On the contrary, I wanted her to fan the flame she had lit the night she kissed me.

The floorboards creaked as I crossed the landing in the dead of night. I knocked on her door softly.

'Dora?' I was whispering when I wanted to shout. 'May I come in?'

'Rose? Yes, yes. Of course.'

I pulled my dressing gown tighter around me as I pushed open the door. She was sitting up in bed, reading. In the soft glow of the lamplight she was radiant.

'Dora,' I said, sitting down on the edge of her bed. 'I have been thinking about you constantly for the past few days. I can't seem to stop thinking about you. You have unlocked something in me. Something I never knew was there. You have opened my eyes. I now see myself for who I really am.' I paused. My head was in such a jumble I couldn't get my words to come out right. 'I am not making much sense.'

Dora placed her book on the nightstand and reached out a hand for mine as a gust of wind funnelled down the chimney and out of the black cast-iron fireplace. This room, at the back of Pebble Cottage, had a wonderful view of the sea and the lighthouse, but it did feel the brunt of the sea wind.

'You're cold,' she said, rubbing my hand with hers. 'Here.' She pulled back her blankets and I slipped in between them.

There was so much that I wanted to say, but the words stuck in my chest. So, I kissed her.

'Rose?' she asked when our lips parted. 'Are you sure about this?'

I traced the line of her jaw with my finger. 'I am sure that I love you.'

# THIRTY-ONE

## SARAH

May 2017

The vice-like grip Rob had on the armrest of his seat as the plane took off reminded Sarah why they'd never travelled abroad together. In the two weeks since he'd offered to come with her, and she'd reluctantly accepted, as advised by Daphne, Heather, and her mother, he hadn't mentioned his fear of flying. It made it all the more puzzling as to why he'd suggested it in the first place.

'I'd forgotten you were petrified of flying,' she whispered. He just grimaced and clamped his lips together to stop himself from screaming as the plane tilted upward and the wheels left the ground. Once the plane levelled off, and the seatbelt sign was switched off, Sarah felt him relax a little. 'Why are you putting yourself through this?' she asked. 'You didn't have to come with me. I would have been fine on my own.'

Rob ran his fingers through his hair. 'I don't really know. I just wanted to.'

'Or did you just want to make sure I came back and didn't disappear into the mountains for another ten years?'

'Maybe.'

Sarah fiddled with her seatbelt. 'Thanks, Rob. And look, I never apologised for the other week.'

'That's alright. You were hammered.' A flicker of something passed across his eyes. Regret? She pushed that thought away.

'I guess this trip will help us work out if we can be friends,' she said. The smile he gave her in reply was weak. Heather had said it was obvious he still had feelings for her. Was that the real reason he'd arranged this trip? Sarah shut her eyes for a moment and laid her head back against the seat. If she could just focus on meeting Dora and finding out whatever she could about Rose, then the car crash that was her own life could be sorted when she got back. Either that or she could up and leave again, return to Manchester. Even if her van wasn't fixed, she could get the train. Maybe she should get out of Dovecote before she hurt people again. Or was it already too late?

Rob's hand was clammy when Sarah held it as the plane came into land at Zurich airport.


The train from Zurich to Chur took them along the shore of Lake Zurich. The sun glittered off the water and the windows of the houses along the steep, forest-scattered hillsides bordering the long lake. Leaving the lake behind, the train wound through a wide, flat-bottomed valley dotted with wooden farmhouses and docile cows grazing on the lush grass. Sarah could only imagine how beautiful it would be in winter, covered in a blanket of snow. As they rose higher, the valleys became narrower, their walls steep and rocky. Jagged mountain-tops loomed ahead, some with a sprinkling of snow still clinging to shaded crevices.

At Chur, they boarded the Mountain Express, a vibrant red train decorated with white Edelweiss flowers. It glided through the town, following a fast-flowing river, on rails embedded into the road. They began to climb steadily through dark tunnels and around tight bends. Rob avoided looking down at the steep drop, but Sarah was transfixed by the tall pine trees that grew poker straight out of seemingly sheer rock faces. Narrow waterfalls tumbled into fast streams, running along deep ravines that had been carved out by slow-moving glaciers millennia ago. The valley disappeared far below as they climbed higher into the mountains, pausing at chalet-style wooden stations. They passed the last station and crossed an impressive viaduct spanning a deep valley. On the other side, clumps of snow lay between the pine trees where the sun failed to penetrate.

Sarah's jaw dropped when they stepped out of Alpensee station, across the road from a shimmering lake. The pine trees and alpine chalets that surrounded the lake were reflected in the crystal-clear water. She gulped down a lungful of fresh mountain air.

'Wow.'

Rob was similarly speechless, only able to reply with a low whistle. Rocky, snow-tipped mountaintops, the shape of Toblerone pieces, loomed behind the dark green forest. The sun glinted off the snow and Sarah pulled her sunglasses out of her handbag. There was heat in the sun and she rolled up the sleeves of her fleece jumper. Away to the left, a road and a path hugged the edge of the lake, leading to a cluster of timber chalets and the forest. To the right, the buildings in the centre of Alpensee were a mixture of old wooden chalet-style houses and restaurants, and square concrete hotels and shops, painted in various dark pastel colours. The main road, where their hotel was, rose steeply before sweeping away up the mountain to the ski lifts. A suntanned couple in their eighties, dressed in full hiking gear, strode past Sarah and Rob, and went through a wooden gate. They were soon lost to the thick forest. Sarah glanced at Rob.

'Why do I suddenly feel very unfit?' she asked with a grin.

Rob laughed. 'You and me both. They must make them tough in these parts. Come on, let's get checked into the hotel and then we can have a look around. I saw online there's a café that does really good apple strudel.'

The wooden balcony from Sarah's single room at Hotel Talblick looked down over the steep-sided mountain valley. Green slopes tumbled to the bottom. She breathed the fresh air deeply as she gazed into the darkness of the pine forest. It was strangely mesmerising. She'd already called Janice to let her know they'd arrived safely. Turning her back on the siren call of the forest, she picked up her jacket. Despite the warmth in the sun, the weather forecast warned that the temperature could get to single figures when the sun went down.

Rob had texted to say he was waiting for her in the lobby. Hotel Talblick mercifully had two rooms left, as every other hotel in Alpensee was eye-wateringly expensive. Despite Rob's protestations, Sarah had insisted on him having the bigger room, seeing as he was paying for them. Sarah, with Janice's help, had taken care of the flights.

Hotel Talblick was halfway up the steep main street. As they'd already seen the bottom half, lined with shops selling equipment and clothing fit for the outdoor pursuits most people came to Alpensee for, they headed towards the top end of town.

'Sorry,' Rob said, stifling a yawn. 'It's either the altitude or the adrenaline comedown after the flight and that train ride, but I'm knackered.'

They came to a halt outside a wooden chalet with red gingham curtains at the windows. Hearts were carved into the wooden window shutters and the balcony running along the upper floor. The weathered wooden sign swinging on chains from the balcony read *Konditorei Gabriella*. The windows were steamed up, and when the door opened, a waft of hot chocolate swirled around them.

'Please tell me this is the strudel place you wanted to go to,' Sarah grinned, elbowing Rob in the side. 'Because that hot chocolate has my name on it.'

They sat down at a small table next to the window. Along the windowsill was a line of ceramic cows. The sugar sachet container on the table was also a black and white cow.

'I'm going to have to bring a couple of these home for Mum,' Sarah said, running a finger along the side of the cow ornament. 'They'd look great in the café.'

'Not sure she'd have space what with the antique teapots all over the place,' Rob said with a grin.

A waitress came over, addressing them in perfect English, and they ordered. Sarah noticed that she glanced back over her shoulder at Rob as she walked away.

Sarah tapped her fingers on the wooden tabletop for a few moments before she spoke again. 'I've been thinking about Dora Müller.'

'What about her?'

'With a name like that, I can only presume she's German, or Swiss. But that must have been awkward for her in Dovecote during the war. Surely she couldn't have wandered around with such an obviously German name?'

The waitress returned with Rob's coffee and Sarah's hot chocolate. Again, her gaze lingered on Rob's toned arms. Rob seemed completely oblivious.

'*Danke*,' Sarah said. She hadn't completely forgotten all her school German.

'I'd not thought of that. Wait though, on the back of the photo, weren't there two surnames?'

'Yeah. Stephens was the other. Do you think it was a family name or something, and she went by that? I had wondered if it was a married name.' Sarah paused as two plates of apple strudel topped with whipped cream appeared. Rob tucked into his enthusiastically.

'This is amazing.' He'd always had a sweet tooth. Sarah smiled to herself. She'd forgotten that about him. It was nice to be reminded. 'Janice definitely needs to start selling strudel at the café. I mean, her sticky buns are epic, but this is next-level.' Sarah tried a forkful. He wasn't wrong, it was delicious.

Fortified by caffeine and sugar, they emerged back out onto the street. At the very top of the road were the ski lifts, cable cars, and gondolas taking people further up the mountain. The ski season was over, but there were still people queuing with walking poles and backpacks.

'I'd love to see the top of the mountain,' Sarah said, watching the silver cable car swing out of the station and begin its slow, silent ascent.

'I'm not sure. You know me and heights. I don't think I could handle flying and going up in that thing in the same day,' Rob said, grimacing.

Sarah laughed. 'Tomorrow then. I'll go up on my own if you chicken out.' Rob visibly paled and swallowed hard. She prodded his arm. 'I'll buy you a beer afterwards.'

There was an outdoor ice rink, shaded from the sun. They watched the skaters gliding across the ice.

'Now that is something I have no urge to try,' Sarah admitted, nodding towards the rink. 'I just know if I did, I'd fall within three seconds.'

'Oh, I don't know. I wouldn't mind.' There was a superior smirk on his face.

'Go on then, Christopher Dean.'

Rob whistled a few bars of Ravel's 'Boléro' and straightened his shoulders. Sarah supressed a chuckle. She knew macho posturing when she saw it. Rob never backed down from a challenge, especially not from her. Maybe that had been their problem? She couldn't help but bait him, and his ego made him rise to it. It was a wonder they'd survived nearly five years together.

Rob appeared on the ice, his sturdy boots exchanged for ice skates. He immediately put his hand out for the wall running along the edge of the rink. Sarah got her phone out. Rob let go of the wall, and promptly fell on his backside. There were tears of laughter in Sarah's eyes. But to his credit, he got straight back up again. He inched his way around the rink, holding onto the wall, until he was level with Sarah. She lowered her phone.

'This is harder than it looks,' he said, panting slightly. His cheeks were flushed and his eyes sparkled. 'But at least I'm giving it a go.' He winked as he pushed himself off from the wall. Sarah mentally brushed aside the tug of longing in her chest. He managed a few feet under his own steam before sliding back over to the wall. At the exit, he turned and gave Sarah a thumbs-up.

'I'll get you back tomorrow on the cable car,' she muttered. He wouldn't be so cocky then.

By the time they'd wandered back down the hill to their hotel, stopping to look in the windows of souvenir shops full of anything and everything a Swiss flag could be stamped on, they were both yawning. It had been a long day, and the mountain air was soporific. They ate an early dinner of *schnitzel* and *rösti* in Hotel Talblick's pine-panelled restaurant and settled in the plush bar for a nightcap.

'What time is tomorrow?' Rob asked, sipping his Scotch.

'The exhibition opens at ten. The talk starts at twelve.' Sarah was struggling to keep her eyes open. 'This is probably all a waste of time. It's not as if we're going to get a chance to talk to Dora.'

Rob scratched his left eyebrow. 'You never know. The exhibition ticket includes a copy of Dora's book, so you'll get to talk to her when you get it signed. Remember, we're doing this for your mum.'

Sarah swallowed a large mouthful of spiced rum and coke. 'Yeah, I know. It just feels like, now we're here, it's a bit mad.'

'I wouldn't expect anything less from you.' He drained his glass. 'And on that note, I am going to bed. I'm exhausted and I've got a bruise from falling on that ice rink.'

'That's what you get for showing off,' Sarah grinned at him. 'I think I might have one more before I turn in.'

He moved as if going in for a kiss but pulled back. 'See you tomorrow, then.'

'Night.' Sarah let out her held breath as she watched him leave the bar. They'd spent a whole day together and neither of them had started a fight. That was progress. She typed a quick message to Heather with a few photos of the view from her room and of the town. Heather's reply was a heart emoji. Her thoughts turned to Dora, and she ordered another rum and coke. Reaching for her wallet in her jacket pocket, she found the photograph of Janice's christening that had been in the shoebox. The others, including the one of Rose and Dora kissing, were in their envelope up in her room. All she could do was hope that Dora would speak to her if she got the chance to show her the picture. She couldn't go back to Dovecote without at least some answers for her mum.

# THIRTY-TWO

## ROSE

December 1943

I was woken by the bells of St. John's Church on Christmas morning. It was the first Christmas since 1939 that had been heralded with church bells, the ban having been lifted in May, and my heart swelled. Lying in bed, wrapped in Dora's arms listening to the distant chimes, was the safest I'd felt in years. I watched Dora sleeping, just listening to her breaths.

The previous three months had been as close to perfect as I could have wished for, considering the times we were living in and that Janice was hundreds of miles away. For the first time in my life, I felt whole, complete, and totally at ease with myself. And it was all thanks to Dora. I would have never considered letting Martin see my bed-tousled hair or bare face, but Dora told me she loved me first thing in the morning, when I was sleepy and warm.

These days I smiled more broadly than ever, although I had to be careful to temper my happiness around other people, or they might think it odd that I wasn't pining for my husband and my daughter. Of course, Dora insisted on taking photograph after photograph of me. She'd even managed to take one of us both sitting on the little patch of lawn in the back garden of Pebble Cottage. The casual observer might not notice, but if one was to look carefully, they would see our little fingers entwined.

In short, I was in love.

'We shan't make the eight o'clock service,' Dora murmured, throwing an arm across my waist. I stroked her shoulder.

'Not to worry. Uncle Douglas is doing another at ten.'

Dora opened an eye and smirked at me. 'Well, in that case there's no need for us to rush at getting up, is there?'


Needless to say, we were almost late for church and arrived out of breath and red-faced. I blamed the redness of my cheeks on the south-westerly wind blowing in off the sea. My aunt and uncle had completely accepted Dora as my friend. The idea of them thinking that we were so much more made me break out in a cold sweat. I was under no illusion as to how our love would be viewed by others, particularly Douglas and Gladys. I tried not to think about what it meant for our future.

There was also the issue of Martin. I was very relieved that, once again, he'd written to say he had to stay at his post over Christmas. The prospect of having him and Dora in Pebble Cottage at the same time didn't bear thinking about. Dora would have to move back into her bedroom, for a start. I pushed those thoughts away as the organ struck up 'Hark the Herald Angels Sing'. It was a day for joy, not fear.

Back home we had a simple, but delicious, lunch. It was mostly vegetables from the garden, but we had a little bit of pork. Dora made *rösti*, a Swiss speciality of grated potato tightly packed into rounds and fried. We listened to the King's speech at three o'clock. His words about absent loved ones made me miss Janice so much it hurt. It didn't feel like a proper Christmas without her. It wasn't until Dora handed me one of the hankies she'd embroidered as a Christmas present that I realised I was crying. Janice's host family had sent a darling letter and card and reassured me that Father Christmas would be visiting. I had hoped for a photograph, but this never came.

Maureen and Stan had given me a bottle of gin. I, in turn, had made them a fruitcake, using whatever I could, plus a little of the café's stock. Well, it was Christmas, after all. Dora pressed a glass of gin and lime cordial into my hand.

'You need a little pick-me-up.' She gave me a kiss before I had a chance to raise the glass to my lips. That kiss restored me more than any amount of gin could have. 'Oh, we need photographs! I should have taken one of that delightful Christmas pudding you made. You are ever so clever with all your baking, Rose. I can only imagine what you will make once the war is over and we're free of this beastly rationing. I shall be the size of a house.'

I kissed the bridge of her nose. 'I will make you anything, and everything, you could possibly want. I just need lots of sugar, an endless supply of fresh eggs, and mounds of real butter. Then you can have anything your heart desires.'

'Hmm. I think I already have that.' Her eyes sparkled in the soft glow of the lights on the Christmas tree. I moved to kiss her again, but she pushed me away and got up from the sofa. 'Photographs first, then you can mess up my hair.' She made me stand by the Christmas tree. It was a poor little thing, with spindly branches that had already shed a good portion of their needles all over the sitting room floor. But the lights and the paper chains I'd dug out of the loft were rather jolly.

'You've taken so many pictures of me this year, I should be used to it. But I do still feel rather self-conscious.' I took a sip of my gin.

'Oh, don't be daft. Now, at least try to look as if you're enjoying yourself.' I heard the click as I was mid-laugh.

'I shall have terrible lines around my eyes in that one. Do

another.' I plumped up my pin curls, struck a pose and smiled. My slightly overlapping front teeth would be visible but I was beyond caring. *Click.* Dora came closer, hiding something behind her back. She produced a sprig of mistletoe and held it up over my head. I glanced upwards. 'It wouldn't do to flout tradition,' I murmured. Our kiss was long and lingering, but was interrupted by an unmistakable click. I pulled away. 'Did you just take a photograph of us kissing?'

There was an impish smile on her face. 'I have no idea what it will come out like. I just pointed and hoped. It might be a picture of the ceiling.'

'Well, as long as no one else ever sees it, I suppose it's alright. Now, put that blasted thing down and kiss me properly, would you?'

1944 was only a few days old when Dora and I wrapped ourselves in our heaviest coats, hats, and scarves and ventured out into town. I checked in on The Seaside Café as we passed along The Promenade. It'd been closed since just before Christmas. I needed a break. Not just from the cooking and the baking and the standing all day, but also from the constant vigilance and anxiety over the never-ending rules and regulations around what could be served and when and for how much. I'd probably broken a few rules without even knowing. If it hadn't been for Dora, who was a constant oasis of calm, I probably would have given up.

I threaded my arm through hers as we meandered through Victoria Park. By the bandstand, a young woman and a man in uniform were standing together, their foreheads touching. As we passed by, we heard him declaring his love for her and Dora glanced at me.

'Shush,' I said, shaking my head. 'I know what you're going

to say, but not in public. Please. We can't. What if someone were to hear?'

Dora frowned and pursed her lips. There was an aching hollowness in my stomach. How desperately unfair it was that that young couple could openly say how they felt about each other but Dora and I couldn't. Inside my mittens, my hands curled in angry fists. I glanced up from my feet to find that delightfully mischievous smile on Dora's lips. She rested her head against my shoulder.

'Even if the well runs dry, we'll always have tea,' she said. I pulled away slightly.

'What on earth does that mean? Are you quite alright?'

She looked over her shoulder; there was nobody within earshot. 'It's code. It means "I love you, and I want to kiss you". We can say it to each other when we're out and about and no one will ever know.'

Now I really wanted to kiss her. 'Are you sure you're not a spy?' I asked. 'Who else would come up with a code?'

'I think it's rather brilliant,' she said, with a little self-satisfied nod.

'Yes, I do too. In fact, I think that even if the well runs dry, we'll always have tea.'

'In that case, let's get a move on and get to the photography shop. Then we can get home and have some actual tea before we freeze to death.'


'Oh, good gracious. What sort of face am I pulling there?' I glanced over Dora's shoulder as I put the teapot down on the kitchen table. She was leafing through the photographs we had just collected. I rested my chin on her shoulder as she revealed the next picture. 'Is that...?'

'I think that's come out rather well. Better than I'd expected.' She handed me the small photograph.

'Would the developer have seen this?' My mouth went dry. Even though my face was mostly hidden, Dovecote residents could probably discern it was me from the set of my hair and the shape of my chin. It was obvious what Dora and I were doing. The sprig of mistletoe above us did rather give the game away. I handed it back to her.

'Don't worry. Developers are incredibly discreet. Particularly these days. Yes, they *see* the photographs, but they don't *look* at them. If you get what I mean.'

'I suppose what's done is done now. Just please make sure it's kept safely hidden.' I poured myself the first cup out of the pot. Dora liked her tea a little more brewed than I did. Cradling the cup in my hand, I looked out into the garden. Dora's reflection appeared behind mine.

'I'm sorry, Rose. I didn't think. Of course, I won't ever let anyone see that picture.'

My head dropped and I put my cup down on the side, suddenly not wanting it. 'No, I'm sorry. It's a lovely picture and I'm glad we have a memento of these wonderful days we're spending together.' The sunlight glinted off my engagement ring. I turned and she placed her hands on my waist. 'What are we going to do, Dora? The papers are saying it's likely the war will be over before next Christmas. That means Martin will be coming home.' I put my hands to my head. 'I'm a married woman, Dora. What am I doing?' Sudden tears engulfed me, and I buried my head in her shoulder. She rubbed my back in long, firm strokes.

'Let's not ruin today by worrying about tomorrow,' she whispered. I let myself slacken against her body, allowing her warmth to seep deep into my bones. The thought of being parted from her was just too much to bear.

# THIRTY-THREE

## SARAH

May 2017

Dora's exhibition was being held in the ballroom of Hotel Bergruhe, a luxury hotel on the lake. Sarah and Rob were ushered through a dark lounge, stuffed with overflowing book-cases and leather armchairs, and into a long room flooded with light streaming in through a wall of glass. A flagstone terrace extended to the edge of the lake. The sun sparkled on the clear water like diamonds. Sarah gaped at the view for a moment before Rob tapped her elbow. He led her over to the first of the displays, laid out to form a snaking path across the room. A small group had gathered by the first set of photographs, and Sarah and Rob waited until they had moved on.

'*St. Hilda's College* – 1938–1940,' Rob read from the caption. 'Is that Oxford?'

'Yeah, I think so. I can't work out any of this,' Sarah frowned.

'Is that Dora?' In the photograph, a young woman was reclining against the thick trunk of an old tree. She had her arms folded across her chest and was looking directly at the camera. Sarah moved closer.

'No, I don't think it is. It doesn't look like the woman with Rose in the photograph taken in the back garden of Pebble Cottage.'

'I suppose, seeing as these are photographs Dora took, she won't be in many,' Rob said.

'Good point. I wonder who this is, then?'

'Friend? Girlfriend?'

'Possibly. See, that's what I don't understand. Rose was married to Martin, but then there's the photograph of her and Dora kissing.'

Rob smirked. 'I would have thought you, of all people, would consider she might have been bisexual.'

Sarah's eyes widened and a shiver ran up her spine. 'Oh!' she gasped. 'Of course. You know what that means, right?'

'Don't jump to any conclusions, Sarah. I'm just saying it's a possibility. They might have just been friends and could have taken that photo of themselves for a laugh or something.'

'But there's a chance my grandmother was bisexual. That's a pretty big deal, to me anyway.' Rob's hand brushed against hers, sending a ripple across her skin. She glanced at the photograph of the mystery woman again. 'I hope we find out who she is in Dora's book.'

Rob moved onto the next display. 'Sarah, you need to see this...'

She hurried to his side and her jaw dropped. The enlarged black and white photograph was haunting. A column of brick rose up from swirling smoke, like a skeletal finger poking out of a grave. A single curtain flapped from half a window frame and a chimney pot tilted precariously. Sarah read out the caption underneath.

'*Blythe Avenue – May 1943. Three people lost their lives and many more were injured when a lone German aircraft dropped a bomb intended for Brighton on the small seaside town of Dovecote, Sussex.* Maureen told me about that. She said she was in the bomb shelter with Rose and...' She swallowed a lump in her throat. 'Mum.'

His hand brushed hers again; this time it felt a little more intentional. 'A few yards to the east and you might never have been born.'

Sarah grimaced. 'And your life would have been infinitely better.'

Rob flashed her a half-smile and elbowed her gently. 'I wouldn't say that.' Sarah forced herself to look away from his blue eyes, that familiar fluttering sensation starting up in her stomach again. She turned back towards the photograph, offering a silent thanks that her mother had been spared. Followed swiftly by a silent apology to those who hadn't.

Rob called out. 'Hey, here she is.'

'Rose?'

'Yeah.'

It was the photograph that had been used in the marketing email: Rose leaning against the railings of The Promenade. Her light-coloured hair fell in loose waves around her shoulders. Rob was studying her with his head slightly tilted, raising Sarah's temperature up a notch. She really needed to concentrate. 'You know, I *can* see Janice in her.'

'Yeah, me too. I think Daphne looks like her.'

'You don't. Look like her, I mean.'

'No, I guess I'm all Portman.'

Rob tilted his head the other way and swept Sarah's fringe back off her forehead. 'Mind you.' He was looking at her lips. 'Maybe around the mouth.'

Sarah cleared her throat, and the outside world came crashing back into focus. They both turned their attention back to the photographs, and Sarah began to breathe again.

'There's another one of Dovecote,' she said, nodding

towards the next photo. The view of the beach, the sea, and the lighthouse was so achingly familiar. 'But the beach is closed off, look.' There was barbed wire along the railings of The Promenade and a large boulder blocked the top of the steps. The photo must have been taken not far from The Seaside Café. The lighthouse was right in the middle of the photograph. It was a view that made Sarah's insides quiver with anger. She bit back the rising tide of memories, and the associated emotional tumult. Almost instantly, the space between her and Rob became cold again. She turned her eyes away; Rob's remained fixed on the picture. How could he even look at it, knowing what had happened, knowing what he'd failed to prevent? Instead, she walked towards the last photograph in the layout. It was Rose again. A small cry escaped Sarah's mouth and Rob turned, startled.

'What?'

'It's Rose. But look.' The platform of Dovecote station was unmistakable. The council had restored it in the eighties to preserve it as it had been built. The station was a listed building now. Someone from 1910 could step off a train there and recognise it. In the photograph, Rose was crying. Even in black and white, the wet lines down her cheeks were clear. She was also holding a baby, whose chubby cheek was pressed firmly against Rose's own. 'Do you think that's Mum? See that little fold at the top of her ear? Mum has one just like that.'

Rob's eyebrows launched themselves upwards. 'Could be.'

Sarah's brain whirred. 'When I put the photos from the envelope in date order, Janice – Mum – was there at the beginning, but then disappeared.'

'Weren't children evacuated during the war? Maybe Rose sent Janice away?'

Sarah thrust her hands into her pockets. 'Maybe. Maureen didn't mention it. Hopefully Dora can tell us.' She nodded at the photos. 'Dora was obviously there to witness all these moments, whatever their relationship was. She *has* to know what happened.'

'Where's Janice's dad, your grandfather, in all of this?'

'That's another good question. It *was* the middle of the war. He may have been away fighting.' Oddly, she cared less about the fate of Martin Wilton than that of Rose. 'I think that's the last of the Dovecote pictures, but let's look at the rest. Rose may still be in them.' The next set of pictures were from mid-1950s New York, and the rest were mountain landscapes or cityscapes. None of them featured Rose or Janice, and Sarah's heart sank. Maybe Dora didn't know what had happened to Rose. Maybe the end of the war came, and Dora moved away from Dovecote, never to see Rose again. Maybe Sarah was going to leave Alpensee with the same questions she'd arrived with.

An announcement in German interrupted her thoughts. Everyone in the room, whether they were examining the photographs or chatting by the window, turned towards the double doors as a petite, elegant woman swept in. Spontaneous applause broke out and Dora Müller looked around with a shy smile on her lips. She was seventy-four years older than in the photograph Sarah had found hidden under her mother's floor-boards, but there was no doubt it was the same woman. Her blue eyes sparkled as she nodded her acknowledgement of the adoration being showered on her as she crossed the room. Her glance skimmed over Sarah, but she hugged a few people and planted kisses on the cheeks of others. An officious-looking woman led Dora over to the far end of the room where a pair or armchairs had been arranged facing rows of plastic chairs. Rob tugged at Sarah's sleeve, and they followed the crowd making their way over. The minute the interviewer began speaking, Sarah turned to Rob with a grin. Of course they should have realised it would all be in German.

Rob whispered in Sarah's ear. 'We can't get up and leave.'

'It's alright,' she whispered back. 'I'm happy just to watch.'

Sarah strained to hear the words Dovecote, Rose, or Janice, but they weren't uttered. There were a few mentions of Oxford and one of Bletchley Park, but as Sarah couldn't understand any of the words around them, it made little sense. So instead, she just watched. It was hard to believe the woman up on the little stage was ninety-five. Dora was so full of life, so expressive. Her laugh was light and airy. She spoke with her elegant, long-fingered hands. Her nails were painted a vibrant cerise that matched her lipstick. Occasionally, she touched her grey curls, and Sarah could see traces of the shy girl in the photo. She was simply glorious, and Sarah drank her in.

Standing in the queue after the interview, having collected her copy of Dora's book, Sarah's heart raced. What if she got her words muddled and all that came out of her mouth was nonsense? She held the book close to her chest as Rob placed a hand on the small of her back and ushered her forwards. The queue shrank until Sarah found herself face-to-face with the woman who might have the answers Sarah and Janice so desperately sought.

'Hello,' Sarah said.

Dora started, almost as if she was mentally adjusting from German to English. 'Hello,' she said, flashing a warm smile. 'Don't tell me you've come all the way from England to see me?'

'Yes, we have.' Sarah glanced at Rob, standing off to one side. He gave her a wink.

'Oh goodness, thank you. Did you want me to sign your book?'

Sarah put the hardback book down on the table. 'Yes, please. Could you dedicate it to my mum?'

'Of course. What's your mum's name?'

'Janice.' Sarah paused. 'I think you may have known her when she was a small baby.' She held her breath as Dora opened the book to find the photograph of Rose and her younger self in the back garden of Pebble Cottage, that Sarah had slipped inside. Dora froze, her pen hovering in mid-air, her cheeks flushed. She blinked a few times. Sarah continued softly. 'Mum grew up believing Douglas and Gladys Legg were her parents. We've only just discovered that may not be the case. I found that photo, and a few others, hidden under a loose floorboard at Pebble Cottage, in Dovecote. Can you tell me who Rose Wilton is, what happened to her, and how and why Mum ended up being adopted?'

Dora opened her mouth and closed it again. 'What's your name?' she finally whispered.

'Sarah.'

'And you're Janice's daughter?'

'One of them. I have an older sister.'

Dora placed a hand on her chest. 'I can't believe it. After all these years. Goodness me. Janice had children. How wonderful!'

'She has grandchildren, too.' Sarah's heart skipped a beat. The officious woman came over and said something to Dora, who nodded and then turned back to Sarah.

'Sarah. Regrettably, I must go. I have an appointment in Chur.' She grabbed a sticky note, scribbled something on it, and passed it to Sarah. 'Come to my house tomorrow morning, at ten. We can talk then. Oh! I never thought... We have a lot to talk about.' There was the shimmer of wetness in her eyes and Sarah could only nod as Dora stood, leant across the table, and lightly kissed her cheek. Her perfume had hints of vanilla and honeysuckle. 'I can see Rose in you. Oh, my!'

And she was gone, whisked away out the double doors. Sarah ran to Rob, and he pulled her into a tight hug as they both burst out laughing.

# THIRTY-FOUR

## SARAH

May 2017

'I can't believe it went so well,' Sarah said as she and Rob made their way back through Hotel Bergruhe and out into the bright sunshine. 'I was so sure she was going to say she had no idea what I was talking about. And that I'd be escorted out by security.'

'Well done,' Rob said, nudging her elbow. 'I could see you were nervous, but you did it.'

'And to get invited to her house!' Sarah straightened her shoulders. 'I mean, yeah.'

'You don't need to act cool with me, Sarah,' Rob said, laughing. 'I like seeing you get excited, dropping that nonchalant act. It reminds me of the you I fell in love with, fourteen years ago.'

Warmth flushed her cheeks. There was nothing she could say to that. 'So, um, how do you fancy that cable car ride? I can go on my own if you'd rather not. I won't make you.'

'Hmm.' Rob stroked his chin. 'I suppose I have to. You'll never let me forget it if I didn't.'

. . .

They were squished close together on the bench of the silver cable car and Sarah felt Rob tense as the car swung out of the station with a slight jolt. She gave his knee a quick squeeze.

'Oh, wow,' she breathed, looking down at the mountain below. There were still a few patches of snow around, but mostly they were flying over green pastures dotted with mountain flowers. 'Rob, seriously. Open your eyes. You can't miss this.' He shook his head vehemently and his eyes remained welded shut. Sarah reached for his hand, which was gripping the bench so tightly, his knuckles had gone white. 'You're alright,' she said, rubbing her thumb across his palm. His fingers closed around hers and he very cautiously opened one eye. 'If you can't look down, at least look out, or up.' Up ahead, the top of the mountain was sprinkled with icing sugar snow.

'Sorry,' Rob said, with a nervous smile. 'Thanks. You're right, it's stunning.'

They travelled the rest of the journey in silence. Green gave way to white, the higher they climbed. At the top, they stepped out onto a snowy plateau. The sun sparkled off the snow drifts, dazzling them. Sarah sucked fresh air deep down into her lungs. All around were jagged rocky mountaintops, their lines sharp against the azure-blue sky.

'I totally get why people were sent to the mountains to recuperate in the olden days. This *has* to be good for you.' The mixture of cold air and warm sunshine made her cheeks tingle.

'Well, I'm not sure that cable car ride did much for my well-being. Think it took a few years off my life.'

'Oh, don't be so overdramatic. You enjoyed it really.' She nodded towards the rustic farmhouse-style restaurant perched on the summit. 'Come on, I promised you a beer.'

There was a table at the edge of the glass-surrounded terrace with a view back down over the valley. Sarah could see the

Alpensee lake shimmering in the sun. She cradled her hot rum punch in her hands and let out a contented sigh. Maybe she could just stay here forever and let all the Dovecote issues sort themselves out. Except, of course, one of the issues with Dovecote was sitting opposite her, taking a cautious sip of something called a *Schümli Pflümli*. According to the menu, it was coffee laced with plum schnapps and topped with frothy whipped cream.

'Ooh,' Rob said, putting down the glass mug. 'That's nice. A few of these and I'll be fine going back down in the cable car. How's the rum punch?'

A waft of the fumes from her drink caught in her throat. 'Potent,' she said.

'I'm sorry I didn't realise that Dora's interview would be in German,' Rob said. 'It must have been mentioned on the ticket site; I just didn't see it.'

'Don't worry. It probably said it on the email I received too. Still, it was nice just to watch her. I can't believe she's ninety-five.'

'And she seemed genuinely pleased to meet you, which is great.' He drank his boozy coffee. 'I really hope she can answer our questions and help us find Rose. How amazing would that be?'

*Our* questions? Help *us*? Since when had this been about Rob? Sarah bit back her retort, remembering how much he'd spent on the trip to Alpensee. The least she owed him was the chance to meet Dora. Maybe it would be good to have him there for moral support. He was looking at her expectantly and she gave him a smile.

'Yeah, I can't wait.'

The conversation turned to the awe-inspiring scenery as they finished their drinks. Setting his cup down, Rob rubbed his hands together; it was quite chilly on the exposed mountaintop.

'Right, we'd better head down. The cable car will be closing soon, and as much as I'm not relishing the thought of getting back in it, I don't fancy a two-hour walk down the mountain either.'

By the time they reached the town and stopped to pick up a bottle of the plum schnapps Rob had clearly developed a taste for, Sarah's stomach was growling. The enticing smell of melted cheese drifted out of warm doorways.

'I don't know about you, but all that fresh mountain air has made me ravenous,' she said as they reached Hotel Talblick. 'What do you fancy doing for dinner?'

Rob blushed slightly. 'Actually, earlier while you were waiting to talk to Dora, I booked the restaurant at Hotel Bergruhe. You don't mind, do you? I just thought it would be nice to have a treat. It's on me.'

'Rob... I... Are you sure? It looks quite pricey.' She ran her fingers through her hair. The cost of this trip was racking up, and she had no way to repay him. The idea of being in debt to Rob, of all people, made her bones ache.

'I want to.'

'As long as you're sure, that sounds lovely. Do I have time to make myself look presentable?'

'You look beautiful to me.' His cheeks flared again. 'But, yes, we have time. I booked for half six.'

The memory of their two kisses, the look in his eyes, and the prospect of a cosy dinner, sent a shiver down Sarah's spine. All she had to do was not get swept away by his dazzling blue eyes and everything would be fine.

The restaurant was a spectacle of jewel colours, brushed gold, and dimmed lighting. At a table overlooking the lake, they washed down beef stroganoff and little eggy dumplings with a robust red wine. They shared a rich chocolate mousse, and only got their spoons entangled once. They laughed and chatted, and, as they walked back up the main street, sated and a little giddy, Sarah wrapped her arm through Rob's. They hadn't mentioned Faith once. Maybe they could learn to exist together without her.

'You know,' Rob said, as they reached Hotel Talblick. 'I've got that bottle of plum schnapps upstairs. If you fancied a nightcap?'

The streetlight glistened in his sapphire eyes and there was no way Sarah could say no.

Back in the hotel, Sarah stepped out onto the balcony of Rob's room as he located a couple of glasses and the bottle of schnapps. Silvery moonlight highlighted the ridges of the mountaintops, making the scattered snow glow a ghostly blueish white. The pine forest loomed thick and dark, but overhead more stars than she had ever seen were strewn like confetti across the night sky.

'Shh,' she said as Rob joined her at the balustrade. 'Can you hear that?'

Rob cocked his head to one side. 'Hear what?'

Sarah smiled. 'Exactly. Nothing.' At that moment, the church clock rang out, shattering the silence. Rob pressed a glass into her hands, and they retired to a pair of sun loungers, laying thick furry blankets across their legs. 'Cheers.' The sip of schnapps burned her throat. 'Wow, that's strong stuff.' They lapsed into a comfortable silence. Not something Sarah had imagined could be possible. There had never been silence between them. There had always been something to say, some niggle to needle, some stitch to unpick.

Rob poured them each another tumbler of schnapps. 'Sarah?'

'Yeah.'

'Can I tell you something? Something I've not told anyone, apart from my therapist.'

Sarah nearly choked. 'Well, that's something I never expected you to say.' Rob raised an eyebrow. 'I'm glad you've had help.' She meant that.

'Yeah, well. It's an ongoing process.'

'Sure.'

'I used to have nightmares.'

Sarah looked away as she put down her glass. He wasn't the only one.

'About Faith.' He turned the glass around in his hand. 'About her fall. I relived it in slow motion, over and over again. I'd see her little feet go out from under her. Sometimes I'd be able to catch her and hold onto her. Other times, I'd grab a scrap of her yellow dress, but it would slip from my hand. Most of the time, I'd relive what actually happened, and I'd see myself snatch a handful of air and watch helplessly as she tumbled down the rocks beneath the lighthouse and into the sea. I'd wake up screaming.' He downed his glass but didn't reach for the bottle. 'I needed you, Sarah. I needed you to help me not see those things.'

Sarah looked out at the endless, star-filled sky. 'I couldn't help you, Rob. I couldn't help you because every time I looked at you, I wanted it to be you. I wanted it to be you who slipped and hit your head, who was lying face-down in the sea. I wished it had been you, not her.' She couldn't look at him. She couldn't bear to see the pain in his eyes, otherwise she'd have to admit that he was hurting as much as she was.

'It was an accident, Sarah. I don't know what else I can tell you to make you believe that. I'm sorry I couldn't save her. I tried, but it all happened so quickly.' His voice hitched. 'It was a matter of seconds between her falling and me puling her out of the water. But it was too late. She was already gone.' He drew a wobbly breath. 'If I could go back and make it me, I would.'

'I know.' She got up from the lounger and leant over the balcony. There was no stopping her tears. They dripped hot onto her hands. A hand softly brushed a strand of hair back behind her ear. She allowed Rob to wrap her in his arms. She rested her head on his shoulder, and he rested his head on hers. When he released his hold, and she looked up at him and saw the sheen on his eyes, she was so close to telling him everything. It was on the tip of her tongue to release the secret she'd been carrying for ten long years. But she couldn't hurt him even more than she already had.

'I love you,' he whispered. And then he kissed her. Her resolve melted at his touch, and she took his hand and led him back into his room.

# THIRTY-FIVE

## ROSE

February 1944

I buttoned up my coat against the harsh winter wind blowing in off the sea. My only customers all day had been Uncle Douglas and Betty. Uncle Douglas was on his way to comfort yet another family who had received *that* telegram. Betty was grumpy, as her latest beau had been sent to a training camp somewhere. Everyone was miserable. The winter was dragging on. The war seemed never-ending. Food was scarce and fun was non-existent. We couldn't go on much longer. But we got up out of our beds every day and carried on. The one bright light in my life was Dora. I simply couldn't have borne it all without her. Endlessly optimistic, and steadfastly resolute, she was getting me through this whole wretched business. I quickened my steps until I was practically running back to Pebble Cottage.

The lively swing rhythm of Benny Goodman's 'Sing, Sing, Sing' accosted me as I pushed open the front door of Pebble Cottage. Before I could object, Dora grabbed my hand and twirled me across the sitting room.

'For goodness' sake, Dora,' I laughed over the gramophone. She put her arms around me and held me close.

'I just needed to let off some steam.'

I kissed her forehead. 'Is everything alright? Has something happened?'

She lifted the needle from the record and closed the lid softly. 'No. Everything's fine.' She kissed me softly on the cheek. I could tell something was bothering her by the way she didn't look me in the eye, but she'd tell me in her own time. You couldn't encourage information from Dora; she only gave it when she was ready. If she had been a spy, she'd have made a very good one. 'Shall I do some *rösti* for tea? I got to the butcher early and picked up some bacon, and we've a couple of real eggs left. Oh, there were a couple of letters for you.'

I picked up the two envelopes from the sideboard. The first was from Scotland and had the obligatory purple 'passed by censor' shield stamped on the front. My heart was heavy as I opened it. I wandered into the kitchen as I read.

'Martin is well. He went to the theatre with Stuart last Monday.' I lowered the thin paper. 'Stuart Smith *again*? Honestly, he mentions him every time he writes. Has he no other friends?'

The letters from my husband had increasingly become more like letters from a brother. The declarations of love and any mention of the hardship of long-term separation had long since vanished from his words. Did I mind? Not really. Well, I did. Any wife would want to be told she was being missed. But there we were again, two jigsaw pieces that just didn't seem to fit together, no matter how hard we tried to. I supposed we'd somehow have to make it work when he came back, for Janice's sake.

I glanced up at Dora, humming softly to herself as she peeled the potatoes. What would that mean for us? My happy little bubble was going to burst at some point. I'd have to learn to live with Martin, and without Dora. In my wilder moments, I imagined running away with Dora, and Janice, and living in blissful happiness for all eternity. But all of that was for another day; I refused to let the future ruin the present. I scrunched Martin's letter in my hand and threw it into the pile of paper waiting for Stan to collect for reuse.

I turned the other envelope over. I'd kept it for last. Bittersweet though it was, at least there was some sweetness. My heart was going some behind my ribs as I read it.

'Janice has learnt to kick a ball. And she can climb the stairs on her own. She runs everywhere.' My voice cracked and I had to swallow hard. 'Oh!'

'What is it?' Dora grabbed my elbows.

'When they show her my picture, she points and says "Mama".' I crumpled into Dora's arms and wept into her shoulder. She rubbed my back in slow, wide circles. I sniffed and stepped out of her embrace. 'Sorry. Gosh, I don't know what's got into me.' I rummaged in my pockets for a handkerchief. Dora handed me hers before I found one.

'The minute we're sure there's going to be no more bombs, you get her home, you hear?' Dora said. I looked up. It wasn't like her to issue commands in such a forceful manner. 'Or anytime you want, Rose. She can come home whenever you want.'

I'd been thinking the same. But there were rumours of bigger, deadlier bombs on the way. I just had to hang on a little longer.

'I'm just so relieved she knows who I am. She was so young when I sent her away.'

'Her host family are doing a wonderful job of making sure she doesn't forget you. Oh, blast.' A puff of black smoke wafted up from the frying pan. Dora scrunched up her nose and giggled. 'I'm afraid the *rösti* might be a little on the crispy side tonight.'

I laughed. 'I don't mind.' I kissed the inside of her wrist as she tried to move away to rescue our supper. 'I love you.'

Later that evening, Dora clicked off the wireless and came back to sit next to me on the sofa.

'I don't know why we listen to the news. It never changes,' I said as she laid her head on my shoulder, and I wrapped my arm around her.

'We listen because some day it *will* change. One day, Mr Churchill will tell us the war is over, that we've won. And we'll shout and jump about. And then the King will make a speech, and we shall all cry with relief.'

'I love you,' I said. 'Do you know that?'

'I do. You tell me all the time. I love you, too.'

'Well, that's good. What was it you said to me once? "Let's not spoil today by worrying about tomorrow". Was that it?'

Dora laughed. 'Sounds like something I might say.'

'It's good advice.' I reached for her hand and lifted it to my lips. Her skin was so soft. She suddenly stiffened. 'Dora?'

She avoided my gaze. 'There's something I have to tell you.'

My mind took off at a thousand miles an hour, flinging all sorts of scenarios at me, each one more awful than the last.

'I've been summoned.'

'Summoned? To where? By whom? Why?'

'By the Foreign Office. I've been told to get a train from Euston to a place called Bletchley, in Buckinghamshire. I don't know any more than that.' Her bottom lip was quivering. This was all so heartbreakingly familiar. Only this time, it would actually break my heart.

'When?'

'Tomorrow.'

My world came to a crashing halt. 'Tomorrow?'

'I'm afraid so.'

'And I'm presuming you have little or no say in this?' I stroked her chestnut hair as she shook her head.

'None whatsoever.'

'Dora.' I cupped her chin in my hand and turned her face to mine. I traced the outline of her lips gently with my thumb. 'In that case, we must make tonight a night to remember.' A fault line cracked across my heart as our lips met.

The following morning was suitably wet and miserable. We kissed behind the closed door of Pebble Cottage and then walked, not touching, to the train station. Its stone walls looked even greyer in the misty drizzle.

'You won't let anyone see those photographs you took last night, will you?' I asked as we entered Dovecote station.

'I'll develop them myself, and they will never leave my possession. I promise.'

We both blushed slightly. It had been quite the daring thing to do, but I must confess, I had rather enjoyed posing for her. Dora climbed aboard the waiting London-bound train and leant out of the window. I stood on my tiptoes and kissed her on the cheek, as though we were relatives. Our eyes met and the last thread holding my heart together snapped in two.

'Even if the well runs dry, we'll always have tea,' she said.

'I love you,' I whispered in her ear. No one else could have heard...

Her postcard arrived the following morning. On the front was an old print of Buckingham Palace. My hands trembled as I turned it over in the heavy silence of the empty kitchen.

*I only made it as far as London before the ache in my heart*

*implored me to write to you. I promise to write a proper letter*
*as soon as I can xx*

I ran my fingers over her words, aching to be touching her instead. This postcard would not be joining Martin's letter on the scrap pile. As I put the kettle on to boil, I had to stop myself from taking two cups from the cupboard. What was I going to do now? As I spooned the tea leaves from the tin, my sigh echoed around the empty cottage. I'd carry on, no matter how hard or lonely it might get. I'd keep going for Dora, and for Janice.

# THIRTY-SIX

## SARAH

May 2017

The low background hum of noise in *Konditorei Gabriella* was just enough of a distraction to prevent Sarah's thoughts from spiralling completely out of control. It had been a mistake, obviously. Possibly an inevitable one, considering how he drew her to him like a magnet. Sarah put down her coffee cup and rubbed her eyes. What now? Where did they go from here? Was there a way back? Or had last night set them on a one-way road from which there was no escape? And what about the thing she had been so close to telling him? Could she keep that secret now? She hadn't waited around this morning to find out Rob's thoughts. He'd revealed enough of his feelings the night before. Feelings that, if she was being honest with herself, she couldn't requite.

The ping of a message alert on her phone sent her heart racing, but her panic subsided at Heather's name on the screen.

*Hey, don't want to sound weird or anything, but I'm kind of missing you. Just got used to having you around again and now*

*you're gone. At least this time, I know you're coming back. You
are coming back, right? Not planning on disappearing off into
the mountains? Anyway, just wanted to say hi. So, hi. X*

The single kiss at the end of Heather's text made Sarah's
heart beat a fraction faster. If Rob sent her into a tailspin,
Heather steadied her. That was the way it had always been.
Heather had been the calm to Rob's storm. She finished her
coffee before typing a reply.

*Hi. I'm wavering on the running away to the mountains ques-
tion. Ask me again tomorrow. X*

As Sarah approached Hotel Talblick, she paused. Rob wasn't
waiting for her in the lobby, and she considered whether to go
and knock on his door. She stuffed her hands into her pockets
and carried on down towards the lake. If he'd overslept or
forgotten they were due at Dora's at ten o'clock, that was *his*
problem. It wasn't as if she was in a hurry to see him anyway.

The address Dora had written on the sticky note was on one
of the winding roads through the pine forest on the opposite
side of the lake. Dora's home was at the end of a steep driveway:
a traditional chalet-style house, with a stone-walled ground
floor, and two wooden cladded floors above. It had a pitched
roof and a wooden balcony running the length of the middle
floor. Window boxes crammed with bright red geraniums and
sage-green shutters provided pops of colour against the dark
wood. Metal silhouettes of cows decorated the walls. A large
Swiss flag fluttered from a pole in the garden. Sarah's hand
trembled as she reached for the doorbell on the dot of ten
o'clock.

'I'm sorry I had to dash yesterday,' Dora said, leading Sarah through a bright hallway and up the stairs into a large, pine-cladded sitting room. 'I'm being pulled from pillar to post for this book.' Grey sofas were arranged around a stone fireplace. The white net curtains at the windows were drawn back to reveal the view through the forest down to the lake. The shimmering lake instantly reminded Sarah of the view of the sea from her own bedroom window in Pebble Cottage on a hot summer's day.

Dora motioned for Sarah to join her on the sofa. There was already a pot of coffee on the table. Dora waggled her head as she poured them each a cup. 'I can't get over it. I must admit, it makes me feel rather old to know that little Janice, who I last saw when she was three years old, is a grandmother herself.'

'You last saw Mum when she was three? I have so many questions, Dora.'

Dora settled back against the sofa, her cup of coffee cradled in her long fingers. 'Why don't you start with what you know? And we'll go from there.'

Sarah drew a steadying breath. 'So, as far as Mum knew, she was born in March 1942 at Bayview Convalescent Home in Dovecote. Her parents were Gladys and Douglas Legg. He was the vicar at St. John's Church. She grew up in Dovecote, at the vicarage. After her mother died, she went to London, where she met my dad, Neil. They got married and, along with my older sister, Daphne, moved back to Dovecote in 1975. Reverend Douglas had moved down to Cornwall, and he died before Daphne was born.'

The sudden lump in her throat caught her off-guard and she coughed.

'My parents bought a run-down, almost derelict cottage, as well as a café that had been closed since the end of the war. I came along a few years later. When I was three, Mum and Dad split up, and he moved away. Mum's been there ever since, running The Seaside Café, and living at Pebble Cottage.'

Dora sucked in a quick breath. 'This is all so incredible. How did you end up finding me? You mentioned some photographs yesterday?'

Sarah sipped her coffee. 'Mum had a fall at the café. She hurt her ankle and couldn't get up the stairs. So we brought her bed downstairs until she got used to her crutches. As I was hoovering her bedroom floor, one of the floorboards caved in, and when I reached down into the hole, I found an old envelope of photographs. Mum and I didn't think too much of it at first, when we looked at them. We thought they had just been accidentally left by a previous owner. But then we came across the one of Rose and a baby. A baby called Janice. With the same date of birth as Mum. My mum thought it was just a coincidence, but I was intrigued.' Sarah gave Dora a small smile. 'Particularly when I saw the one of you and Rose and the sprig of mistletoe.' Dora blushed slightly and hid behind her coffee cup. 'I spoke to an old lady, Maureen, who lives at Bayview. It's a care home now. She used to live next door to Rose.'

'Maureen?' Dora gasped. 'I remember her. She's still alive?'

'Yes, she remembered Rose and told me that she used to live at Pebble Cottage and that she ran The Seaside Café. Maureen misremembered Rose's baby as being named Janet, instead of Janice. She also remembered you from one of the photos I showed her. But it all came to a head when Reverend Clive, who is the current vicar at St. John's, gave me an old shoebox he'd found in the loft of the vicarage. It had Mum's name on it. When we opened it, we got quite a shock. Inside, we found Mum's full birth certificate, her baptism certificate, and her adoption certificate. All of which told us that Douglas and Gladys had adopted her in 1945, and that her parents were actually Rose and Martin Wilton, of Pebble Cottage. There was also a photograph with your name on the back.'

'A photograph with my name on? Gosh. Yes, I remember.'

Dora puffed out her hollow cheeks. 'And so, you thought if you tracked me down, I could fill in some gaps?'

'When I recognised your name from an email I'd had about your exhibition, we guessed you'd be a good place to start. Mum wants to find her mother.'

Dora tapped her cup with her cerise fingernails before putting it down on the table. 'Yes, I suppose she does.'

'What we really want to know is how Mum ended up being adopted by the Leggs – and what happened to Rose, and to Martin.'

'Some of which I can tell you.' Dora paused. 'I would so dearly love to speak with Janice and tell her directly. I have a friend in America, and recently we've started calling each other on our computers, so we can see each other. Would your mother be able to do that?'

'You mean, a Skype call? I don't know how good Mum's laptop is. But I did leave mine at Pebble Cottage.' Sarah pulled her phone from her pocket. 'I think it would be lovely, and Mum would be thrilled. She would have come to Alpensee with me but she's still not great on her ankle. Let me call my sister now and see if we can sort something out.'

Dora's face lit up. 'I'll get us some more coffee. I can't believe it. I really can't.'

Sarah chuckled to herself as she waited for Daphne to pick up her phone.

'Sarah? Is everything alright?'

'Hi, Daffs. Yes, listen. Are you free?'

'Right now? I'm over at Mum's. Why?'

'Perfect! Listen. I'm at Dora's house and she asked if Mum wanted to get on a Skype call with her.' Sarah lowered her voice to a whisper. 'I think she'd quite like to tell Mum what she knows directly.'

'Oh, right. Um, I'll ask her. Hang on.' Sarah strained to hear Daphne's muffled voice as she spoke to Janice. 'Mum's not quite sure what Skype is, but I've explained, and she said yes. I'll need to run home and get my laptop, though. Mum's one is so ancient I don't think it will cope.'

'Mine's upstairs in my bedroom.'

'It was *my* bedroom first.'

'Not that old argument. Look, just go up and get it.' Sarah paused. 'I trust you not to go snooping.'

Daphne inhaled sharply. 'Is there anything in your room to go snooping through?' Sarah could hear her climbing the creaky stairs.

Sarah groaned. 'I meant on the laptop.'

'Oh, right. Are Dad's ashes in that box on the desk?'

'Yeah.'

'You've not scattered him yet, then?'

Sarah chewed her thumb cuticle. 'No, not yet.' Was she ever going to be able to? She pushed that thought away. 'If you set up the laptop on the kitchen table, open Skype, and get Mum in front of the camera, I'll ask Dora to call as soon as we're ready.'

'Hang on, Sarah. I need your password.'

'It's just my date of birth. You do know my date of birth, right?'

Daphne tutted, but Sarah could hear keys being pressed. 'Of course. How could I forget the day you turned up and ruined my life?' A few weeks ago, Daphne would have meant that, but now Sarah could hear the teasing in her voice.

'Love you too, sis,' Sarah said.

'Yeah, well, let's not get carried away, shall we? Right, we're in. Ready when you are... Oh, your background picture.' There was a quiver in Daphne's voice.

Sarah's heart thudded against her ribs. 'Yeah. Like I said, I talk to Faith every day. And having her photo right there means I can never forget.' She breathed away the ball of pain that had lodged itself in her chest. At least she *could* breathe. There had been days when she couldn't. 'I'll go and let Dora know we're ready.'

A few moments later, Dora sat in front of her laptop, her long fingers drumming on the wooden table as they waited for Daphne to accept her call. She glanced at Sarah, who gave her a reassuring smile. This was more than Sarah could have ever hoped for. How gracious and kind of Dora.

'Hello?' Janice's dark-brown eyes stared out from Dora's screen.

'Hi, Mum,' Sarah said, waving. 'Mum, this is Dora Müller.'

'Hello, Dora. I believe you were a friend of my mother's. A mother I've only just found out I had.'

'I can't believe it's really you, Janice. Yes, I was friends with Rose. Sarah has told me how you came to find out. I am sorry it happened this way.' Dora paused and shook her head. 'The last time I saw you, you were three years old, and you had a pink ribbon in your hair,' Dora said gently, her hand on her chest.

'A pink ribbon?' Janice turned to Daphne, who rummaged around out of the camera's field. 'Like this?'

Dora gasped.

'It was in the shoebox that Reverend Clive found in the vicarage,' Sarah explained. 'Dora, who was Rose? And how did Mum end up with Douglas and Gladys?'

Janice looked directly at the laptop's camera. There was a steeliness in her eyes, but Sarah could also see a touch of nervousness in the set of her mother's mouth. 'Yes, Dora, please do tell.' She drew a deep breath. 'Did my mother abandon me, and if so, why?'

Dora glanced at Sarah before turning back towards the screen, not looking directly into the camera. 'Rose didn't abandon you, Janice. I did.'

# THIRTY-SEVEN

## SARAH

May 2017

'Perhaps I should start from the beginning,' Dora said, as the three Portman women gaped at her. 'I know very little about Rose before she came to Dovecote, apart from that she was orphaned young, and grew up in a series of foster homes. I know even less about Martin. What I do know is that they moved to Dovecote from Brighton the day they got married, in 1940. Pebble Cottage, and the café, then known as Ursula's, had been owned by Martin's parents. I believe they were killed early on in the war.'

'Yes, Maureen said the same,' Sarah remarked.

'Within a few months, Rose had got the café – which she renamed The Seaside Café – up and running. Martin continued to work for the Post Office in Brighton.'

'When did you come to Dovecote, Dora?' Janice asked.

'Early 1940. I'd taken a room in one of the large houses on Blythe Avenue. The landlady, Mrs Marshall, had missed her calling. She would have made an excellent drill sergeant.' Sarah's stomach lurched. Blythe Avenue was where the bomb had landed. 'Anyway. I used to visit the café for a cup of tea most days. Rose could see that I was a little lonely, and she made such an effort to speak to me. She was like that with her customers, she really cared about people. Her tea and cakes kept up the spirits of the whole town. She was the closest thing I had to a friend at that time.' Dora stiffened, as though collecting her thoughts. 'But never mind about me. In June 1941, Martin got transferred to Scotland, to work on the trans-Atlantic telegrams. I think Rose surprised herself at how resilient she was without him. She almost seemed to blossom. And then, two months later, she realised she was expecting. You were born on the tenth of March, 1942, Janice. I was one of the first people to meet you. I brought my camera and took some pictures, thinking Rose would like to send one to Martin.'

'This is a lot to take in, Dora. I can't get my head around it all. But speaking of pictures' – Daphne held up the framed picture of Douglas, Gladys, and baby Janice – 'Mum's had this one for years.'

Dora leant closer to the screen. 'That was the day of your christening, Janice. Reverend Douglas asked me to take a photo of him and Gladys with you. You see, Douglas wasn't only the vicar at St. John's, he was also Rose's uncle. Rose didn't know this when she came to Dovecote, and I'm sorry, but I can't remember the circumstances around how or why. He was also Janice's godfather.'

'So, he was my great-uncle? Have I got that right? Well, at least I *was* related to him. This is all very strange, Dora, and getting stranger by the minute. But please do carry on.' Janice took a sip from the mug of tea Daphne had pushed in front of her. She was leaning forward, and Sarah longed to be able to hold her hand. This must be overwhelming for her.

'While Rose was pregnant, I helped out at the café, and we became good friends. In May 1943, Blythe Avenue got hit by a stray bomb, and the house I'd been living in was destroyed. Mrs

Marshall and I managed to shelter in the basement and were dug out of the rubble. The lady in the room next to mine, Rebecca Saunders, wasn't so lucky. She died in Bayview a few hours after the raid. I took myself away from the scene, I couldn't bear to watch bodies being pulled out of the wreckage. Rose found me slumped on the wall of Victoria Park.' Dora tried to disguise wiping a tear from her cheek, but Sarah had seen it trickle from her eye. 'Sorry, it's been a long time since I thought about all of this.' She drew a calming breath. 'Anyway, I found myself homeless until Rose insisted that I move into Pebble Cottage with her.'

Sarah reached for Dora's hand. 'Take your time, Dora. I'm sorry we're bringing it all back to you.' She got a smile in return. 'You moved into Pebble Cottage? I don't suppose your room was the one at the back?'

'With the view of the sea and the draughty cast-iron fireplace? Yes, it was, and I loved that room.'

'Me too,' said Daphne, and Sarah looked at the laptop. She'd almost forgotten her sister was there.

'That room was Daphne's, and then mine,' Sarah explained. 'I was in the small box room until Daphne moved out.'

'Oh! Gosh. Of course.' Dora reached towards the screen as if to touch Janice. 'That little room was yours, Janice. Your cot nearly took up the whole space.'

A moment of silence fell, and Janice frowned.

'I don't remember,' she said, with a frustrated shake of her head.

'You were only a tiny baby, Mum,' Daphne said, placing a hand on Janice's shoulder. 'It's okay.'

Sarah drew a breath and turned to Dora. 'You lived at Pebble Cottage with Rose, and Mum. That explains the photograph of you and Rose in the back garden.'

'Yes. Even back then, photography was a passion of mine, and Rose was such a natural in front of the camera. I loved taking her picture.' There was a hint of pink on the tips of Dora's ears, but Sarah didn't ask the question she was dying to. If Dora wanted to reveal if there was anything more than a friendship between her and Rose, she would. It wouldn't be right to force that out of her. 'But the bombing frightened Rose. She was so afraid that something might happen to you, Janice, that she decided it was best if you were evacuated.'

'She sent me away?' Janice asked, her eyebrows lifting.

Dora nodded sadly. 'It broke her heart. I used to listen to her crying in the dead of night.'

'So that photograph in the exhibition of a woman holding a baby and crying *is* of Rose and Mum? I did wonder.' Sarah's voice was almost a whisper as the pieces of the puzzle began to fit together in her head.

'That was the day Rose had to let you go, Janice. I didn't tell Rose I was taking the picture because I wanted a candid shot. It was such an emotional moment.'

'Where did I go?' Janice rubbed her eyes. 'It feels odd to be saying that. I don't really feel as if any of this is about me.'

Dora squeezed Sarah's hand. From the look in her eyes, Sarah could tell she'd love it to be Janice's. 'You were very young, Janice. Just over a year old. I'm not surprised you don't remember.' Dora paused, trying to recall the details. 'You were sent to a lovely couple in Carlisle. They looked after you well and they used to write to your mother about how you were doing. She never stopped thinking of you. And she missed you terribly. I don't think many people can understand how much hurt and pain a mother can hold.'

Janice and Daphne both glanced at Sarah. She gave them a weak smile in return.

'The next part of the story is a bit vague, I'm sorry,' Dora continued. 'I had to leave Dovecote for a time; I was sent to work at Bletchley Park.'

Sarah opened her mouth to interrupt. Bletchley Park? Did

that mean Dora had been working in intelligence? Had she been a spy? The look on Janice's face made her close her mouth again. This was her mother's story; she could ask Dora about Bletchley Park afterwards.

'But Rose and I kept in touch. Then the war ended, and I was released from my duties. I had to think about what I was going to do.'

'Did you go back to Dovecote?' Sarah asked.

Dora shook her head. 'I was worried for Rose, but I also wanted to visit my parents. I hadn't seen them in almost seven years. They moved to New York just before the start of the war. My father was Swiss German and he realised Europe was about to become dangerous for someone with a German-sounding surname. He made me use my mother's maiden name of Stephens when I applied for university.'

'That explains the two names on the back of the photograph,' Sarah said.

'Yes. Rose was the only person in Dovecote who knew my real name. I didn't start using it until years after the war ended. It was nearly a month after victory was declared in Europe that I was able to leave Bletchley.'

'And I suppose by then, Rose's husband had returned from Scotland and Mum was back in Dovecote with them?' There was a puzzled look on Daphne's face. The thought had occurred to Sarah, too. What had happened to Martin? Maureen said that she never saw Martin return to Dovecote. But then, she and her brother had left Dovecote almost immediately at the war's end.

Sarah watched as Dora took a sip of coffee. The photograph of the kiss under the mistletoe sprang into her mind again. There was more going on than Dora was letting on. Why?

'That's where I cannot help much, I'm afraid. All I know is this: Rose wrote to tell me that Martin had left her and wasn't going to be coming back to Dovecote. She said that if anyone, especially you, Janice, asked about him, I was to say he died in the war. That was what Martin wanted people to think. Whatever had happened, whatever he had done, he thought it best if you believed he was dead.'

Janice raised a sceptical eyebrow, and Sarah placed a hand on Dora's arm.

'Tell us anything you know, Dora, *please*.' The more Sarah found out, the more she yearned to know. Her family tree was being rewritten, and she couldn't bear to leave any branch incomplete.

'I think Rose wanted to tell me more, but may not have wanted to put it in writing. But when I got her letter, I had an idea. What if she, and Janice' – Dora nodded at the screen – 'could come to America with me, for a fresh start? I sent her a telegram asking her to meet me at King's Cross Station, in London. I named the date and time. I came down from Bletchley that morning and waited.'

Janice gasped. 'Did she turn up? What happened, Dora?'

Dora looked from Sarah to Janice and back again. 'Yes, she came. It was so lovely to see her again. But she looked tired, and you weren't with her – she was anxious that you hadn't been sent home yet. The process of returning evacuated children home took a long time. I suppose the authorities were just being careful.' Dora blinked and Sarah could see the beginnings of tears in her eyes. 'Rose telephoned the evacuation service and said she would travel to Carlisle and collect Janice, rather than wait for her to be sent back to Dovecote. She loved my idea of us all going to New York. She wanted a fresh start. We headed up to Carlisle that very same day.'

'I may be jumping the gun here, Dora,' Janice said after a moment. 'But I certainly would have remembered living in America, so I'm guessing something happened to prevent Rose from sailing to New York?'

Dora bit her lip. 'Yes, something happened.'

'I feel as though I'm hearing someone else's story. None of it seems real.' There was a tremor in Janice's voice and Daphne held her mother's hand.

Dora took a deep breath before continuing. 'I promise you it is all true. When we arrived at the house where you were staying, there were lots of tears – mostly from you, Janice. Your host family – I really wish I could remember their names – had made sure you didn't forget your mother. They used to show you a photograph of her that she included with your belongings. I think that helped you understand why you were being taken from what you thought was your home. You were only three, and you must have been so confused.'

'What happened, Dora?' Sarah gave the old woman's hand a light squeeze.

'We planned to sail to New York from Liverpool. But we never made the ship. Just outside of Liverpool, there was an accident. The train we were on collided with a fast-moving freight train.' Dora's eyes fluttered shut and her voice dimmed. 'I can still hear the sound of crunching metal and the screams.' When she opened her eyes again, they were shining with tears. 'As the carriage rolled over, I shielded Janice from the falling luggage and flying glass. But Rose hit her head on something – I don't know what. I tried to help her, but she was badly injured. She was the sole fatality.'

The only sound was a small 'Oh,' from Janice and the rustle of tissue as Dora wiped her wet cheeks. Sarah fought against a wave of nausea. She had the same reaction to any mention of a head injury. The mental image of Faith's broken skull swam in front of her. The nurses at the hospital had tried to hide the damage from Sarah. But she'd seen it when she'd scooped her daughter's lifeless body into her arms and bawled into her hair.

Dora gathered herself and squared her shoulders. 'It pained me so much that I couldn't save Rose. I refused to let you out of my sight after that, Janice. I can only presume the staff at the hospital thought you were my child. Suddenly I was alone, with a three-year-old, who had no idea who I was. I had to make a choice.' Dora released a long breath. 'At your christening, I'd overheard Rose telling Reverend Douglas that if anything were to happen to her and Martin, that he would be your only family, Janice. I gathered your papers from Rose's bag and put them in an envelope, and brought you back to your family. It was a last-minute impulse to write my name on the back of the photograph of your christening. Perhaps I wanted you to find me. Anyway, when I arrived at St. John's vicarage and told Douglas and Gladys what had happened, they immediately asked about Martin.' She glanced at Sarah and then looked down at the table. 'I told him what Rose had asked me to say, which was that Martin was dead. It was wrong, I know.' Dora slowly lifted her head and looked back at the screen. 'For all the years since, I have had this guilt about abandoning you. I should have cared for you; I was your godmother. But I couldn't do it. You reminded me too much of Rose. I am so sorry, Janice.'

Janice let out a deep sigh. 'So that's how I ended up being raised by Mum and Dad. Sorry, I've been calling them that my whole life. I'm not going to stop now.'

'No one expects you to, Mum,' Daphne sniffled, rubbing Janice's arm.

'They were your parents,' Dora added. 'And they loved you.'

'Thank you for bringing me to them. You didn't abandon me. You brought me somewhere safe. You brought me home.' Janice cleared her throat and gave Dora a soft smile. 'Thank you, Dora.'

'I don't understand why Douglas and Gladys didn't tell you about your birth mother. Or that you were adopted,' Sarah huffed. 'I mean, what would have been the harm in telling you?'

'What would have been the point? As far as they knew, both

of my parents were dead. I was only three. They knew I wouldn't remember. And they were right.'

There was a hint of sadness in Janice's voice, and Sarah's frustration softened. Douglas and Gladys hadn't done anything wrong; they were just trying to protect her mother. And what parent doesn't want to do that? Her mind went straight to Rob and how he'd failed to protect Faith. A chill ran through her blood. That wasn't entirely fair. It *had* been an accident, just as much as the train crash that killed Rose. And he'd suffered every bit as much as she had. She had to keep her secret; to tell him would only cause further pain. She looked out of the corner of her eye at Dora. She was keeping a secret too, Sarah could tell.

'Did you ever find out what really happened to Martin, Dora?' Daphne asked. Sarah glanced at her sister and supressed a smile. Daphne was clearly as intrigued as the rest of them.

'No, I didn't. I didn't want to, because if I found out he was still alive, then I'd have to confront the fact that I'd lied to Reverend Douglas. I hope you can forgive me, Janice. If I had told the truth, then maybe someone could have tracked down your father.'

Janice leant forward and rested her chin in her hands. There was a glistening sheen to her eyes. 'There's nothing to forgive, Dora. Please, I mean that. You saved my life and then you found me a loving home. You did the right thing. I had a mother and a father. I was loved. And that is thanks to you.' She stifled a yawn. 'I don't know about the rest of you, but I'm exhausted. This has been a rollercoaster of a morning.' She puffed out her cheeks. 'Dora, thank you so much for taking the time to share all of this with us. I'm glad I know the truth now. How lucky am I to have been loved by two sets of parents, and by good friends? Oh, now look, I'm getting all teary. I think I need a strong cup of tea, and a slice of cake.' She ran the sleeve of her lilac cardigan across her damp cheek.

Dora laughed softly. 'Do you know, Janice, cake was the second word you ever said, after "Mama". Except you pronounced it "ake".'

'Is that so? Well, I have always been fond of baked goods. Now I know where I get that from. That's a nice thing to know. Thank you, Dora.'

'Oh Janice, it has been my absolute pleasure. I am so delighted that I got to see you again. And to meet you too, Daphne. And of course, Sarah.' She squeezed Sarah's hand. 'Maybe we can keep in touch, if you want to?'

Janice smiled. 'Yes, I would like that very much. And if you ever feel the urge to visit Dovecote, please do. I think you're probably overdue a pot of tea at The Seaside Café.'

Dora nodded. 'Oh, that would be wonderful. Perhaps I will manage it, some day. Goodbye, Janice.'

'Goodbye, Dora.'

Sarah and Dora looked at each other in silence for a long moment, each wiping tears from their cheeks.

'Well, there we are,' Sarah said eventually. 'Thank you so much, Dora.'

'Like Janice, I am exhausted.'

Sarah stood up from the table and Dora followed as she went into the sitting room and picked up her tote bag.

'Sarah, will you come back tomorrow morning? I can dig out some photographs that you might want to see.' There was a glimmer in Dora's eyes and Sarah's skin tingled.

'Of course. And... can we talk about that photograph of you and Rose kissing?'

Dora turned pale and Sarah placed a hand on her arm.

'You don't need to be afraid, Dora.'

Dora glanced away, and then back at Sarah. 'I would like to talk about it. I have carried our secret for a long time.'

At the front door, Dora surprised Sarah by enveloping her in a hug. 'Thank you for finding me and for bringing Rose back into my life. I hadn't forgotten her, but I'd not thought about her properly for years.'

At the end of the driveway, Sarah turned to wave to Dora, but she had already gone back inside. She faced the road towards town. She was glad Rob hadn't come. It was right it had just been the four women. But he would be waiting for her. Was it time for her to do what she'd just encouraged Dora to do? Was it time to tell him everything?

# THIRTY-EIGHT

## SARAH

May 2017

Walking back from Dora's, Sarah found Rob sitting on a bench at the edge of the lake holding a takeaway coffee cup and staring into the middle distance.

'That's not got that plum liqueur in it, has it?' she asked, sitting down next to him. He didn't look at her.

'Guess you decided to go and see Dora on your own then,' he said eventually. Sarah flinched. Maybe she should have sent a quick text to let him know she was going to Dora's without him. He invited himself into a deeply personal family matter when he had no right to. He should never have assumed she wanted him there. But, as with so many things, she probably should have told *him* that.

'You weren't in the hotel lobby at quarter to ten, like we agreed.'

'You deliberately snuck out and went without me, Sarah.' He crushed the coffee cup in his hands.

Sarah ran her hand through her hair. 'Are you looking for a fight? Because if you are, then I'm not interested. It's been a long morning. All I want is an obscenely large plate of pasta. And I'm more than happy to get that by myself if you're going to be tetchy and argumentative.'

He finally faced her. 'What I want is to know where I stand, Sarah. Last night—'

'I'm still trying to get my head around last night, Rob. A lot was said, and a lot was done. And I don't know if any of it was a good idea.' She got up. 'I need lunch. I think it's best if I go alone. I just need space.'

'I meant what I said, Sarah,' he called after her. 'I do love you.'

Sarah didn't turn around. She just closed her eyes for a moment. Those were the last words she'd wanted to hear. If it was true, she knew how to change his mind. It would mean hurting him, but she was probably going to do that either way. She was tired of carrying her secret. Maybe she needed to be cruel to be kind.

A small Italian restaurant on the main street had provided the required carbohydrates. Sarah's head was clearer and her mood lighter when she knocked on Rob's door.

'Hi.'

'Hi. Look, sorry about earlier, I shouldn't have started on at you like that.' Rob twisted the hem of his T-shirt between his fingers. 'I was annoyed that you pulled a vanishing act. Especially after, you know.'

Sarah gave him a tight smile. 'I get it. Look, do you fancy a walk? I've just had a truck-load of pasta that I need to walk off.'

'I'll grab my jacket.' He flashed her one of his half-smiles. She hated when he did that; it completely disarmed her. She could not let herself get swept away again. It wasn't fair on him.

They were halfway around the lake by the time Sarah had

updated Rob about what Dora had told her that morning. The sky had clouded over, and the lake was a smoky grey.

'I'm sorry about Rose,' Rob said.

Sarah shrugged. 'I wasn't really expecting my grandmother to still be alive. Not at the age she would have been. But I had hoped that she'd had a good, happy life.'

'So, what now? Are you going to see if you can track down Martin?'

'I don't know. It's up to Mum. But it does sound like he was something of a let-down anyway. I can't imagine what he could have done that his child would be better off thinking he was dead.'

'Yeah, that's kind of shady. But it was a long time ago. Attitudes were different to so many things back then. It could have been anything.'

'We might never know.'

Rob's eyebrows furrowed. 'How is Janice taking it all?'

'Surprisingly well.' She stuffed her hands into the pockets of her jacket. It was chilly without the glare of the sun. 'I'm going to visit Dora again, in the morning, before we leave. She wants to dig out some more photos to show me. You can come along, if you want.'

'No, it's okay. You go.'

'If you're sure?' His nod was accompanied by another of his half-smiles. Her knees gave way as they sat down on a bench that looked back towards the town.

'Sarah, I think we need to—'

'Talk about last night. Yeah, we do. But can I ask you one question first?'

'Go on.'

'You said, a few weeks ago, that you'd been waiting for me. Has there really been no one else in the last ten years?'

Rob rubbed his eyes. 'Well, not exactly.'

'Thank God. That would have been a terrible waste.'

'I'll take that as a compliment.'

'It was meant as one.'

He gave her a crooked smile. 'I did go on a few dates, but my heart wasn't in it. Because of losing you and Faith. I realised I wasn't ready, and that it wouldn't be fair to get involved with someone, only for them to find I wasn't in the right place emotionally. So, while there hasn't been anyone, there hasn't been no one, either.'

'Fair enough.'

'What about you?'

'Kind of the same really, only I did get involved with someone. It was a disaster. She was toxic; I was depressed. We screamed at each other a lot. After that, I gave up. And then Dad got sick, so I didn't have time anyway. Listen, Rob, what you said last night, and earlier – do you really mean it? I mean, are you sure?'

'That I love you?'

'After everything I did to you, how can you possibly love me?'

'God knows. I think it might be against my better judgement. You're right, you really hurt me. You abandoned me when I needed you. But despite all of that, my dumb heart still feels what it feels. And I know I'm setting myself up for a fall again. The minute your van is fixed, and Janice is back on her feet, you'll be gone. If I could change how I feel, I probably would. None of what I've said makes any sense. All I know is that I know I love you.' He put his hands in his hair and leant forward, his elbows resting on his knees, looking down at his feet.

Sarah studied the back of his head for a moment. How many times had she kissed his neck or run her fingers through his hair? A large part of her very much wanted to again, but she couldn't put her hand on her heart and tell him she loved him. Because it wasn't true. And it hadn't been true for a long time.

But was telling him the truth the right way to let him know that? It might give him closure. The truth might hurt now, but it also might make it easier for him to move on in the long run.

'Rob?'

He pulled his head up and looked at her. 'Yeah?'

She swallowed. 'I want to tell you something I've been keeping from you for ten years – actually, for more than ten years.' His look morphed from hopeful anticipation to a mixture of fear and concern. 'I want to tell you where I was the day Faith died.'

'I don't understand. You were away on a bookkeeping course with the other staff from the Bayview office, weren't you?'

'No, I wasn't.' She turned away and looked out over the lake. She couldn't face him while she broke his heart. 'I'd better start at the beginning. Some of this you'll already know, but it only makes sense if I go right back to where it all started. Did I ever tell you that in school I had a huge crush on Heather, and we had a kind of a thing?'

'Um, yeah, you did.'

'Well, after we left school, we both got jobs at Bayview. We started to take our mutual attraction more seriously. We fell in love. But I messed it up. I began to feel trapped and bored. I wanted something more. And when I left her for you, I broke her heart.' Sarah's voice cracked. 'You were everything she wasn't. She was quiet and gentle; you were loud and wild. We went to mad parties and drunken music festival weekends. We were exciting together too, volatile but thrilling. I kind of became addicted to that cycle of arguing and making up, to the point where I would deliberately pick a fight to get that adrenaline rush. You never let me down; you always took the bait. It was like a drug.'

'We weren't *that* bad. Were we?' A hint of a frown creased Rob's forehead.

'I think we were, Rob.' Sarah crossed her arms. 'I'm not blaming you. You didn't make me behave that way. It's a flaw within me, one that's still there. I think what happened last night proved that.' She gave him a soft smile. 'We hadn't had an argument, but emotions were running high. And look what happened.'

His frown deepened. 'But aren't all relationships like that?'

'I don't think so. I think couples in healthy relationships can love each other without tearing each other to shreds. Anyway, then we had Faith and even though, or maybe because, I was sleep-deprived and anxious, I couldn't stop the cycle. Do you remember how much we fought back then? Every conversation turned into a row.' Sarah rubbed her eyes. She hated thinking back to those days, knowing what she'd done.

Rob scrunched up his face. 'Yeah, I remember. I just thought it was the tiredness and the stress, and that we'd come through it.'

'One day, it dawned on me that I didn't want that any more. What I wanted was tenderness, care, patience, and support. But the problem was, I didn't know how to communicate to you what I needed. I only knew how to wind you up. So, I turned to Heather. At first, it was just friendship, honestly. She was someone I could vent my frustrations to about my inability to behave the way I wanted to be treated. But over time, it became something more.'

Sarah shifted her gaze away from the surface of the lake to Rob's face. He looked very confused. The next thing she said would turn that confusion into pain, and maybe anger. But she had to say it. It might be the only thing that would stop him loving her. 'I came to realise... I don't want to say this, but I need to, before we go too far.' She paused. 'I realised that I didn't love you.'

'I see.' Sarah could see the muscles in Rob's jaw working

hard. He was grinding his teeth. 'So where were you when our daughter died, Sarah?'

Sarah clamped her bottom lip between her teeth and folded her hands together. There was no turning back now.

'I was with Heather. It wasn't her fault. She didn't like what we were doing. She didn't like the lies. I wanted to leave you, I wanted to set you free, but I couldn't find a way to do it without breaking you.'

'How long were you cheating on me, Sarah?'

Sarah swallowed hard. 'Almost a year.'

Rob got up from the bench. He didn't shout. He didn't call her things he would have been perfectly within his rights to. If he had, it would have been easier for Sarah to deal with. Anything would have been easier than the tears rolling down his cheeks.

'Rob. I'm—'

He held up his hand to stop her, then simply shook his head and walked away. It was no use her telling herself she'd done it for his own good. There was no hiding the fact that she'd broken his heart all over again.

# THIRTY-NINE

## SARAH

May 2017

It was with a heavy heart that Sarah rang Dora's doorbell early the following morning. Rob hadn't replied to the text she'd sent asking if he was okay. The look on his face when he walked away from her at the lake would be forever etched on her memory, along with the hurt and pain and anger in his eyes when she'd arrived at the hospital the day Faith died.

Sarah followed Dora onto the veranda outside the sitting room, breathing in the scent of the pine forest surrounding the house. Dora's wrinkled hands shook slightly as she poured them coffee. She'd done her nails. The peach nail varnish matched her lipstick.

'You asked about the photograph of me and Rose under the mistletoe,' she said, her eyes settling on a manila envelope on the table between them.

'You were more than friends, weren't you? Kissing under the mistletoe is one thing. But wanting to take her, and Mum, with you to America goes way beyond the actions of a friend.' Dora's cheeks reddened. 'You'll get no judgement from me, Dora. My dad was gay, and I'm bisexual. If Rose was like me, then I'd be thrilled. You've been incredibly kind and generous inviting me into your home and telling us everything you have. So if there are things you would rather not talk about, then I won't force you.'

A slight smile tugged at the edges of Dora's mouth. 'In 1940, I was contacted by the Foreign Office. I was studying languages at Oxford at the time. I was recruited to translate German propaganda and popular publications into English. I was sad I was never able to tell Rose what my job was, but I had signed the Official Secrets Act, and it was a matter of national security. That would have been one in the eye for those who thought I was a German spy. Anyway, I was billeted in Dovecote, the logic being that it was unlikely to be a target for either German bombers or German intelligence. I was released from Oxford and sent to the seaside. I arrived with a broken heart, having left the most wonderful woman behind. Her name was Mariella.'

'Is she the woman in the photograph at your exhibition, leaning against the oak tree?'

'Yes. Most people believed we were just friends.' There was an impish grin on Dora's face, and for a moment Sarah could see the young woman behind the wrinkles. Dora sighed and continued. 'I thought I could never love anyone the way I had loved her. And then I met Rose. Of course, she was out of bounds. She was a married woman. But that didn't stop me completely falling for her. Every day, I went up to Dovecote station, where a man would hand me an envelope full of that day's translation work. On the way back home, I would stop at The Seaside Café and have a cup of tea. Rose would always try to get me to have one of her teacakes, but I was much too nervous around her to eat.'

'And she never realised why you came in each day?'

'No, she never did. I don't think it would have occurred to her that I might fancy her, until I told her. Why would it?'

Sarah put down her coffee cup. 'True.'

'Anyway, time went on. Martin got transferred, Janice was born, and I continued to love Rose from afar.'

'That must have been hard for you.'

Dora tilted her head slightly. 'In a way, I was glad I still had the capacity to love. There was so much hate, so much animosity, so much stress around. It was as though my heart was putting up a little act of resistance all of its own, by refusing to be hardened.'

'What a lovely way to put it.'

'Thank you. I told you yesterday how Rose offered me a place to stay after the bombing. I was a little wary of accepting. On the one hand, living under the same roof as her would be exciting, but on the other hand, I worried about keeping my feelings hidden, being in such close proximity to her. My fears proved well-founded. One evening, there was an unpleasant encounter in the local pub. Some chap, grief-stricken and under the influence, publicly accused me of being a German spy. I couldn't defend myself without giving away the work I was doing. I was very distressed and, back at Pebble Cottage, Rose was so supportive and kind that I kissed her.'

Sarah scrunched up her nose. 'That must have been a bit of a surprise for her. What happened?'

'I was so embarrassed and ashamed of kissing her so suddenly and without warning that I avoided Rose the next day. That evening, she asked if we could talk. She asked me outright if I was a lesbian. I wasn't sure if she knew what a lesbian was. I told her about Mariella. And I told Rose how I felt about her. I said that I understood that she wouldn't requite those feelings and offered to move out at once. She said I could stay. I felt so wretched. I'd spoilt our friendship. Then a few nights later, she came into my room. She said that our kiss had awoken something in her, something she'd never known was there.' Dora blushed. 'She didn't go back to her own room that night.'

'Wow,' Sarah breathed. 'That's quite the awakening, for her.'

'She confided in me that she felt she and Martin didn't really fit together, that she dreaded intimacy with him, and was thankful that he seemed as reluctant to engage in it as she was. She confessed she could appreciate his good looks, and his quiet, gentle nature, but that she didn't feel any sort of attraction to him. She worried what would happen once he returned home. She knew they'd have to play happy families for Janice's sake. They were married, and I know she struggled with the fact that she was, in effect, having an affair. I worried too, but I didn't want to sully our time together. We had to make the most of it while we could. No one knew if we were going to have a future at all. There was a "live for today" attitude.' Dora reached for the envelope, but shivered as a cloud blocked the sun. 'Do you mind if we go inside? I'm a bit chilly.'

'Of course, I'll carry in the coffee things.'

Dora gave Sarah a grateful smile as they sat down on the grey sofas. 'Thank you.' She opened the envelope. 'Now, would you like to see some more photographs of Rose?'

'Yes, please.'

Dora looked at a photo for a long moment before handing it to Sarah. 'This is one of my absolute favourites of her. I took it one summer's day in the garden of Pebble Cottage. You can see how much she loved Janice.'

Sarah took the photograph and nearly burst out crying. Rose was sitting on a blanket, strewn on a small patch of lawn between a vegetable patch and a corrugated iron structure. She was smiling down at Janice, who was lying in front of her, wearing a frilly bonnet. Rose was ticking Janice's tummy, making Janice giggle.

'Oh, what a lovely moment.' She handed the picture back to

Dora. 'The funny thing is that I have an almost identical photo-graph of Mum and me, and one of me and my daughter. Do you have any others?'

'This is the last picture I took of Rose.' Dora's voice quiv-ered as she handed over the next photo. 'I took it while we were waiting for the train to Liverpool. I didn't get it developed until after the accident.' The photo was of Rose and Janice, sat side by side on a station platform bench. Rose was holding Janice's hand and Janice was looking up at her mother, with a slightly confused expression. A sharp pain struck Sarah's chest. Janice was the same age in the photo as Faith was in the framed photo on the mantelpiece of Pebble Cottage. Both children blissfully ignorant of what was to come. The doctors had said that Faith wouldn't have felt any pain. She died instantly when she slipped and hit her head on the rocks beneath the lighthouse, before falling into the sea. There was nothing Rob could have done. Sarah swallowed down the familiar wave of nausea and blinked back the threatening tears.

Dora was looking at a third photograph with tears in her own eyes. 'I don't know whether I should show you this one. I promised Rose I'd never let anyone see it, and I haven't. But I don't suppose that matters now.' Her cheeks were crimson as she handed the photo over. Sarah looked down and let out a low whistle.

'Hmm, I can see why she wouldn't want this to get out.' Rose was lying amongst ruffled bedsheets, completely nude.

'She was the most beautiful woman I have ever known,' Dora whispered.

Dora was right. Rose was as beautiful as any Hollywood starlet of the time. Even in black and white, Sarah could tell her skin was flawless. In other photos, Rose's large, round eyes gave her an air of innocence. In this one, the heaviness of her eyelids made her gaze sultry. 'It was brave of you both to take that photo. Wasn't it illegal, back then?'

'Lesbianism? No. Sex between men was, absolutely. But the men in power felt it was better to say nothing about sex between women, lest it gave wives up and down the country ideas. They presumed most women knew nothing about lesbianism.' She let out a joyously naughty laugh. 'The fools. But even though it was not punishable by law, one's reputation and standing, not to mention job prospects, would be obliterated if there was a hint of any such behaviour.' Dora rolled her eyes. 'They were dark times.'

Sarah rubbed the nape of her neck. 'My generation is incredibly lucky.'

'The rights that exist today were hard-won and shouldn't be taken for granted. There is still work to do.'

Sarah looked back down at the photograph. There was defiance in Rose's smouldering eyes. By allowing Dora to take the photo, she was seizing the opportunity to declare who she was; that she knew who she was. The look on her heart-shaped face was one of power and confidence. But there was something soft and gentle about her features too. And there was no mistaking the love and desire radiating from her. It was one of the most mesmerising photographs Sarah had ever seen.

'I get the feeling that, had she lived, Rose would have been a force to be reckoned with.' A bubble of pride surged in Sarah's chest. She was descended from a fierce, strong, and loving woman. That shouldn't have come as a surprise, really. Janice had inherited some of those traits too, even though they only now knew where from.

'Oh, for sure. She had a stubborn and determined streak. She'd been through so much, and ended up in a loveless marriage to man she felt nothing for. She ran her own business at a time when women didn't do that sort of thing, and raised her baby on her own. All against the backdrop of a seemingly never-ending war that caused so much deprivation and hardship. People forget that, at the time, we didn't know we were going to win.' Her voice trembled. 'We had no idea when or how the war would end.'

'You were both very brave.'

'Well, I don't know about that. Sarah?'

Sarah handed Dora back the photograph, not caring if Dora noticed that the paper was shaking. 'Yes?'

'Yesterday, we were discussing why Reverend Douglas and Gladys never told your mother the truth about her biological parents. Well, there was something I should have said but didn't.' She picked at a loose thread on her grey tweed skirt. 'When I brought Janice to the vicarage, after the accident, Douglas questioned why I was on the train with Rose and Janice.'

'Did he suspect that you were more than friends?'

'I think so. Rose would have been mortified to know he thought that. One of the reasons she wanted to leave Dovecote was to avoid upsetting him. He asked me if there were any "relations of a romantic or physical nature" between us.' She let out a short, sharp laugh. 'I still remember the exact words he used. I should have lied. I should have said that we were just friends, and that I was with her because I knew people in America, and she wanted to go there. But I couldn't betray her like that. I couldn't erase our love. I couldn't deny everything we meant to each other. So, I told him the truth. It didn't go down well. I think that part of the reason why they never told Janice about Rose is because they were ashamed of her, and didn't want Janice to know that her mother had loved another woman.' A tear rolled down Dora's cheek and she wiped it away with a shaking hand. Sarah reached over and took Dora's hand in hers.

'Thank you for honouring her memory and for upholding her truth. That was incredibly brave of you.'

Dora simply nodded. 'I must have more photographs of her. I have so many in storage and all over the place. I need to sort them all out before I die. I will take copies of any I find of her or Janice and send them to you. I know your mother's address.'

Sarah laughed. 'Of course you do. Thank you, that would be lovely. Oh, that reminds me.' She dug in her tote bag. 'I found this in a drawer in the café. It's from you, I believe.' She handed Dora the Christmas card.

'Oh, it's the mansion at Bletchley Park. I'd have been in hot water if anyone knew I'd sent that picture out.' She opened the card and froze.

'What on earth does that inscription mean, Dora? I don't get it.'

*'Even if the well runs dry, we'll always have tea,'* Dora murmured before closing the card and placing it in her lap, her hands crossed over it. 'It was a code I made up. It was our way of declaring our love to one another while in public. You must remember we couldn't say how we felt around other people, or in communications that were being read by the censor. I sent this to Rose at Christmas in 1944. I was at Bletchley Park then.'

Sarah's ears pricked. 'You mentioned Bletchley yesterday. Was it as exciting as it sounds?'

'The level of secrecy about Bletchley Park was experienced even by the people working there. All anyone knew was their own job. I had no idea about the decoding machines, or the extent of the operations being carried out there. I had no idea that the place was crawling with some of the greatest minds of our time, or how we fitted into the war effort. Although we had an inkling that we must have been important.'

'What did you do?' Sarah leant so far forward she was in danger of slipping off the sofa.

'I was a Watchkeeper on Watch Number One. Our job was to translate streams of German words delivered to us from some unnamed department. I know now that we were translating the output of the Bombe machines that were decoding intercepted German communications. As civilian experts in German, we had to fill in the blanks or correct missing letters and words in these messages and then translate them. The communications were frightfully awkward to translate, full of military jargon. Once translated and checked, the messages were sent to the assessors. We had no idea what happened to them after that. We didn't know it, of course, but we were in the run-up to D-Day, and the number of deciphered communications coming through was immense.'

'Do you know that Bletchley Park is open as a museum now?'

'Yes, I had heard. If I wasn't so old, I wouldn't mind going back and having a look around. It would be rather fun to find out what everyone else was doing there. Is the mansion still standing?'

'I think so. I've not been.'

'There was a large ballroom in the mansion, and a kind of recreation room where we could sit and relax. I remember the food being passable, but the tea wasn't a patch on Rose's. There wasn't a day that passed that I didn't miss her, and her teacakes. There was lots of dancing, and such a mixture of people. Lots in uniform, of course, but plenty of civvies too.' Dora gave Sarah a hawkish look. 'Before you ask, I was true to Rose. It wasn't easy, though. Some of the Wrens were very attractive in their Royal Naval Service uniforms.'

Sarah smiled. 'I can imagine.'

'It was there I developed a love of walking. I joined the hiking club, for something to do. If I manage to make it back to Bletchley, would you come with me?'

'I would be honoured and delighted to, Dora.'

'One thing I'd like to know is whether we translated any of the communications intercepted up in Scotland, I expect we did. I do remember wondering at the time if any of the messages I was translating had been intercepted by Martin and his colleagues at the telegram monitoring stations. We could have been working together, without knowing.'

'Wow! How funny. Did you ever meet him?'

'Never. I only saw Rose in The Seaside Café until I moved into Pebble Cottage, and by then he'd been moved up to Scotland. Rose used to tell me what he wrote in his irregular letters.'

'What were his letters like?'

Dora smiled crookedly. 'They were as bland as the eggless cakes Rose was reduced to making at the height of rationing.'

'Was Rose upset by that? The letters, I mean. I presume she was devastated about the cakes.'

'I think she was frustrated by him. It was clear from his letters that he wasn't in love with her, and she just wanted him to say that.'

'So that she could be free to be with you?'

Dora gathered up the photographs and put them back in the envelope. 'We didn't talk about the future. It upset us both too much to think that there might be a day when we'd have to part for good.'

Sarah swallowed the lump in her throat. 'Do you honestly not know why he left Rose?'

Dora smoothed her skirt and glanced out of the window. 'I don't. What I do know, was that marital relations were a struggle. For both of them. Rose confided in me that, on his rare visits home, he slept either in the spare room, or on the sofa. He also made a repetitive mention of a colleague called Stuart Smith in his letters. They seemed to spend much of their spare time together.'

Sarah's eyes widened. 'Do you think he left her for Stuart?'

Dora held up her hands. 'Whatever the reason, Rose didn't appear to hold it against him. She didn't seem angry or sad when she wrote to tell me he'd left her. If anything, she seemed relieved.'

'I guess we'll never know. I hope he was happy.'

'No, I don't suppose we will, and yes I hope he was, too.' Dora patted Sarah's knee. 'You've learnt a lot these past two days about your family. I hope it's not been overwhelming. For you, or for Janice.'

The clock on the wall chimed nine o'clock and Sarah glanced at it, frowning slightly. 'I'm going to have to go soon. And there is so much more I wanted to talk to you about. I want to know more about Bletchley Park, and what you did after the war.'

'After the accident and after leaving Janice in Dovecote, I went to London and met up with a chap I'd known at Bletchley. I was hired as a translator at the Nuremberg Trials. After the horrific things I heard there, and after a brief trip to New York to see my parents, I retreated to Zurich and then came to Alpensee. I started a ladies-only hiking club, which grew into a business offering guided hikes and suchlike. We trained a few women who climbed Everest. It's still going, although I retired from it many years ago. I can't be hiking up mountains at my age. I also developed my love of photography. I did alright at making a living.'

'Did you ever fall in love again?' Sarah asked with a soft smirk.

Dora blushed. 'A couple of times.'

'You never cease to amaze me, Dora. What a life you've had.'

'It's been quite the ride, that's for sure. But it's a shame you have to go. I haven't had a chance to get to know you.'

'Oh, you don't want to do that.'

'I do, Sarah, and I want to know who that rather hunky man you were with the other day is, and why I haven't met him.'

Sarah surprised herself with the sharp, bitter laugh that came out. 'Rob is technically my husband. Although I left him ten years ago when I ran away from Dovecote after my daughter's funeral.'

'Oh, Sarah, I am so sorry.'

'Faith was only three.' Sarah glanced at the envelope. 'The same age Mum was the day you saved her life on that train. Faith wasn't so lucky. Rob had taken her and my sister's little boy out to the Dovecote lighthouse. Faith died after falling and hitting her head on a rock. I left Dovecote full of grief and rage. I only came back last month because my dad made me promise to scatter his ashes into the sea. Which I still haven't been able to do. It's been exactly the disaster you'd expect. Rob and I can't keep our hands off each other. He still loves me, but I don't feel the same way. And... I think I might be falling for the woman I was having an affair with in the months leading up to Faith's accident.' She blinked away fresh tears. 'I was an awful wife, and a terrible mother.'

Dora laid a hand on Sarah's arm. 'Your grandmother and I had a similar conversation around Janice being evacuated. And she felt guilty about our relationship. But accidents happen and hearts lead us astray. Does Rob know about the woman you were seeing?'

Sarah's shoulders slumped. 'I told him yesterday. Carrying this secret had been wearing me down. I've tried to convince myself that I told him for his own good, to help him get over me. In reality, I think I wanted to hurt him. Even though it was a relief to let it out, I feel wretched for hurting him all over again.'

'You didn't ask for my advice, but I'm ninety-five years old; I give out advice whether it's wanted or not.' She pursed her lips, and Sarah held her breath, waiting for Dora to tell her something she didn't want to hear, but already knew in her heart. Dora's gaze softened. 'Talk to him, tell him the truth. Tell him you're struggling to forgive him, that you're sorry you hurt him, but you don't love him. Tell him you want him to move on.'

'How can I forgive him?'

'By forgiving yourself.'

Sarah glanced at the clock again. 'I have to go.'

'I'll send those photos as soon as I can.'

'Thank you, Dora, for giving us our lost family.' Sarah hugged Dora tightly.

'I'll see you again, Sarah,' Dora replied.

'I hope so.'

As she made her way down the road towards the lake, Sarah looked at her phone. Rob had sent her a text.

*We need to get the train at ten o'clock.*

Sarah paused at the edge of the lake. For the first time, she wanted to go back to Dovecote, so she could tell her mum everything she'd learnt that morning. But going back meant a very long journey with Rob. Was she ready to face him?

# FORTY

## ROSE

December 1944

They had said it would be over by now, but here we were. Another year on, and the war was still going. For ten months, I'd lived numbly from letter to letter, only coming alive when the next letter with a London postmark and a purple censor stamp, or a Carlisle postmark, arrived. I had to write back to Dora at a Foreign Office box number, so my letters were probably being censored too. Her letters were full of the hikes she'd been on, the food she was getting at her billet, the dances she'd been to. She never mentioned anything about her work. And she never declared her feelings to me, but I could see them in the stroke of her pen and the loops of her letters. I wrote back telling her the news I'd had from Carlisle about Janice, about all the milestones I was missing. The minute I heard about the doodlebugs falling all over south-east England, I knew Carlisle was still the best place for my baby. I longed to hold both my girls close, to listen to them breathing in their sleep.

As for my husband, the arrival of his letters filled me with dread. Purely because they reminded me of his existence. I didn't wish for anything to happen to him. But each time I unfolded the thin paper, I hoped he was writing to tell me he'd fallen in love with someone else. That would've been rather convenient. But he was going to come home, and I'd have to slip back into the role of his wife. He might even want another child. Having experienced the beauty of nights with Dora, and how right that felt, the idea of intimacy with him felt wrong, and left me cold.

As Christmas loomed once more, I couldn't be bothered with it. What was the point of going to the trouble of sourcing a tree and traipsing up to the loft to retrieve the decorations? No one was going to see it, except me. Even Maureen and Stan wouldn't be around. They were going to Maureen's widowed cousin in Norfolk, who had lost her son on D-Day. Uncle Douglas and Aunt Gladys would be having Christmas dinner at Bayview, at the invitation of Sister Margaret, as usual. I was severely lacking in festive cheer. At least I didn't have to scrabble around for ingredients for a Christmas dinner. A Woolton pie and some mashed potato would do me.

I decided that I'd close The Seaside Café on Thursday the 21st, and I wouldn't open again until the new year. Then I could burrow down in Pebble Cottage and be perfectly miserable. That morning, a telegram arrived, delivered to the café while I was idly flicking through an old copy of *Woman's Weekly*. I never received telegrams, and my hands quaked as I unfolded the yellow paper.

COMING HOME FOR CHRISTMAS STOP BRINGING
FRIEND STOP M STOP

It was a good job I was alone in the café as the word I uttered was not suitable for polite company.

.   .   .

I had to call in favours from all over Dovecote as I hadn't saved up coupons like in previous years. Even if I had, I couldn't have created a Christmas dinner for three adults. I promised fruit cakes in exchange for a few bottles of beer and a bottle of gin from Derek at The Royal Oak. I was immensely grateful for my little community that came through for each other in times of need. I presumed Martin's friend would be the Stuart Smith I had heard so much about. In a way, I was intrigued to meet him. I just hoped he was a nicer sort of friend than Martin's old Brighton pal, Brian. Even all these years on, I could still recall the look of downright hatred Brian gave me on our wedding day.

By the time the train whistle sounded on the afternoon of December 24th, Christmas was back on. There was a tree in the sitting room, bursting with lights and paper garlands. A record of Christmas carols was loaded onto the gramophone. The icebox was fuller than it had been in years. My hair was freshly curled and neatly pinned. I'd unearthed a box of powder and a lipstick from the bottom of a drawer. I plastered a smile on my face. It was only for a few days. And he was my husband; I should have been beside myself with excitement to see him for the first time in years. Perhaps he wouldn't want to share a bed, like he hadn't when he'd come home for Janice's christening. The tension in my shoulders abated.

Like the morning of Janice's christening, I positioned myself at the open front door of Pebble Cottage. It was already getting dark, but the dim-out, introduced back in September, meant that the lights along The Promenade shone again, albeit with shielding and dimmed bulbs. It made the path look as though it was illuminated by moonlight, the actual moon being obscured by thick cloud, and the faint light was better than nothing. Two things instantly struck me when Martin pushed open the front gate – his hairline had receded markedly, and Stuart Smith had very green eyes.

If Stuart was attempting to charm me, it was working. Immediately on being introduced, he produced tins of dried eggs and milk, and some tinned fruit. I hadn't seen a tinned pear in years. He completely won me over by presenting me with a small bar of chocolate, apparently from an American GI he'd run into one evening in a pub in Glasgow. He was a softly spoken man, with a slight London accent, thick dark hair, and those green eyes.

'Thank you so much, Rose, for letting me intrude,' he said, helping me clear the kitchen table and joining me at the sink after a supper of fried liver, carrots, and potatoes. Martin had taken his newspaper into the sitting room. 'I did tell Martin that I couldn't possibly accept his invitation, especially when he hasn't been home for so long. But he did insist.'

'That's quite alright, Stuart.' Any animosity I'd felt towards Martin for unexpectedly giving me an extra mouth to feed, had melted in Stuart's boyish smile. 'I don't like to ask, but...'

He shot me an endearing half-smile that was tinged with sadness. 'Mam and Dad were killed in the Blitz. I've volunteered to work every Christmas since, along with Martin. This year, when I was told I had to take leave' – he paused and shrugged – 'I realised I had nowhere to go.'

Thankfully, Stuart didn't notice the plate slipping from my hands and splashing into the soapy water in the sink. So, Martin could have come home for Christmas, but chose not to? It hurt that he'd not wanted to spend Christmas with Janice.

'You've no brothers or sisters? Or any other family?'

'One brother, but he's in a Japanese prisoner-of-war camp in Singapore. There's an uncle somewhere in the Midlands, but we're not in touch.'

I rubbed his arm gently. 'Oh, Stuart.' I could have cried for him, this quiet little soul. Then I sniffed, and poked my head into the sitting room.

'I thought you'd said you'd given up smoking, Martin

Wilton?' I crossed my arms tightly across my chest. Dash it, though, the cigarette held between his fingers did suit him. He was still a handsome man. I almost wished I could want him.

'I lasted a week. There's stuff-all else to do up in that godforsaken wasteland,' he replied, his brow furrowing deeply.

'He thinks it makes him look like a film star,' Stuart laughed from behind me. 'Rose, thank you for a delicious Christmas Eve supper. If you're not careful, we'll bring you back up to Scotland with us. You'd improve morale no end with dinners like that. If you will excuse me, I'll go up to my room and get out of your way. I'm sure you have a lot to catch up on.'

'There's no need. Honestly,' I spluttered. Martin gave him a look that I couldn't quite interpret, but then turned back to his newspaper.

'I have an excellent book I'm keen to return to. And you haven't seen your husband in a very long time, Rose. Don't let me keep you from him for a minute more. Goodnight.'

'Goodnight, Stuart,' I said as he climbed the stairs. I sat down next to Martin on the sofa, and he put his paper down. His deep-brown eyes had lost their youthful sparkle and there were fine lines radiating from their corners. 'I like him. I'm glad you've made a nice friend.'

Martin glanced at the stairs. 'Yes. It makes it much easier to bear.'

'Is it really awful? You don't say much about it in your letters.'

'It's cold, it rains constantly, and the hut we work in leaks. My billet's not too bad, but it's not home. And I've not had a decent pint in years.' He looked at me and gave me a crooked smile. 'And you're not there.' I had the feeling I was very much an afterthought. 'How are things at the café? Making profit?'

'Just about. Business has been slow the last year or so. I think everyone's just a little fed up and the shortages are biting. I'm down to only serving teacakes, the occasional ginger loaf, and eggless sponges. It's all rather grim, but I think people like to come in for a chat and to see a smiling face as much as they do for refreshments. And that I can always give.'

'I'm proud of you, Rose.' He lightly kissed my nose. That was as much contact as I wanted. But I couldn't let him know that. Even so, I wasn't about to throw myself at him. 'How's Janice?' He'd been home for hours and that was the first time he'd asked about his daughter.

I pursed my lips. 'She's well. Growing like a weed, so I've heard. Her host family sent us a Christmas card from her.' Martin glanced at the mantelpiece, but made no move to get up to look. I swallowed my frustration. It was one thing being cold towards me, but Janice was his baby girl. He should have been dying to see her name on the little card. 'She's safe, that's the main thing. I was thinking of getting her sent home, but then those V-1 bombs started, and I just couldn't.' Martin simply nodded. I needed a drink. 'I got a bottle of gin. Do you fancy one?'

'Actually, I'm quite tired.'

'Right, we can turn in if you want?' Was he after an early night or an 'early night'? I really could have done with that gin.

'Rose, if you don't want me in the bed with you, I understand.'

I shook my head so vigorously I gave myself a headache. 'No, no. Martin, it's our bed. It always has been, and it always will be.' I was going to go to hell, lying to him like that. Dora and I had slept together in my bed for months.

'I don't know if I'd be able to sleep, love. I'm used to being on my own, and I'm sure you are, too.'

'Well, yes. I suppose I am.' Another lie. My bed had felt cold and empty since Dora's departure back in February. 'Whatever you want. But Stuart is in the spare room and Janice's cot is still in the box room, and takes up most of it.'

'Sofa's fine for me.' He pushed down on the cushion. 'More comfortable than my bunk in Scotland.'

'Won't Stuart think it's strange?'

'If he does, he's too damned polite to mention it.'

I got up from the sofa and smoothed out my skirt. 'I'll leave you to get some rest. You've had a long journey.' At the foot of the stairs, I turned back. 'Don't go picking at anything in the kitchen; it's all for Christmas Day dinner tomorrow.'

'Night, Rose.'

'Goodnight, Martin.'

Up in my room, I flopped down on my bed and let out a long, relieved breath. From under my pillow, I withdrew the Christmas card Dora had sent me. On the front was a photograph of an ornate mansion with a tall tree outside. I opened it.

*Dearest Rose,*

*Even if the well runs dry, we'll always have tea. Merry Christmas.*

*Love, Dora*

I kissed her name and clasped the card to my chest.

'I love you,' I whispered.

Christmas Day passed in a flash. By the time we'd gone to church, had lunch, and listened to the King's Speech, it was already dark, so we cracked open the gin. Stuart and Martin had drunk the bottles of beer with dinner. Stuart produced a deck of cards and proceeded to trounce me and Martin at rummy around the kitchen table. In my defence, I was knocking back the gin and having trouble focusing on the cards in my hand.

Despite the coolness between me and Martin, the day was rather jolly.

'This is getting embarrassing,' Stuart declared, gathering up the cards once more. 'You must think I had a terribly misspent youth, Rose.'

I giggled. Pebble Cottage hadn't heard me laugh since Dora had left. 'Not at all. Did you?'

His smile crinkled the skin around his eyes. 'Yes.' He stifled a yawn. 'I'm done in.' He got up from the kitchen table and kissed my cheek lightly. 'Thank you for a wonderful Christmas, Rose.'

'Oh, you're welcome. I'm only sorry there weren't presents. Had I been given more notice, I could have rustled you up a pair of gloves to match Martin's that are waiting for him back up in Scotland.' I'd already posted them before I got his telegram.

'Your delightful company and excellent cooking are more than enough.' He placed a firm hand on Martin's shoulder. 'Goodnight.'

'Goodnight, Stuart.' I gathered up the empty glasses and carried them to the sink. Martin moved into the sitting room. I wiped down the countertop and flicked off the light. 'Are you coming up tonight?' I asked.

He looked at me for a long moment and then averted his eyes. I couldn't help but feel a little rejected. I knew why I didn't want him, but why didn't he want me? Maybe he *had* met someone else.

'I'll just have another cigarette,' he said, eventually.

I kissed his cheek. 'It's up to you.'

He patted my hand.

Later, lying in bed, I heard the back door open. Martin, going out for some fresh air. The door clicked again a short time later. My heart leapt into my mouth when I heard footsteps on the stairs. I waited with bated breath for my bedroom door to open – but instead, I heard the door across the landing creak.

Martin was going into Stuart's room. What on earth could he need to speak to Stuart about that couldn't wait until the morning? I tried to listen, but tiredness overtook me, and I fell sound asleep.

The following morning, something made me pause at the top of the stairs before coming down. I peered through the banisters. Martin hadn't opened the curtains yet, and the sitting room was gloomy. But I could just about make out two figures embracing. I bent down a little further to get a better look, barely breathing.

I clamped a hand over my mouth and crept back into my bedroom. How had I missed the signs? I remembered the creaking stairs and bedroom door the night before. Suddenly, it all made sense. A bubble of excitement burst in my chest. Not the normal reaction a wife might have to catching her husband kissing a man, granted. But I wasn't a normal wife, and I had a deep suspicion that our marriage wasn't normal either. If he and Stuart...

I caught myself before I got carried away. It didn't mean any more than what I had done with Dora, not in terms of the future. After the war, we'd have to go back to putting on a show of being a happily married couple. That was what was expected of us, especially with a child to bring up. The authorities might take Janice away if they found out. But still... Maybe it didn't mean anything to Martin. Maybe it was just – what had Betty said? Any port in a storm? Dash it, they were leaving together; I'd have no time to say anything to Martin. I chewed my fingernail. This made everything more confusing. I couldn't think. I gathered myself together. I had to go and bid them both goodbye, and then I'd ponder what to do.

'Rose, there you are.' Stuart greeted me with a huge smile. Was there something else behind his easy-going compliments? Was he entirely genuine? How could he come into my home, knowing he was... I pushed those thoughts away, wanting to believe he was a sincere man. But what was Martin playing at? My thoughts bumped around my head as I smiled back. If they could put on an act, so could I.

'Do you really have to go so soon? I feel as though you've only just arrived.'

'We're on the early shift tomorrow,' Martin said.

Stuart glanced between us. 'I'll say my goodbyes and leave you to yours. Thank you again, Rose, for taking in this stray. It has been lovely to finally meet you. Martin talks about you all the time.' That was probably a lie.

'It has been my pleasure, Stuart.' Had it? 'I hear a lot about you, too. It is nice to put a face to a name. Have a safe journey, and you are welcome any time.' Now who was lying?

He closed the front door of Pebble Cottage behind him, and I was left alone with my husband. I scrutinised his face for any trace of what he was thinking. He was giving nothing away.

'Well, here we are,' he said.

'Yes, saying goodbye again.'

'I don't think it will be much longer. It has to be over soon. Our boys seem to have the upper hand now. It feels like the beginning of the end.'

'Yes.' I really didn't want to discuss the war. I wanted to ask him if he was in love with Stuart Smith. What would he do if I kissed him? There was only one way to find out. He returned my kiss. Briefly.

'I can't miss the train,' he said, stepping away from me.

'No.'

'It will all be fine once I'm home for good, Rose. And once Janice is home. We can be a proper family then. And if you wanted another baby... Well, we'll see.'

Was it my imagination or did his words sound forced? My pulse thundered in my ears. It would take a few cups of tea to settle my nerves once he was gone. I was too confused to do anything other than nod. 'Stay safe, won't you?'

'I will.'

The minute the door closed behind him I collapsed down on the sofa, my head in my hands. I let out a long, relieved breath. I just had to put it all out of my head. There was no point trying to work it out. It was no use thinking about what might or might not happen. I just had to wait and see. There had to be a solution with which both Martin and I would be happy. I could only hope that it would present itself to me, and that I'd be brave enough to accept it when it did.

# FORTY-ONE

## SARAH

May 2017

The late morning sun flooded the train carriage on the journey down the mountain. Once the stunning vistas of valleys, viaducts, forests, and cute halt stations had been replaced by the urban buildings of Chur, Sarah turned away from the train carriage window. She and Rob hadn't exchanged a single word. Part of her wished he'd done a runner the night before and hot-footed it back to Dovecote without her, or that she could afford to stay on another night and pay for a new flight. But they were stuck together, for a few hours at least.

'I went back to see Dora again earlier this morning,' she said. He raised an eyebrow, but said nothing. 'You were partially right. Dora and Rose were lovers. They were together while Martin was stationed away.'

Rob pursed his lips. 'I guess it runs in the family.'

Sarah raised her eyes from her hands to Rob's face at the venom in his voice. 'Sorry?'

'Cheating on your husband.'

'I... Um.' She closed her mouth. She had no comeback for that.

'Actually, I take that back. If Rose was trapped in a loveless marriage, having to hide her sexuality, then I feel for her. I'm glad she got the chance to love and be loved. I'm happy for her that she got to be her true self.'

The rest of what he meant went unsaid, and Sarah looked back out of the window as Rob stuck his headphones in his ears. A busy train carriage was not the place to point out that she had felt as trapped as Rose had. Sarah's bisexuality didn't come into it. No matter who she'd found to be a shelter from their stormy relationship, no matter who had given her the care and tenderness she'd needed, she would have probably still done what she did.

Once through security at Zurich airport, they went their separate ways – Sarah to the souvenir shop, Rob to the bar. Maybe she could have a word with the person at the gate and see if she could change her seat on the plane. She went to the allocated gate, having picked up a cow-shaped sugar sachet holder and a cow-adorned tea towel for Janice, and boxes of Swiss chocolate for Daphne and Heather. Rob was already there, giving the full charm offensive to the blonde lady behind the counter. He bobbed his head in Sarah's direction, hurt still clouding his eyes, and sat down as far away from her as possible. He'd beaten her to it, then. She buried her head in her book, but the words drifted in front of her eyes as guilt gnawed at her. She hadn't wanted to break him.

At Gatwick, Rob stood at the far end of the luggage carousel, keeping the rest of the passengers from their flight between them. He did the same on the Gatwick train station platform, and at Brighton train station.

It wasn't until they both alighted at Dovecote that they

found themselves occupying the same physical space. Sarah found that this time, the shrill call of the seagulls and the soft lapping of the waves on the pebbly beach didn't grate on her nerves. If she wasn't ecstatic at seeing The Promenade, The Seaside Café, and the lighthouse, the view didn't fan any sort of anger. Could it be that her feelings towards Dovecote were shifting? No, even though the weight of carrying her secret was gone, the town was still haunted by her daughter's ghost, as well as the memory of every wrong thing she'd ever done. Dovecote was still a mirror being held up to her that she was forced to look in, and she didn't like her reflection.

'Rob.' She dug her hands into her pockets. 'I just wanted to say thank you for everything. I couldn't have done all that without your help.' She scuffed the concrete of the station concourse with the toe of her boot. 'I appreciate it.'

'Sure.' He didn't move away. He was giving her a chance to say something else. Sarah chewed the inside of her cheek. Just as he looked like he was going to give up on her, she finally spoke.

'And I'm sorry.' She couldn't look at him, so she kept her eyes firmly on the pavement. 'I'm so sorry for all the lies, for letting you down, and for all the times I picked a fight when I should have just told you how I was feeling. And I'm sorry for blaming you for Faith's accident, and for lying about where I was that day.' She glanced up briefly, to see his face soften a fraction.

Was that the first time he'd heard her refer to what happened to Faith as an accident? If she accepted that Faith's death was an accident, then did that mean she no longer blamed Rob? Had she ever really believed it had been his fault? Or had she held onto that to shield herself from her own guilt? Dora had advised forgiveness. She could forgive Rob; but would she ever forgive herself?

There was more she needed to say, so she drew a breath and

ploughed on. 'I should have been there, and I should have been there for you in the aftermath. I should have let you be there for me, too. I made a mess of everything then, and I did it again when I came back. As soon as my van is fixed, I'll be leaving again, and I won't be coming back. You'll get the closure you need, and you can move on with your life. I'm sorry you've wasted so much time on me. I'll leave a forwarding address for the divorce papers, obviously.' She looked up to see Rob running his hand through his hair.

He puffed out his cheeks. 'I'll get Kev to let you know about the van.'

'Thanks. Bye, then.' She caught a waft of his aftershave on the sea wind, and for the briefest of moments, she could have thrown herself at him, just one last time. Thankfully, he walked away before she could. It would not have helped. With a sigh, she set off down The Promenade, dragging her suitcase behind her.

She did a double take as she passed the large front window of The Seaside Café, and gasped as she pushed open the door.

'Mum! You're back at work.' Janice was behind the counter, still leaning on a crutch. 'Are you sure you should be?'

'Sarah! Welcome back. I got bored at home and I had to make a batch of sticky buns before there was a riot. I've not managed a whole day, and I'm kept under observation.'

Natasha emerged from the kitchen, already in her yellow raincoat with her pink handbag hanging from the crook of her elbow. 'Don't worry, Sarah. I'm keeping a close eye on her. Did you have a nice time in Switzerland with Rob?' Sarah raised an eyebrow at her mum. Natasha headed for the door. 'Right, Janice, I'll head off. See you tomorrow.'

As the door closed, Janice gave Sarah a small smile. 'Sorry, love. It just slipped out. You know what I'm like. I've not said anything to anyone outside the family, though. Even *I* know when to keep my mouth shut.' The bell above the café door tinkled before Sarah could reprimand her mother. Daphne barrelled in, closing the door firmly to stop Treacle sticking her snout in.

'Stay!' Daphne commanded and Treacle retreated, taking up a guard position under the window, from where she could keep an eye on the seagulls. 'Hi, Sarah.'

'Hi. How have things been here?' She nodded towards Janice and lowered her voice. 'Is Mum okay?'

'Surprisingly calm about the whole thing, actually. Did you find out anything more?'

Sarah nodded. 'Mum, come and sit down for a minute.'

Janice hobbled over and sank into a chair.

'I think you're overdoing it, Mum,' Daphne scolded as she sat down next to her.

'Daphne, I'm seventy-five. I'd be tired even if I didn't have a bad ankle. But I'm not giving up the café. It's the only thing I have that gets me out of the house. Sarah, why do you look like you're about to drop a bombshell?'

'Do I? Sorry.' There was no need to be anxious; her mother was an ally. She'd never batted an eyelid about Sarah, and she'd forgiven Neil for leaving her for Pete. Hadn't she? Sarah relaxed her face. 'I went back to see Dora again this morning. There was something she didn't say on our call, because she wasn't sure how it would be received.' She glanced from her mother to her sister. 'I was curious about the relationship between Rose and Dora. The photograph we found of them kissing suggested to me that there was more than a friendship going on. Dora confirmed that she and Rose were lovers.'

'Well, I suppose with Martin away, Rose needed someone,' Daphne said, fiddling with the carnation in the bud vase on the table.

'No, it wasn't like that. Dora explained that Rose had

always felt that she and Martin didn't really fit together, that there was something broken between them. But it wasn't until Dora kissed Rose one evening that Rose realised why she disliked physical intimacy with Martin, and that it wasn't him, but her. The real reason why Dora sent that postcard asking Rose to meet her in London was because they were in love. It feels like a weird thing to be telling you Mum, but your mum was a lesbian.'

'Well, I never,' Janice laughed.

'You're not upset are you, Mum?' Daphne reached over and took Janice's hand.

'Oh Daphne, don't be daft. Honestly.' Janice chuckled. 'You girls forget that I lived through the sixties. There's not much that can shock me. Why on earth would I be upset? Good for her, I say. It's a shame it was cut short, along with her life, but I'm glad she found love.'

'It's lovely to know she was happy. But I feel for poor Martin,' Daphne said with a sigh.

'Martin had already left Rose by the time Dora sent the postcard. It wasn't as if she stole Rose from him. We don't know if he even knew about Dora,' Sarah added.

'Does Dora know anything more about why Martin left Rose?' Janice asked.

Sarah drew a deep breath. 'No. But she remembered Rose had said that Martin mentioned a certain friend, Stuart Smith, a lot in his letters. Dora hinted that she wouldn't be surprised if there had been something going on between Martin and Stuart.'

Janice raised an eyebrow. 'It happens, we all know that.' The silence was broken by Janice getting up and going back behind the café counter. She rearranged the cups on top of the coffee machine and fiddled with the cake tongs.

'Are you okay, Mum?' Sarah asked softly. Maybe she shouldn't have said anything about Martin and Stuart. Of course it would have triggered the memory of what had happened with her own husband. 'It might not have been that. It might have been another woman, or something else entirely. We'll never know for sure.'

Janice put down the tongs she was holding. 'It was a long time ago. I don't hold any of this against any of them. Mum and Dad, or Rose and Martin. It was a different time, and it sounds like they all did what they did because they thought it was for the best.'

Daphne pushed back her chair. 'I have to go and get Jake from football. Will you be okay getting Mum home, Sarah?'

Sarah didn't take her eyes off her mother as she nodded, and Daphne left the café. She reached into her tote bag for Dora's book.

'Dora signed the book of her exhibition for you,' she said, placing the book on the table. 'There are some lovely photographs of Dovecote in it. And of Rose.'

'Are there any of me?' Janice twisted a tea towel in her hands as she came back to the table and sat down next to Sarah.

Sarah swallowed and nodded. 'Yes. There's one of you the day you were evacuated to Carlisle.' She flicked through the book to the relevant page.

'Oh,' Janice said softly, tracing the line of Rose's face with her finger. 'She's crying.' There was a slight wobble in Janice's voice and Sarah gave her hand a quick squeeze.

'She loved you, Mum. She really did. Dora said how much it hurt her to send you away, and Maureen said how besotted she was with you. But she did it to keep you safe. I think that shows how much she cared. She was a good mother who did everything she could to keep you safe. I wish I could say the same about Faith.'

Janice drew a sharp breath. 'You were a wonderful mum, Sarah. God, I didn't know you thought you weren't. It was an accident, love. No one was to blame.'

Sarah glanced back at the open book. 'I think I might be beginning to believe that, but it will take time.'

Janice took Sarah's hand in hers; her skin was soft and warm. 'Tell me more about Rose.'

Sarah puffed out a breath, relieved that her mother had changed the subject. 'She was incredible, Mum. She ran the café, and she raised you, all on her own. The world kept throwing stuff at her and she just kept going. She was strong, independent, loving, and caring. Just like you.'

'And you,' Janice whispered.

Sarah focused on the photograph on the page in front of her. If she looked up at her mum, she wouldn't be able to hold back the tears bubbling in her throat. Outside the café, the waves swished against the pebbles on Dovecote beach. For the first time in years, Sarah breathed in time to their rhythm. Dora was right: the only way to move forward was to forgive.

# FORTY-TWO

## ROSE

January 1945

Getting stuck back into running The Seaside Café and dealing with the associated rules and regulations was exactly what I needed to forget all about Martin, Stuart, and Dora. Well, I didn't want to forget about Dora, I just wanted to forget how much I was missing her – and Janice, too. I still lived for Dora's letters. She always had a funny story, usually about the men in her hiking group, who insisted on leading and then getting lost. I hoped they weren't in charge of mobilising troops across Europe. Our boys would never get to Berlin if that were the case.

Reg Harris was back, in his pinstripe suit and trilby. I'd not seen him around Dovecote for a few months and had hoped he'd been arrested. He'd taken to slouching against the railings on The Promenade, smoking endless cigarettes and watching the café. A cold shiver ran up my spine as he stubbed out his cigarette, touched his trilby, and gave me a nod. I turned away to hide my sneer. He gave me the creeps. He was a criminal, preying on desperate, vulnerable people. Thankfully, Reg was shoved out of my head when Betty swept into the café. I'd not seen her since before Christmas. Her shifts at Brighton Municipal Hospital had kept her busy. Today, she wasn't in uniform.

'Hi, Rose.'

'Betty! Look at you.' She gave me a twirl, and her fur coat fanned out around her. 'That's not real, is it?' Her bright red painted lips twitched. I stepped out from behind the counter and ran my hand along the sleeve.

'No, but it looks it.'

'Where on earth did you get it, Betty?'

'I bought it,' she said, looking away slightly.

'Be serious,' I said. 'You can't buy these, even fake ones. The coupons alone would be ridiculous, never mind the cost.'

'I bought it off Reg Harris.' Her voice was small, and she looked down at the floor.

'Oh, Betty! He's a crook. Whatever possessed you?'

'I've not had anything new for years.' There were tears in her eyes. 'Since Alf Crawford threw me over on New Year's Eve, I've been so down. I needed something to cheer me up.'

'But a fur coat? Betty, it's not stolen, is it?'

'Of course not. Reg said a rich old man exchanged it for a new sofa that Reg had knocking about.' Betty thrust her hands into the coat pockets and when she pulled them out, she had a small piece of paper between her fingers. She looked up at me; her eyes were brimming now. 'Sharp's Dry Cleaners, Brighton,' she read. 'That rat! I'll kill him.'

'What are you on about?'

'Sharp's Dry Cleaners were done over in an armed robbery last week. One of the nurses at Brighton Municipal was telling me the other day. Her uncle owned it. They shot him dead.'

'Oh, Betty.'

'I should have known not to trust that snake.'

I grimaced. 'How much did he charge you?'

'Twelve pounds.' Betty looked very sheepish.

'Twelve pounds? Betty, that's a whole month's salary.'

'It was supposed to be twenty, but he took money off in exchange for...well, you know.' She started to cry, and I wrapped my arms around her. 'I just wanted something nice. Is that too much to ask?'

'There, there. It's not the end of the world. And it *is* a very nice coat.' I handed her a handkerchief, and she dabbed her eyes.

'Do I look awful?' Betty sniffed.

I shook my head. 'You're as beautiful as ever. Do you need a cuppa?'

'No, I'd better be getting on. I'm on night shift.'

'Stay away from Reg Harris and his gang. This war won't go on forever. We'll all be able to have nice things soon. And we won't have to do... You won't have to associate with despicable men like Reg Harris.'

'Do you think very badly of me?'

I tilted my head to one side. 'Of course not. But please don't do things that will make me worry about you.' Betty squeezed my hand and walked out of the café, her head held slightly less high than usual. Poor girl.


The café was very quiet a few days later. No one was venturing out in the cold and drizzle. I was startled when the bell above the door tinkled.

'Be with you in a moment,' I said, not looking up from the ginger loaf I was slicing thinly, to get as many portions out of it as I could.

'No rush, darling.'

I recognised that accent. My mouth went dry. I held onto the knife as I looked up to find Reg Harris leaning against the counter, a smirk on his lips and an evil glint in his eye.

'Reg.'

'Alright, Rose?'

'I was very well until you walked in. What are you doing here?'

'Can't I come in and get a cup of tea like everyone else?'

The memory of Betty's tear-stained face loomed in my head. 'No. I reserve the right to refuse to serve whomever I want.'

'Blimey, who rubbed you up the wrong way?' He leant over the counter. I could smell his cigarette breath. 'Or is that the problem? You not getting what you need, Rose?'

I shrank back. 'Go away, Reg.'

He glanced over his shoulder. 'Nah, don't reckon I will.'

'I'm not scared of you.' Dash and blast, I'd dropped the knife.

He took a cigarette out of a – no doubt stolen – silver case, and put it between his teeth. 'Not seen that girlfriend of yours in a while. The German spy.'

My heart began to pound. 'I don't know who you mean.' I hated that there was a tremor in my voice.

'Yeah, you do,' Reg sneered, taking out a book of matches and striking one. He still didn't light his cigarette. 'I could have you nicked for fraternising with the enemy.'

'And I could have you arrested for selling a stolen fur coat to Betty Jones.'

His grin made my skin crawl. 'I didn't steal it. I found it. There's a subtle difference.'

'If you say so. I am *not* fraternising with the enemy.' Thank God Dora wasn't around to hear this. It would upset her so much. I would have loved to tell Reg that she was doing vital top secret government work, while he hocked stolen goods out of the back of a van outside Victoria Park. That would have shut him up.

'Give it a rest. I've seen you, ain't I? Walking down The Promenade, arm in arm, looking right pally. I reckon you're one of them lesbians. It's not right, that kind of behaviour, not right at all.' He finally lit the cigarette. The smoke caught in my throat, but I willed myself not to cough and tried to still my shaking hands. I couldn't let on that he was right about Dora and me. God knows what he'd do.

'I'll ask you to leave one more time, Reg, before I summon the police.'

He smiled like a crocodile. 'I'll leave when you agree to have a drink with me at The Royal Oak tonight.'

'You'll be waiting a long time, then. Go on, get out of here before you bring my establishment into disrepute.'

He slammed his fist down on the counter. I let out a yelp when he grabbed my wrist and pulled me towards him. 'No one turns down Reg Harris. You hear me?' he snarled. 'You best be at The Royal Oak at eight o'clock tonight, or you'll be sorry.' At that moment, I heard the back door open. Out of the corner of my eye, I saw Stan's large bulk in the kitchen. He'd come to pick up the scrap paper donations I'd been collecting. I gathered every ounce of strength I could and looked Reg right in the eyes.

'There are two very good reasons why I will not be at The Royal Oak with you tonight, or any other night. Firstly, I'm a married woman. And secondly, you're a filthy spiv who robs bombed-out houses and sells stolen goods on the black market. You'd rob your own grandmother if you could make a shilling out of it. You're a despicable, greedy coward and I have no desire to be seen in your company.'

Stan loomed out of the kitchen. 'You best be letting go of this young lady,' he said, making a move towards Reg.

Reg glanced up at Stan and back at me. I could see him deliberating. He let go of my wrist.

Stan's presence gave me the courage to raise my voice. 'For the last time, get out of my café. And don't come back.'

At the door, he turned and jabbed a finger in my direction. 'You'll be sorry. You mark my words, my girl. You're going to be proper sorry that you called *me* a coward.' The force with which he slammed the door rattled the glass.

I massaged my wrist. 'Good timing. Thanks Stan.'

'I'm just glad you're okay. What did he want with you anyway, Rose?'

I sighed. 'Probably money.' Reg Harris's sort wouldn't think twice about blackmailing someone. Well, he had no proof that Dora and I were anything other than friends. 'I know he's got his eye on the café. He's tried offering me special deals on stocks of tea and flour before. I've turned him down, of course. I'd rather go out of business than use his services. Maybe he thought he could flirt his way in. Hopefully that will be the last we see of him.'

'I'll come by at three and walk you home. Just in case he's hanging around.'

'Thanks, Stan, I'd appreciate that.' I glanced back out at The Promenade. Reg's threat to make me sorry rang in my head. Thank goodness Janice and Dora were safely out of harm's way. For the first time since Martin and I had come to Dovecote, it wasn't only bombs I feared.

# FORTY-THREE

## SARAH

May 2017

Sarah paused outside Pebble Cottage as Janice unlocked the front door. In the twilight, the white paint had a lavender hue. What had Rose and Dora thought of the cottage the first time they'd seen it? Had it felt like home to them?

Stepping into the sitting room, Sarah glanced up at the beams crossing the low ceiling. Those beams had witnessed so much. She could see Rose's spindly Christmas tree and almost hear Dora's laughter. The cottage also held memories of her own childhood, and her daughter's short life, too. Their voices were amongst the cacophony of layers of history. This house was part of something bigger. It had been home to so many people, known and unknown. It had been her home too – perhaps the last place that had felt truly like one.

The sound of a boiling kettle roused Sarah from her thoughts, and she went into the kitchen to find Janice sitting at the round pine table, her chin in her hand and a frown on her forehead.

'Something on your mind, Mum?' Sarah took over making

the tea and then reached into her duty-free bag. 'I brought this back for you. They had them on the tables in a lovely little café for holding packs of sugar and I immediately thought of you.' She handed Janice the cow holder. It was black and white with a red map of Switzerland on its side and a red cow bell around its neck. Janice turned it over in her hand.

'It's fabulous. Thank you, love. I'll put it on the windowsill at the café.' She tapped on the table a few times. 'I'm sure I know the name Stuart Smith,' she said suddenly, making Sarah jump.

'Martin's friend? It's not an uncommon name. Maybe you knew someone with that name at school, or when you were in London.'

'No, it's something to do with Pebble Cottage. I'm sure of it. Why can't I remember? Your father would have known; he was good with names.'

'Speaking of Dad,' Sarah said.

'He's still upstairs. I went in and said hello while you were away. Didn't want him to get lonely.'

'You did?' Sarah chewed her lip. What *was* the best thing to do with his ashes? Every time she asked herself that question, she changed her mind. 'Can I ask you something?'

'About Neil?'

'Why don't you talk about what happened between you? Or why you didn't keep in touch with him?'

Janice wrapped her hands around her mug. 'Neil and I should never have got married, Sarah. That's not to say I didn't love him, I really did. And he thought he loved me too. When I fell pregnant with Daphne, he didn't hesitate for a second about "doing the right thing". We got along so well. We had fun together and we made each other laugh. He worked hard, and so did I. But the cracks began to show not long after we moved back to Dovecote. He became a little distant, and didn't seem to mind being away for long periods of time with his work on the railways. We saw very little of each other for years, and when he did come home, it was like he'd built a brick wall around himself, that I couldn't get over, or through.'

Sarah thought for a moment. It sounded very like how Dora had described Rose and Martin's marriage. 'But if that was the case, then how did I ...'

Janice puffed out her cheeks. 'I would never say that you were an accident, Sarah. No child should ever be told that. But, you were unexpected, and I think probably the product of too much Christmas spirit.'

'Fair enough. Did you suspect he was gay?'

'Not in a million years. It crossed my mind that he might have had another woman somewhere, but I couldn't believe that. He was too good a person. Of course, looking back, all the signs were there. But I was quite a naïve, sheltered thing, having been brought up at the vicarage, so I didn't see them. The turning point was when he came home after a couple of months working in Stockport and broke down. He said he'd tried so hard to make himself love me and to be a good husband. He also told me about the men he'd met and how, when he was out in gay bars or clubs, he felt like he belonged. He confessed he and a very special man, called Pete, had fallen in love with each other. Well, what could I say to that? I had to either force him to stay with me, and you girls, and make him miserable, or let him go. To do anything other than let him go would have been monstrous.' There was compassion in Janice's eyes, but Sarah could see there was pain too.

'Oh, Mum.' She reached for her mother's hand. 'That must have broken your heart.'

'I'm not going to lie, it wasn't easy. But I couldn't stop him from being who he was. If I'd made him stay, he would have only kept seeing Pete secretly, and that wouldn't have been fair on anyone.'

'You never met Pete, did you?'

Janice drew a deep breath. 'Your father offered to introduce us, but I said no. There was no sense in muddying the waters. It was better that he had a clean break. What is Pete like?'

'Pete is brilliant. He's funny to the point of being eccentric. He's quite camp. He has a vicious tongue, but also a heart of solid gold. He'd do anything for anyone. When Dad became sick, he looked after him so well.'

'Were they happy together?'

'They really were.' Sudden tears fell from Sarah's eyes, and she grabbed a tissue from the box on the table. 'Dad was so grateful that you allowed him to live his life, but he also felt guilty about hurting you, and he missed us. I think that's why he wanted me to come and tell you he was sorry.'

'We should have kept in touch. We could have been good friends. But it was a different time then, and we thought it best to cut all contact.'

Sarah didn't let go of Janice's hand. 'He regretted not making the effort to see us, especially as times changed. You would have let him see us, wouldn't you?'

'Of course I would. But I left it up to you girls. You were so young when he left that you adapted easily. Daphne was more aware of what was going on and she was angry. She never forgave him for leaving.'

'It's hard to forgive when you're blinded by anger. I'll make sure to have a chat with her and tell her that our dad never stopped loving us both.'

Janice gave Sarah's hand a squeeze. 'I think that would be good for her to hear. Now, I still can't get Stuart Smith out of my mind. Let me think.'

'I'm going upstairs to unpack. Shout if you need anything.'


Up in her room, a shiver ran down Sarah's spine as she looked around, as if seeing the room for the first time. This had been

Dora's room. It was this room that Rose came to the night she realised who she was and told Dora she'd awakened something in her. A whistle of wind from the fireplace drew Sarah's attention to the pinboard hanging on the chimney breast. One of the photos still pinned to the board was of her and Heather, in their nineties vest tops and baggy cargo trousers. Sarah's dark brown hair, which she hadn't yet dyed black and purple, was pulled back from her face in a tight ponytail, just like Sporty Spice. Heather's afro had been teased into Scary-Spice-inspired space buns. They couldn't have been much older than thirteen. Like Rose, it was in this room that Sarah had come to understand who she was and who she loved. She put down the photo and picked up her phone.

She'd just finished writing a text when she heard the creak and click of her mother's crutch on the stairs. She poked her head out of her door. Janice was heading for the tiny box room.

'What are you up to now, Mum?'

'Come with me. I think I remember who Stuart Smith is. But I want to check.'

Sarah followed her into the box room, closing the door behind them. 'I can't believe this used to be my bedroom,' she said. 'It's barely big enough for a single bed.' It was true. The bed was still there, but there were boxes and odds and ends piled up on it.

'Welcome to my filing system.' Janice swept her arm over the small room. 'Believe it or not, I do know where everything is. Now.' She looked around and pointed her crutch at a battered old filing cabinet squashed in between the bed and a dressing table. 'Bottom drawer. There should be a folder labelled "Pebble Cottage". It's the paperwork from when your dad and I bought this place – and the café.' Sarah wiggled the drawer until it slid out. Inside, she found a yellow foolscap document wallet. It was very clearly Neil's handwriting on the front.

Janice moved a box so she could sit on the bed, and

rummaged in the folder before holding up a bundle of papers. 'Here we go. I knew it. I *knew* I remembered his name. Here, look.' Sarah took the paper, and her eyes widened.

'You and Dad bought the cottage from Stuart Smith?'

'In 1975. And the café, too.'

Sarah gasped and looked up at her mother. It was enticing to think this was evidence that proved Dora's theory. 'What are you thinking, Mum?'

'That this Stuart Smith is Martin's Stuart Smith?'

'Wow. Let's think this through.' Sarah took a deep breath and frowned as she thought out loud. 'Martin and Rose owned Pebble Cottage and the café in the 1940s, right? Actually, I wonder if it was only in Martin's name. Maureen said he'd inherited it from his parents. Then in 1945, or thereabouts, Martin runs off with Stuart, leaving Rose, never to return to Dovecote again.'

Janice nodded. 'Sounds about right.'

'He would have still owned the cottage and the café, though. Maybe he intended to sign it over to Rose, but she died before he could.'

'Do we even know that he knew she'd died?'

Sarah chewed her thumbnail as she considered that. 'No, but it probably doesn't matter. Martin and Stuart stay together. Then Martin dies, leaving everything to Stuart, including the cottage and the café.'

Janice took up the story. 'And then in 1975, Stuart sells them to a couple of youngsters with a small child at a very cheap price, because they're pretty much derelict.' Janice fiddled with the chain of her reading glasses. 'The café wasn't too bad. It just needed a good clean and redecoration. Violet Cooper used to come and help me. We spent weeks up to our elbows in soapy water.'

'What state was Pebble Cottage in?' Sarah asked.

Janice laughed. 'Put it this way: you could tell no one had

lived in it since the war. There was even an old Anderson shelter in the back garden. We had to throw out all the curtains and carpets, they were so dusty and decrepit. Some of the furniture was good though, like the kitchen table and the sideboard. We had to get new beds and new sitting room furniture. There was a gramophone that unfortunately we couldn't keep due to the family of mice living in it. The old wireless set that's on the shelf downstairs was left here. It doesn't work, but I've always liked the look of it. There was a baby's cot in the box room, but something about it gave me the shivers, so we threw it out.' Janice's hand flew to her mouth. 'Oh my God. It was *my* cot. No wonder it made me feel funny.' She looked around. 'We didn't find any personal items, though. No clothes, or letters, or things like that.'

'I suppose Stuart, or the estate agent, cleared it out before putting it on the market.'

'I guess so. They didn't check for loose floorboards though, did they?'

'No, and I'm quite glad they didn't,' Sarah said, glancing at her mother.

'So am I.' Janice drew a deep breath. 'The minute I walked into this house in 1975, it felt like home, even though it was a mess.' There were tears in her eyes. 'And now I know why. It's because it *was* my home. Only for a couple of short years, but this was my home.'

'Rose brought you to that Anderson shelter the day Blythe Avenue was bombed,' Sarah whispered. Suddenly everything felt so real. 'Dora showed me a photograph she took of you and Rose in the back garden. It reminded me of the photos of you and me, and of me and Faith.' Janice reached for her hand and Sarah took it; they were both shaking. 'If only these walls could have talked, Mum.' She rested her head on Janice's shoulder. 'I'm glad Martin and Stuart were happy.'

'Me too, love.'

'I wonder if Stuart's still alive?'

'You look if you want. I think I'll leave him be.' They sat lost in their own thoughts for a moment before Janice spoke again. 'Funny how my mother and I both married gay men.'

'Who knows how many unhappy couples there were, or still are, trying to convince themselves that they could, and should, make it work because of social expectations? If things had been different, both Martin and Dad could have lived their lives as their true selves from the beginning. And so could Rose and Dora.'

'Hmm, yes. But then Rose wouldn't have had me, and I wouldn't have had my wonderful daughters.' They lapsed into silence then Janice cleared her throat. 'How was it in Switzerland with Rob, love?'

'I really don't want to talk about it,' she said quietly, picking at her thumb cuticle. She needed time to get it all sorted in her head before she tried to say it out loud. There might have been a chance that she and Rob could have been friends, but she'd ruined that, possibly forever. At least she'd told him she was sorry, that was something.

Janice patted her on the knee. 'I understand, love. But you know where I am if you do.'

Sarah swallowed the lump in her throat. 'Thanks, Mum.'

Janice went back downstairs, and Sarah was pulling the last few bits out of her suitcase when Heather's reply to her text pinged on her phone.

*Come round at nine.*

It was already quarter to. Sarah dumped her clothes and her makeup bag on her bed, grabbed her jacket, and raced down the stairs.

. . .

Sitting on Heather's cream sofa with a mug of hot chocolate in her hand, Sarah tried not to dwell on the fact that the last time she'd been in Heather's flat on Temper Street was the day before Faith's funeral. That day, she'd slumped to the floor, limp and exhausted from a week of non-stop crying. Heather had sat with her, cradling Sarah's head on her lap and stroking her hair. Two days later, Sarah had caught the first train of the morning out of Dovecote, leaving a trail of broken hearts in her wake.

Heather curled her feet, encased in fluffy socks, underneath her while a ginger cat with white paws made himself comfortable on her lap. A tabby glared at Sarah from the armchair on the other side of the coffee table. She must have been sitting in his seat. In a large cage by the window, a blue and yellow budgie whistled.

Heather motioned to them in turn. 'This lump is Rodney, the tabby staring at you is Del Boy, and you'll remember Malcolm the budgie. He's an old man now, just turned twelve.'

''Ello darling,' Malcolm chirped.

Heather turned back to Sarah. 'But enough about my menagerie. Bring me up to speed on the Rob situation.'

Sarah slurped a marshmallow out of her hot chocolate, then put her mug down. Del Boy eyed it. 'He took me for a fancy dinner. We got wrecked on plum schnapps. We both cried. Then we slept together. I confessed I'd cheated on him. Very awkward journey home. I apologised outside Dovecote station. He said he'd make sure my van got fixed.'

Heather let out a long, low whistle. 'All of that was pretty much as expected. Apart from you sleeping with him. What were you thinking?'

'I wasn't.' Sarah said with a shrug, before putting her head in her hands and letting out a little scream. 'He told me he loves me.'

There was a dark shadow across Heather's brown eyes, and she pursed her lips. 'Do you love him?'

Sarah averted her eyes. 'No.'

'Are you sure?' There was something in Heather's tone that Sarah couldn't interpret. It might just have been weariness. She forced herself to meet Heather's gaze.

'I'm very attracted to him. I feel drawn to him, even though I know we're bad for each other. But, no, I don't love him.'

'Does he know that?'

'I told him that, even before Faith's accident, I had realised I didn't love him.'

'Okay, but does he know how you feel about him right now?'

'That's pretty much irrelevant because I took your advice and told him the truth. I broke his heart all over again.' Sarah pressed the heels of her palms against her eyes. 'I'm pretty sure he hates me now.'

'But isn't that what you wanted?'

'I didn't want to hurt him. And I don't want him to hate me.' Sarah flopped back against the cushions.

'Did you want him to still love you?'

Now there was a question. 'I don't know. Maybe.' Sarah thumped a cushion. 'It would have been better for everyone if I'd never come back.'

Heather's glare softened and she gently poked Sarah's arm. 'I'm glad you came back.'

'Please don't be. Please say you hate me too and can never forgive me for the mess I made.'

'I could never hate you.' Heather's voice was soft. She didn't look up at Sarah, focusing instead on stroking Rodney, who purred contentedly. Sarah watched Heather's hand move along the cat's body, slowly and deliberately. Just like how she'd stroked Sarah's hair.

'I never thanked you, for looking after me in the days after Faith's accident,' Sarah almost whispered. 'I wouldn't have survived it, had it not been for you letting me scream and cry and generally be a mess. I couldn't let Rob see me like that, and I couldn't stand to be in the same room as him anyway. I needed you, and you came through for me. So, thank you.' Heather gave her a shy smile. 'And I'm sorry for running out on you. For the record, I did love you, and I knew you loved me too.'

'Yeah, I did. And maybe I...' Heather stopped short of finishing her sentence. Had she been about to say something that a part of Sarah wanted to hear? No, she didn't want to hear Heather say she loved her. No more than she'd wanted to hear it from Rob. She cursed inwardly. Why could she not work out what she wanted? Why was everything so complicated and difficult? Why could she not just let things happen? Why did she break everything she touched?

'I'm not going to be staying around, Heather,' she said. It was better that Heather knew the truth now. Just as, in the long run, it was better for Rob to know the truth. He'd get over it. When he did, he'd realise he was better off without her. Everyone was better off without her.

'What?' Heather's eyes were wide.

'As soon as the van's fixed, I'm gone. Mum's fine now, she can get around. She doesn't need me any more. I've caused enough damage. I'm going to go before I cause any more.'

Heather slammed her mug down on the table, making Rodney jump out of her lap and scurry away. 'For God's sake, Sarah. You can't keep doing this.' She was almost shaking. 'You can't keep running away from situations you cause. You disappear on me for ten years, then suddenly turn up, forcing me to relive all the hurt you caused. And now you're running away again.' She got up and began pacing the room, her palm pressed against her forehead. When she stopped and turned to Sarah, there was fire in her eyes. 'You've made me... I've fallen... I... And you're just going to up and leave without any consideration of anyone else's feelings. You're a selfish coward, Sarah Portman.'

A slap would have stung less. Sarah tried to say something, but nothing came out of her mouth. She bolted for the front door. As it closed behind her, she heard a muffled curse from Heather.

It didn't matter that Dovecote and Pebble Cottage had once been her home; they weren't any longer. Rose had left her home behind; it was time for Sarah to do the same. It was best for everyone.

# FORTY-FOUR

## ROSE

February 1945

A few weeks had passed and thankfully, I'd had no further interactions with Reg Harris. He was still around, though, and if his plan was to frighten me, it had worked. I looked over my shoulder constantly. I asked Maureen to help at the café so I wouldn't be alone. Stan made sure to stop by at least once a day. Reg had really got under my skin, which annoyed me more than anything.

It was yet another grey, overcast day, and the wind swirling in off the sea had a nasty bite to it. Typical February weather. I stomped along The Promenade, wondering why I was bothering. Uncle Douglas might call in. I'd not seen much of him lately; he'd been busy. Betty might pass by on her way to an appointment. She'd cheered up since the incident with the fur coat. A certain American GI by the name of Hunter Carruthers had seen to that. They shared a love of ballroom dancing. I hoped this one would last.

Most mornings, I went in the front door of The Seaside

Café, but this morning, something made me cut down the little alleyway and around to the back door. I stopped short, nearly dropping my keys. The glass from the back window was all over the ground. Just like it had been after the Blythe Avenue bombing. I pushed the door. It swung open. Stepping over the threshold, I let out a scream. There were bowls and utensils all over the floor and counter. The drawers had been emptied; the cupboard doors hung from their hinges.

With a thumping heart, I went into the pantry. The shelves were bare. All my flour, sugar, dried eggs, powdered milk, and my precious stock of currants and raisins – all gone. Even my spices had been taken. One bag of tea remained, with a knife embedded in it. The leaves had seeped out in a trickle, like blood. I opened the icebox and a sob erupted from beneath my rib cage. The margarine, the tiny amount of butter, and a few rare pints of milk were gone. The six priceless fresh eggs had been smashed, their innards smeared across the inside of the refrigerator door.

Tears blurred my vision, and I could barely breathe as I went out into the café. Every chair was broken, every table overturned. The floor glistened with fragments of smashed teapots. The hot water urn had been pushed over on top of the glass display case. Even the net curtains were in shreds. This was no ordinary robbery. No burglar did this much damage. This was a personal attack. This was revenge. And one name immediately sprang to mind: Reg Harris.

With a shaking hand, I pulled open the cash register. Of course it was empty. What made it worse was that he'd taken things he could sell. There were housewives all over the country who would rip his arm off for a bag of flour or a few extra ounces of sugar. It was only when I turned towards the Welsh dresser that I saw the word that had been scrawled in vibrant red paint across the glass doors. It was a word you'd never expect to hear or read, unless you were a professional dog breeder. I only just made it out the back door before I vomited into the shrubbery between the café and the bomb site behind.

'Rose, love. What's the matter?' I could only shake my head at Maureen, who walked around me and went into the kitchen. Her anguished roar drew me inside to join her. She was staring at the wreckage of the café. The minute I appeared at her shoulder, she put her strong arms around me and held me tight. 'Oh, Rose, love. I'm so sorry. I don't know what else to say. I'm sorry.'

I just cried.

A few moments later, she peeled me off her shoulder. 'You stay here, love. I'm going to get Stan, and then I'm going up to the phone box to call the police. Will you be alright for a few minutes? I'll send Stan right up.' I nodded feebly. 'And don't touch anything; the police will need to dust for fingerprints. Although both you and I know who is responsible for this. I'll swing for that scoundrel, I will.' And she went away, fuming and muttering to herself. I thanked my lucky stars that I had friends like her. My hand went to my mouth. What would Martin say?


I was barely aware of Stan arriving and cursing loudly. He was followed swiftly by the police, who took photographs and dusted for fingerprints. Maureen held my hand as I gave a shaky statement. Stan confirmed the previous incident with Reg. The policeman said they'd investigate and get back to me. They were familiar with Reg Harris and his gang. He'd been causing them trouble and was a slippery fish, evading their attempts to arrest him. The policeman gave Stan a permit to bring his van up onto The Promenade to clear out anything I didn't want. I wanted it all gone. Maureen had swept up the broken glass from the back step and she set to cleaning the offensive inscription off the dresser. I just stood in the middle of the floor in a dazed stupor as Stan nailed cardboard sheets to the front window.

'You don't need people looking in, love,' he said gently. 'If anyone asks, you can say you're closed for redecoration.'

'The insurance better pay out,' Maureen huffed, still scrubbing the dresser doors. 'I hope they catch him, and he rots in prison, and then burns in hell for this,' she muttered. She crossed herself and raised her eyes heavenward.

'Hello? Rose?'

I jolted. I knew that voice. I raced to the back door. It was like seeing an angel. I threw my arms around Dora's neck and began to cry all over again.


At Maureen's insistence, Dora and Stan escorted me home. Stan fetched his van and went back to the café, promising to salvage anything he could and throw away anything broken beyond repair. Dora simply put the kettle on and sat me down with a cup of tea. The feel of her hand in mine was all the fortification I needed. She stroked my hair, and when she kissed me, my soul blossomed. I'd waited a year for that kiss, and it was the sweetest moment.

'I've missed you so much,' I said.

'Not as much as I've missed you,' she replied, before kissing me again. 'And I'm so glad I came when I did. Are you okay?'

I snuggled into her shoulder and traced the line of her neck with my finger. 'I am now. How long can you stay for?'

'Only a few days, I'm afraid.'

'We'll make the most of it.' I looked her deep in the eyes as I stood up, took her hand, and led her towards the stairs. 'Starting right now.'

. . .

Thankfully, we were fully dressed again when Maureen and Stan came round.

'We've done all we can, love,' Maureen said.

'Thank you so much. And you too, Stan. What would I do without you both?'

'It's what friends and neighbours are for,' Stan said, handing me a pair of keys. 'I got a locksmith mate of mine to put in new locks, front and back.'

'Oh Stan, that's very kind. How much do I owe him?'

Stan waved away my question. 'He said to sort it out once you get the insurance money. There's no rush.' I was close to tears again. It was the kindness of our community that made me emotional.

'The kitchen isn't as bad as it looked. Most of your pots and pans and bowls and things are in one piece. I've put them back in the cupboards, and Stan fixed the cupboard doors. But you'll probably want to go up yourself and see what's what,' Maureen added.

'We'll go up this afternoon,' Dora said. 'Thank you.'

Maureen squeezed my hand, and Stan gave me a pat on the shoulder. 'You'll bounce back, Rose. You'll be back up and running in no time.'

I gave a feeble nod. 'It will all depend on whether I can replace the stock. I had ingredients stored up that you just can't get any more.'

'Just give us a shout if you need anything,' Maureen said, giving Stan a nudge. 'Come on, you. You need to get up to the farms this afternoon; you were supposed to go yesterday.'

'No rest for the wicked,' Stan quipped, with a wink.


Three days passed in a blur of sorting and clearing the café by day and making love by night.

'I won't come to the station with you,' I said. 'I'll only cry.'

'Not long now, Rose,' Dora whispered into my hair as we embraced. 'I'll be home as soon as I can.' I tried not to think about Martin making the same promise. Having Dora home only served to reinforce how much I didn't want him, and how much I wanted her forever.

'I love you.'

'I love you, too.'

One last kiss and she was gone. I dragged myself up the stairs and flopped down on my bed. It wouldn't be warm again until she was back in it. I buried my head in my pillow and my hands closed around something underneath. It was an envelope. Inside was a small bundle of photographs. Dora must have slipped them there while I'd been making breakfast.

My eyes brimmed as I leafed through them. There was Dora and me in the back garden of Pebble Cottage. I peered at it closely; I could see our little fingers entwined. The memory of Dora's skin against mine sent ripples through my body. The next one was of me, about a month later, leaning against the railings on The Promenade. I picked up one of me in Victoria Park. I could just make out the bandstand behind. That had been the day we'd gone to the pub, and Dora had been attacked by that horrid man. It had also been the day we kissed for the first time. My chest ached at the memory. The next two were from Christmas 1943. One was of me next to the tree and the other was of us kissing under the mistletoe. My pulse thundered in my ears. If anyone was to find these...

My knees went weak at the prospect of Martin coming across them. I didn't even look at the last photograph, but hurriedly stuffed them back into the envelope. In a panic, I looked around the room for a suitable hiding place. Then I remembered there was a loose floorboard under the bed. I lay down on my front and crawled under the bed, feeling for the wobbly piece of wood. I gave it a nudge and dropped the envelope into the cavity. I could look at them whenever I wanted, but no one would ever find them accidentally. I lay on my bed, breathing heavily. At least she hadn't included the one of me sprawled on the bed, wearing nothing but a mischievous smile.

Despite the café, my pride and joy, having been ransacked, there was something good the week had given me: hope. Dora's fleeting visit had reminded me that, no matter how bad things got, I was loved.

# FORTY-FIVE

## SARAH

May 2017

It was a glorious spring day. The sky was clear and cornflower blue. Birdsong filled the air and spring flowers decorated the hedgerows. But the sea wind whipping around the exposed football pitch was cold enough to force Sarah to shove her hands in her pockets and stamp her feet. Despite being chilled to the bone, she wouldn't have missed this for the world. She'd already missed far too much of her nephew's life.

'Thanks for asking me to come along,' she said, nudging Daphne's elbow. 'I know I've been a hermit for the past week.'

'You've been avoiding people, I know. Anyway, I thought it was about time you put in some "aunt" hours. And Jake's been asking about you, so it seemed as good an opportunity to introduce you as any.'

That warmed Sarah up from the inside. Jake was currently hurtling down the left wing, his eyes on the ball coming sailing towards him from Harry in the middle of the pitch. Before Jake could get the ball under control, the opposition's defender slid along the ground, taking Jake out by the ankles.

'Oi! Ref!' Daphne shouted, and Adam gave her a withering glare. 'What?'

Adam tutted. Daphne scowled and Sarah examined her shoelaces. Her phone pinged with a message.

*Hey, look sorry about the other night. I shouldn't have lost my temper. I just don't want you to go. Anyway, how about a drink? H x*

Sarah's pulse quickened. In the week since she'd stormed out of Heather's house, she'd had a dull ache inside. Heather's unfinished sentence played on her mind. What had she been about to say? Before she could begin to formulate a response, her phone pinged again, with another message.

*Hi. Your van's ready to be picked up. Look, I don't want to leave it like we have. I think we should talk. How about we meet in Victoria Park? R.*

No kiss at the end of that one. Rob's choice of venue intrigued her. But then, meeting in public meant they couldn't start screaming at each other, or rip each other's clothes off. Smart move, Rob. She'd give him that. She scrolled between the messages, debating which, if either, offer to accept, but looked up as she felt someone's eyes on her. Rachel was about halfway down the sideline with Ben, and, if looks could kill, Sarah would be toast. Had Rob told his sister about Sarah's affair? She looked back down at the message. Did Rachel know Rob wanted to meet with her? Rachel could glare all she liked.

The final whistle went, and Jake bounded over, sweaty and breathless. His hair was stuck to his forehead, but he was grinning from ear to ear.

'Hi,' he said, eyeing Sarah up. 'I'm guessing you're my Auntie Sarah.'

'Hey,' Sarah said. 'I guess I am.'

'Nice. I like your hair.'

'Thanks.' She'd redone the purple highlights.

'And your nose stud is pretty cool.'

Sarah's finger instinctively went to the turquoise stud. 'Your mum hates it. But don't tell her I told you that,' she stage-whispered. There was something about him that drew her to him. A rebellious streak perhaps? Daphne rolled her eyes.

He grinned back. 'Are you coming back to our house for dinner?' Jake was clearly not like most teenagers. He was chatty and full of questions. Sarah looked to Daphne, who nodded, as though Sarah had passed some sort of test. Maybe her nephew was hard to impress.

'Adam's out tonight at the golf club. You're more than welcome. I was only going to shove a cottage pie in the oven, nothing fancy.'

There was something in Daphne's look that made Sarah think she wanted the company. Jake was giving her very persuasive puppy eyes that completely melted her heart. How could she turn down the opportunity to spend an evening with her sister and her nephew? There was a lot of lost time to make up for.

'I'd love to.'

'Are you any good at Mario Kart?' Jake asked.

Sarah laughed. 'I don't know. I've never played.'


After the second glass of red wine, Sarah got a whole lot better at Mario Kart. But just as she was getting close to defeating her nephew, Daphne sent him to bed. The two sisters sat outside underneath the expensive patio heaters, and Daphne put another log on the fire pit.

'Sorry Jake made you play that blasted game. It drives me mad,' Daphne said, refilling Sarah's wine glass.

'Oh, no, not at all. It was a lot of fun. It was nice to spend time with him. He's a good kid.'

Daphne glanced up at Jake's bedroom window. 'Yeah, he is. He's definitely got that same spark you and Mum have. Maybe it's a Wilton trait. It will take some getting used to, all these new branches on our family tree.'

'From what we've learnt about Rose, I'd say it comes from her. She was quite feisty and determined.'

'I think it missed me,' Daphne said, before swallowing a large mouthful of wine.

Sarah could tell there was something bothering her sister. 'Is everything okay, Daffs?'

It took Daphne a moment to reply. 'Adam's taken the job in Birmingham.'

'You're moving?'

Daphne shook her head. 'Jake and I aren't going with him.'

Sarah nearly dropped her glass. 'What?'

'I told him I didn't want to go. I told him we shouldn't disrupt Jake's schooling or take him away from his friends. He accepted the job anyway. Even though he knew it would make me unhappy, he took the job because it would benefit his career.' There was resignation in Daphne's voice. Sarah recalled the atmosphere between Adam and Daphne the day of Janice's fall. Was this the reason for it?

'You're not splitting up, though, are you? Won't Adam come back at weekends?' Surely, he'd do that at least? Or was he going to break her sister's heart? If he did, Sarah would have something to say about it.

Daphne drained her wine glass. 'I don't know. It's not about the job, really. It's about him not caring how Jake or I feel. He's always been career-focused, I knew that from the day I met him. But it just seems like lately it's all that matters to him. His job certainly seems to matter more to him than I do.' Her bottom lip wobbled.

'You don't want relationship advice from me, Daffs. I mean, have you seen the mess I've created? Have you spoken to Mum?'

Daphne rubbed her eyes. 'Not yet.'

'You know she'll be on your side, whatever happens. Adam might be on the receiving end of one of her stares, though. And we both know that's not pleasant!'

Their eyes met and they dissolved into giggles that the breeze took and carried, up and over the garden fence and out towards the sea.


When Adam's car pulled up on the drive, Sarah made a swift exit, flashing him an evil glare as she went. Poor Daphne. It was one thing when your life was a series of disasters, you kind of got used to it. But it must be hard when your perfect life was suddenly shattered. She paused on The Promenade and leant against the railings, just as her grandmother had done while posing for Dora. The streetlamps cast pools of light on the pebbles, and the moonlight sparkled off the undulating waves. In the distance, the lighthouse beam swept across the bay, warning passing ships of the dangerous rocks at the base of the cliffs. Sarah didn't need the reminder. Neil hadn't really wanted his ashes scattered from those rocks. He'd wanted Sarah to come back, and he'd known she never would unless he made her.

'Thanks, Dad,' she muttered through gritted teeth.

But then, if he hadn't made her come back, she and Janice would never have known about Rose and Dora. She wouldn't have spent a fun evening playing video games with her delightful and funny nephew, and she wouldn't have felt the warmth of Heather's hand in hers again. She also wouldn't have finally come clean to Rob. As much as she knew she'd hurt him, it was for the best – he needed to move on from her. She inhaled a gulp of sea air and, as the salt dried on her lips, she smiled. 'Thanks, Dad.'

A couple walking hand in hand along the beach glanced in her direction and hurried on. Sarah wasn't sure, but it looked like Heather's friend, Emily, and Will Prentice. Every girl in Dovecote had fancied him, even though he went to a posh private school, not the local comprehensive. Sarah had been too busy pining over Heather back then to pay the good-looking rich boy any attention.

But even if she could now face the sea, going out to the lighthouse was a step too far. And it wasn't the right place for her dad. He belonged somewhere he'd been happy. And Pete deserved the honour of scattering the ashes of the man he'd loved so fiercely. She'd take her dad's ashes back to Manchester and give him back to Pete. How lucky had Neil and Pete been, to find a love that survived for so long, and against all odds? She'd never have that.

A hot tear dropped onto her folded hands. Maybe she was destined to be alone. At least then she couldn't hurt anyone. A ripple ran over her skin at the sudden memory of Rob's body pressed against hers. But a relationship founded on conflict and mutual provocation was not sustainable. The thought of having his arms around her, even if it was for one last time, was so tempting.

'Let him go,' she told herself, stuffing her fist into her mouth and biting down on her knuckles. She breathed deeply, tightly grasping the railings again. If she didn't tether herself to some-thing solid, she might start running up the High Street. But would she turn into Courcey Road, or would she keep going up to Temper Street?

The quaking inside suddenly stilled, replaced with calm waters. Heather had always done that to her. A simple touch or a look had brought Sarah back from the edge so many times. If Rob was the fire in her belly, Heather was the deep, calming breath that allowed her to unclench her jaw. But she'd hurt Heather too. What made it worse was that Heather was right; she *was* a coward who ran away rather than face up to what she'd done. So why break the habit of a lifetime? If she collected her van as soon as the garage opened in the morning, she'd be back in Manchester by mid-afternoon. She could drop Neil's ashes off and then head north. Maybe she'd give North Yorkshire a try? She pushed herself off from the railings and walked slowly towards Pebble Cottage. She wouldn't reply to either text; there was nothing more to say to either Rob or Heather. Her mind was made up.

So why did she have an ache in her chest?

# FORTY-SIX

## SARAH

May 2017

If it hadn't been for those couple of glasses of Daphne's wine, Sarah would have heard the storm raging outside her bedroom window in the early hours. Halfway through her second black coffee of the morning, Janice handed her the café keys.

'Can you do me a favour, love? Sue is taking me to my physio appointment this morning. Could you open for me? Natasha will be along after she's done the school run.'

Sarah groaned inwardly. Keeping her eyes open hurt her head. What she really wanted was to go back to bed.

'Yeah, of course I will, Mum.'

After a hot shower, and dressed in her comfiest clothes, Sarah lowered her sunglasses as she stepped out onto Fisherman's Walk. The hanging baskets on the houses opposite were bedraggled; the flowers had been decapitated by the wind. She glanced back: Pebble Cottage looked in one piece. All chimney pots and roof tiles were present and correct, even the ones caked in moss. The Promenade was strewn with leaves and the odd small branch. There were puddles where the waves had breached the wall. It must have been a rough one.

When she reached The Seaside Café, Sarah gasped. A large branch, the size of a small tree, was sticking out of the broken front window. The pavement outside was littered with roof tiles and shattered glass. As Sarah pushed open the door, she stepped into an inch of water that had come in through the smashed window and a hole in the roof. She looked up at the hole. A clear blue sky winked innocently back at her.

'Oh my God!' she shouted, going through to the kitchen. At least that wasn't underwater. She tried the light switch – nothing. No power. She stuck her head out of the back door. The lights were on in the museum next door. 'Is this you again, Dad? Well, if it was, you've got your wish. I can't leave Mum to deal with this on her own. Guess my plan of disappearing this morning isn't happening.'

She got out her phone and started making calls.


The insurance assessor was first on the scene after Janice and Sue, making discomfiting murmuring noises as he typed onto his iPad. Sarah was in the kitchen when she heard Rob arrive.

'What a mess, Rob.' There was a wobble in her mother's voice. How she hadn't collapsed in hysterics when Sue brought her into the café, Sarah would never know.

'Don't worry, Janice. We'll get it sorted for you.' Rob was patting Janice's arm when Sarah emerged from the kitchen. He gave her a curt nod. She flashed a quick smile in return. It was good of him to come and help.

'Why don't you go on home, Mum? We can't have you slipping on this wet floor and damaging your ankle again. Not when it's so nearly healed.'

Sue Prentice put down the chair she'd been righting. 'I

think that's a good idea. Come on, Janice; let the youngsters sort this out.'

Janice let out a long, shaking breath. 'Thanks, love. You don't mind staying? The roofer is on the way, and the electrician will be here within the hour. The glazer can't get here until tomorrow.'

'Of course, Mum.' Sarah clenched her jaw as Rob rolled up the sleeves of his flannel shirt. 'We'll be fine.'

Rob rubbed his hands together. 'Right, then. I'll get that branch out of the way, and put up some boards over the broken window, Janice. We've a load of MDF board down at the garage.'

After Janice and Sue left, while Sarah mopped up the rainwater from the floor, Rob set to the branch with a saw.

'You didn't reply to my text,' he said, tossing a couple of twigs into the pile by door.

'No. I was planning on leaving today.'

He put down the saw. 'Why?'

'Because all I've done since I came back is open old wounds.' She glanced up at him. His arms were crossed over his chest. 'And inflict new ones.'

'Put down that mop,' he demanded. Sarah followed him out of the café to where she'd put the outdoor furniture. He sat down on one of the chairs and motioned for her to join him. 'What's really the problem, Sarah?' he asked after she'd sat down beside him.

She put her head in her hands. 'Me. I'm the problem. I'm just so angry. I can't figure out what I want. Everything I touch breaks. I'm a toxic disaster. I should have one of those hazardous material symbols tattooed on my forehead as a warning.' She waited for him to say something, but he just watched her. 'My feelings for you confused me, too. One minute I wanted to tear your clothes off, the next I wanted to bury you under the patio.'

He still didn't say anything. 'And then there's Heather. I can't even explain what's going on there.'

'That's quite a lot to be getting on with. Firstly, you are not toxic, or a disaster. You've been through a lot, Sarah. And you didn't always get what you needed from those around you. Including me. And I'm sorry, too. I'm sorry for not seeing how damaging and dysfunctional we were, and for not dealing with the issues in our marriage in the right way. You aren't the only one who could have been better at communication. I should have kept my pride in check and not risen to your provocations. I should have been a better man. And I should have been more careful with you when you came back. I shouldn't have kissed you. And I definitely shouldn't have – you know.' There was the slightest of pink tinges to his cheeks.

'I think we're equally to blame for that.'

'Yeah. I'm sorry I freaked you out by telling you how I feel. That was stupid of me. And thank you for telling me the truth.'

'I'm sorry, Rob. I know I should have told you sooner. I should have done the right thing from the start and been honest with you about what was going on with me and Heather. Do you hate me?'

'No. I could never hate you. And I've given myself a good talking to. I don't think I love you. I think I loved the idea of having you back, of going to back to what we had. But the more I've thought about it, the more I've realised that wouldn't be a good thing, for either of us. For all the reasons we've already said. Just to check – you don't love me, do you?'

'I'm sorry, Rob. No, I don't.'

'That's okay.' He looked like he meant it. 'It's time I moved on. Maybe I should accept the invite I've had to meet someone for a drink.'

Sarah grinned. 'Who?'

'Aoife.'

Sarah raised an appreciative eyebrow. 'The Irish hairdresser? She's stunning. And I know she thinks you're fit.'

Rob laughed and kissed her forehead. 'Come on, back to work.'

Back inside, Rob picked up his saw, and Sarah placed a hand on his shoulder.

'Rob?'

'Yeah.'

'I don't blame you for Faith's accident.'

He put his arm around her. 'And you shouldn't blame yourself either. It *was* an accident. I don't think you being there would have prevented it. It was horrific and tragic, but if you fixate on placing blame, either on someone else, or on yourself, you'll never begin to heal.'

'Did your therapist tell you that?'

'First session, and I've never forgotten it.' He squeezed her shoulder. 'There you go, saved you a couple of quid on a therapy session. In all seriousness, Sarah, I'd recommend finding a good therapist. Speak to Adam; he can recommend someone. You've been through a huge amount of trauma, and you deserve to get help with processing all of it.'

Sarah looked down at her feet to hide the tears brewing in her eyes. She sniffed and raised her head. 'I'll think about it.'

They mopped and sawed for a while, an easy silence falling between them. Rob even started whistling at one point. Sarah was cleaning the tables and chairs when Rob extracted the last bit of tree from the window. He leant against the counter, sipping from a flask of tea.

'So, Heather?'

Sarah hoisted herself up onto the counter next to him. 'It was like being whacked with that tree branch when I saw her again.'

'And does she feel the same way?'

'I don't know.'

Rob frowned. 'And you were going to leave without finding out? No offence, but that would have been the dumbest thing you'd ever done.' She slapped him gently on the shoulder. 'You need to find out, Sarah. Before you make any decisions about the future.'

'I can't believe you're encouraging this. Would you really be comfortable with me staying in Dovecote and getting back together with Heather? Would that not be weird for you?'

Rob thought for a moment, scratching his temple. 'Sarah, you are not a bad person. You wouldn't have done what you did for a fling. You must have been in love with her.'

'I really was.' She gave him a lopsided smile. Even after everything that had gone on between them, he could still floor her with how kind he was. Rob deserved happiness. With a bit of luck, it might not be too far away.

'And if you still are, and if she feels the same way, I am not going to stand in the way of that. You deserve a secure, healthy relationship with someone who gives you what you need. Nothing would make me happier than seeing you get that.' His soft smile and the sheen on his deep-blue eyes breached Sarah's dam; she had to hide that she was wiping away a tear by pretending to scratch her nose. She got down from the counter and went back to cleaning the legs of a chair which were caked in an inch of black mud.

'Thanks. Rob. That really means a lot to me. But I don't think it's going to happen. When I last saw Heather, I made her lose her temper. She said I was a selfish coward who ran away from problems rather than facing up to them.' She put down the chair. 'To be fair, she's not wrong.'

'Um, Sarah?' Rob said, clearing his throat. Sarah followed Rob's gaze to where Heather was standing in the doorway.

'I'm going to head down to the garage and get that board to

cover the window,' Rob said, as he sidled towards the door. Sarah might have been mistaken, but she could have sworn he winked at Heather as he left.

'Hi,' Heather said.

'Hi.' Sarah picked up a clean cloth and began rubbing down the counter.

'I can't believe how much damage there is. We had a few small branches come down at Bayview, but everywhere else looks fine. Someone up there must have it in for the café.'

'Or someone doesn't want me to leave Dovecote. I reckon it's Dad. First he killed my van, and now he's done this, knowing I can't leave Mum in the lurch.'

'So, you were still set on leaving? You didn't reply to my text.'

Sarah looked up at the clock on the wall. 'I was planning on being at the motorway services at Oxford having a bacon butty right about now.'

'I'm glad you're still here.'

'You don't mean that.'

'Yes, I do. And would you stop rubbing that counter? You're going to take the varnish off if you keep at it like that.' Heather placed a hand on Sarah's and Sarah let the cloth fall. Heather looked her right in the eyes. 'I'm sorry I lost my temper.'

'I'm sorry I made you lose your temper,' Sarah said with a small smile. The warmth of Heather's hand penetrated Sarah's skin and flooded through her body. 'Heather, I—'

'No, I want to go first. Sarah, listen, I only got so rattled because the thought of you leaving again scared me. Like, proper terrified me. Since you've been back, I've been walking on air. But I need to know what you want, before I lose my mind.'

Sarah swallowed hard. 'I think I might be in love with you.'

'Thank God, because I know I'm in love with you.' Heather

leant across the counter, but just as their lips were about to touch there was a knock on the open door.

A man stood awkwardly in the doorway. 'Um, sorry to interrupt. I'm here to have a look at the roof.'

# FORTY-SEVEN

## ROSE

March 1945

A few weeks after the break-in I stood outside The Seaside Café and looked up at my lovely pink and yellow sign. It was weathered from the wind and the salt from the sea. The cardboard Stan had put over the window had been replaced by a proper board. It looked so sad. It was just another casualty of the war, really. There were hundreds, if not thousands of boarded-up properties all over the country. There were shops that had gone out of business, houses that had been gutted by fire, and all manner of places that no longer had owners. A shiver ran up my spine. What if I put all that work into getting the café open again, and Reg came back? I didn't know if I had the energy.

I turned my back on the café and looked out over the sea. Just one kiss from Dora would make me feel better. But when would I get that? I'd been so buoyed by her visit that I'd momentarily forgotten that an end to the war would also mean the return of Martin. I chewed my bottom lip to stop my tears from spilling over. A tap on my shoulder made me turn around.

'Penny for your thoughts,' Betty quipped, lighting a cigarette and leaning against the railings next to me.

'They're not worth that much,' I replied, giving her a small smile.

Whatever Betty was about to say was interrupted by a loud blast from a policeman's whistle and a shout of, 'Oi!' Reg Harris, minus his trilby, ran out onto The Promenade from the end of Fisherman's Walk, pursued by four police officers, including the one who'd attended The Seaside Café the morning of the break-in. The suitcase in Reg's hand sprang open, spilling packets of cigarettes and boxes of cosmetics all over the path. As he got closer to us, Betty stubbed out her cigarette and stuck out her foot. Reg tripped, tumbling onto the pavement with a tirade of crude language. The policemen were on him in a second, hauling him to his feet.

'Got you now, sonny,' one of the policemen said, clicking a set of handcuffs around Reg's wrists. Reg turned to us with a glare.

Betty smiled sweetly back at him. 'No one sells Betty Jones stolen goods and gets away with it.' Reg's response was taken by the sea breeze as he was dragged away. I just watched, open-mouthed as Betty waved at him. 'Good riddance,' she called out, laughing. She turned back to me and grinned. 'I tipped the police off about where Reg had stashed all his stolen stuff. It's one thing flogging me a nicked fur coat – which, by the way, I've given to the police as evidence, and to see if it can be returned to its rightful owner. It's a whole other kettle of fish when he destroys my best friend's café.'

A tear leaked from my eye, and I wiped it with the sleeve of my coat. 'Oh, Betty, thank you.'

'Don't mention it. I'm just glad he can't scare either of us any more. So, anyway, what's got you standing here with a face like a wet weekend? It's not just what happened to the café that's got you down, is it? Is it Martin?'

I could have told Betty everything. I could have told her that every time I opened a letter from Martin, I prayed that he was writing to tell me he was leaving me. I could have explained that I couldn't sleep without Dora next to me, or that I missed my daughter so much it was like having an arm cut off. But if I started, I wouldn't be able to stop, and if I let all my thoughts and feelings out, there might be nothing left of me, and I might float away on the breeze. So instead, I forced a smile.

'I'll be fine, Betty. It's just, you know, the war, the café, everything.' She nodded, but I could tell she didn't really believe me. We stood side by side for a while, watching the waves lick the pebbles. Betty lit another cigarette.

'Hunter wants me to move to Michigan with him.'

I jolted. That had come out of nowhere. 'Your American GI? Is that a good thing?'

Betty sucked on her cigarette and blew out a cloud of smoke. 'I don't know. His family have money, lots of it. He said I'd never want for anything. And all I'd have to do is keep house and raise his kids.'

'Doesn't sound awful. I hear things are much better in America. There's less rationing for a start. We're going to be clearing up this mess for years, I reckon. Once it's all over, that is. Whenever *that* might happen.'

'Do you think I ought to go?' There was a frown creasing her pale forehead, and it was only then I spotted the dark shadows under her eyes. Clearly the question had been keeping her up at night.

'Do you love him?' I thought instantly of Dora. If only us loving each other was enough to decide our futures. Once again, I was struck by how unfair it was that Dora and I, who loved each other with all our hearts, had to keep that love secret, or give it up, to adhere to what the rest of the world expected of us.

Betty was picking at her red-painted fingernails. 'I'm not sure. How do you know if you're in love?'

The wind ruffled my hair, which I'd left falling loose around my shoulders rather than making the effort to pin up. The wisps tickled my cheeks. Again, it was Dora's face that came to me, not Martin's. The edges of my lips curled upwards, and I closed my eyes for a moment.

'You just do,' I whispered.

'Yeah, I figured that was the case.' She let out a long, slow breath. 'I don't even know if that's what's stopping me from saying yes.'

'So, what is, Betty?'

'I've worked really hard to become qualified as a midwife and a district nurse. And I love it. I love spending time with my patients. Even the old ladies and their varicose veins. Delivering babies brings me so much joy. I'm not sure I want to throw that all away to become a housewife. All these years of us women stepping up and doing all the jobs that men had done before, and doing them well, has made me think. Women have kept this country going, and I feel like I owe it to those women to use the brains God gave me, and to spend my life doing something worthwhile. And I like earning my own money. I don't want to have to go crawling to my husband any time I want a new dress, or a lipstick. What was it you said? One day we'd have nice things, and we wouldn't have to do things with men to get them? Well, isn't that just what marriage is for women? I want to control my own destiny, Rose. And if that means scrimping and saving my nurse's salary, then so be it. Also, I don't want to leave Mum on her own. Not with her lungs in the state they are.'

'It sounds like your mind's pretty much made up.'

Betty stubbed out her cigarette. 'Yeah, I think it is. I'm going to say no. I'm going to carry on with district nursing and midwifery. There's probably going to be a load of babies born about nine months after all the men come home. Might even get to deliver your second, eh?' She elbowed me in the ribs, and I humoured her with a slight chuckle.

As much as I loved Janice with all my heart, I couldn't see how Martin and I would have another child. The thought of him touching me made my blood run cold. That wasn't his fault. He was a perfectly nice man. But he had mentioned another child, too. Did that mean he still wanted to be with me, or had he only said what he thought I wanted to hear? It all made my head hurt.

I tuned back into what Betty was saying. 'There are loads more exams I can do to gain extra qualifications.'

'Good for you, Betty.' The sparkle was back in her eyes, and it swelled my heart to see it.

'Thanks, Rose. Right, I'd better be going.' I watched her strut back down The Promenade. She held her head high again. Betty Jones was back, and everyone had better watch out.

I gazed at the waves lapping the grey stones of Dovecote beach for a few moments more, before heading back to the warm cosiness of Pebble Cottage. It was chilly enough to warrant lighting a fire. I had a sudden urge to re-read Dora's most recent letter. Her words were the next best thing to having her in my arms.

# FORTY-EIGHT

## SARAH

June 2017

'Mind your step, Mum,' Daphne urged as Janice stepped down onto a large, flat rock.

'It's slippery,' Sarah called. 'Please, be careful. Here, Mum, take my hand.' Sarah was down where the rocks met the sea, and although it wasn't easy to be there, her heart hadn't stopped beating. It was a beautiful summer day. The sun reflected off the white paint on the lighthouse above them and threw sparkles across the still, calm sea. It was hard to believe that this was a place of tragedy when the sky was blue and the air was filled with the calls of seagulls. In the distance, Dovecote shimmered in the heat haze, and Sarah could just make out the turquoise railings of The Promenade and the mossy roof of Pebble Cottage.

'Have you got him?' Janice asked, lowering herself down to sit on a rock. Sarah held up the jar as Daphne gingerly made her way down to join them.

A week after the storm, once the repairs to The Seaside Café were underway, Sarah had finally decided, having talked it over with Janice and Daphne, to bring Neil's ashes back to Pete in Manchester. Pete, of course, had sobbed dramatically when she'd pulled up on the driveway. Together, they had brought Neil to his favourite spot in the park, and while Sarah distracted passing dog walkers, Pete had delicately sprinkled the ashes around the bench. But Pete had insisted on sending Sarah back to Dovecote with a small portion of Neil, so she could fulfil his request. As Pete pointed out, Neil clearly already had some sway 'up there' if he was able to cause her van to break down and nearly take out her mother's café, just to keep her from running away again. They didn't want to risk him haunting them both. Tears of relief, gratitude, and love had been shed when Janice and Daphne had refused to let Sarah face the lighthouse rocks alone.

'Is that a marmalade jar?' Daphne asked, squinting at the label.

'We sterilised it first,' Sarah explained.

'How funny,' Janice said, with a laugh. 'Neil loved marmalade. It was his idea for me to brush my sticky buns with it. He'd be tickled pink to know he's in a marmalade jar.'

Sarah and Daphne exchanged a look. 'Marmalade!' they said in unison.

'That's what we were missing,' Daphne said. 'When you hurt your ankle, Sarah and I tried to recreate your sticky buns. But we couldn't get them right.'

'We would never have thought to glaze them with marmalade,' Sarah added. How had she not thought of that? It was obvious, now Janice said it. All their attempts had been missing that citrusy zing.

'Aha! Well, now you know my secret ingredient.' Janice got back to her feet and reached for Daphne's hand for support. 'Are you ready, Sarah? Time to say a last goodbye to a good man who we all loved, and who, in his own way, loved us all too.'

Sarah unscrewed the lid of the jar and slowly tipped her

father's ashes into the waves lapping gently against the rocks. 'Thanks for bringing me back, Dad. I wouldn't have done it without you. You've given me more than you could have imagined, so thank you.' Her voice wobbled. 'Off you go now and rest well. I love you.'

They stood in silence for a moment, each lost in their own thoughts. Daphne and Janice turned to clamber back up the rocks to the path into town.

'You know, I'm glad he was happy,' Daphne said quietly. 'I'm sorry I was so hard on him for so long.'

'That's alright, love,' Janice said. 'He wasn't the kind of person who would have held it against you. Are you coming, Sarah?'

'Just give me a minute. I'll catch you up.'

Once her mum and sister had rounded the base of the lighthouse, Sarah sat down and looked out over the water. She'd done it. She'd come back. And, even sitting here where it had happened, there were only good memories in her head. Her heart still ached, and probably always would. But that burning, stinging pain had gone. She had a way to go yet but, for once, she felt as though she was on the right road. She stood and reached into her pocket for the palm-sized pebble she'd picked off the beach that morning. She had painted a pink heart and a bright yellow sun on it. On the back, she'd written two dates, three years apart. 'This is for you, Faith,' she said, placing the stone down just beyond the reach of the tide. 'I'm sorry, baby. I wish we could have had a lifetime together, and I'm sorry I wasn't here to save you. Your dad and I love you very much, and we always will.'

Heather took hold of Sarah's hand the minute she walked into Victoria Park with Janice and Daphne. Jake ran up and hugged his mum, and gave Sarah a high-five.

Sarah's orange and cream camper van was parked up in the corner, decorated with pink and yellow bunting. There was a long queue outside it and Natasha waved from inside. The van had died the moment Sarah had driven it off the garage forecourt, much to Rob's frustration, and amusement. It was then that Sarah had the idea of getting it converted into a coffee van while The Seaside Café was closed for a full refurbishment after the storm. The local council had said yes to Sarah's idea immediately. Rob and Kev had gutted the van and installed a counter across the sliding side door, and a coffee machine and a hot water urn inside. It was the first weekend they'd been open, and most of the town had gathered in the park for a cuppa and a sticky bun.

'How's it going?' Janice asked, climbing in beside Natasha.

'Brilliantly,' Natasha beamed. 'I love this so much, Sarah! It's so cute,' she called out, and Sarah waved back with grin. The one person that Sarah couldn't see in the crowd was Adam. She wrapped an arm around Daphne's waist. Daphne ruffled Jake's hair, and he took off in the direction of the bandstand, where Harry was waiting with a football in one hand, and Alice's hand in the other.

'No Adam?' Sarah asked.

Daphne pulled a face. 'No. It's only his second week, and he said he had a lot of work to do, so he couldn't make it home.'

'I'm so sorry, Daffs.'

'Well, I'm not giving up hope yet.'

'That's my girl,' Sarah smiled, giving her sister a squeeze.

Daphne inhaled sharply, and Sarah turned to where her sister was looking. There, at the edge of the path, stood a very sheepish-looking Adam. It was like a scene from a film as he pushed his way through the crowd. Sarah took a discreet step away, but not so far that she couldn't hear what was being said.

'I'm sorry,' Adam said. He held his gangly arms tight at his sides, clearly holding back from embracing Daphne. For her part, Daphne just looked shell-shocked. 'I'm so sorry. A week was long enough for me to realise I couldn't stand not seeing you every day. I was wrong to put a dumb job ahead of you and Jake. I've quit the Birmingham job and have asked for my old job back at the Dovecote Medical Centre. Luckily, they hadn't replaced me. I don't care if I never see anything more interesting than varicose veins for the rest of my career, Daphne. I can't live without you. If you'll forgive me, I'd quite like to come home.' Sarah let out a sigh of relief as Daphne nodded and buried herself in her husband's chest. She caught Adam's eye. He looked suitably chastened, so she gave him a smile. He was a lucky man.

Over the heads of the crowd, she saw Rob walking towards them. He gave her a wave, and she waved back. She'd tell him later that she'd been out to the lighthouse. He probably wouldn't believe that she'd finally taken Dora's advice and forgiven herself and the sea. She'd tell Dora the next time they had another Skype call. On their most recent call, Dora and Janice had chatted for hours about Rose, and how she'd brought Janice to The Seaside Café every day when she was a baby. Dora had been astounded that Pebble Cottage hadn't changed that much over the years when Sarah had taken her on a tour via her laptop.

Heather's tug on her arm drew Sarah back to Victoria Park. They were walking away when Reverend Clive intercepted them, the sun shining off his bald head. He really ought to be wearing a hat, Sarah thought.

'Morning, Sarah. Hello, Heather,' he beamed. 'I have good news.'

'Oh?'

He pulled a slightly crumpled letter out of his pocket. 'This came this morning. The Bishop of Liverpool has agreed to our request for Rose's remains to be reinterred in Dovecote.'

A lump formed in Sarah's throat. It must have shown on her

face, as Heather gripped her hand a little tighter. 'Thank you so much, Clive. It will mean so much to all of us to have her home.'

'I'll liaise with the cemetery where Rose was buried after the crash to sort out a date. It may be some time before we can get it all arranged.'

'That's fine. There's no rush. Will you stop by the van and get a sticky bun?'

'That's what I'm really here for,' he said with a wink, before bustling away.

Sarah clutched Heather's hand as Heather guided her through Victoria Park. 'Where are we going?'

'You'll see.' Heather led her up to the cricket pavilion and around to the back. She drew Sarah to a halt next to the wonky heart engraved with their initials. Sarah traced her carving with her finger.

'SP and HR forever. I shouldn't have left you, Heather. Either time.'

'It's all in the past, Sarah. The main thing is we're together now. It's so good to have you home,' she whispered, running her fingers gently down the side of Sarah's face.

'It's good to be home,' Sarah replied. Only a single blackbird in the bush behind the pavilion witnessed their kiss. There was no way Sarah was leaving her home behind ever again.

# FORTY-NINE

## ROSE

May 1945

At three o'clock on Tuesday the 8th of May 1945, we finally got the news bulletin that Dora promised we would. The war was over, in Europe at least. There was no shouting or jumping around in Pebble Cottage. I just simply slumped down on the sofa and wept.

Martin's telegram arrived the following day.

BEING STOOD DOWN ON FRIDAY STOP BE HOME SATURDAY STOP

On Thursday, the smiling postman handed over a postcard.

*I told you this day would come. Love D x*

Friday's post brought an official letter.

*9th May 1945*

*Dear Parent,*

*Please be patient while we work through the arrangements and organise the safe return of your child/children. Further notice to follow. For all queries, please contact your local welfare office.*

*Regards,*

*HM Evacuation Office*

I didn't sleep for two nights.

Martin looked worn out when he trudged up the path to Pebble Cottage. He'd lost more hair, and there were dark circles under his eyes. He'd lost weight too; his Post Office jacket hung off his shoulders.

'Welcome home,' I said, taking him in my arms and hugging him tightly. Whatever else was going on with us, I was glad he was home safe. We'd both survived. For far too many families up and down the country, there would be no homecomings. Even little Dovecote would be adding the names of loved ones to the war memorials in Victoria Park and St. John's Church. Mr and Mrs Ingram, who owned the newsagent on the High Street, had lost one of their sons. And of course, there were the residents of Blythe Avenue, who'd been killed by that lone bomber. However strained relations were between Martin and I, we were the lucky ones.

We sat at the kitchen table, the air heavy with unspoken words. Martin broke the silence.

'The windows of the café are boarded up. What happened?'

I worried the hem of my cardigan between my fingers. 'There was a robbery. In February. The man who did it has been arrested. I filed a claim with the insurance people; the money came in last week. I'm sorry. I was too scared to write to you in case you'd be angry with me.'

Martin reached for my hand. 'Were you there? He didn't hurt you, did he?'

I fought back tears. 'No. It was overnight. I'm so sorry. As soon as things calm down, I'll make a start on getting it up and running again.'

His slight shrug surprised me. 'If you want to. It's up to you.'

'I got a letter from the evacuation office. They're working on getting all the children sent home. I hope it won't be long before we get Janice back. I'm dying to see her.' I sighed. 'Although, I'm a little worried she won't remember me.'

A shadow flitted across Martin's eyes. 'She won't know me at all. Maybe that's for the best.' He rubbed his forehead and drew a deep breath. 'Rose, there's something I need to tell you.' My heart skipped a beat, but I squeezed his hand. He withdrew it. 'There is no easy way for me to say this, so I apologise for my bluntness. I am not the man you think I am.' He looked down at the tabletop. 'I am, and have always been, a homosexual. I am sorry.' I wanted to reach for his hand again, but he'd tucked them in his lap. 'I tried to force myself to love you. I wanted to be the husband you deserve, but I couldn't. I told myself that when we married and moved to Dovecote, I would stop going to the places I had been frequenting. There are places where men like me go to meet other men. But I couldn't stop. That was where I was going after work.' He glanced up at me. I blinked back the tears in my eyes. It was hard to see him so tortured, in so much pain. 'You must believe me that I remained faithful. I never engaged in any intimate activity with anyone else. Not even Brian, much to his annoyance.' Well, that explained the look Brian had given me on our wedding day. Martin looked back down at the table. 'Until I went to Scotland.'

I couldn't bear it any longer; I had to put him out of his misery. 'Until you met Stuart.'

His mouth fell open. 'How did you know?'

I gave him a soft smile. 'I wasn't sure, but I saw you kissing him on Boxing Day morning. I didn't say anything because I wasn't sure how serious it was between you. I didn't know whether you also still had feelings for me, or what your plans were.'

'I am so sorry, Rose. I should have come clean then. I wanted to.'

'Is that why you invited him for Christmas?'

'I had planned on staying for a few more days. I wanted you to meet him and see what a wonderful man he is. I wanted you to like him. Then after he'd left, I was going to tell you the truth. But there was a mix-up in the rota and I had to shorten my leave. It was a stupid thing to do, and you must think I am monstrously insensitive. Please believe me, I had no desire to hurt you.'

'He is a lovely man.'

A shy smile crept over Martin's lips and his eyes began to sparkle. He looked like a man in love. 'Yes, he is. Everyone loves him, including me. I am very fortunate that I am the one he has chosen to love in return. You are very calm, Rose. I had expected tears, and shouting. Perhaps you need some time to absorb this shock and then you'll give me the tongue-lashing I deserve.'

It was my turn to take a steadying breath. 'I can't be angry at you, Martin. If you are not the man I thought you were, then I am not the woman you thought I was, either. I am not the woman I thought I was. While we have been apart, I have also fallen in love. I have fallen in love with a woman named Dora.'

'Dora? Janice's godmother? The woman who took the photos at the christening?'

My cheeks warmed at the memory. 'Yes, that Dora. We lived together as lovers for several months before she was called up to war work in Buckinghamshire. I still love her deeply. Are women who fall in love with other women also called homosexuals? If they are, then I am one.'

Martin sat back in his chair and regarded me with the ghost of a smile on his lips. Then he surprised me by getting to his feet and reaching for my hand. When I also stood, he wrapped me in a tight embrace. When we let go, we looked in each other's eyes, and both burst out laughing. He hugged me again.

'Oh goodness. No wonder we *both* needed liquid courage before we took our clothes off. Oh, Rose.' He kissed me softly on the forehead and we both sat back down. He was still holding my hand.

'In a way, it was better that we both found that difficult. If only things had been different, then we could have told each other what was really going on. Is it awful of me to admit that I was relieved you weren't really interested, even though I didn't understand why I felt like that?' I raised an apologetic smile.

He squeezed my hand. 'I'm sorry if I ever made you feel unwanted or unloved, Rose. I never should have asked you to marry me. I was just so scared of being found out for who I was. I honestly thought that getting married would make my homosexuality go away. And for the record, I was also relieved that you didn't seem bothered that I wasn't pressing you for more intimacy.'

'The worst part, Martin, is that you thought you had to change who you are. That really is the most dreadful thing about all this. If only the world allowed people like us to embrace who we are without feeling as though we are somehow wrong, or broken, or need to be fixed. We really should have just talked about it. But that's not the done thing, I suppose. Do you think we ever loved each other?'

'I think we did. We were both alone and looking for someone. And we found each other. I have always been terribly fond of you, Rose. But perhaps in the way that I would be fond of a close friend.'

'Yes, I think I feel the same. Although I had no inkling of my real feelings until I met Dora.'

'She is a very lucky woman.'

I let out a soft sigh. 'No, I'*m* the lucky one.'

Martin let go of my hand. 'What do we do now?'

'What do you want to do? Have you and Stuart made any plans? Where is he, anyway?'

'In a hotel in Scarborough, waiting for word from me.'

'Then you have to go to him. If that is what you want.' It occurred to me that if Martin left me, I would be free to be with Dora. Here was the solution I had wished for. Both Martin and I would be happy.

'It is. But the scandal, Rose. I can't subject you to that.'

'No one has to know.' Uncle Douglas crossed my mind; he would have a heart attack. There was no way he could ever find out the truth. About Martin and Stuart, or about me and Dora.

'If anyone asks, Rose, blame me. Tell people I left you for another woman. I'll happily be painted as the villain, to save you the burden of the truth.' He paused, a frown creasing his face. 'I can't bear to sully Janice with this, Rose. Will you promise me something?' He took my hand in his again. 'Please?' I nodded. 'If my daughter ever asks what became of her father, please tell her I am dead. It is far better for her to grow up with a dead war hero father, than be saddled with the shame of her father being a homosexual. Promise, Rose, please.'

Tears poured from my eyes, and I dabbed at them with my handkerchief. It was one of the embroidered ones Dora had given me. 'I wish it didn't have to be like this. I promise.'

'Thank you. It is for the best, especially for Janice.' He gave me an encouraging smile. 'Who knows, perhaps one day it won't be like this. Perhaps in the future all love, no matter who it is between, will be proudly and openly celebrated. We can only dream of that world, Rose. But if we hold onto that dream, one day it might become a reality.'

Dora's code phrase swam into my head. 'Oh, wouldn't that be wonderful? I'd like to be able to walk through town holding Dora's hand. It is a little easier for Dora and me. Two aging spinsters sharing a home is not unheard of, even if we must hide our love from the outside world. It is not so easy for men. Martin, your secret is safe with me, but please be careful. If the police find out, you could go to prison.' The thought made me curl my fingers into fists. It was all just so unfair. Martin and Stuart, and Dora and I, weren't hurting anyone. All we wanted was to be allowed to love. Was that really too much to ask?

'I know. We may leave the country. We'll go somewhere where the laws are not so harsh, or where at least a blind eye is turned. Stuart has some family money behind him, and we have good service records. There will always be jobs for men who can operate a telegraph machine.'

'What about the café and this cottage? What shall become of them?'

'Let's see what happens. If you and Dora intend to stay in Dovecote, then I will give both the cottage and the café to you as part of a divorce settlement. Will you commence proceedings?'

'On what basis?'

'Whatever you want. Drag my name through the mud, Rose. I don't care. Just protect yourself and your good name, and the good name of our daughter.'

I looked down at my left hand and over at his. 'We never did get around to buying you a wedding ring.' I pulled his mother's rings from my finger. 'Here. Keep them, or sell them to add to your escape fund.'

When Martin drew a deep breath, it was shaky. 'Thank you.'

'Will you head off tonight? You're more than welcome to stay. Is there anything you need to take with you?'

'I think it's best if I go.' He smiled. 'Both to avoid seeing any acquaintances, and because I cannot bear to be apart from

Stuart for a day longer. No, I can't think of anything I want to take with me. The lighter we travel, the better. I have the photographs you sent me of Janice. I will treasure them forever. I am sorry for everything, Rose.'

'We are both happy, Martin. There is nothing to be sorry for.'

'Please take what I am about to say in the way I intend.' He ran his fingers through his hair. 'I love you.'

We embraced again. 'I love you, too. Now, go. You'll catch the last train. Take my blessings and my best wishes with you. And tell Stuart I said I hope he can cope with your snoring.'

'I wish you and Dora a happy and long life together, Rose. And give Janice a kiss from me.'

It occurred to me as Martin disappeared up The Promenade that that was the most open and loving conversation we had ever had. I looked up at the stars. They seemed to be shining extra brightly.

I closed the front door and went immediately to the drawer where I kept my writing paper. If Martin was brave enough to follow his heart, then I could be too. I had promised to keep Martin's secret, so wouldn't put the full story down on paper, but I could say enough so that she would understand what it meant for us. A happy tear dripped onto the paper as I began to write.

*Dearest, darling Dora...*

# EPILOGUE

## SARAH

April 2018

Sarah gave Dora's hand a gentle squeeze as Reverend Clive made the sign of the cross above Rose's grave, bringing the service to a close. She looked over at the marble headstone on the next plot along. Her grandmother and her daughter, side by side. She swallowed the lump in her throat. Dora's slim shoulders dropped, as though a great weight had been lifted from them.

'For many, many years, I've felt guilty about Rose not being buried where she should be. And now, finally, that has been righted. Thank you for doing this, Sarah. I am very happy that she is home at last.' There was the hint of a tear on Dora's lined cheek, and she wiped it away with a coral-tipped finger. As always, her lipstick matched her nail varnish.

'I'm so pleased you could come. Thank you for making the long journey.'

'Oh, it is my pleasure. It was very kind of you to pick me up from the airport.'

'It's the least I could do. Are we still on for a day out at Bletchley Park?'

'Oh, yes. I am very much looking forward to it. It will be quite the trip down memory lane.'

Janice threaded her arm through Sarah's. 'That was a beautiful service, Sarah. I'm glad I can come and visit both of my mothers now.' Janice had put flowers on Gladys Legg's grave before Rose's reinterment service. They matched the bunch she'd placed on Rose's. 'I explained to Mum what we were doing. I hope she understands that I don't hold any ill feeling towards her and Dad for not telling me about Rose. Whatever their motives or opinions, they did what they thought was right at the time, and I can't hold that against them.'

'I know, Mum,' Sarah said softly. 'You more than make up for them by being such a supportive ally. Thank you for letting me be me, and for welcoming Heather into the family.'

Janice glanced up at the spring-blue sky dotted with light clouds, but Sarah could see the sheen in her eyes. 'All I want is for you to be happy, love. And I'm very proud of you for sticking around and sorting things out with people that you hurt in the past. I'm glad you and Rob are friends. It means he'll still be coming into the café for sticky buns.' She drew a deep breath and squared her shoulders. 'Right, well, I don't know about all of you, but I need a cup of tea. Come on, girls, and you, Clive. The remembrance ceremony isn't over yet. We have a café to reopen.'

A sizeable crowd had gathered on The Promenade and Sarah led Janice through the throng to the front door of The Seaside Café. The signboard above the door was the same, *The Seaside Café*, in looping yellow script on a pink background, but the colours were fresh and lively, and a painted garland of trailing red roses had been added, entwined through the letters.

Climbing roses had been planted on both sides of the main door. One day, they'd form a canopy over the doorway.

'Oh, hello, everyone. Gosh, I didn't expect this,' Janice said, looking slightly flustered as she stood at the café's front door. 'It's a good job I made plenty of sticky buns! Thank you for bearing with us while we've been closed for the past ten months. I hadn't thought it would take that long, but you know how these things go. I will admit, it's been nice to put my feet up, without a great big surgical boot on this time. While I've been resting, I've also been thinking. I'm getting on a bit...' There was a chorus of reassuring 'no's' from the gathered crowd. 'Oh, stop that. I'm seventy-six now.'

'You don't look it,' Rob called from the back of the crowd. Sarah shot him a glare but then laughed.

'Thank you, Rob. Anyway, now that the refurbishment is finished, I can formally announce my retirement. From today, the management and day-to-day running of The Seaside Café will pass to my daughter, Sarah.'

Sarah gaped at her mother as the crowd applauded and cheered. 'Mum? What? Really?'

Janice glanced at Heather and enveloped Sarah in a hug. She whispered in her ear, 'I get the feeling you're not going to be running away again.'

Disentangling herself from her mother's embrace, Sarah turned to Daphne. 'Did you know about this?'

Daphne just smiled.

'But you've been in Dovecote all these years, and you're the oldest. Surely you...?' Sarah's voice faded as her sister shook her head.

'It never really appealed to me. Plus, my tea-making skills are abysmal. I make great cocktails, but awful tea. And anyway,' she added, as Adam slipped his arm around her shoulder and squeezed the top of her arm, 'I've already got my hands full.'

Janice turned the key in the door of the café. 'Well, enough talking. How about a cuppa? Come on in, everyone.'

Sarah walked tall as she stepped through the door and into the café. It was unmistakeably the same café she'd known all her life, but some breathtaking tweaks had been made. The old Welsh dresser had been manoeuvred out of the pantry, sanded down, and now took pride of place along the back wall. A collection of new antique pink and yellow polka dot crockery adorned it. A long plaque had been made from reclaimed driftwood and affixed to the front of the counter. Sarah felt someone come to stand next to her as she looked at it.

'Oh, goodness, look at that,' Dora said, wiping her eyes as she read the chalk-white lettering. *'Even if the well runs dry, we'll always have tea.'* She drew a slightly shaky breath. 'How lovely.'

'It was Mum's idea,' Sarah said. 'I can't wait for people to ask what it means, so I can tell them about you and Rose. If that's okay with you?'

'I actively encourage it.' The smile on Dora's lips touched her cornflower-blue eyes. She looked around. 'It's lovely to see the café again. The last time I was here there'd just been a break-in and it was a mess.'

'A break-in? Oh my goodness. What happened?'

Dora smiled and patted Sarah's hand. 'A story for another day.'

'Hey.' Heather's hand snaked around Sarah's waist, and Sarah turned her head and gave her a light kiss.

Dora sighed softly. 'I can't tell you how happy it makes me to see you two being able to do that,' she said, squeezing Sarah's shoulder. 'Your grandmother would be delighted.' She glanced over to where Harrison Prentice and his partner, Gio, were examining the new artwork on the walls. They were holding hands. 'Your grandfather, too.'

Heather had finally introduced Sarah to all her friends, and they now felt like Sarah's friends too. Sarah smiled. The Pride flag above the front door had been her idea. She thought Rose would approve. Out of the corner of her eye, she saw an elderly woman in a neon pink kaftan and huge orange hoop earrings approach Dora, who had sat down at the table in the window.

'Hello,' the woman said, holding out a thin, wrinkled hand. 'I'm Zeyla. Are those your photographs on the wall?'

Dora had been as good as her word. Not long after Sarah got back to Dovecote, a box of photographs arrived from Switzerland. It took Sarah and Janice a whole afternoon to go through them. When Janice mentioned she wanted to refresh the café décor, Sarah had suggested getting a few of the photos enlarged and framed. They had chosen a mix of shots of Dovecote and ones of Rose, and of Rose and Dora. Sarah had even convinced her mother to put up a few of the ones of herself as a baby. They were perfect.

'Ah, Zeyla's met Dora,' Heather whispered. 'I had hoped she would. Since Maureen passed away last month, Zeyla is one of the few residents left who remember Dovecote during the war. It will be nice for her to chat to someone else who lived through it.' Zeyla's pealing laughter erupted from across the room and Dora reached across the table and touched Zeyla's hand. Sarah shot a raised eyebrow at Heather, who just winked, smiled, and nodded in reply.

Daphne was by the counter, Adam's arm around her shoulders. She'd quit the PTA and she and Adam had taken a second honeymoon. Both had done Daphne the world of good, and she no longer looked permanently stressed and frazzled. It helped that Jake had done better than expected in his exams, even though all he wanted to do was play football and Mario Kart. Sarah still hadn't managed to defeat him, despite their regular Sunday evening chats and gaming sessions. Sarah had the feeling that there was something he was building up to tell her. If it was what she thought, and all the signs were there, all she could do was be there for him when he was ready.

A glint of reflected sunlight flashed in the corner of Sarah's eye. It was coming from the diamond ring on Aoife's hand, which was clasped firmly in Rob's. Aoife turned slightly and Sarah's mouth nearly fell open. There was a definite curve to Aoife's normally ironing-board-flat stomach. Rob caught her eye, and she mouthed, 'Is she?' at him, nodding towards Aoife. He blushed and nodded. Behind the sticky bun he was chomping, there was the biggest, stupidest grin on his face.

'Well, I'll be...' Sarah muttered to herself.

'Did you hear Rob and Aoife have bought Seaspray Cottage on Beachfront Road?' Heather was at Sarah's shoulder again. It took Sarah a moment to process that information, but once it had sunk in, she smiled. Rob had said a few months ago he might be moving out of their old house, for a fresh start. Maybe this baby had been a part of his and Aoife's plans, and he hadn't wanted to bring their child up in the house that reminded him so much of Faith.

A few days after she'd scattered her dad's ashes, Sarah had met Rob at The Royal Oak for a drink. She'd told him about Faith's pebble that she'd placed at the foot of the lighthouse, which made him cry. And she'd confided that she'd taken his advice and found a therapist. He'd told her he was proud of her. She was just glad they were friends.

Once everyone had drifted away and the sun had dipped down behind the cliff to the west, Janice turned the key in the front door of The Seaside Café for the last time, before handing it to Sarah.

'Look after the old girl, won't you?'

'Oh, Mum, you're still going to be around. But yes, I'll take good care of her. Are you absolutely sure about this?'

'I have every faith in you, Sarah. You'll do me, your father, your grandmother, your grandfather, and your great-grandparents proud.'

Sarah swallowed the lump in her throat. To think she was the fourth generation of her family to run The Seaside Café! If she hadn't been slightly nervous before, she was now. Apart from anything else, who would she pass it on to? Maybe she could get Jake into baking. Might she even be ready to have another child of her own? She glanced out at the lighthouse, glowing orange in the setting sun, and her heart skipped a beat. All in good time.

As Janice made her way home to Pebble Cottage, Sarah and Heather leant against the railings, looking out over the sea.

'So,' Heather said, wrapping her arm around Sarah's waist. 'Are you glad you came back?'

Sarah thought about it for a moment, resting her head against Heather's shoulder. The waves swished in time to her heartbeat and the inky sky was strewn with stars. How could she have ever considered leaving? How had she not realised that Dovecote was, had always been, and would always be, her home? That she belonged here, surrounded by people she loved and who loved her. She pulled the salty air deep into her lungs and replied to Heather's question the best way she knew how – with a long, lingering kiss.

# A LETTER FROM LAURA

Dearest Reader,

Thank you so much for choosing to read *My Mother's Photograph* out of the thousands of books out there. It really means so much to me. I really hoped you enjoyed meeting Sarah and Rose, and being immersed in their stories. If you enjoyed *My Mother's Photograph* and would like to find out about all of my latest releases, you can sign up at the following link. Your email address will never be shared, and you can unsubscribe at any time.

*www.bookouture.com/laura-sweeney*

If you've read these letters before, you'll know I like to give you a taste of the research that I've done. For this book there was really only one place that I had to visit – Bletchley Park. Spending a day there really gave me a brilliant insight into the work Dora would have been doing. It's an incredibly atmospheric place, and what went on there is, honestly, mind-blowing. I would whole-heartedly recommend a trip, if you're in the neighbourhood. I also must mention the Imperial War Museum again, whose archives are a treasure trove of articles, photographs, and assorted ephemera which enabled me to bring the 1940s to life. I owe a debt of gratitude to Luke Turner's excellent book, *Men At War*, which shines a light on the complex lives and identities of those men who fought. I went a touch too far in the name of research by spraining my ankle on a quick visit to Switzerland, so I have felt Janice's pain – literally!

As always, I'd love to hear from you, and you'll find me on social media and on my website. Thank you so much for visiting Dovecote. I hope you've had a lovely time.

Laura

www.laurasweeneyauthor.co.uk

 x.com/laura_c_sweeney

 instagram.com/laura_c_sweeney

 bsky.app/profile/lauracsweeney.bsky.social

# ACKNOWLEDGEMENTS

If getting a second book published was my wildest dream, this one, book three, was far beyond that. And it has been a dream, thanks to the wonderful team at Bookouture, who have been brilliant, as usual, to work with. Thank you to Imogen, my ever-patient and enthusiastic editor. This book wouldn't be what it is without you.

I'm writing this just as my first book, *My Grandmother's Secret*, is being released. I can't express in words how immensely grateful I am to everyone who has supported, spread the word, and pre-ordered it. Huge thanks to the early pre-publication readers who left wonderful reviews that made me happy-cry.

A special thank you to the staff at Gladstone's Library in Wales, where a good chunk of this book was written. Gladstone's is the only residential library in the UK and is a truly magical place where words flow like nowhere else. Also, their chocolate brownies are the best writing fuel.

As always, I couldn't do this without the support and encouragement of the lovely authors I have met in person and online. To the wonderful book community I have been welcomed into, you're the best of humanity and a beacon of light in the darkness of social media.

Thank you to Annabel Campbell for providing the inspiration for the painting hanging in Pebble Cottage.

Sorry to my friends who I haven't seen, or spoken to, in

months while on deadline. Thank you for not giving up on me. I promise I'll make it up to you and we'll get together soon.

This past year has been a whirlwind, but thankfully my friends and family have been on hand to help me see which way was up. I couldn't do this without you.

# PUBLISHING TEAM

Turning a manuscript into a book requires the efforts of many people. The publishing team at Bookouture would like to acknowledge everyone who contributed to this publication.

### Commercial
Lauren Morrissette
Hannah Richmond
Imogen Allport

### Cover design
Debbie Clement

### Data and analysis
Mark Alder
Mohamed Bussuri

### Editorial
Imogen Allport

### Copyeditor
Gabbie Chant

### Proofreader
Liz Hurst

## Marketing
Alex Crow
Melanie Price
Occy Carr
Cíara Rosney
Martyna Młynarska

## Operations and distribution
Marina Valles
Stephanie Straub
Joe Morris

## Production
Hannah Snetsinger
Mandy Kullar
Nadia Michael
Charlotte Hegley

## Publicity
Kim Nash
Noelle Holten
Jess Readett
Sarah Hardy

## Rights and contracts
Peta Nightingale
Richard King
Saidah Graham

## RAISING READERS
Books Build Bright Futures

Dear Reader,

We'd love your attention for one more page to tell you about the crisis in children's reading, and what we can all do.

Studies have shown that reading for fun is the **single biggest predictor of a child's future life chances** – more than family circumstance, parents' educational background or income. It improves academic results, mental health, wealth, communication skills, ambition and happiness.

The number of children reading for fun is in rapid decline. Young people have a lot of competition for their time, and a worryingly high number do not have a single book at home.

Hachette works extensively with schools, libraries and literacy charities, but here are some ways we can all raise more readers:

- Reading to children for just 10 minutes a day makes a difference
- Don't give up if children aren't regular readers – there will be books for them!

- Visit bookshops and libraries to get recommendations
- Encourage them to listen to audiobooks
- Support school libraries
- Give books as gifts

There's a lot more information about how to encourage children to read on our websites: **www.RaisingReaders.co.uk** and **www.JoinRaisingReaders.com**.

Thank you for reading.

Printed in Dunstable, United Kingdom

77552727R00211